*It's said that you have to lose yourself in order
to find who you really are…*

What you find might change your life!

Dear Reader,

Carrie Sawyer is a lot like me. She's cynical, stubborn and determined. The last thing in the world she wants to do is go to a ghost hunting convention with her best friend. Carrie doesn't believe in ghosts, and never will. She does believe in having a holiday fling with the sexy and single owner of the hotel.

At first, Carrie gets her shivers from Sam Crider. His touch, his kiss. Even the way he looks at her. But then…mysterious things start to happen, and there are shivers of a whole different kind.

I had a ball writing about Carrie, because I was one of those people who scoffed at ghost sightings and psychic predictions. Now? I rather like the idea that the world is filled with magic and wonder. And love. Definitely love.

Hope you enjoy your time with Carrie and Sam. I sure did. Visit with me at www.joleigh.com or on Twitter @jo_leigh. I'd love to hear about your personal encounters with the supernatural!

Sincerely,

Jo Leigh

SHIVER

BY
JO LEIGH

All the characters in this book have no existence outside the imagination of
the author, and have no relation whatsoever to anyone bearing the same name
or names. They are not even distantly inspired by any individual known or
unknown to the author, and all the incidents are pure invention.

First published in Great Britain 2011
by Mills & Boon, an imprint of Harlequin (UK) Limited,
Eton House, 18-24 Paradise Road, Richmond, Surrey TW9 1SR

© Jolie Kramer 2010

ISBN: 978 0 263 88079 3

14-1011

Harlequin (UK) policy is to use papers that are natural, renewable and
recyclable products and made from wood grown in sustainable forests. The
logging and manufacturing processes conform to the legal environmental
regulations of the country of origin.

Printed and bound in Spain
by Blackprint CPI, Barcelona

Jo Leigh has written over forty novels. She's thrilled that she can write mysteries, suspense and comedies all under the Blaze® banner, especially because the heart of each and every book is the love story.

A triple RITA® finalist, Jo shares her home in Utah with her cute dog, Jessie. You can come chat with Jo at her website: http://www.joleigh.com, follow her on Twitter @jo_leigh and don't forget to check out her daily blog!

To Charlotte.
For writing so beautifully and inspiring me so much.
Also for the LOLs.

Prologue

To: SororitySisters4ever@egroups.com
From: AdventureGirl@FantasyEscapes.com

Okay, ladies, I did it. Fantasy Escapes is opening its doors to the public tomorrow morning and I'm officially trolling for business among my best friends—call me tacky, but I think you all deserve a fabulous getaway!

For those of you who've been under a rock this last year, I've been working on a new start-up business ever since Premiere Properties down-sized me out of a job. I'm putting my extensive travel experience to good use to help clients take one-of-a-kind vacations.

Need a massage on the beach in Miami? I can book you with the best hands on South Beach *and* I know which places have the most luxurious cabanas.

Need a ski trip complete with a sleigh ride?

A bicycle trip to the top of a Hawaiian mountain?

I can make sure you pick the best time to see the perfect sunset while you're there.

You'll recall I'm a bit Type A? Picture the power of Marnie perfectionism at your fingertips! I'll create that once-in-a-lifetime experience you dream about.

So here I sit, brimming with knowledge and ready to send one of my fave foxy friends on an adventure. E-mail me when you're ready to get away! You all know you deserve it... I'm talking to *you*, Carrie Sawyer!

CARRIE CLOSED THE e-mail from Marnie and pulled up her own Web site. Her comic, *Cruel, Cruel World,* needed some new panels since she was only ahead by eight days, but she also needed to check the *CCW* forum, which was a lot easier at the moment since she had no idea what she was going to draw.

Her thoughts drifted back to Marnie's message before she even clicked on the first new comment. She should call Marnie. They hadn't spoken in forever. It was good to see that her old friend was jumping into the deep end of the risk pool. Marnie was too smart to be anyone's flunky.

Man, they'd had some great times way back when. Especially she, Marnie and Erin. They'd met during pledge week freshman year, and the friendship had grown and blossomed as they'd shared their undergraduate years. There were other friends, but none as close. Carrie wasn't sure why she and Marnie hadn't stayed in touch, except for the distance thing. Unlike Erin,

Marnie had settled in Miami, and neither of them was particularly great with the phone calls.

On the other hand, Carrie and Erin spoke three or four times a week. On the phone mostly but in person when they could. It helped that they both lived in downtown Los Angeles. Carrie had found this giant old loft two weeks after she'd graduated, god, five years ago. The neighborhood was a little dicey, but the light that came through the windows in the converted factory was spectacular, and Carrie loved the space.

She'd only been able to afford it because of *Cruel, Cruel World*. The comic had started as an experiment. She hadn't wanted anyone to know about it back then, and she'd written under the name of Carrie Price, but it turned into a marginal hit the first three years of college. Incredibly, the comic had struck syndication gold when she'd become a senior. She'd been picked up by a number of newspapers, and had also built a considerable Web presence with not just the Monday, Wednesday and Friday strips, but the forum, merchandise, her graphic novels and appearances at pretty much every geek and nerd convention across the country. Which meant she was rarely off the clock.

As for Erin, she'd fallen in love with the buildings. She'd come to L.A. to pursue her graduate degree in architecture at USC. Erin had found a place a couple of blocks away from Carrie, which was about the best thing that could have happened.

Left to her own devices, Carrie wouldn't leave the loft for days at a time. She didn't need a lot of live interaction, not when most of her social life was online with all the other comic writers, readers, gamers and bloggers. Not that she had anything against going out in general, but if it wasn't with Erin, she didn't exactly have a smorgasbord of available companions. Especially since her relationship with Armand had crashed and burned. He'd seemed so perfect. A misfit, a musician, a mystery. He'd been great in bed, fun to go out with and a complete cheating bastard.

Despite knowing he was all wrong for her and that he hadn't ever really made her happy, she missed him. It was crazy and stupid and it felt horrible. She *shouldn't* miss him. He was bad for her, and she deserved better. But her brain and her emotions didn't seem to be speaking to each other.

Sadly, the disconnect between what she knew and what she wanted had been going on for a while. In particular, when it came to men. So she was taking a break, a sabbatical from relationships, until her heart and mind joined forces.

The phone rang and Carrie answered without a glance at the caller ID. "Hey, Erin. I assume you got the e-mail from Marnie, too?"

"Lunch at the deli. Ten minutes, max."

Carrie sighed. "Yes, ma'am." As she disconnected, she wondered what Erin was going to get her into this time.

1

THE DUDE'S ELBOW POKED the side of her boob. Again. Carrie couldn't tell if he was doing it on purpose or if he was just clueless. If she had to make a guess, it would be clueless.

It was bad enough the Crider Inn was over an hour from the Denver airport, but the shuttle bus was so packed Carrie hadn't even been able to sit next to Erin. Although Carrie shouldn't complain too hard. At least she was wedged against the luggage rack on one side, whereas her friend was in the middle of a creepy-guy sandwich. The one on her right looked to be in his thirties, sported a world-class mullet and kept pushing up his tortoiseshell glasses with his middle finger, making it look as if he were flipping everyone the bird. Repeatedly. On Erin's left was a nice-enough-looking guy, somewhere in his twenties, who wouldn't be bad at all if he hadn't snorted every two seconds. The postnasal-drip kind of snort that even if you gave him a tissue, it probably wouldn't do any good.

Carrie caught her friend's gaze and scowled at her with evil intent. For her part, Erin smiled brightly as if this were the best shuttle ride ever. Who knew? Maybe for Erin, it was. After all, everyone with the exception of the driver and herself talked of nothing but ghosts.

Ghosts.

Carrie sighed, reminding herself Erin hadn't pointed a gun or threatened her in any way. Carrie had willingly dropped over a thousand bucks of her very hard-earned savings to come to this almost weeklong ghost-hunting extravaganza. She never would have agreed if it hadn't been their last vacation together. Erin was moving to New York three weeks to the day from when they returned, leaving behind her downtown Los Angeles loft to begin her new career as a bona fide architect in New York City.

The two of them had vacationed together every single year since they'd been juniors at the University of Louisville. Last year's trip to Bryce Canyon in Utah had been Carrie's pick, and although Erin hated camping out, she'd gone along with the plan. In return, Carrie had promised she'd go along with whatever, although if she'd known it would have involved ghost hunting, she might have amended the agreement.

Her complaints had fallen on deaf ears, and Erin had booked the trip through Marnie's Fantasy Escapes travel agency. Marnie had been thrilled and grateful, which had helped seal the deal, but the real capper had been when Erin had pointed out, quite cleverly, that Carrie could consider this a weeklong research trip. After all, she was a cartoonist who made her living mocking trends and popular culture. If ghost hunting didn't give her enough ideas for her next graphic novel then she should just quit right now and go find herself a job serving fries with that.

"So, I was sound asleep. I mean, I was out like a light. Nothin' could have gotten me up, not after the workday I'd put in. But then I hear this shriek. It was loud. Like, I don't know—"

Carrie winced and covered her ears as the guy with the elbow issue screamed at the top of his lungs. It was a girly scream, too, high-pitched and weird as hell and far scarier than any apparition.

"Yeah, like that," he said, as if he hadn't almost shattered the windows.

Carrie noted that the shuttle driver hadn't flinched. The bus hadn't swerved or anything. She guessed working for the "Most Haunted Hotel in the U.S." got one used to the odd scream.

"The weird thing was, the people in the living room, like, I don't know, ten feet away or something? They didn't even hear it. But I had my EMF under my pillow, and it was going crazy. Seriously. All in the red. No shit."

Erin had given her a cheat sheet on the ghost-hunting nomenclature. It was far too lengthy to memorize, but she knew that EMF stood for electromagnetic field, and that Elbow Guy was referring to his meter. Carrie'd had no idea there was so much equipment involved in ghost hunting. EMF meters, ultrasensitive thermometers, night-vision goggles and cameras, and a bunch of other stuff she'd zoned out about. Erin had packed her fair share, but Carrie couldn't complain too much. She'd brought not only her laptop, but also her scanner, a bunch of files and her drawing supplies. Thankfully, the Crider Inn had, as Erin put it, "Wi-Fi up the yin yang."

"I've had three important encounters."

The soft voice came from two rows back, and Carrie turned to see it was the pretty woman who was speaking. She was somewhere in her thirties, which seemed to be the median age, and she defied Carrie's stereotypes by being elegant, fashionable and from her reading material—a heavy-duty philosophy tome—educated. Not that Erin wasn't all those things, but Carrie had never lumped her in with the vague group she considered ghost-hunting nut-jobs. Anyway, the pretty woman's voice held a hint of somewhere exotic, perhaps Jamaica, that captivated with its quiet strength.

"When I was a child, my old grandfather came to me after his death. He sat on my bed and he talked to me as clearly as I'm speaking to you. He told me not to worry, that he was in a fine, fine place, and that he would watch over me for all the rest of my days. He also told me that I would travel the world, and see many great things, but it was my family I should treasure most."

Elbow Dude started to comment, but Carrie clipped him one in his side because the woman wasn't finished.

"The second experience was many years later, at a small hotel in Florence, Italy. I woke from an afternoon nap to find an old white woman standing near the balcony. She never turned to look at me, so I didn't see her face, but I watched her shoulders rise as she appeared to take a deep breath, and when she let it out, her head bowed. She was gone the next instant."

The woman smiled at Carrie, maybe because she

was staring so blatantly. "I keep my third experience private."

Carrie faced front once more, wishing she could be one of them. One of these true believers. They seemed to get much more than spooky scares or thrills from these supposedly haunted places. Take Erin, for instance. Something about her belief in ghosts calmed her. It made her world easier to understand, and despite the utter lack of scientific proof, she had no doubts whatsoever.

Carrie wasn't so lucky. She understood the psychology of belief in the supernatural. Human brains were designed to assign patterns and reason whether or not they exist. Ghosts, aliens, conspiracies or even finding evil messages in rock music were all based on assigning meaning to random things. At least ghost hunting was harmless and had been around since the beginning of large-brained hominids, but it wasn't something she subscribed to, and being around people who were so ferocious in their certainty became wearing after a while.

What she found most bewildering was that in all the years and years of ghost hunting, no one seemed concerned that no matter how hard people looked, and damn, there were industries based on people believing in ghosts, there was no repeatable, verifiable proof. She tried hard to keep her opinions to herself when she was around Erin's friends, but it wasn't always easy.

When she heard intelligent, eloquent people expound on their supernatural experiences she tried not to roll her eyes. Whether she could remain a stoic observer after an intense week of pretending to believe in ghosts and goblins, well, that remained to be seen.

Her gaze went to the window as she let herself fall into the lovely Colorado scenery. She'd make the most of her week, especially spending time with Erin. She was going to miss her friend something terrible.

ANOTHER SHUTTLE LOAD of ghost hunters was due to arrive in the next ten minutes, and Sam Crider, current proprietor of the Crider Inn, was ready for them.

Since it was Halloween week and this was the largest and longest convention of ghost aficionados he'd booked since taking over the hotel, he'd gone all out decorating the place. It wasn't hard to give the hotel a spooky ambience. His family had been doing it for generations, ever since the Old Hotel, now condemned but not torn down, had been destroyed by a fire of mysterious origin that had killed a number of his ancestors, who, according to legend, had never checked out.

Personally, he was delighted by this resurgence of ghost hunting and all the television shows that glorified the sport. All the paranormal legends about the Crider property were not only filling his coffers, but they were also a large part of why the hotel and the hundred acres of Crider land were now involved in a bidding war.

Two companies were interested in buying the place. One wanted to exploit the haunted reputation, and the other simply wanted to exploit the land. Sam had no preference as to who won, just so long as the check cleared.

Almost no one who worked for him knew that, of course. All negotiations had been done on the quiet, because a Crider had always owned and run the property and, it was assumed, always would.

He wanted nothing more than to shake the dust of this place off his shoes and get back to his real life. He'd been in the middle of his fifth documentary film when his father had died. Shit, it was ten months ago. The time had gone by in a blur.

He missed the old man. They'd been close. The bond had taken root when Sam was thirteen and his mother had died of breast cancer. It hadn't been strong enough, however, to give Sam a love of the hotel, or a desire to carry on the family tradition. The sale would make it possible for him to continue making films, and no longer on a shoestring budget.

He'd finally have enough money to hire some help, like sound professionals and a full-time assistant. Not to mention the massive upgrade in equipment he'd be able to afford. He could stop thinking local and travel anywhere the stories dictated, film for as long as necessary to get what he needed. He'd have the cash to submit his films to all the important festivals. He'd actually be able to move out of the glorified Brooklyn broom closet he currently called home base.

So ghosts it was, and would be for the next week. Not only to curry favor with the convention people, but also to wow the potential buyers, both of whom were coming to check out the grounds.

That had been a neat trick. As he'd been told by his attorney, his accountant and his real estate broker, no one conducted sales by having the competing parties survey the place at the same time. But Sam had no interest in playing games. Representatives from both companies had already checked out the property, the numbers had been crunched and recrunched, now all that was left was for the CEOs to do a walk-through before actually making bids.

Sam had told the two men that he was having one showing, and that was that. They could take it or leave it. Luckily, they'd both taken it. Turns out they knew each other, had figured they'd both be interested in the place, and were looking forward to seeing each other. But now that it was happening, Sam worried that they'd both say no, and he'd be back to square one.

He surveyed the lobby slowly, trying to see the place with fresh eyes. It wasn't possible. He'd grown up here, had slept in almost every one of the thirty-six guest rooms. He'd eaten in the restaurant—good cooks and bad—learned to shoot pool in the small pub. He'd lost his virginity in the Old Hotel, and had his heart broken sitting in front of the big stone fireplace that dominated the lobby.

He'd miss it all, but not tragically. It was just a building, just land, just a view. He'd already made sure that both the buyers were amenable to keeping the permanent staff, so no guilt there. And he'd found a great retirement place in Denver for his Aunt Grace. If there was one fly in the ointment, it was Grace. She'd lived here all her life, residing in the attached apartment that had once been his parents' home.

But she was getting on in years, and she shouldn't live this far away from medical care anyway. He was doing the right thing, for himself, for the employees, and for Grace. He'd sent her off to her friend's home in Miami for a couple of weeks. She'd been happy to go, to be somewhere warm. He just hoped she'd be half as excited to move when it was time.

He heard the door behind him, and turned to find his old friend Jody Reading bringing him a hot beverage and what looked to be a dessert. Jody was an executive chef, a damn fine one, who'd agreed to come in for the week. She would wow the guests with her superb meals and drive them insane with her prize-winning pastries.

"I thought you'd like to try this before the deluge."

He peeked in the mug to find coffee—a latte, from the looks of it—and a large piece of a layered napoleon, his favorite. "You're ruining me. I'll be a French-pastry junkie and end up living in some alley behind a patisserie."

"As long as it's not my patisserie."

He really shouldn't indulge now, not when the shuttle was due to arrive any minute, but the dessert looked so delicious, he took his plate and the fork and dug in. His moan wasn't particularly manly, but it seemed to please Jody.

"My work here is done," she said. She gave him a friendly swat on the ass, then went back to the kitchen.

Luckily, he was alone, at least for the moment, because he downed the pastry way too fast, which was a crime. But he didn't want to be caught by a guest, and there was a strict rule about eating at the front desk.

Just as he lifted the last forkful to his mouth, the lobby door opened, bringing a gust of cold wind along with eighteen paying guests.

He dropped his fork on the plate, then shoved the plate under a newspaper. He smiled and rang the bell that would bring Patrick from the office. Patrick was the manager of the hotel, and he would handle the registration, while Sam schmoozed.

"You're Sam Crider? The guy who owns the place?"

He nodded at the first person at the desk, Liam O'Connell, one of the conference coordinators.

Liam took the pen and began to fill out his registration card. "Bet you've seen a thing or two."

"Oh, yeah. Things that would curl your hair."

Liam laughed, considering he was mostly bald. "What's the scariest thing you've ever encountered?"

"Oh, I'm not going to give you guys any spoilers. You'll find what you're looking for, but the experience should be untainted." Sam frowned. "You don't have heart trouble, do you?"

Liam shook his head.

"That's good," he said, wondering if he'd gone too far. Seeing the big man's reaction, and the wide eyes of the people behind him, evidently not. "Although we keep smelling salts at the ready. Things can get a little… tense around here."

"Excellent." Liam finished with his card, and then Sam moved on to Gina Fiorello, a friendly-looking young woman who had reserved a single.

"You've probably seen a lot of ghosts," she said.

"Hey, I lived here for seventeen years. What do you think?"

"Wow." Gina filled in her card.

Sam looked down the line, not surprised at the luggage-to-guest ratio. Ghost hunters were big on equipment. The number of gadgets indicated the level of commitment to the cause, and these folks were committed.

The hotel only had four luggage carts and two sturdy part-time students to do the toting. Maybe it would be better for him to put off the talking and help these people get to their rooms.

He slowed down when he caught sight of a tall, striking blonde. She was a beauty and he wondered if she understood what havoc she would cause in a hotel full of conventioneers. Maybe she was with someone; that might help.

She was. Only it wasn't a guy. It was a woman, and Sam stood stock-still the second he saw her. She wasn't very tall, maybe five-four, slender beneath her wool coat and her eyes were as dark as her long hair. Sam had seen her before.

He couldn't remember where, but he remembered his reaction. He'd held his breath. His heart had pounded as if seeing a long-lost lover. He couldn't remember why they hadn't met, and he supposed it didn't matter now.

He didn't believe in reincarnation. Certainly didn't believe in destiny. But he'd be damned if he was going to let another opportunity to meet this woman pass him by.

2

"ARE YOU SEEING THIS?"

Carrie looked up at Erin, bugged that because of Erin's ridiculously huge suitcase, they were at the back of the line. Okay, not quite the back of the line, because there were four people behind them, but she was tired and hungry and she wanted to test her Internet connection. "Yes. The inn is lovely. Great fireplace, very charming."

"God, you are the worst traveler ever. I swear. Why do I keep on taking vacations with you?"

"Honestly? I have no idea."

Erin took hold of Carrie's shoulders and turned her to face the front desk. "I meant are you seeing *that?*" she said, whispering this time.

All Carrie saw was two guys taking reservations. One had impressive silver hair, really thick, and she wanted him to look up so she could see if the face went with the hair. The other guy didn't need to look up. He already was. Staring at her. Unblinking, lips parted. There was no doubt even in this long line that his focus was entirely on her. Maybe. She felt her face heat up, then realized he had to be staring at Erin. Everyone stared at Erin. She turned back to her friend. "You should be flattered."

"Me? He's staring at you, you idiot."

Carrie looked again, and holy crap, he *was* staring at her. She whipped around once more. "What the hell?"

"I know, right?" Erin still whispered and her speech was wonky because she wasn't moving her lips. "Okay. He looked away."

"That was weird." Carrie stole a glance at the desk, grateful whatever that was had stopped. "He must have thought I was someone else. Someone he knew."

"Or maybe he was struck dumb by your beauty and fell instantly, hopelessly in love the moment he saw you."

"Yeah. That's about as likely as actually seeing a ghost."

The three people in front and the four behind turned to her, each one looking appalled. Carrie winced. "Kidding."

Erin shook her head and sighed. "I can't take you anywhere."

Carrie moved closer to her friend and kept her head down, cursing her own big giant mouth. She'd lasted all of two hours before she'd made fun of these people, and they hadn't even checked in yet. Jeez.

So she kept her trap shut long enough to listen in on Mr. Stare's conversations. They weren't actually whole conversations. More like bits and drabs, but each and every one contained a mention of—what else?—ghosts. She suspected that the person he'd mistaken her for wasn't among the living. The man seemed very enthusiastic and utterly convinced that the hauntings in this hotel were one-hundred-percent legit. Verifiable, if only one had the good fortune to be in the right place at the right time.

The single thing provable in this place was that the belief in ridiculous nonsense was utterly egalitarian. Age, race, looks, wealth—none of that mattered. Instead of disturbing her, the realization made her feel happy for Erin. There was a world of folks out there with whom she could share her passion, and some of them were very nice-looking men. Because even if he had stared rather rudely, he was downright hot.

A comment from behind her, something about why some people bothered to come to certain conferences if they were stupid enough not to see what was all around them, made her curse her impulsivity again. Carrie had no doubt that the news of her traitorous talk would spread through the hotel like wildfire.

By the time she reached the front desk she was more concerned about being tarred and feathered than she was about the handsomeness of the guy behind the desk.

That lasted about two seconds.

Sam Crider was tall, maybe six-one, and he wore his slim-hipped jeans and tucked-in, mountain-man flannel shirt well. He looked nothing like the guys she usually hung with, who were mostly cartoonists and always tech nerds, who rarely dressed in anything that wasn't a T-shirt complete with geek-identifying logo and baggy pants. Crider's brown hair was on the longish side, slightly shaggy. His eyes were an interesting hazel and, well, nice. He no longer seemed creepy, despite his propensity for staring and his certainty about ghosts.

Oddly, before she'd finished filling out her registration

information, Crider handed the reins to his compatriot and came around the desk.

"Are these your bags?"

She looked down at her equipment and opened her mouth to explain that none of it was in any way related to ghost hunting, but she stopped herself. "Yep."

"Hang tight. I'm just going to get the luggage cart. Be back in a sec."

As he headed for the cart near the elevator, Erin handed her card to the silver-haired guy and turned to Carrie. "The plot thickens. He's perfect, you know."

Carrie didn't have to ask what Erin meant. The other reason she'd agreed to come on this expedition was the Vacation Rule. Established on their first trip together, Erin and Carrie had decided that when they were traveling, men were always on the menu. As long as they weren't in a relationship, they could each indulge in one-night stands if they wanted. Or even more-night stands if the opportunity presented itself. No risk. No fuss. It was all about pleasure and fun, and dammit, if there was one thing Carrie needed it was some uncomplicated fun.

Two months after they'd made their reservation and Carrie was still hurting over Armand. Ridiculous. Unhealthy. Just plain stupid. So when Erin had suggested that she needed someone to cleanse her palate, so to speak, Carrie had agreed.

"You think?" she asked, watching him walk across the lobby. He certainly had the body of a palate-cleanser.

"Yes," Erin said. "Just don't blow it. The guy owns the hotel. He's a believer."

There was the rub. But it was too soon to worry about that. The staring business could mean nothing. He might have a wife and seven kids or something. A thought occurred. "If he helps with the luggage, am I supposed to tip him?"

"Don't ask me. I tip everyone twice as much as I should. You're the one who's sensible."

"Well, that's not helpful."

"If you hadn't alienated yourself from every single person in Crider, Colorado, you could have asked someone."

"Right. I guess I'll be spending more time in my room than I'd planned."

"Oh, no. You're not getting away with that. Tonight is dinner and then the meet and greet. You're going to both."

Carrie scowled, but Erin didn't seem to care. She just stepped away as the man and cart got closer.

He lifted Carrie's suitcase first, but she stopped him. "You might want to put the *Titanic* on there first, Mr. Crider." She nodded toward Erin's enormous wheeled suitcase. A body could fit in it easily. Carrie knew that there were at least twenty-eight different outfits in there, complete with shoes, scarves, earrings, makeup and anything else her friend thought she might need in the next six days.

Carrie had long ago given up speaking to Erin about her need to take everything she owned on their trips, but Erin never listened. Even last summer when she'd had to lug the heaviest backpack ever, she remained undaunted.

"It's Sam," he said, as he traded luggage. He lifted

Erin's bag with surprising ease. Carrie wondered what he looked like under all that flannel. Vacation Rules were sounding better and better. On the other hand, his handling their luggage seemed to indicate that he was pretty involved in running the hotel, and according to Erin, the ghost hunters had taken over the whole place. So while she was on vacation, he wasn't. Maybe it wouldn't be a problem. If it was even a possibility.

Sam stacked everything in sensible order, and when he was done, he put his hand on the small of her back and smiled at her.

Heat filled her, moving from her lower body to her chest, then her face. He wasn't staring at her now. In fact, he was acting the perfect host. But the hand on her back lingered, as did his smile. She had a really strong, terrifically inappropriate urge to kiss him. Holy crap. This could lead to things. Maybe.

"Shall we?" he asked.

Carrie looked away, because jeez, what the hell? She forced herself to focus. The touch meant nothing. If something were to start, it would have to be started by him, and that wasn't about to happen in the lobby. Also, the only thing she knew for sure about Sam was that he was pretty damn sexy. Vacation Rules didn't mean jumping on anyone at all. She had to actually like the guy, and for that she had to spend more than five minutes with him.

Erin led the way to the elevator. The three of them waited, darting glances at each other. Finally, they climbed on board for their short ride.

There were four stories to the hotel. The underground parking, the banquet level, the lobby, which was where the restaurant and pub were located, and finally two floors of guest rooms. Carrie's room was on the top level, 204. Erin was in 206.

Carrie managed not to look at Crider even after they stepped into the hall. It was way less motel-like than Carrie would have imagined. It didn't seem particularly ghost-friendly, either. Instead, it was calming, with a dark mauve carpet that had a gold diamond pattern, and framed black-and-white photographs of what she imagined were local attractions. Gorgeous pictures, actually. She stopped at a shot of an eagle against a clear sky with a very large, very snowy mountain filling the horizon. Her heart had managed to stop its manic pounding and she was almost herself once more.

"That view's about eighteen miles from here. If you'd like, I can show you."

She looked at Sam and it happened again. Tummy flutters, thoughts of kissing, heat. It was a bit more manageable this time, but still. She wasn't the fluttery, blushing type. Admittedly, it had been a while since she'd had sex, but that fact alone couldn't change her personality. "That's a nice offer, thank you."

"Sure. There's no skiing yet, not enough snow, but the ride out is spectacular. I take people out on the trail from time to time. There's no real schedule to it. Just say when, and I'll make sure it happens."

"That's very nice of you, but I'm not much of a cowgirl. I've lived in big cities my whole life."

"That's a shame. Not that I have anything against major cities. I live in one myself, when I'm not here. But seeing this country on the back of a horse? It's a remarkable experience."

"Excuse me."

Carrie turned at Erin's voice. She was down the hall by her open door.

"I've got a phone call I have to make, so maybe you could drop off my bag?"

No way Erin had to "make a phone call." She just wanted to get unpacked so she could get to the good stuff—the hunting. Or she wanted to leave Sam and Carrie alone. Yeah, it was probably that second thing.

Sam hopped to it, and had the Excessively Large Suitcase on the bed in two shakes. Then it was on to Carrie's room, which was identical to Erin's in all but color. There was a great queen-size bed with wooden head and footboards, a comforter that made her want to jump between the sheets immediately, preferably with the man standing next to her, and a good-size desk that would make working there easy. There was even a small fridge and microwave. All in all, especially for the price, this was an excellent room. "Nice."

"We try." Sam put her suitcase on the bed. When he turned back to the rest of the bags, he said, "I see you're all set to do some serious ghost hunting."

She reminded herself of her role here and smiled. "You bet. I'm all about the ghosts. The more, the better. Bring it on."

He chuckled, a sexy rumbly sound accompanied by a sly sideways glance. His nose, she realized, was on the large side, but it suited him. He also had a dimple in his chin, and how had she not noticed that before? Altogether gorgeous. Which didn't really explain her reaction to him. She lived in L.A. for god's sake. She saw gorgeous men all the time.

"So, L.A.?"

"Yeah," she said as she frowned. "How did you—"

"When you registered."

"Ah."

"What part?"

"Downtown."

He put her laptop on the desk. "Really? You're the first person I've ever met who lived in downtown L.A."

"Lots of us do. Just not as many as say, Chicago, because L.A.'s so spread out."

"That's true. I've worked there before. Not for a while, though."

"Doing what?"

"Documentary films. So, you live in one of those big high-rise buildings?"

"Converted bread factory. It's a loft with a great view of the flower market."

"Sounds great."

"You live here, I suppose."

His lips came together and a shadow crossed his eyes. "Not really. I inherited the place after my father died."

"Oh. I'm sorry."

He put her scanner, which he wouldn't be able to tell was a scanner, on the desk, as well. "It's fine. I grew up here. This is home."

"It's cozy. Pretty."

"Yeah, it is." There was more to unload from the cart, but that was done quickly, and then he put his hands in his pockets and rolled up on the balls of his feet for a second. His gaze wandered the room as if he weren't intimately familiar with the décor.

Her frown came back as she wondered why. The situation was new to her. Always before, she'd met her vacation flings at bars or in the pool, and they had all been fellow travelers. Not that there had been all that many. And she'd never had this kind of immediate full-body flush minutes after meeting. Maybe his lingering had nothing to do with sex at all. He probably wanted to give her some tips about the—

Tips. Dammit. She grabbed her purse and pulled out her wallet. Without a second thought, she whipped out a ten even though it was overkill. "Thank you," she said, holding the bill out to him.

He looked at the money, his eyes widened, then he looked at her. "Um. No, you don't have to—"

"I want to. Really."

He didn't actually blush, but his expression let her know that trying to tip him was a stupid, stupid move. Par for the course, today. Now she didn't know whether to put the money away, or what. She decided to drop it on the bedside table. Casually. As if she'd meant to do that all along.

Of course, it didn't work. Yet, he still didn't leave. Okay, she'd made a mess of everything so far, why not go for the whole enchilada and find out if he, in fact, had any interest in her at all? "Do I remind you of someone you know?"

His head jerked up from looking at the ten-dollar bill. "Excuse me?"

"Downstairs. When I was in line. You looked as though you thought I was someone else."

"No, I didn't," he said, quickly.

Carrie blinked. She responded with a drawn-out, "Okay."

He opened his mouth, showing his very nice white teeth, then closed it again. After a sigh, he said, "I think we may have met before but I can't remember where. It's kind of driving me crazy." He took a step closer. "I don't suppose you recognize me."

"Nope. Not even a little bit."

"Ah. Well. Okay, then." He backed up toward the door. "Maybe I do think you look like someone else." He stopped, took a step toward her. "Do you ever go to San Diego?"

"I've been there."

"Huh."

It didn't seem as if he was going to say any more about that. Instead, he focused on the ten dollars again.

"You used to live in San Diego?"

He shook his head. "No. New York. Still do."

She wasn't sure what was going on here. It probably should have been a lot more uncomfortable than it was, but then, she was used to weird conversations with highly intelligent but socially awkward geeks. "Documentary filmmaker?"

"Yeah."

"Anything I've seen?"

"Doubt it. Unless you go to small film festivals. I've done four major pieces, and a bunch of shorts. Mostly to do with human-rights activism."

"Wow, good cause."

"Yeah."

"No ghosts?"

He studied her face. "No."

"Ah."

He took his hands out of his pockets, then rested one on her suitcase. It was a nice hand, strong, with long fingers and short, neat nails. A moment went by and then he straightened abruptly as if goosed. "You probably want to unpack, and I should let you do that."

"Uh," she said elegantly, watching him back out of the room. He really did know the space well.

"You should try the restaurant. And the pastries. Seriously." He found the doorknob behind him. "Anyway, have a great stay."

"Thank you."

He paused. Again.

As weird as this had become, and she was thinking eleven on a scale of one to ten, she didn't mind. She rather liked it. Him. It. She smiled.

He smiled back. That same great smile. Then he opened the door and slipped into the hallway. She heard the lock click and she sat down on the bed, still certain of nothing, but hopeful. Very hopeful.

3

SAM CLOSED HIS EYES as he shut the door behind him. He supposed he could have behaved more like an idiot with Carrie, but not without rehearsals. He'd recognized people in the past and not recalled the context, but never before had the situation turned him into a complete moron.

With a blink to clear his vision, he made the executive decision to forget everything that had happened in room 204. There was a hotel to run, a hotel to sell, and he had no idea what 204 had even been about, so he wouldn't think about it.

None of the guests were in the hallway at the moment, so he took the time to check that the carpet had been properly vacuumed and the pictures dusted. The wall sconces weren't lit, so he couldn't check for bulbs that needed changing, but then he should know by now that even if there were things about the hotel that needed fixing or refining, the housekeeping staff knew how to do their jobs.

There were few complaints with any of the staff. The lifers had been with the hotel for years, had considered themselves family when his dad had been in charge. The part-timers were paid relatively well and loved the benefits, such as the free ski passes, which meant that they were mostly reliable, and any troublemakers were weeded out quickly.

He skipped the elevator in favor of the stairs, and by the second step down, he was thinking once again about Carrie. He liked her looks, her size, the way she talked. Although he felt sure she wasn't nearly as enthusiastic about ghost hunting as she'd like him to believe. That seemed odd considering she'd signed on for a steady diet of nothing but ghosts. Yet another thing to be curious about.

Where the hell had he seen her before? It wasn't amusing anymore. He tried to picture her with shorter hair, maybe a different color, but that didn't help. Nope, she'd looked like this the last time. He felt sure of it. But then, her looks weren't what had captured his attention. Not completely, at least. It was something more. She seemed to occupy a bigger space than she should. Not her body; her personality. He'd seen it when she was standing in line. Among all the guests, Carrie Sawyer was a singularity.

That's what rang familiar. The way she stood out from the crowd. Maybe it was the contrast between her stature and her energy. Wherever he'd seen her before, he'd been struck by that very thing.

It wasn't unusual for him to pick up on strong personalities. He shot raw footage of people who weren't celebrities. He'd trained himself to see past the superficial, to hone in on unique individuals. His camera would love her.

Once in the lobby, he checked his watch, knowing his buyers would be arriving on-site in a few hours. He supposed he could go check up on the kitchen, or make sure the banquet room was set up properly for tonight's meet and greet.

He'd sent Beverly, the groundskeeper, to make sure that the ghost hunters setting up the camera equipment in the Old Hotel weren't doing anything idiotic, like trying to climb the rickety stairs.

The place was mostly a wreck, and wore its condemned sign like a beacon, but of course his father had made sure that the bottom floor was completely up to code. The insurance company came out yearly to do a check, and Sam had gone along on the last visit.

His dad had done an admirable job of hiding all the safety measures, including the two new load-bearing walls. It would take a very good building inspector to see that what looked like a ruin was very sturdy, and would probably survive an earthquake better than any other building on the property. Not that Sam worried much about earthquakes.

His father and all his family had wanted the ghost hunters to have a good time. That the building seemed condemned was a little extra bonus, but in the daylight it was no more frightening than Disneyland's haunted house. Still, every group that set up equipment in the old place left satisfied that they had, indeed, detected spirits from the other side.

There weren't any tricks put in, either. The wind, the floorboards and the ambience did all the work on minds determined to find it haunted. Everyone's expectations were met, all because they wanted to believe. Of course, that wasn't the exclusive territory of ghost hunters. It was the human condition.

And he supposed it was that very malady that set his thoughts back to Carrie. He wanted to see her again, which was tricky. It wasn't a simple thing for him to view himself as an innkeeper. He knew that the staff were absolutely not allowed to sleep with the guests. He also knew a good half of them ignored that rule at times. But he had the feeling that during the next few days especially, he would be wise to keep his wants focused on one thing alone—the sale.

On the other hand, maybe a distraction was exactly what he needed. There was only so much he could do about the sale. He knew the CEOs didn't want him hovering, and his staff was perfectly capable of handling all the details about the convention.

It had been a long time since he'd been so struck by a woman. That she was only here for a week was a bonus, and if he wasn't mistaken, she was interested. There had been glances, a blush. That shiver when he'd put his hand on the small of her back.

Sam grinned as he headed for the ballroom. This could end up being a far more interesting week than he'd ever anticipated.

CARRIE FINISHED HER roasted squab dinner and had to force herself not to lick the plate. How was it possible that in this little smidge of an inn, she'd had one of the best meals of her life?

The restaurant didn't look like much. Lots of wood, of course. This rustic business wasn't Carrie's cup of tea, but she could see that people would expect it, considering the location and the landscape. There were maybe twenty tables, each with a simple floral center- piece. The silver matched, the glasses were sparkling, the lighting subdued, even though the chandelier was made of horns. Deer, elk, she had no idea. All she knew was they were white and pointy and that she'd personally rather have fluorescent lights, which she despised, than chandeliers made from animal parts.

The best thing about the hotel by far wasn't the décor but the Internet connection. It was fast. Not quite as zippy as her cable at home, but for a hotel in the middle of nowhere, she couldn't complain. Almost as good as her Internet speed was that, in addition to a good-sized shower, there was also a claw-foot bathtub. It was deep and there were candles in little nooks in the tile, and the hotel provided some amazing bath salts. She couldn't wait.

"Oh, my god," Erin said, looking longingly at her empty plate. "That was unbelievably good."

"I know, right?"

"I'm really full." Erin had ordered venison, and had finished every bite. "But I'm having dessert anyway. Can you imagine?"

"I'm thinking about ordering the roast squab all over again."

Erin grinned, then did a sweep of the restaurant. "You can tell how great the food is. Check out how no one's talking. With these geeks, that's a supernatural event."

Carrie leaned back in her chair. "You made a joke. About the supernatural."

"I do have a sense of humor about it," her friend said with a scowl. "I'm not mean like some people."

"Who's been mean? Let me at 'em."

"You're a scream."

Carrie's eyebrows rose. "Is that another joke?"

Ignoring her, Erin got the waitresses's attention with a nod. "I'm going to have coffee. Real coffee."

"What time are you planning to go to bed?"

"The minute after I see my first ghost."

"You're gonna need a lot of coffee."

Erin sighed. "Oh, ye of little faith. I'm telling you, there've been sightings here since the beginning of the last century. Especially in the Old Hotel."

Carrie had read about the extra-added-bonus ghost-filled building in the brochure, and in several articles she found on Google. It had been built in the early 1900s by the newly transplanted Crider family. The ghost stories had begun after the small hotel had burned to the ground. Four families, most of them Criders, had been killed and were said to wander the lower floors searching for a way out. "Don't tell me you're going out there tonight. It's really cold, and I'm positive it's not heated and if I remember correctly, the building is unsafe and off-limits."

Erin grinned. "Of course we get to go inside. That's what we're here for."

"Who's we?"

"You know, Mike, Dean, Liam. The people who put the con together."

"And you're on a first-name basis with them because…?"

"Because I'm not an antisocial loner. We've e-mailed. And chatted. And IM'd."

"Erin, did you send them your picture?"

"No."

"Did you send them to your Web site?"

She hesitated. "Yeah."

Carrie sighed. "I thought so. Did you see pictures of them?"

"No."

"Dear, sweet, oblivious Erin. The reason none of the men are talking in this restaurant isn't because the food is fantastic. It's because they're all too busy trying to come up with witty, obscure opening lines with which to dazzle you."

Erin looked around the room with disbelief.

Carrie noted with smug satisfaction that a good half of the men quickly diverted their attention to either their plates, the unremarkable ceiling or simply closed their eyes, presumably under the impression that if they couldn't see, they became invisible.

"No one's even looking in our direction."

"God, you're naive. New York is gonna eat you alive. Trust me. I bet there are at least ten ghost-related pickup lines thrown your way tonight."

"You're nuts. If anyone's looking it's probably at you."

"Want to bet?"

Her friend's cheeks became pink. "No. But even if you're right, it won't last. The ghosts hold far more interest than I ever could."

"I repeat. Oblivious."

"Look who's talking."

Carrie didn't understand, even when she followed Erin's gaze to the east side of the restaurant. "What?"

"Sam Crider? Staring at you like you're his long-lost soul mate?"

She saw him, but he wasn't looking at her at all. He was checking out an empty table before he straightened the place setting. A perfectly reasonable, if disappointing, thing for the proprietor to do. "You're lying because I'm right. But it won't work. Every single guy in this room wants you. Probably the married guys, too. And who knows, maybe someone will, you know, spark."

"That would be nice." Erin picked up the dessert menu. "I wouldn't mind, you know, getting some hot ghost-hunter booooty. Get it? Booooty?"

Carrie shook her head. "So, so sad."

"Come on. That was funny. Talk about someone needing to get laid. But then, you've already got Sam there locked and loaded."

"I don't know. It was, um, kind of weird in my room."

"Oh?"

"Not sexy weird. Just, I don't know if I'm reading him right. And he's the owner. Owners don't shack up with guests."

Erin laughed. "Now who's being naive? Why bother to own a hotel if you can't sleep with guests? I'm serious, my poor celibate friend, your dry spell is about to be broken."

"Fine. I believe you."

"You don't, but you should. I'm having the hazelnut torte."

Carrie didn't blink at the non sequitur. "I'm having the pumpkin soufflé. It's only proper."

"Speaking of, tomorrow night is the pumpkin-carving thingee. You're going to win."

"I'm not going to enter."

"But you should," a male voice from just behind her interjected, making Carrie jump.

It was Sam. For reasons she couldn't explain, he had gotten even hotter in the three hours since they'd last spoken. It had to be his clothes. Instead of mountain-man flannel, he now wore a silky gray retro-looking long-sleeved shirt that made his hazel eyes seem blue. No tie. He'd stuck with his worn jeans, a decision she could only applaud.

"Sorry," he said, "I was just coming over to make sure you had everything you need, then I overheard pumpkins and, well…"

"That's okay," Erin said. "I hope you can convince her. She's really creative and talented, and I've seen her carve some great pumpkins."

"It's a good prize, you know. A massage in your room."

Carrie wasn't at all sure how to respond. Once again she knew she was blushing, even though she still wasn't sure if he was flirting or not. As a good host, it made sense for him to wander from table to table. Hearing a conversation about a hotel activity made things easy for him, and she could appreciate that, as well. He'd have to be clever and quick to constantly chat it up with complete strangers. It wasn't about her at all. Wait. "An in-room massage for free? Where do I sign up?"

"All you have do to is show up," Erin said, before

smiling up at Sam. "I must tell you this was one of the best meals I've ever had. In my whole life. How is your restaurant not on the cover of every food magazine in the world?"

"We have a special guest chef this week. Not that our regular chef isn't great, but Jody's amazing. We're lucky to have her."

"Trying to impress the ghost hunters?" Carrie asked.

Sam looked down before he met her gaze. "Just lucky. She's an old friend. I'll give you a word of advice. Don't get too full. We're serving dessert in the conference room, and take it from me, these are not ordinary desserts."

"Good to know."

Sam smiled at her and after a few seconds he got that look again. The one that seemed just a bit too focused. It made Carrie turn away as she fought her very physical reaction. He cleared his throat, then said, "Well, have a good night, ladies. If there's anything you need, just give me a call."

"Thank you." Erin closed her menu and put it aside. "It's safe," she whispered a minute later. "He's gone."

Carrie looked up. "So, no pumpkin soufflé. At least not tonight."

"The man is totally into you."

"Stop it."

"Come on, you want him so badly. You're all blushing and touching your hair. I'm trying to think if I've ever seen you like this. I was there when you met Armand, and honey, you were not flirty and girlie. Not even a little."

"He's not Armand."

"Thank god. But you're not exactly you, either. But that's okay. Because—"

"What?"

Erin signaled the waitress again.

"Erin? What are you planning?"

"Nothing."

"Liar."

Erin coughed behind her hand. "Could you have said that a little louder? I'm not planning anything. I don't need to. You're going to be with him, my stubborn friend. Without me lifting a finger."

Carrie ignored the prediction, ignored everything but the fact that Sam, the dutiful host, went straight to the kitchen without talking to any other guests. Before the door swung closed, he looked at her again. A long, piercing stare.

SAFELY IN THE CONFINES of the bustling kitchen, Sam cursed to himself as he headed for the back door. He needed a moment of privacy.

This Carrie business was more serious than he'd thought. He'd known it the moment he'd walked into the dining room and seen her back. Yeah. Her back. He'd have known her even if she hadn't been sitting across from her friend Erin.

He stepped out onto the lit patio. It was an employee lounge, mostly used in the warmer months, but even in the dead of winter people came out here to get away. Some to smoke, although there were few of those left. It was also the path to the trash bins and the storage shed. Well lit, it was difficult to make out much beyond the low fence. Sam went straight for the path that led to the edge of the forest. He had no desire to visit the woods this late, he just wanted to get away from the hotel, from the glare of the spotlights.

The farther he walked, the more detail he could see in front of him. A tree, vague in shape and still more two-dimensional than three. He stopped and smiled when he could discern the forest from the tree.

No wonder there were legends of this place. He'd grown up here and still it seemed otherworldly out here. Shadows upon shadows, the eye suspecting movement, attaching stories to the tricks of the night to ease the fear, as if the explanation alone would take away the danger.

It would be easy to believe that a spirit would come back here. The woods, the mountains, all the secret places. Especially if they'd been loved. Been mourned.

He turned his gaze to the hotel, the illumination from the windows as inviting as a warm bed, a hot meal. *Carrie.*

He wanted her.

He'd been on his own too long. But he had to be discreet. And make damn sure she was amenable. The last thing he needed was a sex scandal when the potential buyers were in residence.

No, he had a strong feeling Carrie was interested. There was something about the way she looked at him.

He shivered, hard. "Well, shit." He felt like an idiot as he started back double time. He hadn't even bothered to put on a jacket. This was what happened when a man who hadn't been with a woman in ten months met someone like Carrie. He got poetic. He got cold. And if he had a brain in his head, he got laid.

4

THE BALLROOM WAS BIGGER than Carrie had imagined. And much more crowded. There had to be at least sixty people milling around, most of them in line for food or drinks. She recognized some of the people from the shuttle, including Elbow Guy, who looked as though he'd showered, and the lovely lady who'd spoken so musically. Most of the crowd would fit right in at Comic-Con, the biggest and most extravagant of the comic conventions she attended. Tonight T-shirts were the hot ticket, ninety percent of them with some kind of paranormal picture, quote, or both. Of course, the TV *Ghost Hunters* show was the most popular, although Halloween itself ran a close second.

Despite Erin filling her in about the hobby, Carrie had no idea there was so much ghost paraphernalia. Not that she was one to talk. She wrote online comics. Graphic novels. She had her own online merchandise store, which did a brisk business. Kudos to the spirit world, although she doubted the ghosts were making any royalties.

Two bars had been set up on either side of the long

room, and she'd bought three tickets for herself at the registration table in the hall. Erin had purchased a couple, but she'd also brought a thermos to fill with coffee, her favorite tea bags, a recorder, a notebook, two different sweaters, a pair of sweatpants, a scarf, a blow-up pillow and three paranormal books to be autographed, all carried in a tote bag that was nearly as large as her suitcase.

"Oh, man, the treats look utterly yummy."

Carrie turned at the rapture in Erin's voice. The food tables lined the front wall by the entrance, and it looked more like a brunch spread from the Four Seasons than a Podunk Inn an hour from Denver. Not only was the fruit artfully arranged, but there was also an ice sculpture in the middle of the biggest table.

As for the pastries, Sam hadn't exaggerated. It was an astonishing array. Éclairs, petits fours, napoleons, *petits pots au chocolat,* tarts, cheesecakes, sponges. It was a veritable cornucopia of deliciousness, and Carrie could already feel the pounds expanding her hips. The closer she got to the table, the harder it was to care.

Not that she could get too close. Those who weren't standing in line for drinks were attacking the desserts like starving wolverines. No one was talking, and if someone didn't back down, there would be bloodshed near the petits fours.

"Think maybe I'll get a drink," Erin said.

"Shouldn't we mark our territory first?"

They both turned to the rows of seats facing the stage. Carrie was impressed by the high-tech equipment on display. A movie-theater-sized screen, several big monitors and a sound board, which was weird. She nodded at the stage. "What's with all the TVs?"

"Only a few people at a time can go to the Old Hotel. Everyone else watches remotely from here."

"Watches what?"

Erin got that look in her eye. "Apparitions, sometimes. Flashes of light. They'll see whoever's in the hotel, of course, and then there are all the monitors for sound, temperature fluctuations, electromagnetic shifts. It can be pretty compelling stuff, if you open your mind. I know there's activity here. I've already felt…things."

"Hands on your ass, perhaps?"

"Carrie. Stop it."

"Sorry. I promise. I'll be good. So when do you get to go to the scary hotel?"

"First shift. Midnight," she said, right before she frowned. "Tomorrow."

"Well, I hope there are apparitions and specters and flashes and everything you've ever wanted, but not until you're there to see it in person. Seriously."

"Don't tell anyone, but me, too," Erin said.

Carrie wondered yet again how she'd gotten so lucky to find such a good friend. The thought was interrupted when she got a load of the chairs set out for those who didn't get to freeze all night in a rickety death trap. They looked intensely uncomfortable, but then Carrie wasn't planning to be in one for too long.

Erin headed out, readjusting her tote as she walked. "I need to put this thing down."

Carrie hurried to catch up, but Erin was tall and she was fast. "As long as we're not…"

Erin put her tote bag down in the front row.

"...in the front row."

"We're at the end. You can still get out when you need to escape."

Carrie waved at her to shush. She'd already gotten dirty looks from people. "Fine. I wasn't going to get alcohol, but you've changed my mind."

"What booze goes with chocolate?"

"Enough of either one, and it doesn't matter." Carrie led her friend to the bar on the right. "But I'm going for a Kahlúa and coffee."

"Oooh, that sounds good. Did you look at your program?"

"Yes. I did."

"So you know about Marcia Williams."

Carrie had no clue. "Absolutely."

Erin folded her arms over her chest. "As often as you lie, you really should be better at it."

"All right. Who's Marcia Williams?"

"Only one of the most famous mediums in the world."

"Oooh," Carrie said, trying to sound as excited as Erin had about the Kahlúa.

"I bought you a reading."

"Erin. You don't have money to throw away like that, especially since you're moving."

Her friend looked wounded. "Really? You've decided to go there on the first night?"

People were looking. But that wasn't why Carrie moved closer to Erin. "I'm sorry. I meant thank you."

The anger disappeared in a blink of Erin's blue eyes. "No fair. I have every reason to be mad."

"There'll be plenty of time for that. And ample opportunities, I'm sure. So let's get drunk and fat and then meet and greet the hell out of this crew."

THE BUYERS WERE ON their way from Denver, and instead of pacing the lobby until he drove himself crazy, Sam headed for the banquet room, which was packed.

He walked through the crowd, checking that the floor was clean, that the glasses and dishes were being bussed, that everyone seemed happy. He didn't worry about the bartenders. Both of them normally worked in the pub, and they knew what they were doing. Gene had worked here over ten years, and he'd met his wife, Felicity, when she'd come on board. They'd been married in the garden right here on the property. Sam had been filming in Atlanta that summer. His father had signed their gift from the both of them.

Carrie was in Felicity's line. She wore slim black jeans and a snug green sweater, and when she turned his way, he felt as if he'd been hit with an electric shock. Just a buzz, diffused through his chest and lower, a reminder of what his trip to the forest had told him. This was a woman he wanted to know better. Intimately. He headed her way.

It was clear the moment she noticed him, and he let out a held breath at her smile. There was nothing forced about it, nothing faked. He'd caught her by surprise and her first instinct was to welcome him. Excellent.

"Hey, you have any pull around here?" she asked. "We've been in line for hours."

He raised his eyebrows. "Hours, huh?"

"At least three. Maybe five. I'm too parched to be sure." Carrie had lost the grin, and replaced it with complete sincerity. It was Erin, and the fact that the ballroom had only been open for about twenty minutes, that gave her away.

"She's like this all the time, Sam. It's awful. You'll see."

"I think I can handle it."

Carrie grinned prettily. "You can get us our drinks?"

"Sure thing. As soon as we reach the bar."

"Oh, you're no fun."

"It's only the first night," he said. "I can't go playing favorites. Yet."

"Oooh." Erin bumped Carrie's shoulder with her own. "You'd better not hog all the good ghosts, missy."

Carrie laughed, but when her gaze caught his, she stopped as if she'd just realized whom she was joking with. A stranger. An innkeeper in a haunted hotel. One who did peculiar things to her mind and her body.

"This looks fantastic," Erin said, filling in what had just begun to feel like an awkward pause. "I can't wait to get my hands on some of that dessert. Who is this chef? Some star of the Food Network?"

"She's been on *Iron Chef* before. And won."

Erin stepped out of line into his personal space and shoved his chest. Kind of hard. He didn't mind exactly, although he was surprised. "You are kidding me." Her voice had gotten half an octave lower, and he took another step back.

"Nope. Not kidding."

"I have to meet her. Can I meet her? I love *Iron Chef*. Almost as much as *Ghost Hunters*. More than *Ghostly*

Encounters. About the same as *Hauntings*. But I love *Hauntings* so much."

He wasn't sure how to respond to these earnest declarations until he looked behind Erin to find Carrie laughing. Hard. Trying to hold it in, and failing miserably. Sam grinned. "I'll see what I can do."

"Thank you. Seriously," Erin said, and she did sound incredibly serious. "Thank you."

"No problem. I think you two are about to lose your place in line."

"She's an architect," Carrie said, as she stepped backward to guard their space. "Honest. A really good one. She makes buildings in between watching TV shows."

"I see. And you're an architect, as well?"

"Nope. Graphic artist. I don't watch enough television to play in the big leagues."

Erin frowned. "Mock all you want. I'm very well-rounded."

Sam wished he was here on vacation. Free to hang out with these two just for the laughs. He couldn't remember the last time he'd felt so relaxed and damn, he was attracted to Carrie. He couldn't stop looking at her. That smile was really something. His cell rang, and he pulled it out of his pocket. "Yeah?"

"Where the hell are you? They're almost here."

Hit with a hard dose of "what was I thinking?" Sam flipped the phone shut. "Gotta go." Then he almost ran out of the ballroom, and did run down the hall to the lobby, cursing under his breath the whole way.

He skidded to a halt on the hardwood floor just before it became the lobby. Putting on his best businessman smile, he walked his most confident walk to the registration desk where Ben Heartly and Kunio Mori were sharing a laugh. As he neared the two men, he thought their good humor looked genuine, that the trip in from the airport had been a good one.

None of this was emotional. It was strictly business for them, just as it was for Sam. Buying the place would work for one or both of them, and it all boiled down to the bottom line. Sam had done extensive research into their companies, and these two men. They had the resources, now all Sam had to do was let the Crider Inn show itself off.

"Gentlemen," he said, putting out his hand. "How was your ride in?"

"Excellent," Heartly said along with his firm shake. "Gorgeous sunset and good company. Although I'd like to take a look around tomorrow to see if there's space for a landing field."

"I'll see to it."

He turned to Mr. Mori.

"I look forward to the scenery on the way back, when it's still daylight."

"It's beautiful country. Would you gentlemen prefer to go straight to your rooms to freshen up? The alternative is to make a quick stop in the ballroom, and then dinner in the restaurant."

"I could do with a meal," Heartly said. "But I'm happy to wait if Kunio would prefer."

"No, I'm starving."

"I'll have your luggage sent to your rooms, and if you'd like, I can take your coats and then we can begin."

Once that had been accomplished, Sam walked with

them, pointing out some of the hotel features, some of its history. He itched to call the kitchen, to make sure everyone was on red alert, but he trusted his staff. The important thing now was not just to know he had no power to alter the outcome, but to believe it.

DRINKS IN HAND, Carrie and Erin stood in their second line of the night, this one a trip to the dessert table, which, as luck would have it, had been replenished. It was like going to Disneyland. Not that there were any large cartoon creatures walking around, but because of the goodies at the end of the wait.

"I'm getting one of everything," Erin said.

Carrie nodded. "I can get behind that."

"Do you think the food's going to be like this every time there's a talk in here?"

"Nope." Carrie sipped her coffee, very, very glad someone brilliant had invented Kahlúa. "I think this is a one-time deal. Next talk, we'll probably get raisins and cold Pop-Tarts. It's the only way they're going to make any money off this conference."

"Hey."

It was a male voice, a little bit behind them and to the left. As a unit, Carrie and Erin turned. Surprise. It was Elbow Guy from the shuttle. His name, according to his tag, was Elton.

"I remember you from the bus," Carrie said.

"Shuttle," Erin said.

"Whatever," Elton added. He stuck out his hand to Carrie, although he stared at Erin the whole time. "I'm Elton." He helpfully pointed to his name tag. "Like the singer. No relation."

Shiver

Carrie managed not to laugh. "Nice to meet you, Elton. I'm Carrie. Like the book. Also no relation."

He nodded, causing his dark, shoulder-length hair to fall forward and back. "So you seen any ghosts?"

"Not so far."

He seemed surprised that Carrie was talking to him. "I mean, ever."

Carrie shook her head. "Not a one. I'm just not lucky like that. But my friend Erin has." She helpfully pushed Erin closer to Elton.

"Yeah? What kind? Like, scary?"

Erin faced her and scowled, but smiled before she turned back. "No, not scary. Why, was yours?"

Carrie left the conversation in Erin's capable hands as she moved closer to nirvana. She'd narrowed down her picks from six to four, eliminating the fruit category. The *petits pots au chocolat* was the current front-runner, with the napoleon inching up.

"Right, Carrie?"

She straightened. "I'm sorry, I zoned out on treat selection. Did you ask me something?"

"Elton was saying that it's really cool to be here where everyone knows that ghosts are real and living among us. Because sometimes, when he tries to talk to people about his experience, they don't get it. And I was saying that he's absolutely right. That every single person here knows ghosts are real."

"Right. Yes. Of course." She looked at Elton, who must have been around twenty or so. He wasn't a bad-looking kid, but his eyes were sad, and his shoulders slumped and his T-shirt was kind of generic. "I'd like to hear about your ghost experience," she said kindly.

Elton smiled. "It was more of a poltergeist than a spirit."

"They throw things around a lot, yes?"

"I'll say. My parents still don't believe me when I tell them, but I swear it's true. The poltergeist knocked over a couple of vases, broke a chair and kept tilting all the pictures in the hallway. It happened for almost a whole year. I kept getting in trouble, and they sent me to the school counselor, but even Frodo, my dog, he used to bark all the time at like, nothing. It wasn't nothing, it was the poltergeist, but even when I showed my dad, he just said the dog was as crazy as—"

A crash of breaking glass and thuds had Carrie spinning around to face the left corner of the ballroom. A big cleanup tray had fallen from a portable stand, leaving a mess of broken dishes. Only, no one was standing near that corner. Not a soul. The closest person was a tall woman with long dark hair who seemed as surprised as everyone else in the room. She couldn't have knocked over the tray and gotten so far away in the time that had lapsed.

Someone must have put one too many plates on the far edge of the unsteady tray. Bummer for the cleanup crew.

Carrie turned back to Erin and Elton, but they were both staring wide-eyed and mystified at each other, then at the spilled tray and back again.

A crackle, a piercing screech of feedback, then a voice from the stage. A low voice, filled with intensity and just a little bit of fear. "Ladies and gentleman," the man on stage said, his gaze sweeping over the crowd. "The party has just gotten started."

5

THE EVENING HAD GONE WELL. Sam slumped into the brown chair in his room. It wasn't the room he'd grown up in, just a room in the hotel, the one that was always rented out last because of the noise from the ice maker and the elevator. He'd been staying in it since he'd come back, having moved Aunt Grace to his dad's apartment.

He could have stayed in what had been his childhood bedroom, but he didn't want to change his aunt's routine. He didn't mind this place. So used to Brooklyn noises, the small sounds in here were like raindrops on a window. Sometimes, though, like tonight, he wished he could sit in his dad's old recliner and lean all the way back. The fire would be going and maybe he'd listen to some Dave Grusin or Brubeck. Sip a little brandy.

Instead, he just closed his eyes in the serviceable chair, too tired to get ready for bed, despite the hour. He checked his watch. It was even later than he'd thought. Just after one. The buyers must be exhausted, although neither one of them let it show.

As he'd planned, the dinner had gone off spectacularly.

Jody had outdone herself with a tasting menu for the three of them, and he'd never enjoyed food more. Heartly had tried to hire her as his personal chef, which she'd politely turned down.

The three men talked about the ghost-hunters conference, the legends, everything but the brass tacks of the property. This was only a viewing; the final piece in a six-month-long process.

Just because they'd laughed, shared wine, broken bread, it didn't mean a thing.

He should really get into bed. There was a lot to do tomorrow, and he didn't relish the idea of the buyers traipsing about unsupervised. He wouldn't necessarily have to go with them personally, but he sure as hell wanted to know what they were doing and when.

He stood, rolled his shoulders, undid his top button. Stopped as it occurred to him that most of the conference attendees would still be in the ballroom, as only a few had been selected to sit in the mind-numbing cold of the Old Hotel. Those inside would also be waiting breathlessly for a spectral vision to float across the monitor screens. Or to hear a disembodied voice whisper something that could vaguely be interpreted as a word instead of the wind meeting wood.

The night staff would make sure there was coffee for the intrepid, tea for the weary, and he was quite sure there was still food to be had. No reason at all for Sam to give them another moment's thought. Except for that one thing.

He still had no reason to go to the ballroom. Even if Carrie were there, he wasn't exactly going to ask her to come back to his room. They'd met less than twelve

hours ago, and just because his mind had gone straight
to the getting-naked part, he couldn't admit it so soon.
Even if she did feel the same way. Which she might
not.

But then again...

No. Going down there was ludicrous. Stupid in every
way. After a heartfelt sigh at what a classic idiot he was,
he turned off the light and headed for the elevator.

CARRIE STARED AT THE blank page of her spiral bound
notebook. It had been blank for far too long, and she was
tired, dammit, so why couldn't she get it done already?
It's not as if she didn't have material to pick from. She
had too *much*. That was it. Too many goofy things, from
the shuttle ride to the programs, to the ghost-hunting
equipment for sale—good god, the equipment—to the
introductions and qualifications of the speakers, there
was simply too much to mock.

Not that it was all mocking, all the time. It wasn't as
if Carrie didn't have a heart. She did, and Erin knew it.
It was just that her job was all about mocking and snark
and being insufferable. That's why her peeps came to
her Web site, why they bought the art and the T-shirts
and the mouse pads and the graphic novels. She'd been
bitchy since childhood, and lucky her, she'd been able
to make a career of it. A win-win situation all the way
around. She wore, as her friend Jeffrey often said, scorn-
colored glasses. But she did try her best to be a compas-
sionate human. It didn't always work, but it happened.
Carrie had actually sat quietly and listened for two solid
hours before she'd bailed. Now, she put her pen down
and went back to her laptop. She'd stopped herself from

doing this when she'd first gotten back in the room, but since she wasn't doing squat anyway…she clicked on Google and typed in Sam's name.

There were a lot of Sams. Once she'd found the right one, there were still a lot of links, mostly to do with his documentary films. Undocumented workers, restorative justice, the American prison system. He sure didn't fool around. She read reviews. Lots of them. All of them with the same general message: his films were intense, specific and illuminating. They were moving and star-tling. He got down to the heart of things and didn't shy away.

Impressed, she went to find his biography on his Web site. No picture on page one, not of him, anyway. The focus was on his latest film and where people could get their hands on it. But there was a hyperlink to his bio, and she leaned forward to read that.

He was older than her by four years. Went to NYU. Worked with some heavy hitters in the documentary field before directing his own. No mention of Crider, Colorado. No mention of his childhood at all. Also no mention of a significant other, but that didn't mean anything.

What she did know for sure was that she wouldn't be averse to spending some time in his company, quite possibly in the bedroom. She wondered if he had an apartment or if he stayed in one of the hotel rooms. That could be weird. But then, maybe he slept with guests all the time.

Shit, she needed to put this away, stop thinking about the hot guy and get some work done. At the very least, she had to get the story concept down. Nothing happened without the concept being clear. She had to narrow her point of attack. Was it the conference as a whole? The "professional ghost hunters?" How hungry people were to have explanations and stories to quell their collective zeitgeist? Until she decided the arc of the series, there would be no series.

Maybe she should have stayed downstairs in the ballroom and watched the monitors with Erin. There was bound to be a ton of great stuff all around her. On the other hand, she was tired from traveling, her sugar rush had ended and so had the buzz from her drink. The smart thing to do would be to climb under that big old comforter and get a good night's rest. Tackle the work again tomorrow.

On the other, other hand, Erin was going to be up all night, and therefore she wouldn't even be around in the morning. No one would. In order for this to work, Carrie needed to be with the natives in their natural habitat. The goal was to blend in. To appear to be one of the loyal believers. They'd all catch on if she went to bed early every night.

But sitting on the floor or on one of those stackable chairs till dawn? No way. No way in hell. Unless… She looked at the comforter, at the big fluffy pillows on the bed. No reason she couldn't observe and be comfortable at the same time, right?

She gathered her notebook and pen and put them in her purse, then she folded up the bedding enough to carry it with her, and she set out for night number one of her new and temporary schedule that began at 4:00 p.m. and would last till 4:00 a.m. Ghosts, it turned out, were night owls.

The whole way down she wondered not about the spooks or the speakers, but if Sam would still be awake. She'd caught a glimpse of him earlier, but he hadn't come back. Funny how disappointed that had made her. Even funnier was how much she hoped he was in the ballroom now.

CARRIE WASN'T IN THE ROOM, which had changed significantly since Sam's last visit. The chairs were gone, or at least shoved to the sidewalls and stacked, at least most of them. The center of the room was now dominated by people on their own fold-up chairs, sleeping bags, cushions, or just pillows. All of them facing the monitors on the stage, which had been moved to give the most folks the best view.

The podium had vanished, the lights were dimmed, the bars emptied of everything but bottled water and pitchers of juice. There was still food on the back tables, but not much, and the big coffee urns would be full 24/7.

It wasn't easy staying up all night, especially when practically every spoken word that was louder than a whisper was immediately followed by a barrage of shushes. Although few of the attendees expected to *see* anything, except perhaps a vague mist, all of them expected to *hear* something. Anything.

The Old Hotel was wired, baby. Infrared cameras viewed the rooms well, but three of the high-end cameras were focused not on the hotel itself, but on the meters placed randomly around the lower floor. Digital and analog audio recorders that picked up electronic voice phenomena were stacked next to a whole hell of a lot of stuff no one needed but everyone in this room wanted. He wasn't complaining. While the gift shop didn't stock top-of-the-line equipment, they did a pretty decent business in various midrange meters and cameras which occupied one whole wall of the moderately large shop, across from the candy bars, magazines and sundries.

Sometimes, Sam wished ghost hunting hadn't become so mainstream. He would have liked to have filmed this, to document the phenomena of the search for the paranormal. This night right here would have been full of opportunities. As they did in gatherings of any kind, the people had formed smaller, more informal groups. Some consisted of only two people, but there were clusters of five or six. Five would be about right, if you had to whisper.

For a documentary, he would have hit up the couples first. Asked them why they were here, what they hoped to see. What had happened in their lives to convince them this wasn't a fool's errand.

Then he'd seek out the family units. Husband, wife and the kids come for a week in the woods to find spooks? Halloween wasn't a legal holiday, so maybe they home-schooled. He'd met a lot of those kinds of folks in the past, dedicated to the pursuit of their passion to the exclusion of almost everything else, including traditional educations for their offspring.

What was happening in those young minds when they stayed up all night waiting? Did the children believe wholeheartedly? When they reached their teens, did they rebel and disavow their parents, insisting that nothing was real that couldn't be proven and tested by science?

His attention was broken not by a word, but by a sensation. The hairs on the back of his neck stood up, and he felt the smallest of shivers. He turned and there was Carrie.

"You're here," she said.

A chorus of "Shhhhhs" followed.

"You're here," she said again, this time in a whisper. "I was pretty sure you'd be sound asleep by now."

She was almost swallowed by the comforter and pillows in her arms, which he managed to take after a fumble. And then it was just Carrie in the same green sweater and jeans from earlier this evening, but she looked even better than she had before. "I should be sleeping," he said, also sotto voce, "but I came down to make sure everything was moving along. Coffee, water, no loud music, that kind of thing."

She smiled, which caused a different kind of shiver altogether. "As long as there's no karaoke, I'm good."

"Oh, there is. In the bar. Every weekend."

"Thanks for the heads-up."

He grinned right back at her, fully aware that he was acting less than the perfect hotelier. "Where do you want these?"

She looked past him, stopping with a nod. "There's Erin. Follow me."

He did so, gladly. Stepping around legs and arms and sometimes whole people as they made their way to what looked like a quiet spot on the left side of the room, not too close to the stage. Erin was sitting with three...no, four young men. The only surprise was that it was only four. Just as he'd suspected, the boys were buzzing around her like bees after honey. He doubted even one of them expected to score, but they would all have plenty of fantasy material for the next time they were alone. He remembered exactly what that was like, and it worried him that it was a little too close to what he was feeling about Carrie as he dropped her comforter on the carpet.

"What are you doing here?" Erin said.

"Shhh." That from about six different people.

Carrie bent to spread her comforter and Sam stepped right in to help. He wasn't feeling tired any longer, even though he knew he was being a fool.

"I'm here to find ghosts," Carrie whispered. "What are you doing here? Hi, Elton."

Sam found Elton via his name tag and his little wave. He was one of the throng surrounding Erin and he fit the bill. Young, thin, ghost T-shirt, long hair. Besotted, but not just with Erin. Sam saw the way Elton looked at Carrie. He stepped in between the two of them, reminding himself that it wouldn't do to threaten a guest.

The other boys were excited about the new female, and damn, he wished he had his camera. They were like a pack of beta wolves, preening and scuffling, even as they sat on the floor with their power drinks, candy wrappers and electronic devices, which were primed for texting. They were all probably trying to figure out how to announce Carrie's arrival in one hundred and forty characters or less.

"So, anything happen?" Carrie asked.

"A temperature anomaly, but nothing significant," Erin said.

It was odd hearing their whispered voices, along with all the other whispers. It made him think of a room full of moths.

"Well, it's early yet," Carrie said, then she turned to him. "Are you going to hang out for a while?"

He nodded. "For a while."

"Great. I'm going to get coffee. I have the feeling it will be necessary."

"I'll go with you."

She led him back across the patchwork quilt of bodies. No one seemed to think it was odd that he was here, and a few even smiled in recognition. Why should they care? Most of them probably thought he was just another guy who worked here. Which was good.

Being with Carrie was better. She poured them each a hot coffee. She put stuff in her cup, then eyed the remaining food.

"Never let this chef go," she said, her low voice causing her to step close to him. "She's unbelievable. I've eaten so much I should be shot for even thinking about taking more."

"It's good to indulge yourself once in a while. You're on vacation. You're supposed to be bad."

The way she looked at him let him know he'd been about as subtle as an eighteen-wheeler. "Even vacations have consequences," she said. But she chose two pink petits fours, both on one plate. "How bad can these be, right?" she asked. "These little things barely count."

He grabbed a big old éclair, more to keep himself busy than because he was hungry. "I have no self-control when it comes to Jody's food. She knows it, too. Once, when she was visiting from Paris, she forced me to eat an entire Bûche de Noël."

"At gunpoint, I assume?"

"No, dammit. Worse. She left it on the counter."

Her laugh wasn't as quiet as it should have been, and she was reprimanded immediately. She glared at the crowd, unsure who'd done the deed. "I mean, come on. If we can't laugh, what's the point?"

He almost laughed, too, but he didn't dare give off even a hint of disrespect.

She handed him a fork and a small napkin. "You say she's going to be here all week?"

"Jody? Yep. All week."

"That is just great. Although I'll pay for it with exercise when I get back home."

"That's what hiking's for. I could show you the prime sights."

"Wow. If I were a person who hiked, I'd jump all over that offer. But with these hours, I intend to sleep through most of the day. I still have to work, too." She closed her mouth quickly, pressing her lips together, as if she'd said something she hadn't meant to.

Of course he wanted to ask her about it, but again, discretion won out. "Then you can take advantage of the sunsets. You can see those from your room. Also, don't worry about having to get up and eat dinner. We're serving late for the rest of the conference, from noon to midnight, breakfast until six p.m."

"Everyone in the hotel is with the con?"

He had just taken a bite of his éclair so he nodded. After he swallowed, he said, "We've only got thirty-six rooms."

"Ah. Lot's of doubles and triples. Been there, done that."

"Really?"

"Sure. I went to college in Kentucky, and we used to go to Daytona Beach for spring break. I mean a whole flock of us. I've slept on couches and floors. A bathtub once. That sucked."

"I know the feeling. I have a very small apartment in Brooklyn. Ever been to New York?"

"So you probably sleep in the bathtub every night."

"Couch. Not a fold-out couch. A short couch. With lumps."

"You must really love Brooklyn."

He ate a bit, as did she, then sipped his coffee before answering. "It's either New York or L.A. Although the options are changing as more of the film business spreads across the country. I use a lot of students for my crew, and it's always last-minute stuff."

"I searched you on Google," she whispered.

"You did?" Dammit, why hadn't he thought of doing that? "And you're still speaking to me?"

"I must not have looked hard enough. Everything I read sang your praises."

He rolled his eyes, but he wasn't feeling quite so blasé. She'd looked him up. He tried to remember everything on his Web site, what pictures she'd seen, but he couldn't think. That happened a lot when he was near her. "Hype," he said. "But I am proud of my films. Some more than others."

"Doesn't it just depress the shit out of you?"

Now he laughed, loudly enough to get his own rebuke. "Not doing something would depress me more.

Not that I'm some massive humanitarian. I just find the real issues to be the most vital. I thought about going into the movie side, but my heart wouldn't be in it. I want to tell stories that matter."

Carrie frowned up at him, although he didn't think she disapproved. More that she was thinking about what he'd said. "How does that work out with you running this place?"

He put his empty plate down, but kept his coffee. "It doesn't."

"There needs to be more of that sentence."

"Right. As much as I'm fond of the inn, it's not my life." He lowered his voice further. "I'm selling it."

"Really?"

"Shhh." He leaned closer. "Uh, that's supposed to be a secret."

"I'll keep it under my hat." She put both her plate and her cup down. "Hasn't the hotel been in your family for generations?"

"Yeah."

"And you don't mind?"

"I'm not very sentimental."

"I imagine not."

"You're appalled."

"No. Not at all. You need to do what you need to do. I'm not a sentimental person, either. Not really. There are only a few things in my life I couldn't live without. One of them, sadly, is my best friend." She looked over at Erin, sitting among her fan boys. "I'm better with her around."

"How so?"

"I live most of my life on the Internet. It's pathetic.

Erin helps me participate in life, as she calls it. Without her I'd go out even less frequently than I do now." Carrie shrugged, took a step away from him. "We should get back to watching the monitors. There could be ghosts."

"Right. Ghosts." He wasn't sure if it was the talk of sentiment or the talk of Erin that had changed the tenor of the conversation. Her body language had changed, even her whisper was different.

Would it be smarter to leave things be for the night and hope for a better tomorrow? Or should he wade back in and try for a recovery?

She took his plate and hers to one of the washing bins, then came back and refilled her coffee. All without meeting his gaze.

"I think it's time for me to say good-night," he said, as much as it pained him.

She looked up then. "Giving up the ghost so early?"

He grimaced at the pun, then smiled. "Big day tomorrow. I can't sleep till noon."

"It was nice running in to you again. I enjoyed it."

"Me, too. Maybe we'll meet again tomorrow."

Her dark eyes were wide and beautiful, and they studied him closely. "Yeah. That would be good. I'd like that."

He believed her. All was not lost. At least, he didn't think so.

6

CARRIE CLOSED HER EYES. Again. For the billionth time. It was four-thirty in the morning, and a half an hour ago, she'd been so dead on her feet that she'd strongly considered paying Erin to put the comforter back on her bed.

She'd managed alone, and to brush her own teeth and get into her pj's, but the moment she'd actually put her head down on the pillow, she'd been alert, awake and, no matter how sternly she'd spoken to her inner monologue, it would…not…stop…yammering.

"Shut up," she said, hoping the aloud version would be more effective than the silent one.

Evidently not, because the next millisecond she was thinking about him. Again. The fact that she'd told him she had to work while she was here wasn't so bad. It was nothing, in fact. They were going to be here for nearly a week. Of course people had to work.

No. What had been bad was that she'd said one hell of a lot more. She'd told him flat out that she was a complete loser who had exactly one real friend, and that the rest of her life was spent playing World of Warcraft and trolling Web sites. Awesome.

Reciprocity. That son of a bitch.

He'd told her his secret about selling the place, which was *whoa*. Major. So then she'd felt the need to reciprocate with a secret of her own.

If she hadn't wanted to sleep with him, it wouldn't be an issue. But, she'd realized the moment he'd taken the comforter and pillows that she did want to sleep with him. She liked him. Nothing earth-shattering, but she was ostensibly on vacation, and Vacation Rules stated that one could sleep with a very attractive hotel owner if one wanted to on the basis of like, which was quite different from Regular Life Rules. She was also allowed to eat at least one dessert a day, she didn't have to work out and she could speak with a British accent if the mood struck.

But Sam had a *life*. He made important films about important issues. He lived in New York and traveled the country, not at comic book conventions, but living with the real people. He was friends with a world-class chef. She was friends with Hobbit107@inbox.com. It was the first damn night and she'd already blown it. Hence, staring at the ceiling in the wee hours of the morning.

The true tragedy was that she hadn't even told him the worst of it. That she was there undercover, her sole intent to embarrass and malign people just like him. Oh, he'd love that. Who wouldn't? She could just see how well that conversation would go. He'd probably kick her right out of the hotel, and who could blame him?

It was a miracle she even had Erin.

Anyway, Sam was going to find out about her. All it

would take was a little Google action, and he'd discover her secret identity. She wrote under the name Carrie Price, but Price was her mom's maiden name, and it wasn't exactly a state secret.

She turned over and socked her pillow a few times, then tried to get comfortable. Fat chance.

Hell, maybe he'd understand. He was a New Yorker, for god's sake. Just because he believed that ghosts were real didn't mean he had no sense of humor. He was probably used to people making fun of him. Film people were notoriously cynical, right?

Crap. Even if he did get made fun of, he wouldn't want to sleep with someone who openly disparaged his beliefs. That would be like her sleeping with someone who thought graphic novels weren't real books.

Worse. Because a lot of people didn't know squat about graphic novels. As far as the supernatural went, she was in the minority. A huge percentage of the world believed not only in life after death, but also ghosts and reincarnation and angels and demons. Most folks didn't go a day without relying on something that couldn't be scientifically proven. It was the norm, and she was the weirdo.

Nothing new there. She was used to being the odd woman out. She just wished she'd kept her mouth shut.

The only thing she had going for her was that he thought she was hot. It was right there all over his face. The way he looked at her? Oh, yeah. He wanted some vacation action.

Her smile fell. It was the first night in far too many nights that she hadn't fallen asleep thinking about

Armand. Was her attraction to Sam nothing but rebound lust?

After giving that a moment's ponder, she turned over one more time. So what if it was? In fact, rebound lust was the whole damn point.

AT TEN TO FOUR IT WAS almost time for the first official event of the day. It, like all their indoor meetings, would be held in the ballroom. Sam had spent the morning with the buyers who continued to make nice noises without saying anything definitive, and left them in Beverly's capable hands for a tour of the stables, the barn and the back fields. Sam had come to supervise the pumpkin-carving contest, which would be loud and messy, but fun. At least, that was the plan.

He wished he'd slept better. Thoughts of his conversation with Carrie had kept him up long after he'd hit the sheets. He'd dissected every word and come up with fifty different interpretations of what had gone down. He'd concluded he hadn't completely blown his chances.

Naturally, he'd looked for her everywhere. At breakfast, although she'd be nuts to come down at eight after her night, in the ballroom, even in the kitchen. He'd been hopeful when they'd gone to the bar to grab lunch, but no go.

After that, Sam had taken Heartly and Mori into Crider City. The trip couldn't have been timed more perfectly, as there were four buses parked at the IHOP and tons of tourists wandering through the decorated town. In Crider, Halloween was as big a deal as Christmas. The local legends about hauntings weren't restricted to the hotel property, but had propagated all through the town. Most probably made up over a beer or two and carefully seeded across Colorado and beyond.

Instead of garlands of pine hanging over Main Street, there were flying witches and cut-out ghosts. Every window had some festive painted depiction of something mildly ghoulish, although appropriate for children. Some stores, like the Gift Emporium, went nuts.

Heartly and Mori resisted buying any ghost-related souvenirs, walked the length of Main and back, then Sam had returned them to the Inn. Mori had fallen asleep on the short ride, but neither he nor Heartly mentioned it.

"Sam?"

It was Wendy, one of the part-timers who was helping with the room setup.

"Yeah?"

"Are we only doing the one prize?"

"Why, do you think we should do more?"

"I think there are gonna be kids here, not many, but enough that we should do something about it."

He gave it some thought as his gaze caught on the wheelbarrow of pumpkins teetering as it was brought down the center aisle. "After everyone's here, take a head count of anyone under eighteen and make a note of the little kids, although I don't think they'll be many. Pick out gifts for all of them, and charge them to the party."

The way she smiled at him was a little surprising. Although he didn't know her that well. So far, she'd been a reliable worker, someone who didn't complain about filling in with double shifts. She probably just liked the idea of looting the gift shop.

His attention went back to the pumpkins. They were being stacked in front of the stage, on two levels, some on the carpet, some on bales of hay. The tables had been equipped with multicolored markers, stencils, ice-cream scoops for the innards, big bowls and lots of paper towels. Of course, each table was covered in thick plastic and paper, and the rules of the contest were in block letters, posted on four walls. Even so, he would read them aloud before the competition got started.

The monitors were on stage, still recording evidence of the supernatural, but during the contest itself, there would be music of the Halloween kind piped in. The food table wasn't festooned with prize-winning pastries, but it was certainly cheerful. Punch and fruit and too many candy treats, all holiday themed, would please guests of any age. The two bars were in the process of being stocked.

The rules were pretty simple. All cutting into pumpkins was done by a staff member. All participants, either as individuals or teams, drew their design on a pumpkin. At the end of the evening, the crowd voted on the winner. Not only did the winner receive an in-room massage, but their pumpkin would also be featured in the Crider City newspaper on the front page.

He heard Jody's voice behind him and when he turned, she was pushing a cart that carried her pumpkin creations. They were so expertly crafted and clever they should have been displayed in a gallery.

Sam went to help her set up. Dry ice swirled in the corner just under the table and around Jody's feet.

"I heard you were all over the place with the buyers this morning." She kept her voice low as she placed the first pumpkin.

"Yeah. They couldn't stop talking about last night's meal, though."

"That was the plan. By the time Heartly leaves, he's never going to forget my name, or my cooking."

"You'd better work fast. He and Mr. Mori are out of here tomorrow. Early."

"I know. And don't sweat it, sweetie. I've got it covered." She placed another pumpkin, then shifted the first. Before she got to the third, she took a long sweeping look at the room. "She's not here yet."

"Who?"

Jody shook her head. "Everyone knows, Sam. Even Mikey, and he never even leaves the kitchen."

"Knows what?"

"That you've got it bad."

He almost argued. Then sighed. "I used to be more subtle than this. How is it possible I've gotten worse at picking up women? It's got to be the sale messing with me. 'Cause this is not how I roll."

"How you roll?" Jody laughed, loudly and long. "Who are you talking to? I've known you since we were freshmen, buddy. I've seen your moves. James Bond, you're not."

He stared at her, openmouthed. "What the hell are you talking about? You're just jealous you didn't marry me when you had the chance."

"We'd have been miserable and you know it. We both had a lot of growing up to do. But you know what?

You've turned into someone I like quite a bit. Not as much as my husband, but still."

"Gee, thanks."

"I heard you were down here last night after one in the morning, when you should have been getting some beauty rest."

"How do you know this?"

"I work in the kitchen. We know everything."

He handed her the next damn pumpkin. "Yeah, well. I'm not sure it did any good."

"Stop. You're gorgeous and wonderful and she'd be an idiot not to like you. Just a thought, though. Tomorrow I'd go back to flannel and hiking boots. Let those big-city boys get a taste of the real Crider experience, and let this woman see that you're a rugged outdoorsman."

"Talk about false advertising."

"What do you care? It's only for another couple of days. And you look damn good in those old jeans of yours."

"Does your husband know you talk like this?"

She grinned at him happily. "He thinks I'm adorable."

"I'll have to talk to him about that."

"Speak of the devil," Jody said, nodding toward the entrance.

He expected to see Jody's husband, but it was Carrie standing by the door. Although he wanted to, he didn't turn. "So, everybody's talking about me and Carrie, huh?"

"You know the kitchen staff, Sam. Biggest bunch of gossips in the world. Except for maybe housekeeping. Or would that be reservations and front desk?"

"Fine. How about using those extraordinary eaves-dropping skills on something useful? Like finding out who's going to buy this joint and for how much."

Jody put another pumpkin in place. "Go talk to her. She keeps looking at you."

"You're just making shit up now."

"Am I?"

Sam studied Jody's face. She was still a beauty. Marriage and having a kid agreed with her. He knew some of that glow was due to working again after such a long hiatus, and that pleased him. He hoped she and Heartly could make a deal. As for her being all-knowing and wise, that was a bunch of bullshit. Nevertheless, he had no qualms about leaving Jody without a second glance.

AND THERE, LIKE A GIFT, was the very man Carrie had been searching for.

He looked good. Skinny black pants, hunter-green button-down shirt all very hotel-ownerish. But his hair, that was all renegade filmmaker. It wasn't quite as messy as just-rolled-out-of-bed. No, it was more just-finished-making-out-in-the-backseat hair.

As he approached his smile swept away all doubts that she'd screwed up her chance with him. She adjusted her sweater, smoothed her hair, although she'd just checked out the ponytail five minutes ago. She was just doing the mating dance of the Prowling Twentysome-thing Female, dressed in her finest plumage. Well, the finest she'd brought, which consisted of jeans, a thrift-store cardigan, navy ballerina flats and an estate-sale broach she'd found in East L.A. Sam looked her up and down, and from what Carrie could see, he approved.

"You're early," he said as he stepped in close. "That means you can have your pick of pumpkins."

"How nicely alliterative. Perhaps I'll pick the prettiest pumpkin."

He opened his mouth, then let it close with a sigh. "I'm just going to give that one to you. I'm not up to the challenge."

"Why not?" she asked as she walked with him to the pumpkin patch.

"I'd have to think. That's probably not gonna happen tonight."

"Ah. How about answering questions? Up to that?"

"Depends. What's the question?"

"Who, exactly, will be giving the prize-winning in-room massage?"

Sam put his hand on the small of her back. They were almost at the pumpkins so this was going to be a fleeting moment. As fleeting moments went, this one was a little bit spectacular. Her body broke out in little bumps, her breath hitched and her step slowed to stretch things out to the last second.

Yeah, she definitely wanted to see how Sam looked when he rolled out of bed.

"We have a terrific masseur who comes up to the hotel. His name is Michael, and he's studied touch therapy for years. He runs a well-known studio and school in Crider. Even if you don't win, you should try and make time for one of his massages."

"Oh," she said, as she looked at the great pile of pumpkins.

"What's wrong? You sound disappointed."

With her heart beating fast, her courage at maximum, she turned to look him straight in the eyes. "I was hoping, if I won, that you'd give me my massage."

His pupils dilated. She'd wager he was blushing as hard as she was, but she didn't move her gaze an inch.

"I think that could be arranged."

"What if I don't win?" she asked.

He smiled. She could tell by the lines at his eyes. By his eyebrows. "It could still be arranged."

She let out her held breath, then turned back to pumpkin picking. It wasn't that she was playing it cool. On the contrary. If she'd kept staring at him like that, and if he'd kept looking back at her with the blatant hunger in his hazel eyes, she'd have kissed him. The last thing she wanted to do was embarrass him or herself, not so early in the evening, at least. Besides, now there was *this* between them. Much stronger than before, when it wasn't a sure thing. Now, it was all tension and subtext and potential. So delicious she shivered with it.

"People," he said, just above a whisper.

"What about them?"

"They're coming. I should…do…things."

She nodded, still not looking at him, smiling at his failure to be the least bit suave. It was tempting to tease him, to discombobulate him as the conference attendees came rushing into the ballroom, eager to snatch the best seat, the best pumpkin. It was quite possible that Erin was among them, and Carrie should have cared about that as she was supposed to have picked out their seats. Not that they'd discussed the contest arrangements, but between them, it was the way things were done. The first one there secured seating or tickets or places in line. But Carrie didn't care where they sat. Or if they sat. She wanted to think about the sex, think about Sam. Think about sex with Sam.

"Have you decided?" he asked, startling her with his volume.

"What?"

"Which pumpkin you'd like."

"Oh. Okay, sure. That one." She pointed down and to the right, which turned out to be not the most perfect of pumpkins. In fact, it was unusually tall, but as soon as she saw, she knew exactly what she was going to draw.

He picked up her selection and when he stood, he met her gaze once more, only something had changed in the few seconds since his question. Somehow, she guessed through some decision he'd made, he'd become far more confident, relaxed. And damn, sexier than ever. "Let's get you a seat."

She followed him, not saying a word as he found a table near the back, on the end. He put the pumpkin on the butcher paper between the markers, then he touched her upper arm. "Do you think Erin has a particular pumpkin type?"

Carrie shook her head. "Oddly, we've never discussed the issue."

"If you had to guess?"

"I'd said asymmetrical. Something interesting."

"I'll be back."

She watched him walk through the burgeoning crowd, and though his hair still rebelled, he was all long legs and easy grace, and Carrie gave herself a quick hug, so proud of herself and her bravery she could just spit. She wasn't one of those women who could snare a man with a come-hither glance. Her confidence was primarily in her pen, on paper. In sharp retorts and wicked double entendres, all the things she'd promised to keep under wraps for the duration of the conference. And yet, she'd managed to say just the right thing at the right time. What would happen from here was anyone's guess, but things were definitely looking up.

7

BY THE TIME ERIN sat down on the opposite side of the table, Carrie was already into her first sketch.

People were still settling in, raising their voices with excited chatter as they found their pumpkins and their seats. According to the program, there would be announcements about the nighttime activities, then a talk about the contest itself, explaining the rules and demonstrating how to make a pattern and transfer it to the gourds.

"You look happy," Erin said, gripping her coffee cup with the strength of one not fully awake. "Did you get laid?"

Carrie darted a glance at the long-haired woman sitting next to Erin, who smiled at her enquiringly. "No," Carrie said, trying to give Erin the eye, which didn't work. "I didn't. But I clearly got more sleep than you. What time did you hit the room?"

"Too late. Or would that be too early? Sorry I missed you for breakfast. I had the best pancakes in the history of pancakes. I think I'm going to put on twenty pounds while I'm here, and I couldn't care less."

Carrie ignored the complaint as she decided she wasn't thrilled with her drawing. She crumpled it, then took another sheet of paper. "So, still no ghosts?"

"Not yet. Some more suspicious temperature readings, though. The honchos are setting up inside the inn for later tonight. I'm going to be in the Old Hotel tonight. I'm so excited. It feels… Something's going to happen tonight. I feel it. You know?"

"Absolutely not, but good for you. Keep that positive thought. I mean, come on, what ghost wouldn't want to meet you? They'd have to be insane to pass up the opportunity."

"Yeah." Erin's voice dripped with sarcasm. "I'm a bundle of delight."

"Shut up. You are."

"I need more caffeine."

"I'll say. What do you think of your pumpkin?"

Erin gave it a look, but her expression didn't change a bit. "It's a pumpkin."

"You don't want to change it for another?"

"I don't care. I'm not gonna do anything with it. You're going to win, and I want to bask in your reflected glory."

"I know just what I want, but I'm not quite getting it," Carrie admitted. "I'm a bit distracted."

"Oh?" Only her best friend would have made the connection directly from that banal sentence to "something happened with Sam."

"Yes, oh."

"Do tell."

Carrie looked at Erin's neighbor. Unabashed, the woman, who had a nice heart-shaped face that shouldn't have been so hidden by her lank dark hair, smiled and waited.

"Later."

"Spoilsport." Erin moved the pumpkin and the supplies to one side, then put her head down in the hollow of her crossed arms. "Wake me when something juicy happens."

Carrie stared at her blank paper, but before she touched it with her pencil, she looked up. Sam was two aisles away, his back to her. Even though she knew it was a little sexist and definitely shallow, she loved the contrast between his broad shoulders and trim hips. With his hair over his collar and the way his black jeans hugged his ass, he was kind of perfect.

There wouldn't be time to discover the inevitable annoying things, for either of them. He didn't have to know she liked to eat her cereal with juice instead of milk, or ketchup on her cold spaghetti. Or that sometimes she would get so involved with her comic that whole days would pass without her realizing it.

He turned just then, as if he'd known she was looking at him. A smile curved his lips, and his right eyebrow arched with their secret. She blushed. Her stomach did that dip-and-swirl thing that hardly ever happened to her.

A part of her wanted to forget everything and drag him off to her room right this second, but the bigger part wanted to keep this feeling for as long as possible. Anticipation, in her experience, always exceeded reality.

One of the few children in the room tapped Sam's shoulder, and the moment was gone except in memory.

She bent to her paper, determined to get what she saw in her mind's eye to come to life on a stencil drawing.

Now, THIS WAS WHY HE had no business hooking up with a guest. At least not right now. Sam was in the middle of dinner with the buyers and Mori was asking him questions about the local skiing and snowboarding. Sam was having a hell of a time keeping focused. Carrie might be hot, but she wasn't multimillion-dollars hot.

What kept tripping him up was that it was almost time for the contest to come to a close, when the group would pick a winner. He felt disloyal hoping it wouldn't be Carrie, but he didn't want her to get the in-room massage from anyone but himself.

He answered Mori's questions without making a fool of himself, glad the three of them were on the tail end of dessert. Of course Jody had outdone herself again, and both Heartly and Mori seemed sated and happy, and not just from the meal.

"Are you going to stick around for any of the ghost hunting tonight?" Sam asked. "They're setting up in the attic and in the garage. Oh, and the storage room, which should be warm. I'm not sure if they've picked out any of the guest rooms to monitor."

Heartly shook his head. "I'm reasonably sure if anyone had actually found evidence of a ghost it would have been in the headlines. I think I'm safe turning in early."

Mr. Mori took a sip of coffee then nodded. "That's the thing with legends and folk tales. Hard to prove, but hard to disprove, too. My family has a long tradition of believing in the afterlife. Personally, I wouldn't mind finding out they're right. There are a few things I'd like to know about what happens next."

"What happens next for me," Heartly said, as he folded his napkin and put it on the table, "is a shower and bed. I'm going to call my wife, hope there's something decent on the tube, and relax. This has been an eventful couple of days. You have a fine property here, Sam. It's well cared for and both your staff and your guests seem happy. I know your father would be proud."

"Thanks. He loved this place. It resonated with him."

"You won't miss it once you're gone?"

"From time to time, I think it's inevitable. But that's the thing about moving on. I've got films of my folks, of the grounds. I've transferred them and all my pictures to digital. They're safe and available when I'm hit by a bout of nostalgia."

"Good," Mr. Mori said. "I have some work to do, so I'll also be heading upstairs. I, too, thank you for your hospitality. And please, don't bother coming down tomorrow, if it's just to see us off. If there's a problem, I'm sure your people can handle it."

Heartly nodded, then stood, and after handshakes without promises, the buyers left the restaurant.

Sam felt relief, but also let down. He'd been hyped up about this for so long that the anticlimax hit hard. The best thing to do now was distract himself. Luckily, he knew exactly how he was going to do just that.

"OH, MY GOD," ERIN SAID, staring at Carrie's finished pumpkin. "You *did* get laid."

"Shhh!" Carrie ignored the woman next to Erin,

knowing she was certainly grinning as broadly as half the jack-o'-lanterns in the room. "I did not."

Her friend leaned over the table, pushed her disheveled hair out of her face and looked at Carrie with wide, accusing eyes. "Liar. I can't believe you didn't tell me."

Carrie turned the pumpkin so that her art couldn't be seen. It wasn't as if she'd drawn Sam naked or anything. No one would even know it was Sam. All she'd drawn was a back. The rear view from thighs up. Narrow hips, broad shoulders, hair scraping a collar. A hint of arms, a sense of movement. She'd paid particular attention to the butt, but that was an artistic statement. Nothing whatsoever to do with Halloween, but she liked it. She wanted to carve it, see if she could make it come alive on the pumpkin itself. "I have no idea what you're so *loudly* talking about."

"Come on. Tell me. I've got nothin' here. No ghosts. No sparks, and I'm getting fatter by the second. I need you to tell me what happened."

After a dramatic sigh, Carrie leaned forward. "We kind of made plans."

"What kind?"

At least they were whispering, although Carrie had the feeling they weren't quiet enough. "For later."

"Details, woman. Details."

She lowered her voice further, put her hand in front of her mouth. "He promised me a massage."

"What?" Erin asked, her voice a veritable trumpet.

"Shhh. Dammit. I'm going to get coffee. You sit here, young lady, and think about what you've done."

"The hell with that." Erin got up and followed Carrie

to the back of the room to the giant coffee urns. The second they were reasonably alone, she poked Carrie in the side. "Spill."

It was a damn good thing she didn't know anyone in the place, or plan to ever see any of them again, because she was certain that in approximately ten minutes, the word around the conference would be how the nonbeliever was also a total slut. "All we did was talk. I was interested in the in-room massage prize. He said that could be arranged." She smiled at Erin. "Even if I didn't win."

"Ha. I knew it. From that first minute. Didn't I tell you? Didn't I say? Oh, I'm so jealous. He's like the only doable guy in this whole place. Except for maybe Liam."

"Liam, the conference coordinator? The married conference coordinator? His wife is here."

"I'm not gonna jump him. Sheesh. I'm just making an observation."

"That's what you get for hanging around ghost hunters."

"Hey, Sam is a believer. Remember?"

"He can believe in whatever he wants," she said, cupping her coffee between her hands. "As long as he's as great underneath those clothes as he is in them."

Someone behind Carrie coughed. Not a real cough. The kind of cough that said she was busted. Even before she turned, Carrie knew who it was. Yep. The woman from their table.

"I like your pumpkin," she said sweetly.

"Thanks."

"I'm sure you'll win the prize." The woman, whose

white T-shirt said Dude, Run in big black letters, gave her a grin, then walked away without even the pretense of getting a beverage.

"This just keeps getting better," Erin said, taking way too much pleasure in Carrie's embarrassment.

But Carrie's attention was diverted when she saw that Sam had come into the room. In fact, he was standing by their table, looking at her pumpkin. And he was grinning with all the subtlety of a tree falling on a house.

"He," Erin stated, "is hot. Very, very hot."

"I got dibs," Carrie said, which was probably obvious from the blush warming her cheeks.

"Come on." Erin took her arm with her free hand and led Carrie to the table. To Sam. As soon as she was in range, Erin said, "Hey, *Pumpkin*. How you doin'?"

Carrie didn't sock her friend, even though she wanted to. Instead, she smiled as innocently as she could. "Here to start the judging?"

He nodded. "I just announce, the group will judge."

Erin set her cup down. "I'll bet the female faction will vote for Carrie's. Although it's not at all scary."

"Really?" Sam asked. "You don't find that frightening?"

Erin touched his shoulder. "Sorry, babe. It's the best-looking thing in these parts. Except for the inspiration."

"Erin." Carrie couldn't have put more nuance on the name if she'd tried. It said *Shut up, stop it, go to your room,* and *we may be on vacation, but I can still kick your ass.*

Erin just laughed. She took her seat, crossed her arms

over her Ghosts Do It in the Dark T-shirt and stared at the two of them as if they were on high-def TV. The Soap Channel.

"Go do your thing," Carrie said, abandoning all hope of getting through tonight with any dignity.

"I'll see you after?"

She nodded.

Sam hesitated, then took her hand in his and gave it a gentle squeeze. "Good."

Carrie watched him as he meandered through the crowd, commenting to the participants, especially the younger ones. It occurred to her that this was all her own damn fault, and if she hadn't wanted the hotel populace to know she wanted to sleep with the owner, she should have drawn a spooky little ghost and kept her mouth shut.

So she sat, resigned. "You can stop looking so delighted. I admit it. All of it." Then Carrie turned to Erin's neighbor. "And you can stop it, too."

The "Dude, Run" woman burst out laughing. "You have to admit. I didn't have to work very hard."

"No, you didn't."

"I'm Lulu," she said. "I'm here with my old man, who is busy watching some sports thing in the bar. He doesn't believe in any of this stuff, and he wasn't supposed to come, but since the bar has more ESPN than we have at home, he insisted. I gather you two are friends?"

Carrie nodded. "Nice to meet you, Lulu. I'm Carrie, that's Erin. I'm not sure about us being friends, though."

Lulu shook her head. "I can see that's not true. Sorry

for sticking it to you over by the coffee, but man, that pumpkin. Did you think you'd get away with it?"

"I guess not."

"Personally, I don't blame you a bit. He's a cutie."

A shiver went through Carrie, not big enough that anyone would notice, but she felt it move straight down her back until it made her cross her legs. This was becoming very real. Very close. Thank god she'd shaved her legs.

As she sipped her now-cooled coffee she tried to do a quick run-through of the coming night, despite having no idea of the actual logistics. His place? Where was his place? Her room? No one too close there, but he'd have to make the call. She supposed she could insist that it be her room. At this point, she doubted the game would be called on account of venue.

She'd brought condoms because she always brought condoms on the off chance. But it had been a while since Armand, and she was feeling surprisingly gun-shy. Normally, she had no qualms about her sexuality, but with Sam, she wanted him to like it. Her. A lot.

"Carrie."

She blinked at Erin. "What?"

"You're not in the bedroom yet, so please pay attention to the person sitting across from you."

"Sorry. Zoned."

"I guessed. Your squeeze is asking for pumpkins to be brought onstage."

"I told you, I'm not entering."

"You have to." This, from Lulu. "It's adorable and everyone'll get a real kick out of it. It's not as if the whole room doesn't know."

"Have I thanked you guys for that yet? No?" She leaned forward. "There's a reason."

"Honey," Lulu said, as if she'd known them for years. "Half the people here were talking about you the minute you checked in. Some said you didn't believe in ghosts. Personally, that's fine with me. You can believe in whatever the hell you want. Others said you and Sam got into a little staring contest in line. Sherry said it was like you two were having sex right there in the middle of the lobby."

"Oh, my god." Carrie put her head in her hands.

"It's kind of sweet," Erin said. "No reason for you to be embarrassed. You're both consenting adults and you're not breaking any rules. They're all just jealous. I know because I am, too. Do yourself a favor. Own it. If someone doesn't like it, too bad."

Carrie lifted her head just enough to stare at Erin. "Own it? Who the hell are you talking to?"

"The new you. The one who's going to be brave and daring and fierce even when I'm in New York. The one who's not going to lock herself in the loft and only come out when there's no more milk."

Carrie's stomach swooped again, this time unpleasantly with the reminder that soon her life was going to change so dramatically. "I shouldn't be hooking up. I should be spending time with you."

Erin gave her a lopsided grin. "I love you, but not that much."

"You know what I mean."

"I do. But please, I beg of you, do this. He seems like a really nice guy. He's not about to do something hinky. He's the owner, he's got staff, guests. If it's terrible, so what? You both get a little itchy when you see each other and then you move on. It's the perfect time and place to take a chance, trust me."

"And how do you know that?"

Erin tapped her temple with her index finger. "Psychic."

Carrie leaned over and tapped her friend's other temple. "Insane."

Lulu laughed as she picked up her contest entry. "Well, I'm planning on winning the sanctioned massage. But whatever happens, I think I can safely say that someone sitting at this table is gonna be real happy with their prize."

Carrie didn't argue. As she looked up at the stage, she was hit again by how deeply she was attracted to Sam, even though she hadn't known him for long. She couldn't remember the last time this had happened. There was something about him that pleased her. A lot of somethings, from his looks to his humor to the way he interacted with the guests and the staff. Nothing psychic about her opinions, but her intuition told her that being with Sam was a good move. There was chemistry at work, the good kind. Whatever tonight would bring, she knew at the very least they'd have some laughs. The only thing she had to be careful about was the whole reciprocity thing. Seeing each other naked would take care of that issue nicely.

She shivered again, and it wasn't because she was spooked.

8

ONLY SIXTEEN PUMPKINS were entered into the competition. Four of them were from kids. Sam had encouraged the crowd, which wasn't nearly as large as they had anticipated, to come on up, but most of them seemed to want to move on to the actual ghost hunting.

He tried to keep his attention on the contest, but his thoughts were so captured by Carrie he stumbled over his words, and in one case, a boy. They'd almost lost his pumpkin, but Sam had made a precipitous catch. All that was left was the voting, the winner determined by applause. He'd best get on with it, as moments ago the conference team had entered the ballroom, ready to rally the troops.

"Settle, people," he said into the microphone. "Settle. There's a remarkable massage at stake here, and fabulous prizes for our younger contestants."

A smattering of claps followed as he walked over to the first pumpkin on display. "Here's number one. Let's here it for Johnny Newland's horrible ghost!"

The family of Johnny Newland hooted and hollered

although it was obvious that the young entrant would win something other than the massage.

"Here's our second entrant. Lulu Foster's witch!"

The well-done, very traditional witch drawing got a lot of support. As Sam went down the line, he thought Lulu might just get the prize, but then he got to number twelve and that one, a gruesome face painted with lots of red blood, earned such praise that Elton, Erin's admiring fan, stood up and took a bow.

The voting ended with Elton the clear winner, and it was no surprise to Sam when Elton announced he was donating his prize to a friend. The young man blushed furiously when he smiled at Erin.

For her part, Erin winked at the kid, then laughed loudly at something Carrie said.

Sam was pleased that Carrie hadn't entered. That pumpkin was personal, although far more people were in on the secret than was comfortable. He couldn't imagine his father flirting so blatantly with a guest, but who knew? His dad hadn't ever mentioned a particular woman in his life in the years following Sam's mother's death, but he didn't imagine his father never looked. Sam had long ago decided that if his dad had found someone else, it would have been a good thing. Now, he'd never know if that had happened.

Sam pulled himself out of the melancholy dip with another look at Carrie. She smiled up at him, and he centered himself. The sooner the rest of the prizes were doled out, the sooner he could make his escape.

Wendy had chosen the kid's prizes well. They were stickers and pens and ghost stories for young readers, and everyone seemed thrilled with their loot. Finally,

Sam was able to hand the mic off to the conference committee. The moment he stepped off the stage, his body stirred in anticipation.

She looked so fine in her jeans and blue cardigan, her dark hair put up in a loose ponytail that showed off her graceful neck. But it was her red lipstick that kept drawing his attention. The idea that he would be tasting her soon not only made him damn aware of his dick, but also made him feel as if he'd had too much champagne.

He already knew she smelled good, but he had yet to discover the details. There was a world to discover waiting across the ballroom. A whole person, beautiful and unknown, smiling as she dipped her head, shifted her gaze.

An announcement from the stage made him turn. It was nothing, just a logistics thing, a heads-up for folks to fill their thermoses and get ready. When Sam turned back, Carrie had stood up and she wasn't alone. Erin's gang of guys had come calling, Elton blushing like a schoolgirl. Sam saw Carrie search him out, shrug her shoulders, then turn back to the conversation.

It was okay. He could wait. But not in the middle of the room. He walked to the far corner and grabbed a bottle of water as he passed the beverage table.

There was so much excitement in the room that he could lean against the wall with no worry of being bothered. He should have looked over the crowd, made a call to Patrick to check on things, but he didn't. He watched her instead.

How could that woman not have dozens of friends? She'd seemed almost distraught when she'd confessed her fear of Erin's leaving. From the bits he'd gathered, and he knew there wasn't sufficient evidence to justify most of his wild speculations, Carrie's relationships were primarily online and yet she didn't think of them as relationships at all.

If she left her downtown loft, it was on an errand or at the behest of Erin. With Erin in New York, it would be easy for Carrie's already narrow world to become narrower. He'd seen it a lot, primarily in big cities. The lost people might have been that way even without the Internet, but now, jeez, it was easier than ever to keep one's distance. To live just outside of the real world.

He wanted to understand this. Carrie was not only attractive, but she also laughed easily, seemed comfortable in her skin, and she was funny, smart. Okay, so maybe he was projecting again, but he didn't believe he was far off the mark. A woman like her would normally have a broad circle of friends. He'd expect to see her at clubs, at movies, at the very least in bookstores or flea markets, but with a posse. Something didn't fit with her, and it made him enormously curious.

It was his curse, this need to get to the truth of people. That singular drive was behind all of his films, all his life's work. Even with his weird schedules and guerilla filmmaking, he'd still managed to have friends. They were mostly work related, but that's how most people hooked up in every walk of life.

He supposed there were worse habits to have. He'd met so many amazing individuals in his dogged pursuit. The journey had put him in close contact—intimate contact—with people so different from himself it was as if he'd met extraterrestrials. He'd soon learned to step outside his comfortable first-world existence to experience how all different kinds of people lived, whether they were from Colorado, the mountains of Appalachia, or living in tar-paper hovels in Tijuana.

Even with all that experience, Carrie was still a puzzle. A mystery. He liked mysteries.

CARRIE DISENGAGED HERSELF from the fawning boys around Erin, mouthing "Sorry" for leaving her to her minions. She just wasn't able to be polite for one more second.

That's what she loved about forums and blogs and fan groups. The arrow keys. If she didn't like the conversation, she could skip past it with no guilt whatsoever. She also was very fond of the delete key. What was so satisfying as to make something unpleasant or unwanted vanish at the touch of a button?

It was probably good though that she couldn't make things disappear in real life. Her world would be awfully repetitive. She liked her routines, her day-to-day made her feel comfortable and safe.

Tonight didn't feel safe at all.

Well, it felt safe enough in the physical well-being sense of the word, but routine? Same old? Just another walk in a ballroom? Not by a mile. Every step of her ballerina shoes took her closer to Sam. If this had been a computer game, she'd have gotten the cheats and read ahead. Not knowing was scary as hell, but it was also kind of wonderful. He just looked so damn happy to see her.

Okay, so maybe she wouldn't have hit the down arrow

on this one. Maybe she would have ventured in with no expectations, except to have herself an awesome time.

Her hands went to the bottom of her sweater and she gave it a tug, which made her think about the getting-undressed part. It might be a good move to get to know him a little better. Talk before getting naked, 'cause once they were naked the conversation tended to get a little stilted. Not that there was anything wrong with that, but in her experience, she was better if she knew who she was getting in bed with. Normally that meant what kind of comics he read, if he was into Halo, which blogs he regularly followed and when he'd admitted he was a card-carrying geek.

Good lord, she lived a weird life.

Her pace slowed as she approached him, standing all loose and handsome as he leaned against the back wall. He'd done something odd to his hair at some point, but she liked it sticking up. She also liked the way his big hand held that little water bottle. That was an artist's hand, and she knew what she was talking about. Hands were important to her and his were elegant, blunt-ended and strong. She just knew they'd feel wonderful skimming down her naked back.

"Is that blush all for me?" he asked, his voice low enough that stragglers around them wouldn't hear.

"Evidently," she said, touching her fingers to her cheek. She hadn't realized.

"I'm glad." He pushed off the wall, but he didn't move to touch her. "I know you got up late, but what would you think about visiting the bar? I know I could do with a drink."

"That's an excellent idea," she said as her body let

go of some tension that had been in her shoulders. "I'll warn you though, I like them sweet and girly. I can live without the little umbrellas, I suppose, but only if I have to."

"I don't know if we stock umbrellas," he said, only now putting one hand just above her elbow. "But I bet we have enough cherries to make up for it."

His touch wasn't even skin-on-skin, but it still felt incredibly intimate. She looked up at him, surprised again at how tall he was.

"Just so you know," he said, bending just a bit to get closer to her ear, "I asked Wendy to take special care of your pumpkin."

"Oh." She'd forgotten about it. It had been sitting right on the table, and she'd meant to take it with her, but seeing him waiting had knocked everything out of her head. "Thanks. I wanted to carve it."

"Later," he said. "Now, let's find ourselves a nice, quiet booth. I've got questions to ask, and I'm willing to answer a few myself."

She smiled the whole way to the bar, taking a deep whiff of the wonderful smells coming out of the restaurant. She wasn't hungry, not really, but the scent was seductive. Perhaps this bar served appetizers. That would be a good idea anyway. She didn't want to be drunk tonight, and she was a lightweight at the best of times.

The bar, which carried on the rustic theme of the ballroom and restaurant, had people in it. Carrie didn't know why that surprised her, but it did. It wasn't packed or anything, and there were empty booths lining the far wall, but still. People. Even though they'd passed several ghost folk on the way from the ballroom, it had felt as though he'd been taking her somewhere private. His bar.

Which it was, technically, but it wasn't closed now. In fact, there was some sporting event playing rather loudly. She looked to see if she could pick out Lulu's husband, but he could have been one of three likely contenders. Carrie hoped it was the good-looking cowboy, though.

Sam stood by the farthest booth and waited for her to slide in until he took the seat across from her. "We hardly got to speak today. How was your night?"

"Fine. No ghost sightings, but there were a few more temperature fluctuations," she said, shamelessly stealing not only her words from Erin, but also the attitude. "It's early yet."

"Are you planning on hunting later?"

"That depends."

"On?"

"Don't play coy, Mr. Crider. It doesn't work with those knowing eyes."

"Coy? Me? Never." He leaned forward. "I promised a massage, and I give a damn good one. But there are all kinds of massages, and I would never presume to pick out the one that's best for you."

"Well played, sir."

A cute blonde waitress dressed in black and orange came to the booth flashing a toothy grin. "Hey, Sam," she said, in a very Southern drawl. "What can I get y'all?"

"The lady likes her drinks sweet and girly. What do you recommend?"

"We make a milk punch that I swear tastes like the

best vanilla milk shake you've ever had. If you want something more tropical, go for the daiquiris. Whatever flavor, you won't find a better one in the state."

"Milk punch? Made with cream or ice cream?"

"Ice cream, darlin'. I am not foolin'. It's like you're drinking a piece of creamy heaven."

Carrie grinned. "Sign me up."

"What about you, Sam?"

"I'm not nearly that adventurous, Debbi, but if anyone could have gotten me to drink a booze milk shake, it would have been you."

Debbi laughed. "People tell me I have a gift."

"People are right. I'll just have a Balvenie, please. On the rocks."

"Comin' right up." She turned back to Carrie. "You interested in some appetizers?"

"I might be."

Debbi nodded. "Here's a tip. The buffalo wings go really well with that milk punch, but you won't find anything in this place that isn't delicious. I'll be right back with the menu and your drinks."

Carrie turned to Sam and found him looking at her with the most interesting expression. Completely at ease, yet curious with a hint of wicked in his slight smile. She swallowed, fought the temptation to look away. She wasn't used to being studied, not by a man she hardly knew. Who was she kidding? If she wasn't at a conference or an expo, she wasn't particularly used to being near people, whether she knew them or not. Maybe because she went to so many conferences, from Comic-Con to Wizard World to WonderCon, she seemed to spend half her life selling merchandise, speaking on panels and bonding with her fellows. At least here, no one knew that she wrote *Cruel, Cruel World*. It was liberating. She smiled, felt the tension leave the back of her neck. "How goes it with your secret sale?"

He darted a look around, and seeing it was all clear, came back to her. "It's over. Technically, the buyers aren't leaving until tomorrow, but the dog-and-pony show has ended. What happens next is anybody's guess. It's now officially out of my hands."

"Must be a relief."

"It'll be a relief when I cash a check. I admit I was anxious, wanting everything to be perfect. Then I realized the property is the property, and no fancy meals were going to change anyone's mind."

"That's a lot of expense to go to if it wasn't going to swing the deal."

"Jody?" He shook his head. "No, she's a gift of circumstance, not expense. We've known each other since college. She hasn't worked for over a year, what with having the baby and all. She wanted to get in the groove again before she went back to New York. It was a good situation for the both of us."

"I can't imagine any restaurant not wanting her. She's incredible."

Debbi came back carrying the drinks. Carrie's was tall and frothy, Sam's looked like a double. Carrie took a sip of the drink before she opened the bar menu. It was better than advertised. "Oh, my god."

"I know," Debbi said. "Why don't y'all take a look at the menu. I'm gonna go get a drink order, but I'll be back in a quick minute."

"Thanks." Sam didn't even look at the waitress, didn't

pick up his drink, either. "I've been thinking about you. A lot."

Carrie met his gaze. "Is that a good thing?"

"Very. Do you like oysters on the half shell?"

She blinked at the non sequitur. "Uh, yeah. Do you like bunnies?"

He laughed. "Yes. A lot. But not to eat. I was going to order the oysters, but some people don't care for them, so..."

"That was nice. Also nice is not eating bunnies. I'm a total hypocrite about all that, though. I eat chicken and fish, and sometimes even beef, and I always tell myself that I'm going to be a vegetarian, but that only lasts for a couple of days. It's horrible. I convince myself that buying free-range, organic food is enough, when I know damn well it's not."

Sam nodded. "I've gone through that. I was a vegetarian for three years. I don't know what made me go back to meat. Actually, I do. I was pissed at someone, the person who got me to be vegetarian in the first place. So I ate meat as a screw-you. Not very effective. Or mature. Especially since I was twenty-seven at the time."

Carrie liked him better for the confession. She understood human frailty. It's what her comics were all about, in the end. She wanted to tell him about them, to spill it all and share it all, but she couldn't. He believed in ghosts. He believed a lifetime's worth. Honestly, that wouldn't have stopped her if she'd met him under different circumstances. If he wasn't a rebound guy. But her heart was still vulnerable, so she didn't dare tell too much or like too deeply. She was only here for five more days. Then they'd never see each other again, so why spoil it when it was just getting good? This…this thing with Sam was a blip, a moment. A nice one that she didn't want to screw up.

"What's wrong?"

"Hmm?"

"That frown. What happened?"

"Oh, nothing. Really. Nothing. Odd thoughts of home and things I have no business dwelling on when I'm here on vacation. I have to try the wings, but I also want the artichoke-and-spinach dip. If you're willing to share."

"I'm in," he said. Then he reached across the table and took her hand. "I'm very glad you're here. It hasn't been the best year. Losing my dad, taking over the hotel. The damn sale has swallowed me whole. I've spent too much time in my own head. I want to hear about you, about your life, about Erin moving, about your loft. Just about anything you'd be willing to tell me."

"That could take some time."

He nodded as his thumb drew a lazy circle over the back of her hand. "I'm extraordinarily attracted to you. I know it's old-fashioned and if I ever admitted this to my male friends, they'd revoke my guy license, but I prefer to have sex with more than just a smokin' body. Which you have, by the way. I'd like to know you better."

"Dammit," she said, closing her menu. "I just wanted a quick fuck."

Sam didn't move. Not a muscle.

She grinned. "I'm joking. Mostly."

His smile started small, ended wide, and his eyes told her there would be nothing quick about it.

9

SAM SIPPED HIS BALVENIE, savoring the smooth single malt. The combination of his favorite scotch and Carrie was the best thing that had happened to him in months. It helped that her little joke had not only started him on the road to a nice hard-on, but he could also safely infer that said hard-on would come to a satisfactory conclusion. All he had to worry about was focusing too much on his dick. "How come you don't have more friends?" he asked, opening the door widely on distraction.

She blinked at him, lifting her pursed lips off her straw. "I have friends. They're just online, is all, which is a perfectly legitimate form of friendship, you know. In fact, sometimes I think those are the most honest relationships. There are so many ways to connect online, based on interests and passions. Without worrying about all the physical stuff."

"I can see it as an addition to real interaction, but not as a replacement. We do too much communicating through body language. There's so much room for misunderstanding online."

She nodded. "You have a point. But some people are better at real life than others."

"I think you're pretty damn great at it."

Her expression was doubtful. "That's because you want to have the sex."

"Doesn't mean I'm wrong."

Carrie tilted her head slightly to the right. "Now that you mention it, I have been pretty great. With you, I mean. I'm not usually. I wonder what that's about?"

"Could it be because you, too, want to have *the sex?*"

"No. I mean, I do want it, but I don't think that's it. I've wanted to, occasionally, sleep with other vacation guys, but frankly, if they hadn't spoken a word all night, that would've been fine. Even preferable. I like you. I want to talk with you."

"I'm glad."

"I was comfortable with you really quickly. Especially after that whole staring thing at check-in. That was just weird."

He wasn't going to be embarrassed about that, not when the end result was her across the table. "I still haven't figured out where I know you from but I swear it wasn't a line. I have seen you before. It'll come to me."

"Maybe you haven't actually seen me before," she said, lifting both eyebrows and leaning forward dramatically. "Maybe we were destined to hook up this week. You know, paranormally."

He laughed, he couldn't help it. "Paranormally?"

She sniffed. "It's a word. And if not, it should be."

"Okay, let's say you're right. Maybe you were brought

here for a reason. Maybe we were lovers in a past life. Interesting notion. Not sure I'm convinced, though." He sipped his scotch again. "We should ask what's-her-name."

"Yeah," Carrie said. "The medium. I haven't seen her around. I thought she was part of the package."

"She's been having private consultations in her room."

Carrie looked at him slyly.

"Not that kind of consultation. I don't think. I could be wrong. That would actually be smart. Illegal as hell, but still, smart."

"What would?"

"Hiring a hooker for these conferences. Some of these guys looked pretty desperate. I feel badly for Erin. She's surrounded."

Carrie leaned forward again. "Don't be fooled by their looks. You know what they say about geeks and nerds, right?"

"That they're geeky and nerdy?"

"Please," Carrie said with a sniff. "Everyone knows geeks and nerds are amazing in bed."

Sam barked out a laugh. "What?"

Just then, food arrived. It was a lot. More than usual, she felt sure, which meant that the kitchen knew he was here with Carrie. He wasn't surprised, although he didn't think either one of them wanted to eat this much.

"Wow. How do you make any money in here? Do you charge triple for the booze?"

"These aren't standard portions."

Carrie nodded. "Buttering up the boss."

"Something like that."

She took a chicken wing and dipped it in the ranch dressing. After one bite her eyes rolled with happiness.

He took a swallow of scotch, followed by an ice-cold oyster that slid down his throat. Another perfect combination. "Thinking geeks and nerds are great in bed is not common knowledge. I have never heard that, and what makes you think it's true?"

"First off, you must live under a rock because, come on. And second, geeks and nerds think more about sex, more *creatively* about sex, than jocks on their best days."

"That's an insane theory." Sam took a chicken wing and pointed it at her. "All guys think about sex all the time, especially young ones, but I'll tell you a secret, oh, woman who lives her life online—guys in their late twenties and early thirties think about sex just as often as guys at seventeen. They're just better at making it into a team sport."

Carrie laughed and the sound of it made him smile. "Spoken like a jock who's what, I'd guess, thirty, thirty-one?"

"Thought you looked me up."

"Of course I did." She put her red lips around her straw once more and sucked. On purpose. When she finally lifted her head again, she licked those lips. Also on purpose. "Know why I looked you up?"

"Because you're nosy?"

Her lips curled up and he didn't need any damn oysters to bolster his libido.

"Because I, sir, am a geek and a nerd," she whispered, her voice like a long slow lick up the side of his neck.

"And while I may not be able to prove my hypothesis in regard to guy geeks, I'm dead-on positive it's true for us girls."

Sam finished off his scotch without choking then slapped down the glass. "We need to-go containers for this food."

She leaned against the high back of the booth. "I believe I won this round, Mr. Crider."

"The hell with that. You've won the whole shooting match."

Carrie smiled like an evil genius, then held up her hand to signal the waitress.

THE QUICK BEAT OF HER heart had nothing to do with the fact that she and Sam had practically run to the second floor. It had everything to do with what was going to happen after their brief stop at his room.

He had a bit of difficulty with the key card to 214, but it worked in the end, and she followed him inside and closed the door behind her. His was a regular room, not unlike her own. Different colors, same idea. She put the bag of goodies on the dresser. "Why do you have a room? Don't you live here?"

"I do. But so does my aunt. She's been staying in my folks' old place, though she's away for a couple of weeks."

"You have an aunt living here? What's going to happen if the place sells?"

Sam had put a backpack on the bed, and he disappeared into the bathroom for a moment, returning with toothbrush, et cetera, a few moments later. "I've found a great assisted-living place in Denver. Twenty-four-hour care, hospital next door, really good food. She'll love it."

"How long has she lived here?"

Sam punched the backpack open and shoved his toiletries inside. "Her whole life."

"Really? Wow."

"It's the best thing. I'd have wanted her there even if I weren't selling the place."

"No, it's a good idea. You're pretty far away from a hospital here."

He looked at her. "That's right. Too far. It isn't safe."

Carrie wasn't the most intuitive person in the world but even she could see there was a massive amount of guilt in the air. The subject needed a reboot, and fast. "You going to change into something more...comfortable?"

"What? Why?" He looked down. "Is something wrong? Did I spill?"

Carrie sighed. "That was me attempting to be alluring. I was so good in the restaurant, too. I mean, come on, I aced that."

He smiled and the tension eased out of his shoulders as he walked to her. "You certainly did. And I've been meaning to do this ever since." He lifted her chin and as she closed her eyes she felt his warm breath, then the brush of his soft, dry lips against hers. It was a sweet introduction to the intimate part of the evening. Nothing scary and yet the next gentle touch made her shiver in anticipation.

He teased her until she was forced to grab his shirt and pull him closer. He cut off a soft moan to swipe the crease between her lips with his tongue. Then again. She opened to him as she flattened her hands against his chest.

He might not have been a geek, but he must have put a lot of thought into kissing to have been this good at it. He moved her back until she rested against the door. Still exploring her, letting her do the same, he began a tactile journey with his hands starting with an unhurried exploration of her cardigan-covered arms. It was just this side of maddening not to feel his skin on hers, but she didn't mind. They had all night, and she had always been a sucker for a good slow build.

As he pulled back in order to find a new angle, she felt his fingers at the tie holding up her ponytail. With the dexterity of a safecracker, he managed to free her hair without the slightest discomfort. She'd been right about his talented hands. What would they do to the rest of her?

He pulled away again, only this time he didn't return, forcing her to open her eyes. "I want you to hold that thought. Exactly that thought."

She nodded. He touched her cheek with the back of his knuckles just before he continued his packing. Not that there was much of it. A change of clothes, his cell phone charger, some things from his bedside drawer that she assumed were condoms.

For her part, Carrie just held up the door and watched him, liking the way her breaths were short and her nipples were hard. This was so much better than just sleeping with him for his body, as nice as that body was. They hadn't been long in the bar, but she'd learned a lot. She'd guessed at his sense of humor, but now she was sure. His eyes weren't faking their kindness, and even the huge amount of food had clued her in to the staff's affection for him.

It had been good to see his guilt, as well. Not that she wanted him to be uncomfortable, but she did want to know that he felt things deeply, that he cared. More than he wanted to. And that was something she understood from the inside out.

"Carrie?"

She blinked at his voice, at the realization that he'd said her name more than once. "Sorry."

"It's fine. Holding that thought?"

"Variations on a theme," she said. "Ready?"

He nodded. She got the food and he opened the door to a blessedly empty hallway. "Come on. I don't relish the idea of being caught."

"As if there's not a person in this hotel who doesn't know we're doing this."

"Next time, when I pretend to be stealthy, lie."

"Sorry. Got it. Will do."

They hurried down the hall. Carrie brushed her fingers against Erin's door, although she wasn't sure why. She wasn't superstitious. But she did know her friend wished her well.

"Key?"

She pulled it out of her front pocket, shoved it in the slot and received a nice green light in return. Sam shut the door the second they'd crossed the threshold.

"Phew. Made it."

"Quiet as ninjas."

He smiled. "You're making fun of me."

"Affectionately," she said, putting the food into the small fridge before pulling him closer.

He dropped the backpack with a thud, then his hand was in her hair, her lips open in welcome. After a nice long kiss that made all the fun parts of her body wake up, he leaned back. "Dammit, I was going to ask you to do the hair thing. Like from the movies."

"The hair thing? This worries me. What's the hair thing?"

"And you think I've lived under a rock. You know, the 'Miss Jones, you're beautiful without your…glasses…' You have no idea what I'm talking about."

"Not in the slightest. Who the hell is Miss Jones?"

Sam sighed. "Never mind. It doesn't matter."

She eyed him suspiciously, hating that she didn't know a cultural reference. "Explain it, please."

"Later," he said, "I'll be happy to go into detail."

She brushed his bottom lip with her fingertip. "You know what? I really do like you," she whispered as she trapped that same lip between her teeth. When she let it go, she kissed him and his hands moved from the small of her back to her shoulders, then down again. It felt wonderful, but it wasn't enough. She moved her kisses to the side of his mouth. "Bed?"

He nodded. "Naked would be good."

She nipped his earlobe. "So undress me."

"Pushy."

"Want me to stop?"

"Nuh-uh. No, not even for a second, please, no."

Carrie laughed and decided that pushy wasn't a bad thing. She maneuvered until she reached his top button. He tried to return the favor with her cardigan, but the logistics called for a redirect, so he went instead to the waist of her jeans.

Somehow, even as they continued to make out, she managed to suck in her stomach as he grappled with getting her out of her pants. She kind of lost her concentration for a minute when the zipper came down and Sam lingered in the general area, cupping her between her thighs.

"Hot," he whispered, right before his tongue plunged between her teeth.

She moved her hips, riding his hand. His moan pleased her very much. But she needed to see him. He tried to stop her from pulling back, but she got far enough away that she could meet his gaze.

This was odd, all of it. Wanting to see his expressions, wishing they could talk and kiss simultaneously. None of her other vacation hook-ups had been remotely this interesting or exciting. Her reactions were off, and she could only attribute that to the differences between Sam and Armand.

He stopped unbuttoning her at the bottom of her sweater. "What's wrong?"

She'd been frowning, and she hadn't noticed. Hadn't noticed him moving from button to button, either. "Nothing. Sorry. Just, I didn't expect this."

"What?"

"You."

His lips quirked in a lopsided smile. "I'm right there with you."

"I'm thinking you might have a point about us having met before. Ever been to Louisville?"

"Nope."

"Daytona Beach for spring break?"

"Nope."

She sighed as she tugged his shirt out of his pants. "I'll think on it some more."

"Think on your own time. I want you here. Now. In fact, it's my goal to turn you into a puddle of mindless bliss."

"Wow. Going for the gold. I approve of your boldness."

"Then you won't mind if I do this." He crouched down, bringing her jeans down with him. Since he hadn't quite gotten the last button of her sweater undone, she did the honors. He smiled up at her before turning his attention to her white panties. She wondered if he cared that she hadn't worn a thong. Because she didn't own a thong. Hated the damn things. She preferred panties that actually covered more than a postage stamp, and couldn't really care if she had a panty line. Whoever didn't like it could kiss her fabric-covered ass.

Nope, Sam didn't seem to mind. Not if his kiss was any indication. He didn't even move the material to the side, which felt oddly naughty. His hot breath made her tremble as he carefully nipped the silk between his teeth, then pulled up, giving her the sexiest wedgie in the history of wedgies.

He moved his head a bit more, and her panties rubbed between her lips, right up against her clit. It wasn't more than a suggestion, a whisper of friction, but standing there with her sweater unbuttoned revealing her white bra and her jeans puddled around her ankles felt altogether wicked.

She couldn't help touching him, running her hand

through his thick, unruly hair. He parted his teeth, then moved in, licking between her fold.

She hummed her approval as his hands moved slowly up her legs to her thighs. Closed her eyes when he pulled her underwear down. Then he barked out a surprised laugh.

"Oh," she said. "You noticed."

"It's purple," he said. "Hard not to notice."

"I have a lot of me time."

He looked up at her, then back at her purple-dyed lightning-bolt pubic hair.

"Mostly I just do a regular landing strip, but I was feeling festive."

He leaned in again, running his tongue next to her topiary. "I love it," he said. "And I intend to extol its virtues in detail, but my pants just got exponentially tighter." He rose slowly, licking and nipping her skin as he made his way up. Her breasts stopped his progress, though, and just as he'd done below the waist, he used his mouth over the silk of her bra, wetting the center until her nipples were erect. Then he took the left one, the wet one, between his teeth, and applied suction.

"You are very good with your mouth," she said, rising up on her toes as the suction got stronger.

His response was to give her right breast equal attention.

Somehow she made her hands move purposefully. She finished unbuttoning his shirt, then manhandled him until his chest was bare.

He was even prettier underneath than she'd hoped. At least, from this angle. It was a difficult choice, but she eased away from his wonderful lips so she could get a good look at Sam. Oh, yeah. It wasn't one of those impossible six-packs, but his skin was firm, his chest well-defined, and his shoulders looked even broader now that she could see his trim waist and narrow hips. The jeans needed to go. Now.

"You didn't like what I was doing?"

She grinned at him. "Loved it more than kittens. But you need to get naked."

"You're right. I do."

She looked down to see a nice-looking bulge under his zipper. While she watched him deal with that, she kicked out of her jeans and panties, sent her shoes flying. All movement stilled as his pants and boxers lowered to reveal one hell of a nice cock.

He lacked neither in length nor girth, had done some judicious trimming himself, although he wasn't as artistically inclined as she was, which was fine. His thighs were good, too. He looked like a real man, a considerate man. A horny man.

"Sweater," he said, as he lowered himself onto the bed so he could remove his shoes.

A glance down reminded her not only of her cardigan, but also the state of her nips. Goodness, between the two of them, they just couldn't be more pointy.

She let her sweater drop and her bra followed quickly. By that time, he was naked, too, and she couldn't stop herself from climbing on top of him as he sat on the edge of the bed.

"This was a wonderful idea," she said, just before she kissed him.

"I concur," he said, his breath heating her lips as he

switched the angle of their kiss. His hands were warm and strong as they moved all over her back.

She pulled away, just a bit. "I'm going to lean over to that drawer," she said, nodding at the bedside table. "Don't let me fall."

He held on to her as she stretched. It was quite a maneuver, and she'd have been better off getting up, but screw it. Which was why she was grasping the box of condoms with the very tips of her fingers.

Finally she snagged it. Sam helped her sit up straight. She took one packet out, tossed the box and had that sucker open in a flash.

He scooted them both back on the bed, probably for stabilization, but as soon as he was done, she rose up on her knees, rolled the condom down, which earned her a nice reverse hiss, and took hold of him by his shoulders.

"Get ready," she said.

"Wow. When you want something, you don't waste any time."

"Don't fret. This one's just to take the edge off. We'll revisit your special talents in a bit."

"Beautiful *and* practical."

"Seriously. Get ready."

He splayed one hand over the small of her back while the other positioned his cock just so. Her eyes closed and her head fell back as she sunk, as slowly and tightly as she could, to the sound of his long, low moan.

10

SAM DIDN'T MOVE. He wanted to. Oh, lord, he wanted to. But her sitting on him, pressing against him, around him, with her head back and her neck the most beautiful thing he'd ever seen, forced him to stay as still as he could, barely even breathing.

The concept of overstimulation had never been so clear. His balls had tightened and he was skating so close to the point of no return that it was sixty-forty, not in longevity's favor. Now would have been a good time to cite baseball statistics or picture something dick-withering, but Carrie had swamped all his senses. Even without her touching him, he probably could come from the sweet spicy scent of her. Hell, he'd almost come from the way her nipple looked under the wet translucence of her plain white bra.

Best thing she could have done was go on the offensive. He was pretty sure she hadn't meant for him to come this quickly, but at least he wasn't going to explode while doing something ridiculous, like reaching for the light switch.

"You're getting awfully red," she said.

He hadn't noticed that she'd lifted her head.

He opened his mouth, but then she shifted on him, and it was so close…almost…he let out his breath. "It's okay," he said, his voice barely audible.

"Something's wrong. Are you in pain?"

He cried out as Carrie squeezed him. "Stop. Wait. Don't move."

"Why? What's wrong? Cramp?"

He let out a laugh which nearly did him in. "I'm fine. I just need you to stop. Doing anything. Just. Don't."

"Oooooh," she said as the truth hit.

He closed his eyes. If he could have, he would have plugged his ears. His nose. Although he guessed there wasn't a practical way to stop his skin from feeling or his nerve endings from sending urgent signals to his brain. This was insane.

He opened his eyes again and decided to go out with a bang. Finesse was overrated, and besides, it was all her fault.

He moved both his hands to her hips. Luckily, she grabbed hold of his shoulders, and therefore didn't fall. Then he lifted her, that wet heat sliding up his cock until just the head was left inside. After a great gulp of air, he lowered her again, his arms shaking with the effort, not because she was heavy—she wasn't—but the tortured feeling of holding off. All he knew was this thing might not last long, but it was going to be epic.

Carrie had caught on and was doing her part for the cause. She helped lower herself oh, so slowly, and dammit, she used those inner muscles of hers to make the journey an exquisite torment. He took a breath when she reached bottom, and he could feel the itch of sweat trickle down his temple.

He had maybe one round trip left in him. He looked at her. She looked at him. He nodded. She pressed those beautiful red lips together.

Up she went, and okay, she was some kind of Kegel exercise champion, because damn, she was killing him. Carrie leaned over and actually did lick a long wet stripe up the side of his neck. And that was that.

He let her go. She came down a hell of a lot faster than the last time, and by then, he'd come. It was his head thrown back this time, a completely different set of muscles strained to the breaking point, and he only stopped an ear-splitting howl by biting the crap out of his lower lip.

When he finally could see without spots before his eyes, he raised his head to find her smiling at him. A wide-eyed grin.

"Feel better?" she asked.

"Much."

"Good," she said, as if the quickie had been the most normal thing she'd done all day. "I was afraid you'd hurt yourself."

"So was I. Sorry about, well, you."

"Oh, piffle. I had a fine time, thanks for asking."

He laughed. "You did say I'd get another chance, right?"

Carrie nodded. "We've got all night."

"What about the ghosts?"

"Let them find their own. You're mine tonight, hot stuff."

He kissed her. Because he was the luckiest son of a

bitch in Colorado, she wrapped her arms around him and kissed him back. He didn't really have the breath for such a prodigious kiss, but he wouldn't have stopped for the world. In fact, she was the one to finally pull away, although not far. "Let's get cleaned up so we can really get dirty."

"You just keep having one stunning idea after another," Sam said. He lifted her again, and with her help she dismounted. He excused himself and headed for the bathroom, his thoughts as unsteady as his legs.

He'd never expected this. He wasn't a man known for hyperbole, but this woman, this night, was the best goddamn thing that had ever happened to him. He'd had good sex before, sure. And he'd met great women who made him laugh, who made him think and who were beautiful, some who were all three at the same time. Carrie was in a league of her own.

He looked at himself in the mirror. Yeah, it was still just him looking back. "Lucky bastard."

CARRIE WAS IN NO PARTICULAR rush to get to act two. She knew Sam wasn't, either. She liked being under the covers with him, his arms all tight and manly holding her close, their bodies touching wherever possible. The light from the table lamp let her see his expressions, which made it even better. "Tell me about your first time," she said, and not just as filler. She wanted to know about Sam's love life, and she might as well start at the beginning.

"I was seventeen. She was nineteen."

"Ooh, an older woman."

He nodded. "Her name was Trish, and she was from

Toronto. Her family was vacationing at the inn. Mostly for the ghosts, but they did manage to fit in a lot of skiing. She asked me to show her the Old Hotel."

"She was pretty, wasn't she?"

"Gorgeous. Of course, I was a seventeen-year-old virgin. She could have looked like a Picasso painting, and I wouldn't have cared, so take all this with a grain of salt."

Carrie grinned and snuggled. She had no doubt the girl had been a beauty. No way Sam hadn't been a total babe at seventeen. "Go on."

"It was the middle of the afternoon, not prime lovin' time, and honestly I was just hoping for a little under-the-sweater action. She got scared by something, I have no idea what, but she fell on me. I'm pretty sure she kissed me first. Not because that's how I remember it, but she was the one who had the condom. I wasn't a very bright seventeen-year-old. I lasted about as long as I did tonight, but I had an excuse then. First time and all."

"No excuse tonight?"

He tweaked her nipple. "Well, it is you."

"Good answer. Was that it with Trish? Or was there a repeat performance?"

"Nope. She left the next day. I moved to New York to start college. Fell in love with the city, and with my film courses. And then I discovered documentaries. I mean, I'd seen them, but not very often, and not very good ones. I knew from the first semester that's what I wanted to do. My life became pretty narrow. Films and women. If I could combine the two, all the better. To tell the truth, I spent a lot more time watching films."

"Was there anyone special?"

"Nope. Jody came closest, but even then I knew I wasn't going for the kind of life that would accommodate a serious relationship. The minute I could, I was working on student films, any films that would hire me, usually not for pay. I slept on couches, in vans. Earned barely enough to live, socking all I could away so I could continue to be a vagabond. After graduation I traveled extensively, kept my options open."

"You've never been tempted by love?"

"No, I never have been. Probably because I never stuck around long enough to let it happen. I think I loved Jody, but she was too smart to fall for me. She's responsible for the friendship, though, and I'm grateful for that."

"Do you still have other friends from college?"

"Some from college, most from after. There's a group of us who tend to work on each other's projects, and that's good. I have a few folks I can count on to bail me out of jail if the need should arise. But I'm mostly on the road. At least, I used to be. Since my father died, I've been here."

"I'm really sorry about your dad."

"Thanks. So what about you? What was your first time?"

"Wait."

Braving the cold, she got out of bed and rescued their appetizers from the fridge. There were napkins in the bag, and she brought two water bottles back with her.

When Sam saw her intent, he moved around pillows so they could lean against the headboard and snack as they talked.

The spread looked wonderful, and she settled in to

eat, ravenous and thirsty, too. After two chicken wings, she took a swig of water, then said, "I was sixteen, and frankly, I was way too young. I was at a party with seniors, and I got drunk. I was cripplingly shy, and everyone thought I was weird. I ended up with this gawky nerd guy I knew from science class. We were both terrified and terrible at it. It put me off sex for a good long time."

"When did you change your mind?"

"That would be around the time I met Randy Oliver. Also a senior, but in college, while I was a junior. He was a brooding artist. I liked comics. I thought we'd paint beautiful pictures together, and for about three months, we did. Then he dumped me for a cheerleader. But it was okay, as I'd met Erin by then. We've been friends ever since." She took one of the oysters, squeezed some lemon, dabbed it with hot sauce, then let it slither down her throat.

"I know you hate the idea of her leaving."

"I want her to be happy. I do. I'm just scared. I don't fit in easily. At least not in person, unless I'm with my fellow comic aficionados. You can see how something like that has to be planned, though. So I spend most of my time online, working, chatting. My favorite media tool is Twitter, which should give you a clue about my social skills."

Sam laughed. "I tried Twitter, but it's not really my thing."

"Yeah, I can see that."

"It's hard for me to imagine you in such tiny bites. I'm amazingly comfortable with you. As if I've known you—wait a minute." He put down a half-eaten wing. "San Diego. Comic-Con. Last year. You were there."

"Yeah."

"That's where I saw you. Christ, I knew it. I knew I wasn't crazy. You were selling comics. I was working with a camera crew. I don't think we got you on tape, though."

She winced on the inside, hoping this didn't out her as Carrie Price. Not yet, at least. "Why would you tape me? I wasn't anyone important."

"But I remember you so clearly. You had on some weird wrestling T-shirt."

That stopped her cold. Wrestling. All she'd worn were *Cruel, Cruel World* T-shirts because she was selling them. CCW. Celebrity Championship Wrestling. She'd been teased about that. "Well. I'm glad that's settled. You were right all along. It was such a madhouse there. I'm amazed you remember anything."

"It was fun. I was helping out a director friend of mine. We got to film a lot of pretty big interviews. I made some connections. The weather was sweet."

Carrie nodded as her blood pressure tried to go back to normal. She thought she might squeak by on this. "It was a good time. Erin came with me. She mostly stood in line."

"I think that's what everyone did. Wow. I remembered. I got a tripod in the back because of you."

"What?"

"You stopped me short. Just a look at you, and I couldn't move. The guy behind me was carrying his camera and tripod. He bumped into me. Gave me a hell of a bruise."

"Really? Me?"

He nodded. "There was something... I know this sounds crazy. And I'm not. Crazy, I mean. It was as if you had a spotlight shining on you. Like you were in focus, and everything else was one frame off. Just like yesterday when I saw you in line."

"Why didn't you say something? At the convention, I mean."

"We were running late. I never even had time to look for you."

"And you're sure it was me?"

"Absolutely."

She bit her lip and looked down at her lap. In a second she was going to burst into tears, dammit. No one had ever... It wasn't even possible...

Sam sighed. "Wrestling T-shirts. Bizarre."

There was only one thing to do. She gathered all the boxes of food and shoved them in the plastic bag. Didn't bother putting it away because the floor was much closer. Soon, he was, too. She climbed on his lap once more and she kissed him.

She still couldn't make sense of it. There had been thousands of people wandering around Comic-Con. Utter chaos. People were dressed in costumes, major celebrities were everywhere, there were huge, expensive displays all over the place. Her booth had been the smallest one she could get.

How was it possible he'd remembered her? She wasn't the type. She was reasonably pretty, she guessed, but no one had ever walked into a pole, or run a red light or even tripped before. He'd gotten a tripod in the back. That was...she didn't even know what that was.

He leaned back, blinking at her. No wonder. She'd practically eaten him up. "You okay?"

She nodded. "Want you."

He smiled as his hand ran up her back. Everywhere his lips touched, he lit a slow fire. Good. She didn't want this to be over before it had a chance to simmer.

She ran her hand down his chest, enjoying the feel of his smattering of hair, then down his smooth belly. He seemed to like that, or at least the direction she was heading. Just to unbalance him a bit, she switched to running that same hand through the hair on his head.

She really liked the way he always seemed to look as though he'd just had wild, passionate sex. It would be kind of funny if after the real thing, he ended up all neat and tidy.

"What are you grinning about?"

"I'm happy," she said, liking the way his eyes had darkened and how his lips were wet.

"Me, too."

Her breath hitched as his finger slipped inside her. "Oh."

"You seem to be very, um, enthused."

She discovered he was just as ready as she was. "I'm not the only one."

His gaze wandered over her face at the same leisurely pace as his thick finger. She matched his rhythm, letting herself enjoy how extraordinarily soft his skin was, and yet so hard. Nothing else felt like a penis, which was a fine thing. Nothing should. She wondered what she must feel like for him. Soft, warm, wet. It would be nice to be a guy for a night, just to really know.

"You're thinking."

She nodded. "I'm always doing that. I drive people crazy. Stopping in the middle of sentences, changing topics midstride. It's annoying."

"I don't mind. You're wonderful to watch. And to touch. I feel like I've won an all-access pass to the most interesting place ever. And you don't even mind if I touch all the shiny gadgets."

"My shiny gadgets like to be touched."

"Remember that private massage I promised you?" She nodded.

"My specialty is being focused and specific. I find the exact place you need a good rub. And then I only use one finger."

His thumb settled into a nice slow circle on her clit. She wiggled, a pure reflex at the sensation, and grinned as she kissed him. She continued her own brand of massage, her hand sliding down to the base of his cock, back up and over, spreading his pre-come as she did it again.

For a while, it was enough. But as her tongue explored his taste and her free hand roamed over the curve of his jaw, the fire built and soon she wanted more pressure, and his hips met each swoop of her palm.

Their breathing lost its languor and became the sound of want, then need. He pulled back from her mouth and kissed her chin as he traveled down the bed. He paid his due to each nipple, making her moan and her hand stutter. He sucked just hard enough, licked her like ice cream.

But he didn't stop there, even though it meant he moved his cock out of her reach. There was still lots of him to play with. He seemed to like that she tugged gently on that soft chest hair, that she tweaked his little flat nipples. But they were roadside attractions in his journey down her stomach to her lightning bolt. He got comfy when his tongue took the place of his thumb.

That got her attention. One hundred percent of it. Because Sam knew what he was doing. Holy...

He jerked the covers off their bodies as he enjoyed her, and there was no question in her mind that he was having almost as good a time as she was. He nudged her legs farther apart, used one hand to spread her, the fingers of the other to fill her and his tongue to drive her insane.

She fisted a pillow and groped around for his hair, but he was too low, so she toyed with her nipples, instead, at least for a minute. Soon, though, she couldn't concentrate on anything but the orgasm that was just starting to build.

Sam must have felt her muscles tighten because he got focused and fast. As it hit, she arched up, cried out. When she opened her eyes, she met his smug gaze. He moved up the bed, running one hand lightly over her skin as he opened a condom packet with his teeth. She vaguely wondered when he'd gotten it, but her thoughts were looser than normal as her body continued to be hit with delicious aftershocks.

Sam sheathed his cock then settled between her thighs. With one arm braced, he lined himself up and slid inside, moaning at the unbelievable sensation. Immensely glad that he'd come earlier, he bent over to kiss her as he stilled, feeling her tremble around him.

Her eyes were shiny and unfocused. The look suited

her and if she were his, he'd make it his business to keep
her that way as often as possible.

He had to move. Needed more. In fact… He shifted
so he could lift her thighs, lift her so he could go deep,
hard. Pulling almost all the way out, he stopped, just
for a second, just to make sure she was with him, that
she understood he wasn't going to hold back.

Her mouth opened as he thrust. The way she gasped
stirred something in his chest, or maybe it was the way
her head thrashed on the pillow, her long dark hair a
wild tangle. Nothing existed but his hard cock and her
soft pussy, the sound of his grunts and her harsh breath.
He wanted to stay there forever, to feel this and only
this.

Her hands went to his shoulders; her fingers dug into
his flesh.

He hated that his eyes were going to close when he
most wanted to see, but it all came down to a moment
of perfect tension, sparks behind his eyelids, tendons
stretching, everything he was concentrated in a pinpoint
of intense pleasure and release.

When he finally met her dark brown gaze, he felt as
if he'd been winded by a blow, tilted on his axis. Breathless, speechless, he was confused, happy, and not just
because the sex had been great. It was…

He didn't know what the hell it was.

_11_

THE NEXT AFTERNOON, when Erin opened her door, she was still in her pajamas, her hair was a mess and last night's mascara was smudged under her eyes, but she didn't yell at Carrie for waking her, probably because of the large coffee Carrie shoved at her. "When did you get in?"

"I don't know," Erin said through a yawn. "Seven? Maybe? What time is it now?"

"Two."

"Shit." She sipped her coffee and kind of choked as her eyes widened. "You. Last night. Sam."

"Me. Sam. Bed. _Awesome._"

"Oh, my god." Erin went to the unmade bed and sat down, curling her legs under her, gripping her coffee like a lifeline. "Tell me every last detail."

"You'll get broad strokes and you'll be glad for them." Carrie pulled one of the chairs from the table and sat. She also smiled.

"So it didn't suck…so to speak."

"No, it didn't. It didn't very much."

Erin's mouth fell open. "You haven't butchered the

English language that horribly since what's-his-name junior year."

"What's-his-name was an amateur."

"My, my. You don't say."

Carrie rolled her eyes, but not at her friend's response. It was ridiculous to like Sam this much. They'd just met. "It's crazy. I'm crazy. None of it makes sense."

"You'll have to give me a little bit more information here. What's crazy and why doesn't it make sense?"

"I hardly know him."

"You've seen him naked. I'd say you two were on friendly terms."

"You know what I mean, smart-ass. It wasn't the sex, either. Well, some of it was the sex. Okay, a lot of it was the sex. But it was also the talking. The talking was…"

"Fantastic?"

Carrie nodded. Drank some coffee. Stared at Erin. Drank some more.

"I'm still too tired to coax you through each sentence, Carrie. Talk."

"Right. We went to the bar and had food, which we hardly touched. Until later. But that's not important. He has a great sense of humor. And his employees like him a lot, did you know that? It says something about his character. Oh, and he was kind of in love with Jody, the chef, in college, but he's never wanted to get serious because he likes his freedom, but I think there's more to it. Anyway, he got into film in college and he has a place in New York, and if I come to visit you, I could, you know…" She shooed away that thought because that was just stupid. "He really wants to sell the hotel, but that's a secret, or, wait, did I tell you already?"

Carrie took another sip of coffee, but the second she swallowed, she said, "He got some stuff from his room, then we went to my room, and we talked and laughed, and he figured out that he had seen me at Comic-Con. Remember that stare when we first got here? Of course you do, well, that's where he'd seen me before. He was working with a film crew, interviewing people and stuff, and he passed my booth. They didn't even stop. He stopped, though, and the guy behind him poked him with a tripod."

Erin held up her hand. "Wait. Stop. Just…stop."

Carrie closed her mouth. It wasn't like Erin to shut her down. "What?"

"Too much all at once. I'm on my first cup of coffee."

After a deep, cleansing breath, Carrie nodded. "Sorry."

"No prob. Now, let's see if we can concentrate on the chronological events of the evening. You got to your room. Did you immediately jump each other?"

Carrie grinned. "Yeah. We pretty much did."

"Good kisser?"

"Fabulous. Astonishing. He should go on tour."

"Carrie," Erin said, but the way she said it was significant, as were her uplifted eyebrows.

"What?"

"You really like him. I mean *really* like him."

Carrie deflated. Not that she wasn't still over-the-moon about the night, but Erin was right. She really liked Sam. More than she should. There were only a few days left of vacation time, then it was back home to her life. "I know."

"That's great!"

"It's not though, is it? We're leaving in a few days, and besides, he's a rebound vacation guy. I'm emotionally vulnerable. And I'm using him, you know, for the comics."

"Ah, sweetie. Let's take that last thing first. Just tell him. He'll understand. It's not that huge a deal."

"It is a big deal. How would you like it if someone came to stay with you, and you found out they were writing comics about how you're an idiot?"

Erin's face, hell, her whole body went into "are you kidding me?" mode. "You do that to me all the time."

"I do not."

"Carrie!"

"Okay, but we're friends."

"Yeah," she said, again, with the significance. "Trust me. Tell him."

Carrie shook her head. "No. I'll just enjoy him while I have him, and leave with happy memories. That's what's supposed to happen on vacation."

Erin cocked her head to the side. "You're pretty," she said, as if it talking to a very small child. It was an old routine between them, one that never ceased to be annoying.

"Shut up. So I got excited. It happens. I'm hungry."

Erin took a long drink of the last of her coffee, then put the cup down on the bedside table. "I have to shower and dress. But you're right. We need to get to dinner by four."

"Got a hot date, do we?"

"Not me, cookie. You."

Carrie stood up, confused. "We didn't make any plans. Sam has to do something or other, and he won't be free until eight tonight."

"Not with Sam. Tonight's your appointment with Marcia."

Carrie stepped back as if slapped. "Oh, no, no, no. Not a chance. I'm not going to see a medium, Erin. It's ridiculous and a complete waste of money."

"You are going. At six. There's no choice involved. You are doing this because you're my best friend. And I'm moving across the country. So you have to."

There was nothing Carrie could say to that. Actually there was, but what was the point? Erin had pulled out the biggest of guns. While Carrie could have argued, could have bitched about the blackmail, she didn't because her friend wouldn't have pulled out that gun if it hadn't been a huge honkin' deal. "Fine. How long do I have to stay?"

"I bought an hour."

"An hour!"

"Yes. And you're not going to sneak out early because I booked myself into the hour right after you."

Carrie sighed with intent. "Why are you doing this to me?"

"Because you're my best friend. And if you'd stop being so rigid in your certainty you might just learn something."

"There's absolutely no proof that anyone can see the future, can see the dead. Even if someone claims to have done any of those things, it's never been repeatable, and any greater-than-average results have always been and

will always be within the accepted norm. The woman
is a charlatan, and I can't—"

She stopped herself. It was ludicrous to have this
discussion again. Erin would continue to believe in this
hokum no matter what Carrie said, and no amount of
logic would change that. "Fine. I'll go, but I hate to see
you waste your money. You'll need it in New York."

As Erin collected some clothes from the dresser, she
shot Carrie a look in the mirror. "You think it's a coincidence that I'm moving to New York and Sam just
happens to have an apartment there?"

"Yes. It's the definition of coincidence."

"Right. I don't know how you get through each day
with that closed mind of yours. Don't you get it?" Erin
turned, clothes held to her chest. "Aside from everything
else, you're missing half the fun."

"I don't consider people being fleeced of their
hard-earned cash to be fun and games. Do you know
how much some of that ghost-hunting crap costs? Did
you see anyone in that ballroom who looked like a
millionaire?"

"I'm astonished we're friends at all," Erin said as she
headed to the bathroom. "Doesn't stop me from adoring
you, though, and if that isn't destiny, I don't know what
is."

Carrie stared at the closing door and didn't move until
she heard the water turn on. It was true. Their friendship
laughed in the face of Carrie's beloved logic, but it was
one of the best parts of her life.

Maybe she was the crazy one. Maybe there were
ghosts all over the damn place, and there was an af-

terlife, and angels and demons and soothsayers and paranormal pooches.

Nah. She didn't care how much she wanted to share this with Erin, there was no way she was ever going to believe in hocus-pocus. Ever.

SAM STARED AT THE BACK of his office door, pen in hand, checks ready for signing. He wasn't thinking about bills or menus or the staff meeting at five. His thoughts were in room 204, with Carrie. He wondered if she was in the ballroom yet, or if she and Erin were having dinner. He and Carrie had agreed to meet up at eight. Sadly, not in room 204 because she'd committed to spending the evening in one of the "haunted" rooms. Not a terrible plan, as that meant sitting in the dark, in the quiet, waiting for ghosts who would never appear. As long as he was sitting next to her, Sam was cool with that. Couldn't hurt to be seen getting into the "spirit" of things, and there was no one he'd rather hang with. He only wished they could be alone. Naked would be even better. Sadly, there weren't enough haunted rooms in the hotel, or the Old Hotel, or even the stables or the staff quarters to assign only two people to a location.

Maybe Carrie wouldn't want to stay for long. It still surprised him that a woman that sane could believe in ghosts. Why, he wasn't sure. Everyone in his family had, everyone who checked in to the Crider Inn did. More than half the world believed in reincarnation, so it wasn't a big leap to believe that in between lives spirits might want to get in touch with those they left behind. All romantic bullshit. Dead was dead. Everything else was wishful thinking. He'd become inured to the ghost

crap in the last ten months, but he had to admit he was
a little disappointed in Carrie. Guess he was doing a bit
of his own wishful thinking.

None of it mattered. She was leaving in three days.
The likelihood of seeing her again was slim. The thought
was depressing.

He couldn't remember the last time he hadn't been
grateful for an end date. Time limits were his friend.
He'd crafted his life around escapes and exits. Being
stuck in the hotel this long had made him stir-crazy, and
maybe that's all this was. Crazy thoughts. He couldn't
like her this much. Not *this* much. He believed in love
at first sight as much as he believed in ghosts. Besides,
it had nothing to do with love.

From what he'd seen in his life, love at all was at best
unlikely. He used to think his parents were crazy about
each other, but as he'd gotten older and further away
from the trauma of his mother's death, he'd realized
the stories his father told were just that—stories. More
what his dad had wished than what it had been.

Personally, Sam was a hell of a lot more comfortable
living in the real world. It wasn't as pretty or comfort-
ing, but it was what was true. And the truth was, he and
Carrie had hit it off. They were compatible sexually, and
his first impression of her was great. But she was on
vacation and they were both on their best behavior. At
their age, feeling that vibe with each other had kicked
off a hell of a chemical storm. The urge to mate was
strong, and people were notoriously fantastic at fooling
themselves that a couple of nights of laughs and orgasms
could turn into fifty or sixty years of wedded bliss.

The only thing that was reasonably certain in his life

was that he would get to see Carrie again. Would they have another night of amazing sex? Possibly. Would she appeal to him in the same way? He hoped so.

But he wouldn't bet the farm. Shit happened. All the damn time. To good people and bad. To kids and to nice old ladies and to young mothers.

He'd better pay the bills. Money exchanges, he liked those. They were clean. No hidden agendas, at least the way he conducted his business.

He focused on the paper beneath his hand, the grip of the pen. The stuff he could count on.

MARCIA'S ROOM LOOKED LIKE a regular room, only bigger. It was a suite, one of only a few in the hotel, and the sitting room had been set up to accommodate the telling of lies for fun and profit, although not very cinematically.

As far as Carrie could see, the only nod to B movie–type mediums was swapping a red lightbulb for the regular one in the lamp by the table. There was a tablecloth, yes, but it was a white one with absolutely no tassels at all. No crystal ball, no tarot cards, not even a crow sitting ominously outside the window.

Marcia came in from the bedroom, having only kept Carrie about two minutes. "I'm going to make some tea. Will you join me?"

"Ah, you read the leaves?"

"No, I drink the beverage."

Carrie felt herself flush.

"Common mistake, don't sweat it. I've got some apple cinnamon or green."

Carrie was going to be there for an hour, she might as well have something to drink. "Apple, thanks."

Marcia busied herself boiling water in the microwave. Again, nothing spooky about it. Nor with the woman herself. She was younger than Carrie had imagined, maybe in her late thirties? Her hair was short but cute, her makeup looked professional, and she wore a great curve-hugging maroon sweater over jeans.

The microwave dinged, and Marcia put a ceramic cup of hot water in front of Carrie, then a tray with sugar and sweetener packets, a spoon, the tea bags, both kinds, and even some sliced-up lemon. No milk...wait, Marcia opened the fridge and there was a little carton of milk.

"Thanks."

"You're welcome."

By the time Carrie finished stirring and steeping, Marcia had taken her seat, and was looking at Carrie as a shrink would.

"What would you like to talk about?" Marcia asked. She sounded incredibly reasonable.

Carrie wanted to talk about the fact that she didn't believe any part of this nonsense, but she couldn't blow her cover. It still amazed Carrie that Erin had thought this was a good idea.

"And don't worry," Marcia said, dipping her tea bag into the slightly blushed water. "I know you don't believe in what I do."

"Erin told you?"

The older woman smiled. "I haven't met Erin."

"Oh."

"That wasn't a message from beyond, by the way. You don't hide your cynicism very well."

"Oh," Carrie said again. "I don't. It's true. I'm usually not very cynical. I mean, the people I hang with, they all know what I believe in. And what I don't."

"Like mediums. And ghosts."

She could backpedal. Say that ghosts were the exception. Although… "Do you keep this stuff confidential? You know, medium-client privilege?"

"Not quite like that. I don't get kicked out of the profession if I say the wrong thing, but yes, I keep things confidential. People tend to open up around me. Especially after I tell them something that hits very close to home."

"How long have you been doing this?"

"A long time. Long enough to recognize diversionary tactics." She put her tea bag on the little saucer and took a sip. When she put it down, she again smiled at Carrie. Gently. "I have a proposition for you."

"What's that?"

"I know and understand and even respect that you don't believe in any kind of mystical explanations for things that occur. But perhaps you can believe that I read people very well."

"Oh, that I do believe."

"There, that's a beginning." Marcia leaned back. "There's sometimes a benefit from speaking to someone who doesn't know your history or have any kind of preconceived notions about you. I'm not a therapist, and I promise not to offer any advice whatsoever. But if you ask me questions, I can offer some responses based on your body language, your silent tells. That's not mysticism. That's biomechanics. Neurolinguistics. You're here for an hour, for heaven's sake, and I don't have a deck of cards."

"I can already tell you're good at what you do."

"Is that a yes?"

Part of Carrie wanted to say no, that it was just another bunch of bull, but… "What the hell. Let's go for it."

"Great." Marcia sipped more of her tea, then put her hands flat on the table. "What was the first question that came to mind?"

"Huh," Carrie said, surprised that it wasn't about Erin. "I thought about Sam. Wondered if I'd see him when this was over."

"The session or the conference?"

"Both, I guess."

"I know you'd like to. More than you care to admit. You and Sam connected. Quite meaningfully."

"See, I'm already not really…comfortable."

"Why's that?"

"Because good con artists are good because they tell people what they want to hear. There's no way to verify anything you say."

"Sure there is. You can record the session, then see what happens."

"I don't have a tape."

"I do. I'll let you buy the tape for one dollar. You can start recording now, if you'd like."

"One dollar. Is this the only thing you're going to try and sell me?"

"Yep. I've already collected my fee. I won't even charge you for the tea."

Carrie picked up her purse and handed the woman a dollar bill. "Let's rock and roll."

"Okay." Marcia took about three minutes to get things all set up, and the first thing she did was repeat what she'd already told Carrie. "Have anything to add?"

Carrie shook her head. "Another question, though. What if you're wrong? What if it's all crap, then what?"

"Then you get to be right. And tell all your friends."

"So I win, either way."

Marcia nodded, her eyebrows high and her head cocked, as if this was all a delightful game, and she already knew who the real winner was.

"All right. Let's get the girly stuff out of the way. First, am I going to get married? To whom? When? What about kids? Will I have one, two, more? None? And then there's Erin. Is her move to New York going to be the end of our friendship?"

"Whoa, let's slow down a bit there, Ms. Sawyer. It's not a race, and I'm not a machine. Let's go back to question number one. Will you get married?"

Carrie forced herself to sit back, to school her expressions and not give it all away. She wanted Marcia to work for her money. No vague answers that could apply to anyone. Carrie wanted specifics, dammit. And when Marcia started talking, she got them.

12

THE ATTIC WAS BIG, the size of a double garage at least, and pretty clean as far as attics went. Stacks of old chairs teetered against the back wall alongside a slew of old paintings that had probably once graced the walls downstairs. Carrie kind of liked the first one, a landscape of the woods with a mountain rising majestically in the background. There were metal buffet tables, lamps and dusty shades, fake flower arrangements that had seen better days. At the far end, in front of two wooden dressers, stood two cameras, one infrared, the other thermal imaging, along with a gaggle of meters that measured god knows what. Sadly, nothing comfortable to sit on, except the blankets and pillows brought by the eight of them assigned to the room.

It wasn't Carrie's idea of a perfect late-night hot spot, but Sam and Erin were with her, so it was better than it could have been. Sam had assigned her to bring pillows. He'd come with the good stuff, though. A big comforter, plus a blanket, a picnic basket full of snacks and two thermoses of coffee, which she'd need if she was going to stay up for the rest of the night. Actually, morning, as it was just past midnight.

Erin had brought a couple of her fan boys who were busy making her as comfortable as a queen bee. Four people she didn't know, but had seen, rounded out the group. All signs pointed to boredom, with a slim chance of some groping in the dark. She and Sam would have to be careful, though, what with all the equipment.

Evidently he was thinking the same thing as he led her to the far wall, behind the eyes of the cameras. They moved some tables away from the wall and spread out their comforter. From their vantage point, they'd have a semiblocked view of one of the monitors. Not that there would be anything to see.

"Why are you all the way over there?" Erin said. "What's the matter, you don't like hanging out with the riffraff?"

"No," Carrie said. "Just you."

"Ha. You're a scream."

"Oooh, ghost-hunting humor."

Erin made a face, then turned back to her love slaves, giving them benevolent directions as to pillow placement.

"So, there's no talking, right?" Carrie asked the group at large.

"Nope. When the red lights are on, the mouths are off." This from Elton, who had either started to grow a mustache or needed a good washing.

"And we're here until...?"

"Three," Erin said. "Or four. Depending."

"On what?"

"Ghosts."

Carrie nodded. "Ah."

"Come on." Sam maneuvered her onto the comforter. "Sit. If you're a good girl, I'll give you a treat."

She scowled, but didn't mean it. He was simply too gorgeous in his flannel shirt, jeans and hiking boots. She hummed "The Lumberjack Song" as she lowered herself to the floor.

"I can hear you," he said.

"I know."

"I guess I'm going to eat all the cookies myself."

"Cookies?" Erin's voice from across the room sounded kind of hollow, echoey. Carrie wondered what caused that. Something about the rafters above them? Had to be. So that explained why the attic was "haunted." God, this was dumb.

Sam sat down next to Carrie. Close. "I thought you were a veteran ghost hunter."

"Nope. Long-time listener, first-time caller."

"I'll bet you're all excited."

He was so not talking about ghosts. "Very."

"Me, too."

"But Sam, you grew up here. Surely you've seen all the ghosts in this place, right? You probably know all their names."

"They're pretty cagey, but then, knowing my family, that makes sense."

"Really? Do explain."

Sam settled in, then smiled. "You want to know about the ghost in the attic?"

Everyone nodded as if by mentioning the word *ghost* itself, Sam had mesmerized them all.

He leaned a bit forward, as Carrie watched the man

standing at the door turn the overhead light to dim. She kept her cool, though, wanting to watch Sam in action.

"It was in 1939, during a long, hot summer. My great-grandparents were running the hotel. They had a full house, folks who'd come to Crider to enjoy the good fishing and swimming in the lakes and the cool shade in the forest. One couple, they were called Thomas and Constance Mapleton, had a young child with them, two-year-old Francis."

Carrie blinked in astonishment at Sam's complete ease and expertise at bullshitting these nice people. He was like P. T. Barnum in his ability to play the room, to emphasize the right word, provide the telling detail. As she watched, it was as if everyone around her became children. Eager, open, completely willing to fall under his spell.

"Francis was having a rough time with his teeth. Crying kept up not just his parents but the other guests, as well. My great-grandpa, Robert B. Crider, was sent up to this very attic by my great-grandma, Eleanor. Robert took Constance with him, for there was a large wooden chest sitting right where you are, Erin, filled with old toys from over the years. The hope was to distract Francis, although according to my dad, Grandma Eleanor planned on using a finger dabbed in whiskey on the child's gums come nightfall."

No one seemed to give a moment's thought to the fact that Sam had completely changed the cadence of his voice, that his accent had somehow become more Southern, which didn't make a great deal of sense except that it worked.

She'd been to story times at libraries and conferences before, and Sam was the best she'd ever heard. He was a natural, probably because he believed every word. Hadn't he told her he believed that the most compelling stories were true?

"When Robert and Constance were in this very room, looking at abandoned dolls and hand-carved miniature wagons, a woman neither one of them had ever seen before was suddenly right behind Constance. It gave them both a frightful scare, but Robert, being a good host, asked if he could help the woman.

"She was dressed plain, no hat, her hair was dark and very long, and instead of shoes the woman wore tattered slippers.

"'I left it here,' she said.

"'What's that?' Robert asked.

"'I left my Sara's doll here. She's crying for it.'

"Robert and Constance reached back down into the toy chest to find Sara's doll," Sam continued. "When they looked up again, the woman had turned. She raised her hand as if to ward off a blow, then vanished right before their eyes."

Carrie heard the group exhale, couldn't see, but knew there were goose bumps and shivers all around.

"She didn't stay away, though. People still hear the attic steps creaking, the soft tread of her slippers. Some have said they've heard her call out, sometimes for Sara, sometimes in alarm."

"Have you seen her?" Elton asked.

"Oh, yes," Sam said.

"Come on," Erin said. "Tell us."

"Can't." Sam nodded at one of the couples Carrie

didn't know who were standing by the equipment. "They're going to start up any second."

She leaned into him, shoulder to shoulder, wanting to talk about his performance, wanting him to turn and give her a wink or a sign that it had all been well-rehearsed nonsense.

He gave her a smile that didn't give her a clue, but if the lights had been turned off, he'd have kissed her. She knew it, because she would have met him halfway.

The guy by the monitors started going into his spiel, and Carrie lost interest in seconds. She tried not to stare outright at Sam, but she did dart a few glances.

They'd connected at eight as promised. She'd been in the ballroom not listening to a lecture on analyzing the evidence after an investigation. Erin had been taking notes, but it was clear she was distracted because they hadn't had a chance to talk about their individual sessions with Marcia.

Carrie had been glad of the delay. She would talk to Erin about what had happened, but she needed time to digest what she'd heard.

No wonder Marcia was a famous medium. For someone so inclined, it would be a simple thing to believe her impressions had come from a mystical source, because they were remarkably spot-on. Carrie had met people who had that gift of observation, but no one as astute as Marcia.

She'd nailed Carrie on her hermitlike existence, on her dependence and love of living virtually. She'd also seen that Carrie didn't make friends easily, and that she was worried that she'd end up tragically alone.

"You okay?" Sam whispered.

She nodded. "Peachy. Can't wait to get this show on the road."

"I've been meaning to ask," he said, keeping his voice low and close. "What got you into ghost hunting?"

"Erin," she said, glad at least that part wasn't a lie. "She loves old buildings and goes wandering all over L.A. in search of hidden treasure. Great molding or an architectural detail that's of this style or that. She told me once that it's more than just seeing bits of long-forgotten beauty. She feels the people who walked down the halls and worked and lived in the old relics. And when I'm with her, and she's showing me around, I can see them, too."

That wasn't a lie, either. She saw them in Erin's eyes, in her changing expressions. The stories Erin told sounded like the truth, and for her best friend's sake, Carrie hoped they were.

"That's nice. I wonder if she'll feel anyone up here tonight."

"She might. Especially after that story. So you've seen a few ghosts yourself, have you?"

Sam leaned even closer, but his response would have to wait. The woman by the cameras called for attention, and stared straight at Sam and Carrie.

"Okay. We're about ready. The lights are gonna be out in a minute, so make sure you have all your stuff where you can grab it. No crunchy foods, dudes, and no crinkling paper. Nothing distracting, all right? Just sit, meditate, ask the spirits to come. In about an hour, me and George here are gonna do some talking, but in the meantime the more calm energy we can put out there, the more likely we are to have a sighting. Oh, and listen,

like we said earlier, we'll have bathroom breaks every
two hours. Make use of them. It's a drag to have to stir
things up because someone didn't visit the restroom.
All right. Any questions?"

There were none. This wasn't anyone's first time,
except her own. George and his lady friend did some
last-minute tinkering, then the lights went off.

The room swooped into the kind of darkness that
had a presence. There were no windows up here, and
the only light sources at all were small red and yellow
buttons coming from the equipment and a few of those
little flashlights. She made the mistake of looking at
one of the buttons too long, and the light burned a trail
across the little vision she had. It would dissipate soon,
but she'd learned her lesson.

She jumped when she felt something brush her thigh.
Luckily she hadn't cried out, because it was Sam's hand.
She grabbed it, glad for his warmth, for his company.

He leaned over, slowly, working, she thought, at not
scaring her as much as not making noise. She marked
his progress by the feel of him against her hip, her side,
her shoulder. Then she felt his warm breath heat the shell
of her ear.

"I'm going to cover us," he whispered so softly she
felt sure no one else had heard.

She squeezed his hand to let him know that was
fine.

The blanket settled across her lap, and in the dark
room with the eerie lights, even something as mundane
as a blanket became weird. Once more, Sam found her
hand and moved as close as he could. Carrie let her head
rest on his shoulder.

The quiet changed from peculiar to cozy, helped along by the heat of the man next to her. She felt him kiss her head, and it made her smile.

It didn't seem to matter if she closed her eyes, but she did anyway. It reminded her of how it had been to fall asleep next to Sam last night. He'd curled around her body like an apostrophe, and she wasn't at all surprised to find that they fit together perfectly.

Time ticked by in silent seconds, and she drifted in the twilight between sleep and awareness. Twice, Sam shifted, but so gently, he must have known she was dozing. She wondered, briefly, if she snored, and that's why he'd nudged her awake, but she couldn't seem to care very much either way. Sleep beckoned once again.

But not for long.

A male voice, at once nasal and sluggish, woke her. It was George, and she supposed this was the talking portion of the program, which struck her as particularly useless. If there were in fact ghosts in the attic, or even just outside the attic, they would surely know there were a bunch of living people inside the room. They didn't need an invitation, as they were incorporeal. So, was the message that began most of the late-night stakeouts she'd seen on TV, and was listening to live and in person, for the ghosts' sake or those hoping to see ghosts? Carrie figured it was the latter. After all, there was something ritualistic about the whole damn exercise.

The singsong cadence seemed universal, the words more formal than anyone would use in casual conversation. But people liked ritual. They liked all the trappings that lent credence to ceremony and weight to beliefs. Ritual brought people into agreement and collusion.

What could be more appropriate for those seeking contact with the other side?

Odder than the voice itself was the night-vision view of the man on the monitor. His eyes glowed as did the white parts of his T-shirt. Nothing anyone in the room hadn't seen before. Yet the atmosphere had changed. Not because of spectral visitations, but because of the sheer amount of want coming from the people.

Behind George, something clattered to the ground, making everyone, including Carrie, jump.

"Whoa, did you see that? What the hell?"

A little flashlight went on, making her wince. People stirred, someone whimpered. Carrie thought it might have been one of Erin's boys.

"Shit, man," George said. "That was the EMF meter. That was just sitting there, we weren't anywhere near it. It flew off the goddamn chair."

"I knew it," Ann said. "I told you we were gonna find something tonight. Did it get on tape? Did anyone feel anything?"

Carrie leaned into Sam. "Because there couldn't possibly be any other explanation for a meter sitting on a rickety chair to fall."

"Shhh," he said, but he wasn't scolding.

It wasn't easy to see, but she'd swear he was smiling. Ah, the flashlight beam came their way, and sure enough. He was grinning like a fool. But did he just find the immediate assumption that a ghost was responsible for a piece of equipment falling ludicrous, or the whole concept?

"There's a cold spot!" Erin said.

"I feel it, right there!" That was Elton.

Then Carrie heard the sound of a high five, and some high-pitched laughter.

"Man, this is awesome," George said. "I bet we got that on tape. What's your temperature reading, dude?"

She couldn't hold it anymore. Laughter bubbled up, and she pushed her mouth onto Sam's sleeve, trying to stop. The harder she tried, the more hilarious it became, and she ended up faking a coughing fit just to cover it.

"Will you stop?" Sam whispered, his lips close. *Now* he was scolding.

"I can't help it," she said, keeping her voice as low as she could. "It's not that I don't believe in, you know, stuff. But it's chilly in an old attic? I mean…"

"Quiet, or we're going to get kicked out of here."

"Hey, what's going on over there?" Erin said. "Did you guys get something?"

Carrie couldn't answer. She had most of one fist shoved in her mouth.

"Nope. Thought we did, but it was just Carrie knocking over a thermos. She got kind of excited."

"Well, who wouldn't?" George asked. "But hey, man. Be careful. It's just the beginning of the night, and we've already got some excellent movement. Okay, okay. Let's all chill. In fact, let's take a break now, calm down. Go on out if you need to. 'Cause when we get back, man, it's gonna be all business. I'm gonna check the monitor, see if we caught that meter hitting the floor."

Carrie got up so fast she was afraid she'd knock every meter to the ground. But she made it outside lickety-split, then headed straight for the stairs. She needed to stop laughing, or they really were going to kick her out. Not just out of the attic, but out of the conference. She'd make up something for Sam, although who was she kidding? She'd already blown it with him. Maybe if she told him the evidence wasn't hard-core enough for the likes of her, he'd buy it.

Then she burst out laughing again. A cold spot. A meter falling. No wonder the equipment sellers were making a fortune. Talk about gullible. Talk about reaching.

She got to the bathroom, and it was mercifully empty, although her hysterics had calmed down in her mad dash. Thank goodness. She'd never make it through the rest of the night if she didn't take control. It was funny, yes, but not to them. At least, not to most of them.

Sam had been grinning, though. She hadn't made that up. Maybe he was just laughing at her. Or maybe he completely believed in ghosts, but recognized George, et al, were full of crap. She couldn't take any more chances, though. There were so few days left, she'd gotten no work done at all, and much more importantly, she didn't want to strain things between her and Sam.

She got comfy in a stall and thought again about Marcia. The parts the woman had gotten right were impressive. The prognostication, however, seemed off by a mile. As much as Carrie would miss Erin, there was no way Carrie was moving out of her loft, not now or in the foreseeable future. She loved that loft. It was perfect for her. The light, the space, the convenience. She felt safe there, and while she wouldn't mind an occasional visit to New York, living there was out of the question.

Marcia hadn't actually said Carrie would move to

New York, but then, she didn't have to. No, Marcia had said she would move to follow someone very important to her. Someone who would be a major part of the rest of her life. While it was nice for Carrie to think she and Erin would be friends forever, she wasn't convinced of it. People changed. Erin had changed from the girl she was in college, and so had Carrie.

Lost in thought, she went to the sink to wash, and as she pumped the soap, the mirror started to steam up. She turned off the hot water, afraid there was something wrong with the plumbing, but the steam kept on building. It didn't have an odor. It was simply ordinary steam, like what happened during a hot shower, only there wasn't a shower.

She rinsed her hands and turned off the taps before backing up. It wasn't that she was spooked. Something was clearly wrong with the plumbing, and it could be dangerous in there. Just as she was turning to find a paper towel she noticed that the steam wasn't evenly distributed over the entire mirror. It was centered in front of where she'd been standing. But that wasn't the weirdest thing about it. There was a word etched in the condensation. Four letters that spelled STAY.

A shiver went up her spine, but a second later, she laughed at her own foolishness. Someone had marked that part of the mirror earlier, that's all, and the steam only adhered to the surrounding glass. It wasn't supernatural, it wasn't ghosts. But she needed to tell Sam right away. This could be a real problem for him.

She hurried out to the stairs and met Sam, among others, coming down.

"There you are," he said. "You ran off in such a hurry I was worried."

"Had to go to the bathroom. And speaking of, you've got a plumbing issue in the ladies' room."

"Crap," he said. "No pun intended. Show me."

She led him to the ladies' restroom. She went in first to make sure no one would be surprised, but it was still empty. "It's safe."

Sam entered and she pointed to the mirror. To the perfectly clean, steam-free mirror.

"I'm not sure what you're pointing at," he said.

"The mirror."

"What's wrong with it?"

"There was steam."

"Steam? On the mirror?"

Carrie nodded. "I know what steam looks like, and there was steam. Quite a bit of it."

Sam frowned. Looked around, then up. "There's a vent up there," he said. "I'll call maintenance to have a look. I really don't want the place to blow up. That would be bad."

"Yes, it would." She wasn't looking at him, though. She went up close to the mirror, to where she'd seen the word so clearly. Standing on tiptoes, she leaned forward and put the side of her hand up against the mirror where the *S* had been. She huffed a breath. It worked, insomuch as she got the mirror to steam, but there was no partial *S*. No partial anything. She moved a little to the right and repeated the experiment.

"Carrie?"

"Yeah?"

"What are you doing?"

She stepped back. "Nothing." No way she was going to tell him about the word. In fact, while she was certain there was a perfectly logical explanation, she wanted the subject dropped *tout de suite*. "We should get back. You can call the maintenance people on the way."

He looked at her suspiciously. "You sure you're okay? Maybe it would be better to skip the rest of the investigation. Have you lie down."

She rolled her eyes, when she saw his eyebrows waggle. "Cut it out. I'm not nuts. Something went wrong with your plumbing, and you're going to be sorry when some other lady you aren't sleeping with gets a face full of hot steam, and sues you for billions."

"Billions, huh? I promise I'll have it looked into first thing tomorrow, and for tonight, I'll make sure this bathroom is put out of service."

"Thank you," she said.

"You're welcome."

Then she stood once again on tiptoes, but this time it was to kiss him. He seemed pleased, if the tightness of his arms was any indicator.

"Ahem."

She jumped away from Sam, and he jumped back from her, only he banged his head on the stall door behind him. Loudly.

"I'm sure," Erin said as she crossed her arms, "you two could find somewhere a little less public to make out in this hotel *that one of you owns and where the other has a private room.*"

"Sorry," Sam said. "Plumbing issue. Don't use this bathroom." He crossed to the door with as much grace as a man with flaming cheeks could muster, but to his credit he stopped there, instead of abandoning Carrie to her fate.

"And as for you, missy," Erin said, giving her a wicked stare. "I heard you laughing. You are hereby excused from participating in tonight's adventure. Go find another way to amuse yourself." She gave Sam a sideways glance. "The opportunities are boundless."

Carrie lost her smile. "I'm sorry, Erin. I just got the giggles is all. I can do better. I want to be there."

Erin eyed her, the debate clear on her face, as was the moment she gave in. "Promise to behave?"

Carrie held up her hand. "I swear."

Erin pointed at Sam. "I'm holding you responsible."

"Me? What did I do?"

"Aided and abetted." Erin looked from Sam to Carrie then back again. "We clear?"

The two of them answered at the same time, and in the same penitent voice. Carrie had to bite the hell out of her lower lip so she wouldn't laugh.

13

SAM WOULDN'T HAVE MINDED skipping the rest of the investigation in the attic. Too many silly people on a fool's errand. But it was a chance to be with Carrie, and he would take what he could get. Even sitting next to her when they couldn't speak made him… *Happy* was the word that came to him, but it didn't make much sense. The things that made him happy with Carrie were all forbidden in the attic, so why, precisely, was he willing to stay up all night just so he could sit near her?

Pheromones weren't exactly a proven fact, but that side of things made sense. They were chemically compatible, so he wanted to be near her scent, to feel her. Besides, she smelled really good.

They settled down in the dim light as the others trickled in. George and Ann were working on the machines, Erin's boys were staring at the door as they drank caffeinated power beverages, and he decided now was a perfect time to surprise Carrie with a treat. Jody had come through again, this time with the best cheesecake he'd ever eaten. He had two large pieces in the picnic basket, and he brought them out with as much flourish as he could in the weird circumstances. "Ta-da," he whispered.

"Cheesecake!" she whispered back. Not even. She mostly mouthed the word. But the way her face lit up was better than a shout.

He gave her one plate, then a fork and a napkin. Before he took the wrapping off his own piece, he poured them both drinks from the thermoses. The lights were going to go off any second, and he wanted to be ready.

George took a head count, then said, "Quiet, people. Here we go." And just like that, it was dark. Sam managed to get his fork to his mouth without making a mess, and he rolled his eyes even though no one could see. A few seconds later, he felt Carrie's warm breath at his ear. She made a sound that was exactly like the one she'd made in bed, but much, much quieter. He grinned. Orgasmic cheesecake. If anyone could do it, Jody could.

They remained as quiet as mice as they finished their food and sipped their coffee, then Sam put things away. Now came *his* treat. The slow move to press himself against Carrie. To feel her heat from thigh to shoulder, to hold her hand and bring it to his lips.

She met him halfway. He buried his nose in her soft hair and inhaled her scent. He should put the blanket over them, but he'd been so preoccupied with the snack he wasn't really sure how to manage it. Well, no one could see them in the dark, and if they needed to keep each other warm, so much the better.

Her hand slipped from his and came to rest on his thigh. Her breath was back at his ear, but not to whisper.

He had to hold back a gasp as she took his lobe between her teeth.

So she wanted to play, did she? Here in this dark room full of people? He could deal with that. He found her face, her jaw to be precise, which gave him his bearings. Finding her lips was no problem at all. It wasn't easy to keep silent, though. Everything about this woman made him want to moan.

She shifted into the kiss, he moved his hand down her arm, heading in the direction of her breast, but taking his time. By the time he reached his destination, he fully understood the folly of the enterprise. He needed to take her out of here. *Now*. If she so much as breathed in a downward direction, it was quite conceivable that he would come. Not the image he wanted to leave with his guests. When her hand moved higher up his leg, he had to stop her.

She made a noise. Not a loud noise, probably, but it felt loud, and obvious. They should really stop this. Go back to sitting and watching the monitors. Hope like hell that a ghost did something so dramatic, it would make everyone run screaming from the room. Or if not everyone, just them. That would work.

Carrie trapped his lower lip between her teeth and the nip was just shy of painful, which would have been great if the sensation hadn't gone right to his dick. This was torture. So why couldn't he stop?

Carrie let go with an audible gasp, much louder than the noise from before, and it made him jerk back and gasp, too. Then he saw something behind her, and it took him a few seconds to realize it was a person, not a spirit. Someone was talking to Carrie. He imagined it was Erin, but it might have been someone else. But how had she made her way to Carrie? Shouldn't there have been some fumbles along the way? What the hell was going on?

The shadow person rose like a specter of darkness. A second later, Carrie turned his head and leaned in close enough that her lips touched his ear. "That was Erin," she said in the softest tone possible. "People are wearing night-vision glasses. They've all been watching us make out."

It was probably good that he had to be silent. His curses out loud would have made his ancestors blush.

It was much later and Carrie couldn't catch her breath. Not from ghosts. There'd been no ghosts, except the invisible, nonexistent kind. They were in her room, finally naked, and Sam hadn't been content with one orgasm from her, even though she'd told him—no, probably *because* she'd told him—she was a one-orgasm kind of gal. The big surprise wasn't that he'd gotten her there, but that he'd gotten her there so quickly. Wow.

"You okay?" he asked, through his gasps for air.

"'bout the same as you."

"I need resuscitation."

She smiled. "You're on your own."

They panted for a bit. Carrie thought about snagging the water from the bedside table, but no way she was moving that far.

"Don't take this the wrong way," he said, "but I have to be awake and alert in three hours."

She let her head fall to the side so she could see him.

"What other way is there to take it? *I* don't have to get up in three hours. So it's fine."

He was still faceup, eyes closed, chest heaving, but he grinned. "It must be love."

His words were a joke, a cute one at that, and yet her breath hitched and she turned away, grabbing the water bottle as she got up to go to the bathroom. She had no idea why her stomach clenched and it was harder to breathe. It had to be sleep deprivation, that's all. She wasn't used to being up till four in the morning. She wasn't particularly used to being up till midnight. That Sam had teased her about love didn't mean anything. If he'd said it seriously, now that would have scared her.

She shut the door behind her. Unfortunately, the bathroom was small and it was impossible not to see herself in the big mirror behind the sink. Her hair was a fright wig, her makeup had smeared under her eyes and standing hunched against the door was not her sexiest look. The best thing to do was wash up and get back to bed. The man had to be up in three hours, for god's sake.

Instead, she turned on the shower. The second it was at temperature, she stepped inside. The moment she was drenched it occurred to her she should have brought in a robe. Screw it. She just needed a minute, that's all. Water always had calmed her.

Whatever she was feeling for Sam Crider, it wasn't love. Not that she'd been in love, but at least she knew that love took time. Love was about trust, respect, getting to know someone's habits, moods, likes, dislikes. It wasn't some mysterious thing bestowed by Cupid or destiny or whatever myths floated one's boat. She wasn't even sure the construct existed except in fiction.

What people called love was friendship and sex.
Compatible chemistries melding with compatible interests. She was very sexually compatible with Sam,
but she didn't love him. All the feelings she had, the
quickening of her heart, the flush she felt all over, the
way she almost ached to see him… Simple enough.
Humans were designed to procreate. Didn't mean they
were meant to live as mates for fifty years. Or even five.
She was far too practical to let herself go off on some
fantasy called love.

Even if she did think that one day she'd be married,
have a kid or two, she wasn't searching for any kind of
fairy-tale romance. She'd read a study once where the
number of happily married love matches were equal to
the number of happily married arranged matches. Which
just proved her point.

She grabbed the bar of soap and washed herself, satisfied that her emotions were back under her control.

The sound of Sam entering the bathroom only made
her drop the soap because she wasn't used to sharing.
When he stepped into the shower with her, she could
barely breathe, but that was adrenaline. Or epinephrine.
Or one of those other chemicals.

When he kissed her, the blossom of heat that spread
through her body had nothing to do with forever. Even
though a forever of this…thing…called to a part of her
that was utterly new. She grasped him behind his neck
and held him steady as she kissed him back. They were
both too wrung out to actually do it again, but that's not
what her kiss was about.

She wanted him close, to feel the way he made her
heart pound.

She held him tight because she needed to make sure he understood this was more than a vacation fling, even if she didn't know what to call it.

She turned them so he was under the spray of the water, the urge to wash his hair strong, but, she realized, not all sexual. She hated that he'd have so little sleep. She wanted to take care of him. The thought brought a strange pressure to her chest, a yearning she couldn't explain.

Freaked out, she let him go, stepped back, searched for the soap, her hands flailing about, her wet hair slapping her in the face. When she found it, she shoved it in his hand without meeting his eye. Then she stepped dripping out of the shower to cover herself with a towel.

"Carrie?"

She looked at him through the glass shower door. Put a smile on her face. "Wash. For god's sake, you have to be up and alert in three hours."

SAM KNEW THE DAY WAS GOING to be a long one. He hadn't had nearly enough sleep, and he'd been away from the crazy schedules of filmmaking long enough that his body wasn't accustomed to weird hours and time shifts. It was worth it. The only thing he regretted was the make-out session in the attic. He'd didn't like the idea of compromising Carrie's reputation. Coming in at a distant second was his own reputation, but he was here temporarily, and while he wasn't in favor of behaving unprofessionally, being with Carrie felt necessary. Even getting dressed this morning, he'd come up with a dozen excuses why he should take the day off. Some of them were damn good, too.

It wasn't as if his staff couldn't handle things. Maybe, after he'd signed paychecks, he'd make sure the plans for tonight's activities were all in place, check in with reservations, housekeeping, Jody, then go back to Carrie's room. Leaving her as she slept had been painful.

The prospect of her leaving for good even more so.

Tonight was Halloween. The afternoon and evening were packed with a hayride, a ghost tour of the stables and a dinner and dance in the ballroom. A band was coming in from Denver, and dammit, there was too much to do for him to take off any more time. They had to decorate the ballroom before six. The dinner alone was going to be a massive event, but at least the restaurant and bar would be closed at five so Jody and her people would only have to do the banquet.

He was asking a lot of his employees and he had to pitch in. It would be an exhausting day, ending with a lot of drunk and crazy ghost hunters wandering the hotel.

He didn't know when he'd be able to see Carrie. Tomorrow was their last full day and night together since she was leaving first thing Tuesday morning.

It wasn't enough time. Not by half. Maybe after he'd sold the place, he'd spend a week or two in L.A. He'd be able to afford it, and he could put off setting up his new life for that long. He could even look into getting some equipment while he was there.

If she wanted him to come.

No use getting ahead of himself. Although he didn't like to think about it, there was a chance that Carrie wanted this to end the moment she was in the airport shuttle. She had her own life, and she'd be dealing with Erin's move. Why wasn't it Carrie coming to New York?

Long-distance relationships never worked, which was an excuse he'd used to break things off more often than he cared to admit. Just because it was his go-to relationship ender didn't make it untrue.

He grabbed some coffee from the kiosk in the lobby, then went to his office, struggling to get his mind into work mode. Mail from the last several days had piled up on his desk, and he separated it quickly. The stack of his aunt's magazines was considerable. It wouldn't be a bad idea to take it all back there and check to make sure everything was as it should be. He had the key to her apartment, of course, although he really didn't like visiting the quarters often.

He opened the door slowly, hit at once with the familiar scents of pine and roses. His aunt had dozens of candles, all rose-scented, and she kept pine wreaths and small plants year-round.

Those were fine, no problem. The thing was, whenever he walked into the residence he couldn't stop himself from searching for the one scent he knew wasn't there. His mother had loved Boucheron perfume. It had been one of her few indulgences, she'd said. Worn to make her feel like a princess. Sam could recognize that scent anywhere, and every time he smelled it, memories crashed into him like rogue waves. Sadly, the memories weren't of the good times, but of the afterward, the days and nights in her sick bed, when nothing at all made her feel like royalty.

He put the magazines on the sideboard where Grace liked them, and did a quick tour. Nothing had been disturbed. Not just in the two weeks she'd been gone, but in years. Every picture on the wall was a picture he knew intimately. Every stick of furniture was hope-lessly old-fashioned in homage to the ancestors, and had been often patched, never replaced. Except in the master bedroom. There was his father's bed, now his aunt's. Bought a few months after his mother had died.

He wasn't sure what compelled him to open the room least likely to have changed. His old bedroom was in stasis, a monument to a child long gone. Even though he'd lived in the apartment until he was seventeen, the décor was from his preteen years. He'd been a slave to *Star Wars,* and posters hung on each wall. Even the bedspread had Wookies and lightsabers. His father had told him he'd hoped one day that Sam would come back to the hotel, that he'd have his own children, and they could redecorate if they wanted to.

That thought led to another, although he wasn't sure why. He was sorry Carrie wasn't here with him. There were good memories here, memories that had been over-shadowed with pain, but now his thoughts went back to hours spent building scale models with his dad, having his friends over, hiding out in the Old Hotel when he wasn't supposed to. Listening to his mother laugh, to both his folks telling the guests all the ghost stories. So many Halloweens before his mother had gotten sick. Happy times. He would like to tell Carrie about them. Show her the places outside the inn where he'd played. Where he'd learned to ride a horse, and how to ski. Where he and his parents had built snowmen.

There wouldn't be time for any of that. She would be gone in the blink of an eye.

He turned and stepped on something hard and small. Moving his foot, he bent, hardly believing what he saw.

It was a die, an old Dungeons & Dragons polyhedral d20, exactly like the one he'd played with all those years ago. But that set hadn't been touched since he was thirteen. How did the die get on the floor?

He opened the closet door. Up on the far corner shelf were plastic storage bins, and he knew which one had been dedicated to D&D because of the stickers on the front.

He put the bin on the bed, opened it, and there was the original game book, a big black bag of dice, maps, character sheets, everything he'd loved so much as a kid. He poured the bag onto the spread, onto the *Millennium Falcon*. The d20 was missing.

Who the hell could have been in this room? No one would want any of this old crap. He could have understood someone taking the whole bin to sell on eBay or something, but one die? It was crazy.

He put the dice, all but the d20, back in the bag, returned the bin to its rightful place, left the room and his past behind. As mysteries went, this wasn't much of one. But it occupied his thoughts all the way to his desk.

His phone rang minutes after he'd opened the first of his correspondence. The number was familiar. "Sam Crider."

"Sam. It's Kunio Mori."

"How are you, Mr. Mori? Your trip went well?"

"Yes, very. I wanted to give you a heads-up. I was impressed with your property. So were my money people. You should be receiving the offer any minute."

Sam's eyes widened, but he made sure his voice

sounded perfectly normal. "That was a lot faster than I anticipated."

"You were smart to see both of us at the same time. It lit a fire. Now go take a look at the papers. Talk to your people. I know it's a busy time for you there, so I'll expect to hear from you the beginning of next week."

"Absolutely, Mr. Mori. I appreciate the quick response."

"It's a good place you have there, Sam. Not quite Vail, but good in its own way."

"It is, yes. I'll get back to you." Sam hung up the phone. He should get his ass over to the fax machine, see what the offer was. It would be low, but the first offer always was. Then there would be negotiations, and he would let Heartly know right away that an offer was on the table. This was going to happen. His future would be secured.

As he leaned back in his dad's old chair, Sam's hand went to his pocket and he pulled out the d20, not even sure why he'd kept it. He turned it over and over. He hadn't been able to play D&D often. Sam lived so far from town, he missed a lot of games. But his folks, they would let him have sleepovers, and he and his pals would stay up too late, get too excited. Damn, they'd gotten lost for hours in a world of trolls and hidden doors and magic spells. Always, in the background, was the faint sent of Boucheron.

14

CARRIE HAD COFFEE in one hand, her notebook in the other, and a frown on her face. She'd gotten up too early, far too alone, pulled on her cowboy flannel pajamas, made terrible coffee from the in-room service, and hauled out her work.

She'd done nothing for too many days. It was Sunday, Halloween already. They were leaving first thing Tuesday morning. She'd finished exactly nine panels, total. Enough for an introduction to the graphic novel, or three days of her online comic. She should have done four times as many, and even the panels she did have pretty much sucked.

Her black-and-white sketches were good. She'd captured the essence of the conference in a few key props like fake ghosts and tourists overburdened with too much ghost-hunting equipment. But the words, the truly important part, they were…flat. Bordering on nice.

Not only had she wasted precious time she could have spent with Erin, but she had also fallen into lust with a guy whose whole history was tied up with ghosts. It would have made so much more sense for Erin and Sam to hook up. They could live happily ever after in New York, spook hunting to their heart's content.

All Carrie felt was confused. That she hadn't told Sam about her comic was the least of it. That moment in the shower had spun in her head as she'd examined it from every angle. She didn't love him, she barely knew him, and yet she'd felt something so deep, so… frightening it made her question her sanity.

It wasn't her first trip around this particular block. She'd had vacation sex before, and she'd had rebound sex, but never simultaneously. Perhaps it was the combination that made this feel so weird.

In her twenty-six years, she'd had crushes, obsessions, friends with benefits and tragic seductions. She'd experienced a lot of emotions around men and being a couple, and she thought herself reasonably savvy. But this was new territory, and she couldn't even pinpoint why. It was a good thing she was leaving soon. If she stayed, she could get in trouble. Find herself falling into an unwise relationship with a man who wasn't interested in a relationship, who lived across the country…

Oh, she was the most idiotic person in the universe. In a relationship with Sam? In love? *Please*. She was far more likely to be hit by lightening. *Twice*.

It could turn into love, though, she thought. Maybe. Possibly. *Definitely not.*

Marcia the Medium had told her that her life was about to take a dramatic turn. But that was about Erin leaving for New York. Carrie being on her own again. To entertain any other interpretation was as crazy as believing in ghosts.

She sighed again as she looked down at her sketches.

She'd done the thing with the falling meter where everyone immediately assumed spooks were responsible. And the bit where the change in temperature was a "sign." But they both seemed lame. Neither would stop anyone from reading *CCW,* but it wasn't close to the sarcasm she was capable of.

Maybe she should forget this whole damn idea and come up with something new. Either way, she was still so far behind on work she was going to be a crazed woman when she got home. That might not be so bad. The less time she had to obsess over Erin leaving and missing Sam, the better.

It occurred to her, and not for the first time, that the two things were connected. Solace, thy name is Sam? She truly liked being with him. He was really funny and sexy and great. But when she let herself think too much, when she got really panicked about Erin's departure, the doubts came at her from all sides.

Wasn't she too old to be worrying so much about a friend leaving? It wasn't as if Erin was going to the moon. They'd still talk, use Skype, visit.

Only, without Erin's prompting, Carrie was afraid she'd turn into someone she didn't want to be. The trouble was, she wasn't sure who she *did* want to be. Except that if she could, she'd be more like someone who could picture herself in love. In a healthy way. With a guy who loved her back.

She sipped her coffee, grimacing at how cold it had gotten. She put her notebook down and stuck the cup in the microwave. The smartest thing she could do now was go back to bed. Nothing was going to happen until tonight, and she wasn't even sure when she was going to see Sam. He would be busy as hell getting things set up for the Halloween extravaganza. Erin was all over the costume party at the ballroom. Carrie wished she could skip it. Just stay here in the room and sleep.

The ding happened, and yep, the coffee was now hot. How pitiful that it felt like the only success of the day. She put the cup down and fell onto the bed. Sam's scent filled her senses and a stab of want took her breath away. She hated that she'd slept through his leaving this morning. Hated that he had so much to do they probably wouldn't be able to spend any time together tonight. She burrowed her face in his pillow and wished that she'd met him in Los Angeles. It would have been so great to show him around, to share her comic with him. To share her life.

God, she had to stop. It was useless to wish for things she couldn't have.

Dragging her butt up, she meant to get her laptop, but picked up her notebook instead. Turning to a new page, she started to write. Not about ghosts, but about her best friend in the whole world. Her best friend leaving.

She and Erin were in the comic all the time. They had different names, but it was them, and it was time for her to tell her faithful readers that Sheri, Erin's avatar, was leaving. Jessie, Carrie's comic self, was going to be crushed. Rudderless. *Cruel, Cruel World* wasn't always about sarcasm and glib one-liners. It was about life. All of it. Even the part where the best friend disappears.

At some point, she shifted her position, stuffing pillows behind her back. She forgot about her coffee, about everything but telling this story.

Carrie wasn't surprised when Sam entered the drawings. She called him Steve and drew him tall and handsome with his broad shoulders and sexy hair. While Jessie was still heartbroken at the loss of Sheri, she found such comfort in Steve's arms, Carrie found herself sniffling.

Her hand was just starting to cramp when a knock brought her out of the zone. She had no idea how many panels she'd done. They were rough, sure, but they were honest. Whatever she'd written and drawn in this mad frenzy was important, at least to her.

"Just a minute." She ached when she stood, having been too long in one position. The light had changed as well, and she glanced at the small clock on the table, surprised that it was almost five.

She opened the door to find Erin wearing the sexiest Corpse Bride outfit in the universe, complete with long dark wig, enormous fake eyelashes and a dead flower bouquet.

"You're in your pajamas."

Carrie looked down. "Yep."

"We're supposed to be having cocktails right now. You were supposed to be ready fifteen minutes ago."

"I was working. Sorry. Hey, why don't I go dressed as a person who just got out of bed? I could be ready in two minutes."

"Um, sweetie, you'd need more than two, even if I did let you go in that. Luckily, I have the perfect costume because I am just that good." Erin brought in a really large bag, then retrieved her own pair of knee-high patent-leather lace-up boots.

"Oh, no. I told you I wasn't going in costume. We agreed."

"*We* did no such thing." Erin stepped inside. "Come on. You'll look sexy. Sam's gonna go crazy when he sees you."

"I don't want Sam to go crazy. Besides, he's not going to dress up."

"How do you know?"

"I just do."

"Stop arguing," Erin said. "It's Halloween. We're in ghost central. There's going to be a band. You've even got a date. What the hell are you complaining for?"

Carrie closed her eyes for a second. Then she smiled at Erin. "You're right. It's a perfect night, and we're both going to enjoy every minute of it. Let me see the costume."

Despite her attitude switch, Carrie moaned when she got a load of the outfit. She'd be damned if she was putting that on, best friend or not.

"ARE YOU IMPLYING WE can't do our jobs?"

Sam frowned at Beverly and Patrick, who were standing in his office doorway, blocking his exit. "Don't be ridiculous. Of course you can, but I have a job to do, too."

"Not tonight, you don't," Patrick said. "We've got it covered."

"All you have to do is go get dressed," Beverly added.

"I haven't checked the ballroom, or talked to Jody. I have no idea what I'm going to say to start the evening off—"

Patrick, who was Sam's senior by a good fifteen years and had worked at the inn for longer than that, held up his hand. "Take the night off, Sam. Everything's covered. Enjoy yourself. This isn't the first or the last Halloween you're going to see at the hotel. Just have a good time."

Sam opened his mouth, but shut it at Patrick's glare.

"We have work to do, so let's not belabor the point. Go get dressed. Eat. Dance with your lady friend. And do not, under any circumstances, get up before ten tomorrow morning."

"You've been talking to the kitchen staff."

Beverly grinned. "The kitchen staff has been talking to us."

"It's none of your business, you know."

"Uh-huh." Beverly moved in back of him and gave him a gentle shove. "We're all terrible snoops. Deal with it."

"Fine. But don't be surprised if your Christmas bonuses are pieces of coal."

His employees didn't even acknowledge the threat, they just made sure he made it to the stairs. He could have ducked down to the ballroom, but the truth was, he didn't want to work tonight. For that matter, he didn't want to wear a costume, or go to the dinner or party. He wanted to spend every minute he could alone with Carrie.

It should have been a night of celebration. Kunio Mori's offer wasn't as low as he'd feared. It wasn't as high as he'd hoped, either, but it was real, and Mori's company had the money to back it up. So why wasn't he elated? His hand went back in his pocket, to the inexplicable die. Maybe leaving this place was going to be harder than he'd anticipated. Mori planned to demolish the inn and the Old

Hotel, probably every other building on the property. His plans included a pro-circuit golf course and a world-class spa in addition to a new, much larger hotel.

Sam was fine with that. He had schooled his expectations to the realm of possibility, not wishful thinking. But as he closed his door behind him, he was doing exactly that. He pictured himself in the Crider Inn, years from now. In a house built just down the road. A house he shared with Carrie, with two daughters, a dog and a custom editing bay in the basement. The picture was vivid and visceral in his mind's eye, even as the logical part of himself knew it was absurd. It wasn't like a dream, but a memory, which was…nuts.

He wasn't the marrying kind, he'd never wanted to keep the hotel, and he was the last man on earth who should have kids. It was the reality of the sale, that was all. The fact that he was tired. Meeting Carrie and liking her so damn much had mixed up his signals. He shook it off as he went to his closet.

He hated that he'd agreed to wear a costume, but he was glad he'd at least put his foot down when it came to applying makeup. He pulled out the black tuxedo, rolled his eyes when he looked in the bag hooked over the hanger and found a toy gun and a fake martini. Those would be staying in his room. The tuxedo? That he didn't mind so much. If no one realized he was supposed to be James Bond, that would be fine by him. There was only one person he wanted to impress tonight, and she liked him for who he was.

IT WAS ALMOST SIX WHEN Sam walked into the ballroom. He smiled as he was assailed with scary sound effects, outrageously great decorations, lit jack-o'-lanterns, and the happy chatter of excited guests. The big room had been transformed from a classroom to its namesake. Everyone here looked like they were having a ball. The band wasn't due to go on until nine, but they'd already set up. His staff, who had decided to all dress up as zombies, didn't have the shuffling gait of movie zombies, thank goodness. They did, however, look pretty disgusting.

The costumes of the guests, however, made his zombies look like amateurs. There were vampires and ghouls, mummies and monsters. All the tropes were represented extravagantly. Serious time had been spent on everything from shoes to hairdos.

There were long lines at the bars, and that was fine, since no one had to drive home. People were finding their seats, and Sam relaxed now that he knew everything was running smoothly, and let himself hunt for Carrie. He had no idea what she would be wearing, although she'd threatened no costume at all. He kind of hoped that was the case because he was clearly the only noncreepy character in the room. If he'd added a little fake blood dripping down the side of his mouth and a pair of fangs, he could have been a vampire, he supposed. But the hell with it. He wanted the guests to shine.

He spotted Erin first, and man, she looked great. He recognized the Corpse Bride, but hadn't realized a skeleton could have so many nice curves. He even liked the black wig, at least for the night. Her fan club hovered, of course, each of them bloody and maimed in some horrifying way. It was to be expected, he supposed.

Sam stopped dead in his tracks when he finally spotted Carrie. She was the sexiest thing he'd ever seen.

She wore shiny black boots that laced up to her knees. Above that, he could see her black stockings. Thigh-high stockings that showed off her superb legs and her very, very short red dress.

He walked toward her, glad for his tux. He hadn't cared a few minutes ago, but now he wanted her to like what he'd worn. He wanted her to feel proud to be with him.

Her dress was cut low and tight, revealing a lot of skin. It was sleeveless and snug. A black lacy thing covered the dress and her arms, making her appear to be covered in spiderwebs. Her hair swept across her back, her makeup was bold, and her lips bloodred.

Even Erin's boys were eyeing Carrie. Oh, they'd noticed her before, but Carrie had always underplayed her sexuality. Now that it was out in the open like this, Sam wondered if he'd have to stop any duels tonight. Or if he'd be in one himself.

She smiled as he approached, giving him a low, sexy whistle. "Well, hello there, handsome. I think you might be at the wrong party. Shouldn't you be gambling in Monaco or sipping champagne on a yacht?"

"I should," he said, "but I heard you needed protection from every male in Colorado."

She came close, but stopped herself halfway to a kiss. "Oh, uh, sorry."

"It's okay. I think our secret is out."

"Really? Is that bad?"

"The staff doesn't think so. They kicked me out of

my office. Made me promise not to do anything but enjoy the night with my lady friend."

"Who is she?" Carrie said, raising two fists. "Let me at her."

He laughed as he pulled her into his arms. "Am I going to ruin anything if I ravish you?"

"Only my cool, calm exterior," she said, looking up at him. Her lashes were absurdly long and ridiculously sexy. But then, everything about her was sexy, with or without her costume.

He bent to kiss her, and now that she had the all-clear, she took no prisoners. Her tongue slipped between his lips, her body pressed against his and her arms held him tight. The ballroom slipped away, and all that mattered was Carrie, and her heat, and how the taste of her made him feel like an intoxicated seventeen-year-old.

He ran his hands down her back, but felt thwarted by the black lace. If he'd had her alone, he'd strip her slowly, leaving her in her stockings and not another stitch.

She pulled back. "Oh, my. We probably shouldn't do too much of that when we're in public."

"I don't care where we are. I just want you."

She touched his lips with her red-tipped nail. "I know. And I promise, we'll leave the moment we can. This is Erin's big night, too, and she's only got her groupies to hang with."

"Right. Absolutely. And there's dinner coming. So we should…" He cleared his throat, a little wary of stepping back as his cock was half-hard. "How about I get us some drinks? That actually might help."

"Good. I suppose they don't have milk punches here, huh?"

"Doubt it. Do you like melon?"

She nodded.

"Midori cocktail it is. What about Erin?"

"She likes bourbon and 7-Up."

"I'll be back. Don't go anywhere."

IT WAS TEN-FIFTEEN AND Carrie was ready to go. The dinner had been a gastronomic triumph, the conversation hilarious, even the band was outstanding. But she wanted to be with Sam. Alone. Naked.

"Go, already," Erin said, making her jump at the words so close to her ear. The band was really loud.

Carrie spun around. "I don't want to leave you here alone," she shouted.

"Alone? I'm having a blast," Erin shouted back. "I love my boys. They're adorable and they all want so badly to dance, and they're all terrified to ask. I've decided to take them all out on the floor at once. We'll have our own mosh pit."

Carrie hugged her friend, careful of wigs and spiderwebs. "Happy Halloween, you ghost-loving freak."

"Ah, you say the sweetest things. Now go have fun with Bond. James Bond."

"He's hot, isn't he?"

"Smokin'."

Carrie smiled before she turned, determined to find Sam and carry him off to bed. Last she'd seen, he'd been dragged out on the dance floor by Marcia the Medium, who made a very convincing Elvira.

He wasn't on the dance floor or at either of the bars. In fact, Carrie couldn't find him anywhere. She wasn't worried he'd been swept away or anything, but he could have been called to work. There was that vent in the second-floor ladies' room, which she'd forgotten to ask about.

Carrie made her way through the crowd. Lulu stopped her with a hand on Carrie's arm. She was sitting between two of the guys Carrie had seen in the pub, so she still didn't know which one was her husband.

"You look great," Lulu said, and she didn't even have to shout as the band had stopped playing.

"You do, too." The woman had come dressed as a witch, but a pretty one, and Lulu didn't need a wig.

"How are you and Sam doing?"

Carrie guessed Sam had been right. Everyone knew about them. "He's a great guy. I'm looking for him now."

"Can't help you there, but listen. If I don't see you again, I'm glad you were here. It was fun."

"Thanks. It was. I've really enjoyed myself."

"I'm glad, hon. This was always meant to be a hoot and a holler. Travel safely."

Carrie wasn't much for hugging, but she did squeeze Lulu's shoulder, bummed she hadn't had more time to talk to her. Carrie had been such a damn snob, she'd probably missed out on a lot of nice people. The same people she wanted to make fun of in her comic. Actually talking to people changed everything.

She finally made it to the door, looked behind her once again, then left the ballroom. She spotted Sam and Marcia just down the hall, standing close to each other, Marcia's hand on Sam's arm. Carrie didn't want to intrude, so she ducked back inside to wait.

The band came back. Five invitations to dance later,

Sam walked in. The smile he gave her made her insides flutter. He looked so incredible in his tuxedo, she'd want him to wear one all the time. Or maybe rotate the tux and his mountain-man flannel. Yeah, she'd enjoy stripping him out of both of those.

"That's an interesting look," he said, putting his lips right against her ear.

"I have evil things planned for you," she shouted.

"What?"

She grabbed his hand and pulled him not just to the hallway, but all the way to the stairs. He didn't complain. By the time they made it to the second floor, he was in the lead, hurrying her along.

"My ears are ringing," he said.

"Mine, too. I haven't been to a loud party like that in a long time."

"Me, neither," he said, shaking his head. "I don't miss them much."

She pulled her key card out from under the top of her right stocking. It was the only place she'd found to stash it. Sam seemed amused. And aroused.

The moment they were inside her room, she pushed him against the door and pulled his mouth down to hers. He kissed her back, the way they'd been wanting to all night. When they finally parted, they were both panting and anxious.

Carrie reached for the button on his tux, but he captured her hands. "Please," he said. "Let me do this."

She thought he meant to strip for her. Not the other way around. Sam lifted her arms and carefully pulled the lace thing over her head. He put it on the dresser, then pulled her near the bed. He stood right in front of her, eyeing her hungrily. As strenuously as she'd objected to wearing this barely there costume, that's how glad she was now that she'd given in. The way he looked at her made her feel like the sexiest woman on earth.

When he ran a fingertip down the low *V* of her neckline, she broke out in goose bumps and had to squeeze her thighs together. Sam continued to touch bare skin. Her arms, her jaw, and bending down so his lips were inches from her own, he ran his fingertips across the skin above her stockings, then up her inner thighs.

Her eyes closed as she became sensation, quivering at his warm breath and his nimble fingers. Before she knew it, he'd taken off the red dress, the kisses to the back of her neck distracting and wonderful.

Finally, he knelt before her. He unlaced each of the boots. They belonged to Erin, who'd brought them in her giant suitcase just for this night, but maybe Carrie would buy them from her. They certainly were a big hit.

But he liked the stockings more.

With black panties and thigh-high stockings all that was left of her clothes, she felt more naked than naked. Especially because Sam was so elegantly dressed. When he dragged her panties down, letting them fall, he sat back on his haunches, his gaze moving slowly from her toes all the way up to her very hard nipples.

Then he met her gaze, and it wasn't just lust she saw in his expression. She didn't have words for what was happening between them, and that was scary because all she'd ever had was words. She knew, a moment before it happened, that he was going to stand, to cradle her face in his hands, to kiss her closed eyes as gently as a whisper, then her nose, and finally, her lips.

He stripped for her, but it wasn't a dance or a tease. She took off the stockings, and together they got in bed, fitting their bodies together, twining their legs, touching everything in reach, and in between kisses and the whole time he was in her, their gazes stayed locked. In the end, when he'd taken her beyond the ability to hold back, she had to close her eyes. But still, she saw him.

15

SAM RAN HIS HAND OVER Carrie's stomach, then up to her breast. He stroked her softly as they lay in the dark.

Carrie sighed.

"What's wrong?"

"I have to get up. I don't want to. But I have to."

"I wish I could do it for you."

She laughed. "Some things can't be delegated." With that, she got out of bed, and he wished he'd left the light on so he could see her more clearly as she walked across the room. There was a moment after she reached the bathroom when she was magnificently backlit, but that ended quickly with the closing of the door.

He was tired, but he didn't want to sleep yet. He coveted his time with her and didn't want to miss a moment of it.

She came out of the bathroom quickly enough, then hurried to the bed.

"Ouch."

"What happened?"

Carrie bent over and picked up something from the

floor. "What in the world?" She carried her small object to the bed as Sam turned on the lamp.

"How did this get here?" She got under the covers, then held out what looked like his d20 die on the palm of her hand. "Someone played Dungeons and Dragons while I was out?"

He took it from her, bewildered. He'd left the thing in his jeans. "It must have fallen out of my pocket, but I don't remember putting it there in the first place."

"You were in a D-and-D game and you didn't invite me?"

He smiled, loving that she knew D&D, and that she'd recognized the die. "My last game was about eighteen years ago."

"And you carry the die around for good luck?"

He handed it back to her. Carrie put it on the bedside table, turned off the light and snuggled against him. Her hands and feet were cold, but he didn't mind. "I stepped on it, too. I was checking the apartment my aunt lives in."

"She's a big player, huh?"

"She's eighty-two and she cusses like a truck driver. She's more the poker type."

"She sounds like my kind of relative. It'd be nice to meet her."

"You two would get along." He smiled before he kissed her hair. "I got an offer today."

"To do what?"

"For the land. The hotel."

"You're kidding?" Carrie turned to face him, leaning on her bent arm. "That's incredible, Sam. I thought it would be months before you heard. Who was it, Heartly or Mori? Oh, my god, this is so exciting."

He couldn't help but grin at her exuberance, even as he wondered where his own excitement was. "It's not a deal yet. Just an offer. A lowball offer. From Mori. If Heartly's going to play, it'll be soon."

"Mori's the one who wants to change everything, right? Tear down the hotel?"

Sam nodded. "Yeah. He's got big plans. It'll be beautiful once it's done."

"It's beautiful now."

He tugged her down so her head rested on his chest. "Every amenity you can imagine. A spa, a pool that's open all year, fancy restaurants, concierge service twenty-four hours a day. It'll be the kind of place most people can't afford. There's even going to be a private airstrip. Did I mention the professional golf course?"

"No more ghost-hunting tours."

"Nope." He tickled her ear. "We can never make out in the attic again."

"Maybe the new hotel will have an attic."

"Would you want to come here if it did?"

She looked up at him. "I suppose, but only if you were here, too."

He smiled, but not for long. "I thought I'd be more excited."

"Me, too. Are you having second thoughts?"

"Not really. No. It just got me thinking about this old place. It's home. It's where my parents lived, where I played D-and-D with my friends from school. My mom died here."

She cupped his cheek and kissed his shoulder. "I hadn't asked, I just... How old were you?"

"Thirteen. You know, I was raised on ghost stories. The ghosts were my family tree. I believed in them the way I believe in cars or dishes. I never even questioned that there was life after death, or that the people you loved always came back."

He shifted down a bit, hugged her closer. "After my mom died, I was certain she was going to come back. It was the last thing I thought about every night, and the first thing every day. When it didn't happen right away, I thought I'd done something wrong. Like there was an incantation or something that had to be said before she'd show up. I wanted to ask my dad, but he was having such a tough time. Then I figured if Mom was going to come back, she should probably go to Dad first. He'd gotten so quiet, so sad.

"It took a full year before I suspected she wasn't coming. Another year to accept it." He caressed her cheek with the back of his hand. "I hate to spoil the illusion, but I knew then that all the stories were just stories. Lies. And I continue the lies every day here. But then again, who am I to tell people what to believe, huh? I could be completely wrong."

Carrie ran her hand up his chest, curled her leg over his. She didn't say anything, just held him, cared about him. He'd never told anyone about his disillusionment even though it had changed him fundamentally. He'd become a cynic. A naive cynic at that age, but from that time on, he never took things or people at face value.

He hadn't expected to tell Carrie. He was glad he had,

though. The telling of it had shifted something inside him. He smoothed her hair, closed his eyes.

He thought about his brief conversation with Marcia after their dance. She'd offered to give him a reading, and he'd declined. She'd looked at him with concern. Told him to stop fighting. That he should try saying yes, that yes would give him peace.

Yes would give him peace. It was just that kind of bullshit he hated about the supposed supernatural. It could mean anything, probably meant nothing. As generic as a fortune cookie.

Yet, the only thing he could think of when he held Carrie close was *yes*. He had no idea what the question was, the context. The word would never have come up, he was certain, if he hadn't talked to Marcia, if she hadn't planted the suggestion, but that didn't negate what he felt.

Yes. Carrie belonged here in his arms.

Yes. He wanted her to stay.

Yes. This was the second time he'd been changed forever.

CARRIE HAD NEVER WISHED so hard that ghosts were real. The truth was often unkind, but it hurt to think what it had been like for that little kid who missed his mom.

She'd grown up with her own family's myths, and each realization that her parents had painted the world through a skewed point of view had been difficult. None of the stories had been malicious. They'd told her she was the most beautiful little girl in the world. That life was fair, that she could accomplish anything if she tried hard enough.

After all these years, she still wanted those things to be true. Felt personally affronted when faced with evidence to the contrary. Well, not that first thing. She had been lucky in the looks department but for whatever reason, she'd stopped comparing herself to others in high school. Guess she was lucky that way, too.

Right now, though, she cared far more that Sam had been betrayed so young, and so powerfully. It was easy to connect the dots to his choice in career. Of course he made documentary films. Of course he lived to show others the truth, unvarnished.

"Hey," he said, just before he kissed her hair again. "It's late. You should go to sleep."

"I don't want to."

She felt him nod. "I know."

"I have something to tell you." It was that reciprocity thing again. He'd confessed, now it was her turn. She wondered if she'd have told him anyway, if she'd have told him now.

"What's that?"

"I don't believe in ghosts, either."

"Yeah, I kind of figured."

She lifted her head, although she couldn't see him very well. "Really?"

"Since that first day. No offence, but acting isn't your forte."

"So, everybody—?"

"I think so. Not that anyone particularly cares, at least that I've seen, but you weren't all that subtle."

"Shit," she said, laying her head down again. "That's not the worst part."

"Oh. What is?"

She tried to move closer to him, but unless she wanted to climb on top, she'd maxed out. "I don't work with Celebrity Championship Wrestling."

"No?"

"I didn't back in San Diego, either. I write a Web comic and graphic novels called *Cruel, Cruel World*."

"Why is that worse? I think it sounds terrific. I'm sorry I didn't know before. And how come when I looked you up online, I didn't see that?"

"You looked me up? Awwww."

"That was a sidebar. Continue with your confession."

"I write under the name Carrie Price. I didn't tell you because I came here to get material. To make fun of the whole thing."

"I thought you came here to be with Erin."

"That's true." She moved her hand to the middle of his chest and started to mess with his hair. "She wanted to come so badly. She really thought she'd see ghosts. She told me she feels things, but in terms of evidence, not so much."

He laughed. "Not too surprising."

"I know. Even so, her confidence is unshaken."

"That's the way it works. People who come to Crider looking for ghosts find what they're after. Every time."

"Maybe that's a good thing."

"You think I'd be happier if I still believed my mother was coming back?"

"I don't know. Do you?"

He didn't answer. She continued to run her fingertips across his chest as she tried to memorize everything. The way the bed dipped, the warmth of his body, how he made her feel safe.

"I can't answer that," he said, finally. "I do wish I'd spent less time being angry."

She sat with that for a moment. "I don't say it's the Crider Inn you know."

"Hmm?"

"In the comic. I didn't malign your hotel or this conference in particular. I'll let you see the panels."

"I'm glad. I want to see your work. I have a feeling I'm going to like them very much."

"It was kind of shitty, though. To come here purely to mock the proceedings. Not to put too fine a point on it, but I'm not that nice. I mock a lot of things. It's kind of my shtick."

"Okay."

Maybe she hadn't been clear. "I lied to you. To everyone here. Not Erin, she knows. Still. I lied. That's not a very good quality."

"You're being too hard on yourself. It's a fan convention. About ghosts. Personally, I'm grateful. You might not have come if there hadn't been something to mock."

Carrie shook her head, as much as she could in her position. "I've been torturing myself over telling you this. I thought you'd be mad. I'd have been mad if the situations were reversed. It's because we're having sex, isn't it?"

"No, it's not. I'm thrilled that we're having sex, but it

doesn't change my opinion. I think a lot of things should be mocked. You heard me out there. For ten months, I've been lying for profit. I needed the business, and I had no shame whatsoever in propagating all the ghost crap. I could have told them the truth, but they wouldn't have believed me. They'd have been pissed, but nothing would have changed."

"Wait a minute. Is this why we hooked up? Because we're both liars?"

"No. It's because we share important views. For example, you like purple lightning bolts, and so do I."

She smiled at the change in topic and liked him even more for letting her off the hook.

"You're creative," he continued. "You work in the arts and so do I."

Her hand moved slowly down his chest, with purpose. "You like comics. I hope."

"I do," he said. "Seriously. I've still got vintage comics in my old bedroom. I'll show you. After I see yours."

She had passed his belly button and was now reaching another patch of hair. She skimmed that section and found his penis had already started to wake up.

"I like you," he said. His voice cracked a tiny bit right at the end.

Carrie closed her eyes. "I like you back. A lot."

He moved then, even though it meant her hand dropped to the side. He stayed next to her, but scooted down so he could look into her face, and she could see his. It was dark, but her eyes had grown accustomed and she saw enough.

"It's going to be over too soon," he said. "I hate that. I feel like I just found you and now you're leaving."

She touched his cheek, ran her thumb near his mouth, along his jaw. It wasn't enough. She kissed the same trail, up and back. She breathed in his breath, he breathed in hers. His lips were dry and soft as she brushed against them, reveling in this part. The part before tongues, before arched backs and curled toes. "What is this?" she whispered.

"If I believed it existed," he whispered back, "I'd say it was magic."

Right then, right that second, with those words still swirling around her, she knew she loved him. That it wasn't a question of if, but how. She had another life, he had another life. Neither of them were supposed to be there. She didn't want him three thousand miles away, but in her bed, with her leg slung over his hip. With his breath in her mouth. She wanted to see him wake up every morning in the light of her loft. Despite all logic and reason, she wanted him not for a night, but for keeps.

16

THE EGGS BENEDICT looked really good, but Carrie pushed the plate away.

"Are you sick?" Erin asked through a mouthful of Belgian waffle. "This is our last breakfast here."

"I'm not hungry."

"You're depressed. I get it. You don't want to leave Sam."

Carrie looked at her friend, wanting to tell her everything in her head, but it was all a jumble of fears and hopes and craziness. Screw it. Erin would eventually make sense of Carrie's rambling. She always did. "I like him so much," she said. "I might even be in love with him. But I'm so ripe for a raging case of transference it's not even funny. The breakup with Armand, you leaving. I'm anticipating loneliness, which is never a good thing, so I'm putting all this emotional energy into Sam.

"How can I trust it? I don't believe in soul mates, or destiny or anything that could begin to explain how badly I want to be part of his life. He lives on the other side of the country, I've got my work, he's got his. It's ridiculous to even think of us being together, but that's all I am thinking of. I know. I'm completely insane. Maybe I'll just have myself committed, and that'll take care of everything."

"No, if anyone's going to commit you, it'll be me," Erin said. "But you're not even a little bit nuts when it comes to Sam. I think you are in love with him. The real thing, not transference. I've seen you with every man you've been with since freshman year, and this, my dear friend, is the real McCoy."

"You're not telling me this out of guilt, are you? I know you feel horrible about leaving me."

"Well, of course I feel horrible. But not because I think you'll wither away and die without me. We've been best friends for years, and we count on each other. It's only natural, but it doesn't have a thing to do with your feelings for Sam."

"It's so fast, Erin. Things like this always look good in the movies, but—"

"My mom knew she was going to marry my dad the first day they met."

"You're making that up."

Erin held up her hand. It had a fork in it, but still, Carrie understood. "You can call her and ask her right now if you want. They got married five months after they met, and they're still really happy together. It can happen."

"To me?"

"Love happens whether you believe in it or not."

"Like ghosts, huh?"

Erin smiled. "Yeah."

"This week has been kind of disappointing for you, hasn't it?"

"What are you talking about? It's been fabulous. I'm so glad you came with me. I loved the lectures and the parties, and being with my peeps. I don't need the kind of proof you do, Carrie. There have been spirits here the whole time. I've felt them."

"That's enough for you?"

Erin nodded. "I kept smelling this great perfume. No idea what it is, so I can't shop for it, but it was all over the place."

Carrie kept her cynicism to herself. If Erin believed she smelled a spook, then so be it.

Erin ate some more, but only after pouring a great deal more syrup on her waffle. It looked good, and Carrie ended up pulling her own plate closer, and when she took a bite of her eggs, she knew she'd done the right thing.

"Marcia told me I was going to be happy in New York," Erin said. "She sees me with someone. A man who'll surprise me."

"She told me my whole world was going to turn upside down."

Erin held up her cup of coffee. "Here's to upside-down worlds and surprising men."

Carrie clicked her cup against Erin's, but before she'd brought it to her mouth, she was already thinking of all the reasons she shouldn't get her hopes up.

THE FAX SEEMED SLOW, but that was probably because there were so many pages to it. The first page had told Sam it was Heartly's offer, which the man had told Sam to expect. This one was for less money than Mori had offered, which Sam had also expected. Heartly wanted basically the same deal, but he had no intention of tearing down any of the existing structures.

Only days ago, Sam had thought the decision was a no-brainer. He'd planned on taking the most money. Now, he wasn't so sure. He felt foolish for his indecisiveness, for feeling so sentimental after all these years. His life plan had been set in stone. Sell, go back to New York, work on films until he was too old or too tired to make any more. It seemed the stone was more like sand, and as the faxed pages slid into the tray, his certainty crumbled.

He loved his work. His real work. Now that the sale had turned from a wish to a reality, there was no ignoring that he also loved his old home. What he'd never dreamed of, though, was that another love could overshadow everything he prized.

He had fallen in love.

The fax stopped. Sam gathered the papers and sat at his desk, but he didn't look at them. His thoughts were on his past and his future, and his hand went to his pocket, where he'd placed the old d20 this morning.

It was a coincidence, him finding the die. As far as coincidences went, it was killer, but it wasn't a portent or a sign because there were no such things. It had, however, shaken off dusty memories.

For years, when he'd thought of home and of the hotel, he'd only focused on the bad things. His mother's death had hit him profoundly and he'd needed something to blame. The irony struck him that he was furious that his mother hadn't turned into a ghost, something he said he didn't believe in. And he'd vilified the hotel, Crider, everything about this place because he'd been a scared, angry young man.

So much time wasted. He'd loved his parents very much, and only now could he appreciate how charmed his childhood had been. The foundation of his life had been built right here. And it looked as if the building wasn't complete.

He wanted to keep his family hotel. He wanted to continue to make films. Most of all, he wanted to be with Carrie. Impossible to have everything. So, what was he willing to fight for? To live for?

It was almost three-thirty, and he wanted to see Carrie, but first, he put on his jacket. He needed to think, and to walk, and there was no better place to do that than the grounds of the Crider Inn.

IT WAS NEARING FIVE, and she hadn't heard from Sam. Carrie threw her underwear, minus what she'd wear tomorrow, in her suitcase. Every minute without Sam was terrible, and yet she knew selling the hotel was way more important than hanging out with her. Even if it was their final night. Even if he did think they'd found magic.

"Magic my ass," she muttered. She got the room service menu and wondered if Jody would make her a dozen assorted pastries, and if she could manage that by five-thirty, latest. Probably not. Well, there were other desserts that were on the menu, and she should be used to getting what she could instead of what she wanted.

She rolled her eyes at her pathetic self and sat down on the bed. Whatever she'd imagined love to be, this wasn't it. This sucked. This hurt. This...

She fell back, arms spread, misery growing with every heartbeat. Online friends were good. They were great. It didn't matter where they lived, they were right there, on her computer. Talk about magic. She'd been happy as a clam for years with her online friends. Erin living nearby had been a wonderful bonus, but they'd probably never have a chance to miss each other. There was texting, Facebook, Twitter, Skype, IMs, direct messages, LiveJournal, Digg, the *CCW* forum and a hundred more ways to keep in touch every second of every day.

She and Sam could even, you know, have phone sex. Internet sex.

Tears burned her eyes and she turned over, feeling very much like a petulant child, and not giving a crap. She didn't want an online relationship with him. Not with Sam. She wanted his physical body. She wanted to hear him laugh, feel his kisses. Touch him whenever she wanted, and make love to him until they were old and wrinkled and neither one of them could get it up anymore.

Was that so much to ask?

Evidently, yes. Because she sure as hell couldn't think how that was gonna happen.

She'd even come to terms with the fact that she wasn't transferring a damn thing. She loved Erin and she loved Sam, and they were two very different kinds of love, and it was merely a coincidence that the three of them were in the same place at the same time. Coincidences happened all the time, and signified exactly nothing.

There was no such thing as fate or destiny. But there

was love. She knew that now, because she was in it up to her eyebrows.

Her heart nearly leapt out of her chest at the knock on her door. She was on her feet so fast she nearly fell, and she didn't even bother to look through the security thing before she yanked it open.

Sam. He smiled at her, and she jumped into his arms, knocking him back a bunch of steps as he grabbed her legs and held on tight. She kissed him, hard. He kissed her back.

Someone somewhere slammed a door. She and Sam didn't stop kissing for a second. He got them inside, then kicked her door closed, but she wouldn't have cared if the whole conference was watching. This was her last night with Sam. She was going to wring every drop of him she could before she had to get on that shuttle. She was going to leave them both empty and gasping for air.

His kisses were as desperate as her own, his hands gripped her too tightly, and it was achingly sad and brilliantly wonderful.

Like all good things, it came to an end as Sam let her down. She wiped her mouth with the back of her hand, turned toward her suitcase for fear of breaking down into a crying mess. "Did you get the offer from Heartly?"

"Yeah. It was less than Mori's."

"Well, that makes things easy." She went to the dresser and pulled out all her sweaters.

"Actually, this decision was remarkably easy."

That hurt. It was a fact, and she'd known it, but hearing him speak so blithely about it was like a stab in the gut. "I'm happy for you."

"Are you?"

She sniffed, turned to face him. "You wanted this. You'll be able to make your films now without worrying about money. That's great."

"I didn't take Mori's offer."

"What? Why?"

"Because I liked Heartly's better. With a few changes."

She put her sweaters in the suitcase, confused. "What kind of changes?"

"Well, for starters, I'm going to still own the hotel."

"What?"

He nodded, looking at her closely, as if he wanted to examine her reactions carefully. "This is my home. I had sex here for the first time."

"I know."

He wasn't all that close, but she could feel him tense, and she knew if she looked down, his hands would be fisted. She didn't look down.

"I played Dungeons and Dragons here for the first time."

"I know."

"I fell in love here for the first time."

"I—" She stopped breathing. Her heart pounded in her chest.

"Carrie, I love you. I'll understand if you say no, but I hope you say yes. Or at least think about saying yes."

"To what?" she said, her voice barely above a croak.

"I want to build us a house. Build you a place to write your comics, to be online with all your friends. I want you to live there with me, just down the road. I want to build an editing studio in our basement. I'll still own the hotel, but Patrick will be the general manager, and I'll still make films, just not as many as I'd thought. I want you to travel with me on location. And I want to go with you to Comic-Con and all those other geek conventions. I know it's fast, but I also know it's real. I love you. You've changed everything. I don't want my old life anymore. I want you, every day. Every night. Please." He took a step closer, and his eyes, his whole body, showed his yearning. He opened his mouth, shut it again, took yet another step. Then he whispered one word. *"Stay."*

She could hardly believe what she was hearing. She felt like laughing and crying, and her whole body shook. "I..." She swallowed, tried again. "I..."

A hand pushed her hard, a hand on her back, as real a hand as she'd ever felt, shoved her toward Sam.

Just as he lurched forward.

His eyes got really big, and her mouth opened in disbelief. "What the—"

"Hell was that?" he finished for her. He spun around, but there was no one there, and she knew there was no one behind her, either.

But she'd felt it.

He'd felt it.

And there was this wonderful scent in the air. Like nothing she'd ever smelled before.

"Holy shit," he whispered.

"I know," she said. "Marcia told me we're being

guided. Pushed toward each other. There goes my entire belief system."

He laughed, but he kept on staring at her. Waiting.

She smiled. And then she said the only thing she could say. The truest and surest thing she'd ever felt. *"Yes."*

Epilogue

The following Halloween…

THE GHOST HUNTERS had come again. Just as many as last year, even though there was a ton of construction going on all over the hundred acres.

Carrie was dressed in her costume, the same little red-and-black number she'd worn last year. Sam, who'd had to pick up some equipment in Denver, had arrived home late, so he was still getting into his tux.

She was in her loft, the one on the top floor of their recently completed house. The light was magnificent, and so was her Internet connection. She sat down at the computer and dialed the Brooklyn number.

A second later, there was Erin, smiling at her from her own computer. "You look gorgeous!" her friend said.

"You're not the Corpse Bride? What happened?"

"I decided to change things up. Don't you like it?" Erin stood up so Carrie could see her costume through the camera lens. She was a pirate, almost complete and perfect.

"No eye patch?"

"Have you ever worn an eye patch? They're annoying as all get out, and I want to have fun tonight." Erin sat down again. "And no peg leg."

"True. But your buckle is fabulously swashed."

"Thank you. Where's your honey?"

"Getting dressed. Sam says happy Halloween, and we both wish you were here."

"Work is insane, and for some strange reason, Halloween is not a national holiday."

"Weird."

"Is Elton there?" Erin asked.

"He is. And mourning that you're not."

"Tell him for me he should find himself a nice girl who lives in Arizona. And tell him I'm thinking of him."

"Think that's wise? He'll be on the next plane to La Guardia."

Erin smiled. "I miss you."

"I know. But we'll be there in two months."

"I can't believe you guys are coming from Colorado to New York for Christmas. You're insane."

Carrie adjusted her spiderwebs. "Aren't you glad?"

"I'm jealous. Why doesn't Sam have a brother?"

"I don't know. But I do know there's someone out there for you. He's coming. Soon. And he'll surprise you."

"So now you're a soothsayer?"

"No. But it's impossible to believe that anyone as wonderful as you won't find the right guy."

"She's right, you know."

Carrie looked behind her as Sam stepped into the

loft. He looked stunning in his James Bond outfit. She'd never tell even Erin, but he wore it from time to time, even when they weren't going to a costume party.

"Hey, Sam. I miss you."

Carrie felt him behind her, then his hands were on her shoulders. "I miss you, too. Did Heartly call you?"

"Yeah. Thanks. I don't know if we'll get the bid, but just being asked gave me major points with my boss. I really appreciate it."

"You're welcome. I didn't have to do much convincing. He loves the house."

"It's a great house."

Carrie put her hand on Sam's. "Go knock 'em dead at your party, Erin. We've got to go. Jody's going to start serving dinner soon, and I don't want to miss a bite."

"Oh, send me a goodie basket. I can't believe you guys aren't fat as pigs having her restaurant right there."

Carrie grinned. "Did I mention she's going to cater the wedding?"

"Wedding?" Erin leaned forward, her mouth open. "You set a date? When were you going to tell me?"

"We haven't set a date. I'm waiting to hear when you can take a week's vacation. Figure it out already. I'm anxious."

"I love that you're waiting for me." Erin sniffed. "I love you guys."

"We love you back," Sam said. "Now go on. We're really late."

"And whose fault is that?" Carrie asked.

"Mine. It's all mine." He kissed her cheek, then waved at Erin. "We're hanging up now. You two can chat tomorrow."

"Okay, bye!"

Carrie hit the button to disconnect, then she spun around in her chair. "You look so hot. Why don't we skip the party and just make out?"

His eyebrows rose. "I'm game."

"Maybe we'll skip the dance part. Leave after dinner."

"You love Jody's food more than you love me."

She stood up into his arms. "Impossible."

Sam kissed her, and she shivered all the way down to her toes. When he pulled back, he looked at her in that way of his. "I love you."

"I know. I love you back."

"Wow. Spooky."

She smiled. Kissed him again. "Maybe we'll stay for a couple of dances. Just to show 'em how it's done."

He turned his head, looking around the room. "You talking to me?"

"What? You're a good dancer."

"I'm a terrible dancer."

She sighed. "I know."

"Come on. Let's get your coat. It's cold out there."

She let him walk her down the stairs, to the first floor, past her custom kitchen and gorgeous living room. She supposed she'd eventually get used to it, but she still felt as if she were living in a dream.

As he went to get the coats, she looked out the big windows to the woods. Their woods. She loved that the ghost hunters had never stopped coming. That the hotel was still going, that the Old Hotel was still condemned. It would be another year before the luxury lodge would be complete, and several more for all the condos, the shopping mall, the spa and all the rest were finished. They wouldn't see any of it, not from that window. Their world was private. She was free to work on *Cruel, Cruel World,* even though she wasn't quite the sarcastic mocker she used to be. And Sam worked on his films.

She'd never dreamed this could be her life. That one person could mean so much to her. It was the best thing she'd ever been shoved into.

Sam held her coat, took her hand, and they set off together down the winding path, as she silently thanked her mother-in-law for her push in the right direction.

* * * * *

Dear Reader,

There's just something about a strong, bad-boy hero who can rock a business suit, isn't there? He may try to conceal his true character, but once you get this guy between the sheets…oh, my!

Private Sessions is the first in our three-book PRIVATE SCANDALS series and focuses on hot businessman Caleb Payne, who embodies all of what bad boys are made of. He knows exactly what it takes to get what he wants; especially when it comes to sexy Bryna Metaxas, who not only provides an opportunity to glean a bit of enjoyment out of the disaster that is Caleb's current business life, but to wreak a bit of revenge. But there are some sins that are unforgivable… Has he finally gone too far?

We hope you enjoy every sizzling, heart-stopping moment of Caleb and Bryna's journey toward happily-ever-after. We'd love to hear what you think. Contact us at PO Box 12271, Toledo, OH 43612, USA (we'll respond with a signed bookplate, newsletter and bookmark), or visit us on the web at www. toricarrington.net.

Here's wishing you love, romance and HOT reading,

Lori & Tony Karayianni
aka Tori Carrington

PRIVATE SESSIONS

BY
TORI CARRINGTON

First published in Great Britain 2011
by Mills & Boon, an imprint of Harlequin (UK) Limited,
Eton House, 18-24 Paradise Road, Richmond, Surrey TW9 1SR

© Lori Karayianni & Tony Karayianni

ISBN: 978 0 263 88079 3

14-1011

Harlequin (UK) policy is to use papers that are natural, renewable and
recyclable products and made from wood grown in sustainable forests. The
logging and manufacturing processes conform to the legal environmental
regulations of the country of origin.

Printed and bound in Spain
by Blackprint CPI, Barcelona

Multi-award-winning, bestselling authors Lori Schlachter Karayianni and Tony Karayianni are the power behind the pen name **Tori Carrington**. Their over forty-five titles include numerous Blaze® mini-series, as well as the ongoing Sofie Metropolis comedic mystery series with another publisher. Visit www.toricarrington.net and www.sofiemetro.com for more information on the duo and their titles.

We dedicate this book to bad-boy-loving women everywhere...

And to Julie Chivers and editor extraordinaire Brenda Chin: you guys rock!

Prologue

"GREAT SEX IS NOT ENOUGH for me, Caleb. Not anymore."

Damn. There it was…

Caleb Payne stood in front of the floor-to-ceiling windows of his penthouse apartment, his attention not on the reflection of the beautiful woman who had uttered the words, but on the sight beyond the glass. Seattle's skyline twinkled against the inky late-night backdrop. His fingers tightened around the crystal tumbler that held an inch of the best whiskey the civilized world had to offer. He downed the smooth liquid in one swallow and then slowly dragged the back of his hand against his mouth, finally considering Cissy's image in the window.

How was it possible such an attractive woman suddenly emerged unappealing? Despite the low-cut, curve-hugging long red dress she wore, her white-blond hair floating around her smooth shoulders, he wanted to look everywhere but at her.

His gaze fell to her full breasts. Correction: he wanted to look everywhere but into her pleading, hopeful face.

She instinctively crossed her arms, impeding his view.

"Sex is all I have to give you." Caleb slowly turned, considering her reaction from beneath his brows. "I told you that from the beginning."

He'd seen this coming since earlier that evening, when his limo had stopped at her downtown apartment to pick her up for the charity ball they'd attended.

Actually, if he were honest, he'd seen this coming since the day they'd first met.

It gave him no pleasure to know that he'd been spot-on when it came to the timeline he'd imagined when he'd met the pretty socialite six months ago. Around about month three, she'd started talking exclusivity. Which hadn't been a problem, considering it was in his cautious nature to stick to one sexual partner at a time. Month four brought talk of combining households, a conversation he'd artfully avoided.

And tonight, a week before the end of month six, she had launched her plan for even more.

"I've never lied to you, Cissy," he told her now. "You knew the score from the beginning."

"But things change. People change."

He shook his head. "Not me. Never me."

Pain crumpled her face, an emotion that left him unmoved.

He wondered if she'd say the words countless others had said before her and call him a heartless bastard.

If she did, she'd be right. He'd been raised by a single mother, never knowing his father although the man had always been nearby, present without being a presence. While Caleb had never wanted for anything materially…well, one therapist he'd dated had suggested he'd been stunted emotionally by his upbringing.

He'd been a bastard child within a socio-economic class that still frowned heavily on such things. And his peers had never let him forget it.

That's where the heartless part entered in.

Oh, Cissy might want more now, but in a week, maybe two, she'd be thankful she hadn't been successful in her efforts. Out there somewhere was a man who would improve her standing; not detract from it.

He walked to the bar and poured another finger into his glass, waiting for the other shoe to drop.

"Is marriage anywhere in the cards for us?" Cissy asked quietly.

He inwardly winced.

Once, just once, he'd like to be proven wrong. He'd like to date a woman who was unpredictable. Someone who would surprise him. Someone who'd enjoy whatever moments they could spend together without planning, scheming, plotting for something more.

Someone who wouldn't want something he was incapable of giving.

He shook his head. "No."

He heard her moving around. Imagined her picking up her wrap. Checking inside her purse. Perhaps getting a tissue with which to wipe her nose. Then stalking toward the front door.

"Well, then, I guess this is goodbye." Her voice was half accusatory, half hopeful.

He nodded again without turning. "Goodbye, Cissy."

Silence. Long moments later the door closed behind her. Caleb downed the whiskey, tapping his fingers against the expensive crystal. Shame. He'd liked Cissy. She'd been nice to have around. Nice to have in his bed.

He sighed and then headed for his home office and the only thing that never asked him for anything more, that never complained or questioned or demanded, or failed to hold his fascination: work.

1

THE MORE THINGS CHANGED, the more they stayed the same.

Bryna Metaxas weighed the old axiom, feeling exasperated by her job, by the current stagnancy of her love life—or, rather, the lack of one at all—and frustrated by everything in general.

She sat in her small office at the old lumber mill where Metaxas Limited was located in Earnest, Washington, blind to the view of the lush, pine-covered hills visible through the window behind her. She was too busy trying not to think about the weekly Tuesday meeting she'd attended that morning where she'd been marginalized yet again. She couldn't help wondering why her older cousin Troy included her if he wasn't going to have her do anything more substantial than take notes and follow up on minor details. She was half-surprised that he hadn't asked her to serve coffee to the dozen attendees while they brainstormed ideas on where to go now that the deal they'd been working on with Greek billionaire Manolis Philippidis had fallen through.

Fallen through. Now, that was a print-ready description for what had happened. *Disaster* would be more fitting.

Bryna drew in a deep breath. How long had she been working at the company? Nearly two years. And while every six months she was given a positive review and her salary was increased incrementally, she was doing basically the same mundane tasks she had done since the day she hired on.

At any other company she would have quit long ago. But this was a family operation…and she was part of the family.

Besides, as a resident of Earnest, she had a vested interest in seeing the plan succeed for the good of the community. Hell, she'd minored in green energy at university and had a better working knowledge of the emerging technology than either of her cousins.

Bryna sighed and pushed her straight black hair back from her face. On her desk sat three different versions of a proposal—variants on the original she'd put together months ago, but had never seen the top of her cousin's in-box. A proposal she'd thought stood a chance when the Philippidis debacle happened. But, no. If anything, Troy was even less interested in looking at her ideas. No matter how many bricks walls he continually ran into.

Ultimately, she'd decided she'd have to fly solo.

It was just after eleven and she'd been at the old family mill offices since six, moths fluttering their wings against the walls of her stomach at the thought of going this alone. If some of that wild flapping was also associated with the very attractive person she'd decided to approach first…well, she wasn't admitting to it, beyond allowing that it had been a while since she'd enjoyed male attention…and this particular hot, single male not only appeared skilled in that specific area, he was renowned for it.

At any rate, if her plan worked the way she hoped, she'd be a major player in the business rather than the second fiddle to which she'd been relegated.

Of course, if her cousins Troy and his younger brother Ari found out what she was up to, they'd probably fire her sorry butt on the spot, family ties be damned.

She heard Troy's voice in the hall outside her door. Bryna quickly put another file on top of the proposals and picked up a pen, pretending interest in the routine accounting job she'd been given to do the day before.

"Hey, Bry," Troy said, leaning against the door-jamb the way he always did.

Everything that the gossips said about both of her cousins was true. They were powerful and impossibly good-looking, walking, talking Greek gods, a double whammy to any single female within grinning distance.

Of course, Ari was no longer on the market. And Troy...

"You look like shit," she said.

And he did. It was the height of summer and he looked pale as a ghost. And tired beyond what any amount of sleep could cure.

The reason for that was closely tied into Ari's change in bachelor status. A month ago the two brothers had traveled to Greece, not so much for the Philippidis wedding, but to close the deal with the wealthy groom that would put the company on a fast track. And save Earnest, the old mill town that they all called home that had recently chalked up a twenty-five percent unemployment rate, the highest in its hundred-year history.

Needless to say, the deal hadn't gone through. Not through any fault of Troy's. Rather, Ari's infatuation with the bride had resulted in the collapse of not only the deal, but contributed to the downward spiral of what was left of the company itself.

And that broke Bryna's heart. Metaxas Limited was a true family business. Troy...well, what would he do without the company his grandfather and then father built? He lived, ate and breathed ML. The cash flow reflected his blood flow.

Both Troy and Ari were much more than cousins to her: they were her brothers. She'd been an only child until she was twelve and the Cessna her father had been flying had crashed, killing him and her mother as they'd been returning from a weekend trip to San Francisco. Her father's brother had generously provided a home for her along with his two sons, his own wife having died long ago.

It hadn't been easy being the only female in a house full of males. But it had been interesting. She remembered the first time she'd brought a boy home to "study," when she was fifteen. Troy and Ari had invited Dale Whitman out back for a talk after they'd caught him and Bryna enjoying a first kiss over their chemistry books. When Dale hadn't returned to the dining room within ten minutes, she went looking for him. And found him trussed up by his ankles, suspended from a branch of the old oak tree out back.

Her cousins had scared him so badly that not only had he not returned, no other boyfriend had dared show up at the Metaxas estate again, the ankle story having taken on a life of its own and grown to mythological proportions that would do the Greeks proud.

And this company was their Mount Olympus.

Which is why Bryna had decided it was long past time she took action to defend and protect the same.

Her cousin chuckled quietly at her comment and rubbed his freshly shaven chin. "Gee, thanks. Exactly what I needed to hear this morning."

Bryna grimaced. "Just calling 'em as I see 'em."

"Yeah, well, maybe that's one of the reasons why you haven't earned that promotion you've been angling for."

"Oh, so unfair. I'm speaking to you cousin to cousin now. Not employer to employee."

"And the difference in the Land of Bryna?"

She flashed him a bright smile. "I'd be much nicer if we weren't related."

She successfully concealed her true reaction to her recent promotion denial. She wanted to be included on an equal level, damn it. Was that too much to ask? Okay, so she was only twenty-four. But she'd graduated summa cum laude from WSU with her master's in business administration. And she was up to the task.

She'd even told them she didn't need a hike in salary. Just give her anything that was above junior associate, essentially a glorified office assistant, and she'd be happy.

Troy had told her no. Again. That the company was putting a freeze on all promotions for the time being.

She'd half expected him to ruffle her hair and tell her to go out and play like a good girl.

She needed to convince him that she wasn't their cute little cousin anymore. Or merely their cute little cousin; she had no intention of giving up her special spot in the family.

Troy said, "If that were true, I'd give you the promotion in a blink."

She twisted her lips. "I'm never going to live down that Bainwright incident, am I?"

"Bainwright incident? Oh, wait. Yes, now I remember." He shook his finger at her. "Maybe it's just me, but dumping the contents of a water pitcher in a supplier's lap during a meeting is not exactly good work etiquette."

"Neither is his copping a feel while I was pouring his water."

"He said it was an honest mistake."

"An honest mistake would be if he'd removed the hand in question the moment it made contact. Not leave it there and give a couple of squeezes for good measure."

She remembered the slimy man's fingers on her breast and gave an involuntary shudder.

Troy sighed heavily. "When you realize that perhaps you could have handled the situation more diplomatically, maybe then we'll have another talk about that promotion."

Bryna sat back, prepared to say something along the lines of "So I suppose offering him my other breast for a tweak would have been preferable."

Instead, her gaze fell on the files on her desk. More specifically, on the proposals that she was scheduled to pitch to none other than Manolis Philippidis's principal consultant in…

"Oh, my God, is that the time?" Bryna launched herself from her chair.

Troy blinked at her. "What, do you have an appointment?"

"Yes," she confirmed, pulling on her suit jacket and buttoning the front. "Yes, I do."

"May I ask with whom?"

She struck a pose. "With the hairdresser in Seattle. Would you like to attend, act as my wingman?"

He chuckled. "Thanks, but I'll pass."

"You may want to rethink that. You could probably use a good spray tan."

She discreetly stuffed the proposals into her briefcase and began to pass him.

"Very funny."

"See you later, then."

"Since it's Tuesday, why don't you just stay there? Come back on Sunday?"

Her usual schedule was to head to her small apartment in Seattle every Wednesday night, spend two days working from there, then return home to the Metaxas estate Sunday morning for brunch, starting the cycle over again.

"No, I'll be coming back this afternoon," she told him.

As Bryna headed toward the old steel stairs and the parking lot beyond the mill doors, she wasn't sure which bothered her more: that she was nervous as hell, or that Troy hadn't even thought twice about her leaving in the middle of the morning.

Just went to show you how much her cousin really thought of her and her work ethic.

She smiled to herself. If everything went the way she planned, that would all change soon enough....

2

To the victor the spoils....

Caleb knew who Bryna Metaxas was. She was related to the same man indirectly responsible for the collapse of his latest business deal. But given the fact that his position or personal wealth hadn't been impacted, he was still the victor.

And she was very definitely the spoils. Because he had absolutely no interest in pursuing anything of a business nature with her.

They'd met once. During a meeting at Metaxas Limited. While Manolis Philippidis had droned on about a catch in the contract, Caleb had allowed himself to appreciate Bryna's remarkable beauty. The type of looker who would be right at home sunning herself on one of Philippidis's yachts, a white, barely there bikini playing up her physical assets, large sunglasses perched on her petite nose, her long, dark hair combed back while a formally clad waiter served her a dirty martini. He remembered thinking that she could easily challenge any of the goddesses her Greek ancestry boasted on the sexy meter. Why she would ever want to be associated with her loser cousins was an intriguing mystery to him. Especially since whatever ideas she'd proffered were immediately squashed by her cousin Troy, her thoughtful frown as he did so making her all the more appealing.

And she looked even better now, staring up at him with a wide smile.

Although for the record he'd prefer to see her in that barely there bikini rather than in the too-stern navy blue suit she had on.

He openly appreciated the pretty young woman who'd stormed his office after he'd made her wait for half an hour. She was a little on the young side. He was maybe a decade her senior. But if his recent experiences had taught him anything, it was that seeing women closer to his own age came with baggage he was no longer interested in carrying. Biological clocks and measuring sticks were tucked in their designer handbags, always nearby, always dictating their actions.

Bryna was young and had yet to hear the distant ticking. And her handbag of choice appeared to be a briefcase.

The fact that she was a member of the Metaxas family added a certain illicit appeal to her attraction quotient. It had been Ari Metaxas who sank one of his prized deals. Oh, not the business proposal that bit the dust with Philippidis's marriage plans. But the contract Caleb had been working on for two years with a Dubai company that would have resulted in one of the largest conglomerates currently operating today.

The same contract that Philippidis's single-minded lust for revenge against Metaxas and his unfaithful bride had mucked up beyond repair.

"Thanks for taking my appointment," Bryna said, moving her briefcase from one hand to the other and then extending her right.

"No problem." Was her skin really that soft? Caleb shamelessly held on to the feminine digits, rubbing his thumb slowly along the back.

He watched her pupils grow large in her dark green irises at the unabashed liberty he took. But rather than immediately try to pull away, she held his gaze, allowing the fiery spark that ignited between them to flare, running from her skin over to his. The heat sped downward and settled pleasantly in his groin.

He allowed himself a moment to imagine removing that barely there bikini in his fantasy to leave her fully bare...

Bryna cleared her throat and slowly withdrew her hand, taking the sexy image with her.

"I have three proposals I'd like to submit to you," she said, sitting in one of the two high-backed visitor's chairs and putting her case down at her crossed ankles. Slender, shapely ankles that drew his attention.

She took documents out of her briefcase and held them out to him.

He made no move to take them. Instead, he permitted his gaze to rake up her calves to where the hem of her skirt had hiked up to just above her pleasing knees.

Bryna placed the proposals on the desk he stood next to.

"I'm sure that once you've had a chance to review them, you'll see that a partnership with Metaxas Limited would be in everyone's best interest."

Having her open her knees a little wider would be in his best interest. Would she be wearing plain white panties, he wondered. Black? Red? Or would she surprise him by going commando?

The idea nudged his temperature gauge up more than a few notches.

He lifted his telltale gaze back to her face. "Does Troy know you're here?"

He'd met both brothers on several occasions, but he'd gotten the distinct impression that the elder was in charge of all business dealings. And a control freak. Much like he, himself, was.

He was intrigued by the way Bryna avoided his gaze.

If he were to guess, he'd say that no one was aware that she was there.

Caleb knew himself well enough to recognize his growing attraction to the young woman sitting in his visitor's chair. And judging by her reaction when they'd touched, he knew it would be all too easy to draw her into a sexual liaison. A few carefully placed caresses, whispered words, and she'd melt like butter on his toast.

The telecom buzzed.

His secretary. He'd instructed her to interrupt the meeting at minute five.

The problem lay in that he wasn't all too sure he wanted to end his time with Bryna Metaxas.

"Excuse me," he said.

"Sure. Go ahead."

He picked up the phone and listened for a moment, his gaze roving hungrily over Bryna's soft curves, before hanging up.

"I'm sorry," he said, going for feigned reluctance and surprised to actually be feeling it. "But there appears to be an overseas call I really must take."

She twisted lips that were full and lush and made for a man's kiss. "Of course." She got up from the chair. "I'm grateful for the time you've extended me. Just give my office a call when you've had a chance to review the proposals so we can set up another meeting." She began to turn away, then lifted a finger and swiveled back. Her mouth was slightly open, as if prepared to say something, but his expression—which he was sure revealed his naked interest in her—must have caused her to hesitate.

Her pink tongue darted out and moistened those provocative lips.

"Actually," she said quietly, then cleared her throat, "I'll, um, call you."

Caleb found himself crossing the room to be nearer to her. The musky scent of her perfume filled his senses. He dragged his gaze away from her mouth up to her eyes and then crossed his arms over his chest, as much to keep from touching her as to maintain the distance he wasn't sure why he suddenly required. "Why did you choose me, Miss Metaxas?"

She was clearly as aware of him as he was of her…and thrown by his close proximity. He watched her elegant throat work around a swallow. "I don't understand?"

"Why didn't you go straight to Philippidis himself?"

Her smile was soft, tinged with a bit of wryness. "I thought my chances of putting together something with you were better, considering the circumstances." She took in the width of his shoulders, his height. "I mean, you're an independent consultant, right? While you're associated with Philippidis, you're not his employee." She shrugged, the action looking anything but nonchalant. "We can't sell Philippidis, but perhaps we—you and I—can work together to sell the idea to someone else."

He liked her confidence…her awareness of herself as a woman. And he admired her poise; obviously she'd put a lot of thought into her approach, even though she knew the chances of him taking her up on her offer were remote.

He picked up the folders, glanced at the top one, then held them out to her.

"While flattered, Miss Metaxas, I'm afraid I'm not interested."

Inaccurate to the nth degree. The problem lay in that he was very interested in her…only on a much more personal level.

She hesitantly took the proposals, but the look in her eyes told him that she saw him; possibly saw right through him.

Caleb cocked a brow.

"Are you sure there isn't…something I can do to persuade you differently.…" she asked quietly, leadingly.

He'd been playing the man v. woman game for long enough that he understood some had the killer instinct, were born with a natural understanding of basic human need and how to bend it to their advantage, and some didn't.

Sexy Miss Bryna Metaxas had been born with it. She might not understand exactly how best to use it, but she knew enough to make her very enticing, indeed.

He smiled. "I'm sure."

He drew closer to her, estimating that he had a good five inches on her and years of experience. While she demonstrated good instinctive skills, she was no match for him in any department.

Why, then, did he want to see just how much of a challenge she'd present?

He was a breath away from her. She didn't blink. Didn't move. Didn't indicate one way or another if he intimidated her. To the contrary, she appeared equally as enthralled by the chemistry that existed between them.

"I feel it only fair to tell you that this won't be the last you hear from me," she said so quietly it was nearly a whisper.

Caleb's gaze slid over her face, taking in the hint of heated color and her decadent mouth before returning to her eyes.

"I certainly hope not, Miss Metaxas."

He watched as she gave him one last smile and then turned to leave. He stood for long moments after the door closed behind her.

Fascinating.

He walked back behind his desk and picked up the phone to ask his secretary to place a call for him. Then noticed that the sly bird had left the proposals on his desk despite his handing them back to her.

He grinned, giving her points for moxie.

And scoring her highly across the board...

3

BRYNA SAT IN HER CAR in the parking lot of Metaxas
Limited. Despite the routine forty-five-minute drive
from the city back to Earnest, she felt oddly shaken,
as if she'd just escaped being run down by a speeding car…and she wanted to step right back into its
path.

She'd heard that Caleb Payne was not a man to
fool around with. And when their paths had crossed
before she'd certainly seen firsthand that he could
be darkly suggestive. But this morning…wow. She
couldn't have been more affected by him had he lit
a flamethrower and aimed it in her direction. Even
now her skin tingled and her panties were damp from
their brief face-to-face. Oh, his words may have been
straightforward and dismissive. But his dark eyes
had held wicked invitation. One that she found she
wanted to take him up on, despite all the bells and
whistles going off warning her against just that.

Okay, so maybe it wasn't a good idea to be entertaining thoughts of seducing the man she wanted to help pull Metaxas Limited back from the brink. If she were being honest, it was a very bad idea. She'd never mixed business with pleasure before and now, with the stakes as high as they were, she shouldn't even be thinking about it.

Which was probably part of the reason she was.

Her younger cousin Ari had once told her that she had a dangerous streak to her. Opting to date the bad boys over the good. Taking imprudent risks with her job that found her struggling for acceptance and advancement.

She closed her eyes tightly, both hands gripping the steering wheel, and took a deep breath.

Go away, go away, go away, she ordered the image of Caleb Payne etched into the back of her eyelids.

A knock on her window caused her to knock her head against the roof of her late-model Mustang GT. Which was no less than she deserved, she thought wryly as she stared out at Ari standing next to her car.

She slid the keys from the ignition and opened the door too fast, hitting his legs.

"Ow." Ari chuckled as he stepped back. "Sorry. I didn't mean to startle you."

Bryna pushed the door lock on her key fob twice, engaging the alarm. "That's why you knocked on the window and gave me a robin's egg on my head."

"A robin's egg?" He lifted his hand to touch her hair and she playfully batted it out of the way.

"Don't you dare."

His grin was one-hundred-percent pure Ari.

When it came to the charm and looks departments, it was joked within the family that Ari Metaxas had hit the genetic lottery. If he smiled at you, you were required to smile back. It was as simple as that.

That it had been that same irresistible charm that had landed the company in trouble wasn't surprising.

"Where you coming back from?" Ari asked as they walked toward the offices.

"I should be asking you the same thing."

"I asked you first."

"So you did." Abruptly, Bryna had a hard time remembering her excuse for being away from the office.

She absently rubbed at the bump on her head and then remembered. A hair appointment. Yes, that was it.

"Salon," she told him. "And you?"

"Lunch with my fiancée."

Bryna tried not to let her feelings register in a visual way, but Ari must have caught her frown.

"Uh-oh," he said quietly, his smile vanishing. "Are you still having trouble accepting that Elena and I are together?"

Bryna opened the door for him. "Did I say anything?"

"You didn't have to. It's written all over your face."

All right. So she might have to forgive her cousin for his tawdry behavior. It was an unwritten rule in the familial contract. But the woman at least half—if not fully—responsible for what had happened a month ago in Greece…well, it didn't say anywhere that she couldn't hold a grudge against her for life.

"She's carrying my child. Your niece or nephew."

Bryna softened. He hadn't said *second cousin*, which was actually what would be the case. But *niece or nephew*. Her heart expanded with fondness.

This was exactly the reason it was easy to forgive Ari's charming little heart.

"How'd the doctor's appointment go?" she asked.

Ari's grin made a bouncing comeback. "I heard the baby's heartbeat. It has to be the second-best thing I've ever heard in my life."

"Second?"

"Elena's soft sighs are the first."

Bryna held up her hand palm out. "TMI."

"Get your mind out of the gutter, Bry."

They climbed the steps to the second floor of the old mill offices and walked down the narrow hallway. "Who says my mind's in the gutter?"

She would. Ever since the meeting with Caleb.

"TMI includes mushy sweet moments, as well."

"Ah, I get it."

She walked through the open doorway to her office and then turned toward him. "Don't you have some work to do?"

He slid his hands into the pockets of his khaki pants, his crisp, navy blazer draping back in a way that made him look as if he'd just stepped from a Calvin Klein ad.

He opened his mouth to say something and she closed her door in his face, staring at him through the glass.

He laughed and shook his head, continuing on down the hall toward his own office.

Bryna placed her briefcase on her desk, then opened the door again, looking up and down the hallway. She didn't see one of the dozen people who worked there.

Good. She needed a few moments to herself to get her thoughts together.

And to scheme exactly how she was going to sneak a meeting with Caleb Payne again…one that might include indulging in the vivid fantasies that were forming in her mind at the mere idea of acting on the intense attraction that existed between them.…

AS MUCH A LONER AS HE WAS, he hated eating alone.

Caleb lingered in his office after five o'clock that Friday, checking his watch and thinking about whom he could invite to dinner at such a late hour. Someone who wouldn't expect anything beyond a good meal. He wasn't up to anything more.

He had a couple of male colleagues he could call, but both were married. And while the thought of eating alone didn't please him, less appealing was dining solo at a couple's house. Especially a young couple convinced they were in love.

"Mr. Payne?"

His secretary opened the door after briefly knocking.

"I have the New York attorney for you on line one."

Caleb looked at his watch. That would make it after 8:00 p.m. eastern time. Which was pretty much par for the course for their conversations. He didn't hire anyone who wasn't two hundred percent committed to their careers.

"Thank you, Nancy. Any word yet on Manolis?"

Philippidis had been avoiding his calls all day.

"No, sir. I'm still trying."

"Thank you."

She left the office, closing the door behind her. He turned his attention to the waiting call from his personal attorney.

How long had this case been dragging on? Two years? And the last time he checked, it was no closer to being resolved than when he originally brought the suit.

Of course, the unusual nature of his petition was partly responsible. Most courts didn't know what to do with a thirty-two-year-old man's request to force a DNA test. Especially when the parent in question was deceased.

"Harry," Caleb said, picking up the extension.

"Caleb."

He sat back in the chair and closed his eyes; he could tell by the sound of the attorney's voice that this wasn't going to be good.

"I've received an offer."

He listened as an amount in the mid-seven digits was named.

"Are you still there?" Harry asked, reminding him that he had yet to respond.

"No."

A slight pause and then, "No, you're not there? Or, no, no deal?"

He sighed and sat up straighter. "This has never been about the money."

Money he had. In spades. He'd made three times more than his father ever had by age thirty. And the Payne family was just as old and wealthy a New England clan as the Winsteads.

The thought brought his mother's face to mind. As her only child, they'd always shared an especially close bond…drawn tighter, he suspected, by the details surrounding his birth.

He had yet to tell her he was pursuing this lawsuit; of course, that meant little—she was probably already well aware of what was going on. The upper one percent was like a small town with lots of acreage. Still, she had yet to say anything to him. He suspected she was waiting for him to come to her and allowing him to do what he needed to do.

The way he saw it, he was doing this as much for her as for himself. She'd sacrificed so much for him…surely he owed her at least the return of her good name.

"They're anxious for you to let this go."

Of course they were. The Winsteads didn't want an illegitimate child to sully up the late, great Theodore Winstead's good name.

He realized he was gritting his teeth and forced himself to stop.

"You don't have to make a decision now. Sleep on it. I'll call again on Monday."

"No need," Caleb said. "Refuse and go to the next step."

"Will do." Not even a hesitation.

Satisfied, he hung up the phone and sat back again, his every muscle coiled and tense.

He didn't know how long he sat like that until there was another knock and Nancy appeared in the door.

"Any luck finding Philippidis?" he asked.

"No."

He stared at her for minute. It was understood that when he was in the office she was to be present, as well. Unless she requested otherwise, or he dismissed her.

"These messages came in while you were on the phone."

He rubbed his face, noting the stubble there. He'd use his en suite bathroom to shave and clean up before leaving.

He accepted the five slips of paper, leafing through them once, and then again, stopping on one in particular.

He held it up. "Is this her office number?"

"Her cell phone."

Even better.

"Thanks, Nancy. That'll be all. I'll see you on Monday."

"Very good, sir. Good night."

Caleb rounded his desk, waiting until his secretary gathered her things and left the office before sitting down and picking up the phone, dialing the number on the slip.

She picked up on the second ring.

"Our meeting was interrupted the other day. I'd like to continue it."

He waited for Bryna Metaxas to reply. "I'd like that," she said, a low, groin-tightening purr in her voice. "Next week?"

"A half hour. At Giorgio's."

HALF AN HOUR wasn't nearly enough time for a girl to put on her evening best. But when the invitation was accepted, she was bound by business etiquette to follow through.

But as the taxi pulled up to Giorgio's forty minutes later, Bryna knew that business had nothing to do with agreeing to meet Caleb Payne at the upscale restaurant.

She adjusted the heel strap of the gold Grecian-style sandals that Ari had brought back from Santorini for her, paid the driver and stepped out, pleasantly surprised to find Caleb waiting for her outside the doors. She'd expected him to be ensconced in one of the plush booths enjoying a drink, possibly even having ordered already.

Instead he'd waited outside.

Every sensation she'd experienced during their meeting the other day returned...tenfold. She felt... breathless, somehow. Like he was already touching her everywhere she wanted to be touched by him... and she was responding in a greedy, uninhibited way....

Over the past couple of days, she'd tried to convince herself she was overreacting to what had really happened, imagined that he had been attracted to her, shelved any sexual notions with a Post-it that read *harmless flirtation*.

But now she knew she hadn't amplified anything... if anything, she'd downplayed it.

She walked in his direction, watching him watch her. Despite her business argument, she was dressed for sheer pleasure. There was nothing innocent about her choice of little black dress. The clingy material was too intimate, her bare shoulder moist with lotion and perfumed, her hair down from her usual twist and finger-curled around her face.

Bryna hesitated slightly as she drew near enough to speak. In the waning evening light, he looked a dangerous black figure, more shadow than light. And for reasons she was ill-prepared to identify, she felt as if she was walking into a trap. A nicely appointed trap, but one the man across from her had designed to his advantage…and one she fully intended to enter, the hell with the consequences.

Finally, she stopped in front of him, clutching her small purse. Whatever words she might have said dissolved against her dry tongue as Caleb's gaze lingered on her legs and then slowly made its way up the snug fit of her dress until he finally looked into her eyes. Bryna jutted her chin out the tiniest bit and smiled suggestively, waiting for his thoughts, which she was sure he was about to share.

"Intriguing."

Bryna shivered. She'd never been referred to as intriguing before; she decided she liked it. More, she was determined to prove herself exactly that.

She asked in a voice she hardly recognized, "Shall we?"

The upward quirk of the corners of his mouth made her own water. "We most definitely shall.…"

4

CALEB HAD CERTAINLY KNOWN his share of women. And prided himself on being able to pigeonhole them within five minutes. Who they were. What they were after. How long their liaison would last.

But Bryna Metaxas was proving a charming enigma.

Throughout dinner she was by turns openly flirtatious and smartly businesslike depending on which way he slanted the conversation.

She even seemed to realize exactly what he was doing with each turn, a small, acknowledging smile letting him know that he wouldn't always get his way.

Little did she know that he always got exactly that, he reflected as he sipped his post-dinner coffee.

"So, tell me, Mr. Payne. Since it's obvious you didn't ask me here to discuss business matters—in fact, I'm certain you haven't even looked at the proposals I left at your office—then why did you ask?"

Direct. Fresh. Another woman might think the reason for his invitation unimportant, instead focusing on what she could gain from it. Not Bryna.

"Is it a sin to want to enjoy the company of a beautiful woman?"

She licked the side of her fork in a decidedly sexy manner that they both knew was done for reasons other than enjoyment of the slice of chocolate mousse torte she'd ordered for dessert.

"I should think you'd have at least a dozen beautiful women you could call."

Caleb leaned back in the leather booth, his suit pants feeling tight around the crotch at the sight of her tongue darting out of her red painted lips and drawing slowly along the silver. He could think of one place in particular where he'd like to see her do that, and the idea was so tempting it was more intoxicating than the snifter of cognac he'd ordered along with his coffee.

"I could also ask why you were free on a Friday evening." He hiked a brow. "Or did you cancel something?"

"You're redirecting the conversation. Again."

Caleb chuckled and narrowed his eyes as he considered her.

"Okay." He leaned forward, placing his hands on the table between them. "I recently found myself at the end of six-month relationship," he said. "And

hadn't thought about not having company this weekend. And, the truth is, I do not like to dine alone."

She appeared surprised that he'd offered up what
he had. She leaned forward, as well, their hands
nearly meeting on the table. "I appreciate the honesty,
but that still doesn't explain why you called me."

"I called you," he began, turning his hands palm
up, aware of the way they itched to touch her, her
cheek, her neck, her breasts.... "Because I was
reasonably sure that you wouldn't sleep with me
tonight."

That apparently surprised her as she sat back. But
she recovered quickly.

She didn't appear in any hurry to offer up a response. And he liked that. Indeed, he enjoyed watching her face as she turned his explanation over in
her beautiful head, her eyes growing dark, her smile
provocatively sexy.

He'd bet she was slowly rubbing her foot against
the calf of her other leg under the table.

"Reasonably?" she asked, her voice quiet and
loaded with suggestion.

Nice. "Mmm."

"Because?"

"Because you wouldn't want me to get the wrong
impression."

She smiled. "Ah, because of our business connection."

"There is no business connection."

"Yet."

He grinned. "Yet."

"So you think I'm above sleeping with someone for business gain," she said quietly, putting another forkful of torte in her mouth. A mouth that was driving him to absolute distraction.

"I think you're very much above it."

"And if I invited you back to my place?"

"I'd have to insist we go to mine.…"

OKAY, SO HE'D CALLED her bluff.

And Bryna practically shivered from head to toe at the thought of going through with it.

It had been sweet torture sitting across from him, wanting to know more, but unable to find the words with which to ask him.

Oh, they'd talked. But she'd been too distracted by the line of his jaw…the strength of his hands…the length of his fingers…the sureness of his dark gaze to challenge him to a verbal rather than visual duel.

And now she had the chance at a physical contest…

The heat of his hand where it rested on her arm as they walked toward the restaurant door seared her bare flesh.

At the curb, a limo instantly pulled up and the driver came out to open the door for them.

If she got into that car, she knew she'd be a goner. She would be unable to stop herself from going as far as he intended to take this. And while an elemental, wild side of her was all for it, her mind cried out that it was too fast, too soon. To sleep with him would be placing the advantage in his court and swipe all the balls from hers.

Instead of entering the car, she turned toward him, finding him so close that her thigh ended up pressing against a certain, nicely rock-hard part of him. She shivered and looked up into his eyes, her hand resting against his chest.

"As tempting as the invitation is," she whispered, her breath grazing the jaw she'd been wanted to taste all night, "I'm afraid you're right. There's no chance I'm going to sleep with you tonight."

He smelled of limes and one hundred percent hot male.

She watched the corners of his mouth turn up. "Shame," he said, his fingers brushing against her hips and then resting there, pulling her imperceptibly closer to him, crowding her against his arousal.

"Mmm," she agreed, her heart pounding a loud rhythm in her chest.

She leaned in as if to kiss him, her gaze moving from his eyes to his mouth and back again.

She stepped back instead and waved for a taxi.

"Thank you for dinner," she murmured.

"Thank you for the company."

"Anytime."

His eyes sparkled dangerously. "I might just take you up on that offer."

She hoped he did.

SO SOFT…SO WARM…

Her body throbbed with yearning, wet, needy. She arched her back, reaching for Caleb as he leaned above her. But he always seemed just out of reach, smiling that knowing, wicked grin.…

Her own moan woke her up.

Bryna rose quickly to her elbows and pushed back the tangle of hair in her eyes. She blinked her old bedroom at the Metaxas estate into view. White-curtained canopy. Pink-and-white wallpaper. A white marble fireplace. Stuffed animals stacked up in one corner.

She blew out a long breath. It had been two days since she'd said goodbye to Caleb at the restaurant, and ever since he'd haunted her dreams. Always there, always just within reach, yet outside it.

Bryna whipped the covers back and maneuvered her bare legs over the side of the bed, paying little mind that her simple cotton nightgown was bunched up around her thighs. She reached for her cell on the nightstand and clicked it open. No calls. No texts. She closed it again and put it back down and then padded across the large room toward the connecting bathroom.

Friday night it had taken all of her will after getting into that cab not to direct the driver to turn around and follow the limo instead. The reaction had surprised her. She'd never met a man who'd gotten under her skin to such a mind-robbing degree. She

wanted to feel his hands on her. Wanted to put her
mouth on him. Wanted to spend the night exploring the seeds of sensation their dinner together had
planted in her. So much so that to prevent herself
from pursuing him the next day, she'd driven back
to Earnest for the night when usually she drove up
Sunday morning for family brunch.

Within twenty minutes Bryna was showered and
dressed in a white slacks and a purple short-sleeved
blouse, no less bothered than she'd been when she'd
awakened. But determined to shake off the peculiar
feelings any which way she could.

She slid into her sandals and went downstairs.
It was nine and brunch wasn't until ten-thirty, but
she wasn't surprised when she found her uncle Percy
and Troy already up and on the back deck enjoying
coffee.

"Good morning." She kissed her uncle on the
check and squeezed her cousin's shoulder as she
passed on the way to the chair next to him.

"Well, good morning to you, too," Percy said, fold-
ing the business section of the paper and placing it
on the table. "Nice to see you here so early."

"I actually came in last night," she said, pouring
herself a cup of coffee.

"Oh? Any particular reason for that?"

Just that she couldn't seem to get a maddening
man out of her mind, that's all. "No. Just decided I'd
like to wake up at home this morning, that's all."

And the grand ol' estate was that, wasn't it? All

800 acres of land and 25,000 square feet of house. Plenty of room for them all to reside without living on top of each other.

Home. It was odd, sometimes, to think that for her it had once been a simpler place just outside Seattle. The past twelve years since her parents' deaths, this had been where her old grade cards, school photographs and swim meet medals were stored. This sweeping mansion that sat on a hill overlooking the town of Earnest. And no matter how much she claimed independence, this was where she went when she needed to find peace. When she needed to touch base with her foundation.

And it was her uncle Percy and cousins Troy and Ari who were her immediate family. They were always there for her.

"Have you added enough sugar?" Troy asked now.

Bryna looked at where she was stirring in yet another teaspoonful. She frowned and took a sip, making a face.

"Uh-oh. Looks like man troubles to me."

They all turned as the more outspoken of them had stepped out onto the deck.

Ari.

Bryna smiled and then grimaced. "Correct me if I'm wrong, but you usually have to have a man in order for there to be any kind of trouble, don't you?"

"Not necessarily." Ari reached over her and

plucked a grape from a bunch on a tray. "Trouble enters when you want a man you can't have."

Troy rustled his section of the *Seattle Times*. "Look who's the expert suddenly."

Bryna looked behind Ari. Could it be he'd come to the brunch alone this week? She knew a spot of hope.

Then Elena came outside, apologizing for her delay. "I'm not even showing yet, but I swear my bladder is the size of a pea."

Bryna frowned as she watched the other woman greet her uncle the same way she had and then say good morning to Troy, who actually grinned at her.

Where was the animosity? The anger?

Oh, well. It looked as if the job would have to fall to her. When the other woman took the chair next to her, Bryna focused solely on her coffee.

Even she admitted to being surprised at her reaction to her cousin's intended…especially since Elena was pregnant with what they all hoped would be the first of the next Metaxas generation. But so much had been riding on that deal with Philippidis. To just throw it all away because of a woman was unthinkable to her.

She frowned. If only Elena would have kept her legs closed, and her hand on her ex-groom's arm, right now the first production line would be running and the second would be under construction, employing at least two hundred of the town's hurting residents.

The thought made her mind drift back to Caleb and her own conflicted feelings for him.

Of course, the difference lay in that she wasn't engaged to marry someone else so no one would be hurt if things spiraled out of control and then went south.

She swallowed hard.

Other than herself, that is....

5

WAS IT TIME YET?

Caleb looked at his watch as the presentation dragged on. There were ten men in the room for the weekly Wednesday meeting that had been scheduled for that morning, then delayed until afternoon because Manolis Philippidis was late flying in.

He glanced at the modern-day Greek tycoon at the end of the table. Manolis held a small coffee cup in his meaty fingers, his dark eyes on the acquisitions head who was talking about the pros and cons of buying a small business out of Minnesota that made public buses that ran on natural gas.

The new business was green business.

He looked at his watch again.

"Are we keeping you from something, Caleb?" Manolis asked, interrupting the speaker.

He sat back, grinning easily. "No. Not at all."

"Perhaps we're boring you, then?"

Caleb's smile grew tight.

It was well-known that there was no love lost between the two men. Which was why Caleb had never worked directly for him. Would never hand that kind of power to a man who would just as soon fire you as look at you.

No. Caleb liked that he was a well-paid consultant to the company. A very well-paid consultant. Which sometimes required him to sit through trying meetings that had nothing to do with him. And suffer a man who was otherwise insufferable.

"To the contrary. I was thinking about the three other more viable gas-powered bus ventures that are looking for investors rather than to be bought outright." He raised a brow. "Would you like me to continue? Or shall we get back to the meeting agenda?"

As expected, Manolis glowered at him, finished off his coffee and then looked at his own watch. "I believe this meeting is concluded."

If there was one man who hated wasting time as much as Caleb it was Philippidis.

The Greek stood and everyone else at the table hurried to do the same. All but for Caleb, who took his time getting to his feet.

He extended his hand toward Manolis, who shook it. "You have information on these other companies?"

"I sent proposals to the ventures head a month ago."

Manolis nodded. "Let him know I want to hear more about them at next month's meeting."

"Very well."

The other man straightened his tailor-made suit jacket as if having just made an important decision and muttered his goodbyes before leaving the room.

Caleb followed him out, heading directly for his own office.

"Has…" he began as he neared Nancy's desk.

She interrupted. "Miss Metaxas is waiting in your office, as you directed, sir."

The sun had just emerged from the heavy gray clouds.

BRYNA READ THE SPINES of the books in the cases that lined Caleb's office. Business tomes were interspaced with leather-bound classic fiction novels and philosophy titles. She wondered if he'd read them or if they'd come by way of a professional decorator. He was, after all, a consultant with the Philippidis company, meaning this wasn't his permanent office, but rather a temporary one.

But how temporary? How many years had he been working with him?

She moved down the bookcase, squinting to read the script on a recognition-of-excellence plaque that had been propped against the books.

She looked around. There were no photographs, personal or professional. It seemed to her that everything was purposely displayed to reveal very little about the office's inhabitant beyond his power and success.

She'd moved to where she could see behind his desk and now looked over her shoulder, eyeing the drawers there.

The door opened and she jumped.

Caleb seemed to take in the situation in one glance. He slowly closed the door even as Bryna walked to the visitor's side of the desk.

"Nice to see you again, Miss Metaxas," he said in that low, deep way he had of speaking.

She cleared her throat. "The pleasure's all mine, Mr. Payne."

He stood looking at her for a moment, not long, but long enough to encourage that longing to wend through her veins anew.

"We'll see," he said, but whether it was a threat or a promise, she didn't know.

He walked toward his chair.

Did he know what effect he had on her? She'd offer an unqualified yes. He gave the impression of being a man who was aware of everyone and everything in any room he inhabited. And likely commanded the gazes of every female within a half-mile radius, along with a majority of men if just from sheer envy.

"I was pleased when you called for this appointment," she said. "Would you like to go over the proposals?"

He opened the right desk drawer, watching her face as he did so. "Only one of them has possibilities."

"Oh? Which?"

"The second."

She smiled.

"That's the one you intended me to choose."

"It's the one I'd hoped you'd choose."

Of the three, the proposal was the most solid and followed the basic tenets of the original, only scaled down. Instead of four production lines, they'd begin with one. Rather than go whole hog, she proposed starting with a limited offering. Troy's plans were large, ambitious, much like her cousin himself. But as she'd tried without success to explain to him, perhaps it was better to start small with the potential to grow big than big with the possibility of failure…if he succeeded in selling the grand idea at all.…

Caleb walked to a polished table near the window that held four chairs. He put the proposal in question down. "There are a number of things we need to reconfigure."

Bryna followed him and pulled out the chair next to the one he stood behind. But he didn't sit. Instead, he shrugged out of his jacket, hung it on a hanger inside a door that she suspected led to a full bathroom, and then undid his cufflinks, sliding them into his pockets before rolling up his sleeves.

Her mouth went dry. Even though he was going for comfort, he still looked more elegant than any man she'd ever seen. And that was saying something because her cousins weren't exactly slouches when it came to the man department.

He'd begun talking, presumably about the proposal, but Bryna couldn't make a word out. Her ears had stopped accepting input as her heart rate sped up. She was too caught up watching him take off his tie and undo his top three buttons. His waist was narrow where his Egyptian broadcloth shirt was tucked into his slacks, the belt further emphasizing the difference from his wide chest and shoulders.

"Is something the matter, Miss Metaxas?" he asked, leaning a large-palmed hand on the table on the other side of her.

The pungent scent of limes assaulted her senses, and his sudden nearness made her lick her parched lips.

"Bryna…please," she said, sounding more in control than she felt.

Dear Lord, how did any woman manage to conduct official business with this man?

She gathered her wits about her and smiled up at him. "I thought we moved beyond formalities the other night."

A hint of a grin. A shadow of stubble.

He was ten, maybe twelve inches from her. So easy to lean in and run the tip of her tongue along his jawline…

He stood suddenly. "You're right. It's late. Perhaps we should reschedule this meeting."

Bryna's eyes widened. "No." She forced herself to

focus on the notepad she'd laid on the table before her. "I'm fine. Sorry. It's been a long day. I just drove in from Earnest after putting a full day in…"

He grasped her chair back.

Bryna silently cursed herself. Had she just put the kibosh on a business deal because she couldn't control her runaway hormones?

So she'd spent the past six days imagining the many ways Caleb Payne knew to please a woman. And had explored a couple of those ways with her own hands. She could separate business from pleasure.

"Very well. I'll have my secretary call yours to reschedule," she said.

He pushed her chair back in after she rose to her feet.

"I'm afraid you misunderstood me, Miss…Bryna. I'm not ending this meeting. I'm merely suggesting we move it."

To your bed? her mind offered. "Oh?" she fairly croaked.

"To a restaurant. Preferably one that offers up a good pinot noir."

Relief flushed her system. "Ah. How much of this has to do with your not liking to eat alone?"

"Nothing. I merely see an opportunity for us to kill two birds with one proverbial stone."

Was it her, or had he just leaned in closer to her?

Limes.

He'd definitely moved nearer.

Her mouth watered.

"I know just the place...." she offered.

SO IT WAS AGREED. They would split up. She would go home to freshen up and he would pick her up at her place in an hour.

Bryna tried not to run down the hall outside his office in her hurry to lessen the time between now and when they'd meet again.

God, when was the last time she'd felt this kind of charged anticipation? It had been so long ago she couldn't remember. She could scold herself for acting unprofessionally later. Right now she was enjoying the zing of awareness, the hungry longing between her thighs, the rasp of her nipples against her bra as she walked.

"Oh!"

She ran headlong into someone coming around the corner to the elevators.

"Pardon me. I wasn't watching where I was going," she said automatically.

Then she brought the man into focus and all apology left her.

Manolis Philippidis.

Stupid, stupid, stupid.

This was his company. She should have taken into consideration that the chances of running into him here would be greater than average.

Still, she was unprepared for facing the man

responsible for so much of the trouble her family's company was in.

His face registered nothing and then it seemed to dawn on him who she was. They'd met more than a few times at the mill offices and he'd tried to pick her up at least once.

The guy gave her the creeps despite his Greek Sean Connery good looks.

"Miss Metaxas, isn't it?" he asked, looking behind her as if to see who she was with.

"Mr. Philippidis. Hello."

"It's nice to see you."

His eyes told her it was anything but.

She realized that the hand he'd put on her sleeve to steady her was still there, now caressing her.

She shuddered.

"Are you here alone?"

"Yes. Yes, I am."

"Well, then. Why don't we go into my office where we can…catch up."

The last thing she wanted was to catch up with Manolis Philippidis. She'd intended to put this deal together without having anything to do with him, in essence employing Caleb's services as a consultant to help her to attract investors.

"I'm sorry," she said, "but I'm late for an appointment. Maybe another…"

His hand tightened on her arm. "I insist."

She stared at him. He wasn't insinuating that he'd physically take her to his office, was he? He'd better be careful or she'd have to use some of her Tae Bo moves on him.

"Miss Metaxas came for a meeting with me."

Caleb.

Bryna instantly relaxed as he came to stand next to her, his tie tightened, his jacket back on.

She watched as the two men indulged in one of those stare-off things that she sometimes saw Troy and Ari do even as she discreetly shrugged off Philippidis's hand.

"Oh? And why wasn't I apprised of the situation?" Manolis asked.

Caleb's smile was just shy of threatening. "There's nothing to apprise you of."

"If you'll excuse me," Bryna said quietly. "I really must go."

Her gaze flitted to Caleb's face.

"I don't want to be late for that meeting."

She moved around them.

"It was…nice to see you again, Mr. Philippidis."

She couldn't have hurried for the elevators faster had she dived for them, and was relieved when the doors closed, blocking out the two men staring after her.

Cripes.

6

FROM HERE ON HE AND BRYNA were going to meet outside Philippidis's offices.

Damn. Why hadn't he thought that the Greek might bump into her?

Why hadn't he considered what his reaction to seeing the old man's hands on her might be?

He and the wealthy businessman were already a drop of bad blood away from parting professional company altogether, no matter the consequences to his own business ambitions. But he didn't want it to be over a woman. No matter how tantalizing.

Even though he'd spent a great deal of his career acting as the Greek's wingman, facilitating deals that would have otherwise fallen through without some careful finessing, he'd always remained independent, working solely on contract, never directly for him. The professional relationship had fattened his accounts and allowed him room to spearhead his own deals. As far as everyone was concerned, the only person he was loyal to was himself and the deal.

Which was likely why Bryna Metaxas had sought him out; if she'd thought for a minute that he might screw her over out of allegiance to Philippidis, then he would have been the last person she'd approach.

"Sir?"

He blinked at the driver who spoke to him over the intercom in the back of his limo.

"Would you like me to ring for the lady?"

They were at Bryna's apartment already.

Caleb scratched his face. He'd meant to shave before leaving the office but had been too preoccupied to do more than return a couple of urgent phone calls. He looked through the window to find Bryna already coming through the lobby doors.

Some of the tension coiled in his muscles loosened. A woman with no pretenses. Who was ready when she said she'd be and didn't make him wait.

Refreshing.

The driver immediately got out and opened the door for her and she slipped in.

Despite the daytime summer heat, the night was cool. She wore a light white pashmina over her dark fuchsia dress.

"I'm sorry if I made you wait," she said.

Caleb relaxed farther into the rich leather seat, enjoying the view of her. The deep V of the sleeveless sheath. The length of her smooth legs. "Not at all."

The driver got back behind the wheel. "Sir?" he asked over the intercom.

Caleb held Bryna's gaze. "I'd like to suggest some-place different if you don't mind?"

"Sure. Whatever you like."

He grinned. "Dangerous comment, that."

Her chin came up a fraction of an inch, telling him that she stood by her words.

Whatever he liked…

An intriguing prospect, indeed.

He reached up and pressed the intercom button. "Home, James."

THE LAST THING on Bryna's mind was the proposal. Or food, for that matter. From the moment she slid inside Caleb's limo, she'd felt as if she was in a cocoon, a cottony blanket that muted sounds, but somehow made colors more vibrant. And heightened her sexual awareness of the man who'd played the lead role in many a dream as of late.

His penthouse apartment was as impersonal as his office had been, but no less sumptuous. A wall of windows overlooked the Seattle skyline, the view mesmerizing her as the glowing orange ball of the sun sank behind the Space Needle. The main room was combination sitting and dining area, with a rounded corner of glass devoted to what could be called an entertainment area. There was a top-of-the-line stereo system that was revealed behind an etched panel as Caleb switched on an instrumental jazz CD, filling the large room with the sound of a smoky sax from multiple unseen speakers.

A man that knew what he liked, and liked what he knew.

She ran her hand over a gleaming black grand piano, tinkling a few of the keys.

"Do you play?"

He poured them two glasses of wine at a nearby antique liquor cabinet. "I play."

She rounded the piano. "I'd like to see that."

He held out a glass and she accepted it. "It's generally something I do in private."

"Why am I not surprised?"

He cocked his head slightly.

"I'm guessing you don't let many people see you with your guard down. And…" She touched a key again. "Music takes passion."

His eyes glimmered darkly. "Plenty of…people have seen my passion."

"I bet." She smiled into her wineglass. The smooth, bloodred liquid flowed lightly over her tongue, leaving just the faintest essence of lavender. "I'm not talking about sex, Caleb." The moment the *s* word was out of her mouth, her entire body reacted to the prospect of having some of it with him now, tonight. "I have no doubt that you're very, very good at that." She cleared her crowded throat. "You're probably very, very good at everything you do."

An image of his mouth leaning in to claim hers made her lips tingle.

"I'm talking about doing something that bares you to someone else, from which you have nothing to gain."

He paused, weighing her words, obviously intrigued. "I've played some in front of groups. However small."

"Mmm. That's performing. Not revealing."

He followed her path around the piano, running his finger over the keys much as she had, but the sounds he elicited were much more pleasing than her unskilled pokes. "Perhaps."

She shivered, the one, quiet word traveling like a sigh over her skin.

"And perhaps there are some things that I like to claim for myself alone."

He'd stepped up behind her, and his last couple of words exited as warm breath against her bare shoulder.

"However briefly," she whispered.

"Meaning?"

He moved his head to hover over her other shoulder, making her hyperaware of his nearness, his intentions.

"Meaning that you can play the piano as long as you want…and then you can leave it to sit without paying it another thought until the desire moves you to play again."

He was silent for a long moment and then he made a small humming sound. "You smell good."

She moved her head to the side, giving him access

to her neck if he so chose to take advantage of it. "Thank you."

"So, Miss Metaxas, are you suggesting that I might treat people the same way as I treat my piano?"

She lifted her wineglass to her lips, her fingers trembling ever so slightly. "From what I've seen of you so far, I'm guessing that you're a man of strict control."

She felt his lips against her shoulder. A shiver shimmered through her, followed by a flash of heat.

She turned almost abruptly and smiled up at him. "I bet you make love the same way you conduct business—with methodical thoroughness."

He held her gaze. "Would you like to put that theory to the test?"

She leaned in until their lips were the width of a butterfly wing away. "I'd like to see you lose control."

His dark right brow rose slightly.

She'd surprised him. And knowing that turned her on all the more.

She ran her tongue along her bottom lip and then breathed a light kiss on him.

Caleb reached toward a square panel in the wall to his left and pushed a button.

"Sir?" a male voice immediately responded.

"Lionel, put dinner in the warmer. I'll see you in the morning."

"Very good, sir. Good evening."

"THE WINDOWS CONTINUE in here…"

Caleb stood in the open doorway of his master bedroom, absorbing Bryna's soft silhouette against the golden, waning light. He didn't paint, but if he did, he thought it would be this image, this moment he'd like to commit eternally to canvas.

She moved her head to the side. "As does the music…"

He couldn't remember the last time a woman had found her way to his bedroom so quickly. Last week's impromptu dinner aside, they hadn't even dated. And even this evening, the plan had been to continue the meeting that had begun in his office.

Her proposal was long forgotten in his briefcase by the front door.

He watched as she reached behind her, slowly unzipping her dress.

"I figure—" her voice was soft and low "—that we're both adults. Whatever this is…this thing that's crackling between us…it need not interfere with our business dealings.…"

She turned, allowing the dress to fall in a puddle to the ground, revealing that she wore absolutely nothing underneath. No lacy bra. No expensive underwear. It was just Bryna and a simple gold necklace bearing a small cross and her high-heeled sandals.

His brow moved upward again at the thought that she'd been bare-bottomed since the moment she slid into his limo.

There was no game playing with her. No angles to work or rules to obey.

And his throbbing hard-on told him that her naked honesty appealed to him on several levels.

He placed his wineglass on the credenza next to where she'd left hers and crossed the room, coming to stand directly in front of her. She looked up into his face, her expression needy and challenging all at once.

Caleb took her in, inch by tantalizing inch.

Her breasts were small and pert, untouched by a plastic surgeon's knife. Dark nipples puckered, as thick as the tip of his pinky finger. Her waist was narrow and her hips flared…her womanhood neatly trimmed but left natural.

He'd taken his jacket off in the other room, but now he systematically loosened and then took off his tie and began unbuttoning his shirt. It joined her dress on the floor along with his slacks and within moments he stood facing her, as naked as she was.

And feeling oddly emotionally bare.

He leaned in at the same time she did and they kissed. She tasted sweet as he slid his tongue against hers, desire mingling with the fine wine.

She murmured something he couldn't make out and then she was swaying into him, her nipples grazing his chest, her hips against his. His hard-on throbbed against her soft belly and her musky, female scent filled his senses.

Caleb recalled thinking that he'd like to be surprised by a woman for a change.

He believed he just had been....

7

BRYNA'S ENTIRE BODY trembled, tautened, waiting for her to exhale.

Everything about Caleb Payne was long and lean. And his expression was so intense that she couldn't look anywhere but into his mesmerizing eyes.

She'd never bought into the vampire myth. But if she had, she would have suspected he was one.

He lifted a hand to her shoulder and slid it up over her collarbone, then her neck, threading his fingers into the hair at the nape of her neck. He tilted her head back and then kissed her so thoroughly her knees nearly gave out from under her.

She'd known he would be good. There had never been any question that he would see to her every need even as he quenched his own. But it was one thing to anticipate something, quite another to experience it.

Her heart thudded so erratically in her chest that

she was concerned she wouldn't survive her reaction
to him. Her lungs would accept nothing but shallow
intakes of air. Her body was on fire, seeming to seek
a fundamental meeting with or without her coopera-
tion as she pressed her hips harder against his, the
crisp hair on his thighs rasping against her smoother
skin.

Before she'd realized he'd moved, she felt his
fingers against her bottom. Bryna shifted her feet,
giving him better access. The instant his fingertip
touched her swollen folds, she nearly collapsed altogether, the sensation swirling with the anticipation.

He supported her weight against him, his index
finger dipping into her saturated channel and using
her own fluid to lubricate the attention he focused
on her aching core.

Bryna grasped his shoulders and threw her head
back.

She heard his groan and then he was sweeping
her up into his arms and carrying her to the mam-
moth bed across the room. He carefully laid her down
against the white comforter, but didn't immediately
follow. Instead, he collected a box from a nightstand drawer and tossed it to the bed beside her. She
reached for the condoms, then forgot them altogether
when he spread her knees with his, standing above
her next to the bed.

Bryna restlessly licked her lips, allowing her gaze
to move over his magnificent form. His penis was
stiff and thick, the head nearly hitting his navel. She

swallowed hard, filled with the need to press her tongue against the turgid flesh.

But Caleb had something else in mind as he slid his hands up her legs to her inner thighs.

She automatically opened to him, spreading her legs and bending her ankles. He leaned in and she surrendered her ability to breathe altogether as he parted her folds and pressed his tongue against her tight bud.

Bryna twisted her fists into the bedding, holding on for dear life as her hips bucked involuntarily. Caleb flattened a palm against her trembling stomach, holding her still even as his other hand caressed and tugged and stroked her, his mouth hot and knowing.

This couldn't be real. She had to be dreaming. Sex was never this good. The earth stopped spinning and she hovered somewhere between this world and an alternate universe. A place where everything was white and sweet and so very, very exquisite. One didn't need food or water in order to survive, only this…this incredible facet of being.

He slid a finger inside her dripping opening, stroking her with a touch so skillful that she burst into yet another realm, this one red and gold and hot…so very hot. She reached for him, wanting, needing, to feel him inside her, now.

She'd never known such a complete urgency. Inhibition and thought were left far behind. There existed only a greedy desire to claim him.

He granted her wish and lifted to kiss her. She tasted her musk on his tongue as she slid her head one way, then the next, wanting to swallow him whole even as she reached for his erection. Her fingers curved around the hard flesh, barely meeting around his thick width. She guided him to her sex and bore upward against him.

He slowly slid in to the hilt.

Everything halted. Bryna's gasp emerged silent; her heart contracted and then stopped. They were no longer two separate entities but one, joined, together.

Then her heart beat again, her gasp echoed through the air and time started back up in a sort of slow motion animation.

At some point, Caleb withdrew and finally sheathed himself.

Finally she could no longer take the chaos building inside her and Bryna surrendered to what easily rated as the best orgasm of her life.

LONG HOURS LATER, Caleb watched Bryna unabashedly coax a bit of lobster meat from a stubborn claw with her tongue, the sucking sound making his manhood stiffen all over again.

It was a source of amusement and consternation that he seemed to be in a highly aroused state whenever he was near her.

"Which restaurant did you say this was from?" she asked, licking her fingers.

They were sitting at the butcher-block island in his penthouse kitchen on two stools, a single candle lighting the room, her wearing his white shirt, two buttons strategically holding the material together, while he wore a pair of black silk drawstring pants. At somewhere around one, after hearing her stomach growl, he'd suggested they finally see to that dinner they'd intended to have earlier.

That meant they'd indulged in five straight hours of mind-blowing sex.

And he wanted more....

He told her the name of the restaurant and she nodded, although he suspected she hadn't truly heard him. She was openly gazing at his abs and then down lower to where his hard-on tented the material of his pants. Her pupils were large in her green eyes, her hair a tangled mass around her head. He'd never seen anything so sexy in his life. She hadn't dived for the shower before coming into the kitchen like other women he'd known. Hadn't stopped to reapply makeup or squirt perfume. She looked wondrously natural and open and well sexed, her scent—their combined scent—teasing his senses.

How long had it been since he'd felt, truly felt, a woman around him? When he hadn't pulled on a condom before entering? He wasn't sure what had compelled him not to do it now. But he'd been filled with an urgent need to sample her, unimpeded.

He'd wanted to feel her. Pure and simple.

She picked up her wineglass with sticky fingers

and nearly dropped it. Laughing, she took a sip, considering him over the rim.

"You've barely touched a thing," she murmured.

That's because all he could think about was hauling her back on top of him. Right now. Where he sat on the stool.

"I had a big lunch."

The corners of her mouth turned up. "So did I. But I'm still ravenous."

"I noticed."

Her chewing slowed and she began to put the claw down.

"No, no. Please don't alter your behavior because of me. I'm enjoying watching you eat."

And he was. She did it with such childlike enthusiasm that he was fascinated. She used the back of her wrist to push her hair back, baring the perfect oval of her face to his gaze. Her lips were slightly swollen, her color high. And she couldn't have been more beautiful to him.

She looked around the kitchen. "Nice place. Own or rent?"

"Own."

"Are you from Seattle?"

He shook his head. "New England."

"I thought I detected a bit of an accent."

"Oh?"

"Yeah. Sexy. JFKish somehow. But more subtle."

"Thank you. I think."

Her soft laugh did something odd to his stomach. "You're welcome." She wiped her hands on the linen napkin and picked up a fresh roll. "So...are you planning to stay here? In Seattle, I mean?"

He lifted a brow. Funny, but no one had actually asked him that before. Perhaps they just assumed that he would. Or maybe they weren't interested one way or the other.

"Depends on what the future brings."

She nodded. "Businesswise."

"Yes."

She chewed thoughtfully. "I've lived here all my life. Well, here and in Earnest. After my parents..."

Her sentence abruptly ended and she grimaced.

"After your parents..." he prompted.

She put the roll down and sipped from her wineglass. "After my parents died."

Silence reigned for a few moments.

She cleared her throat. "Sorry. I usually don't share things of that nature on a first date. I hate when people offer up their life stories." She made a face. "Poor me. My parents died in a plane crash when I was twelve and I had to go live with my uncle and cousins in Earnest." She drank again. "Talk about darkening the mood."

"So this is our first date, then?"

She looked at him without saying anything. Then, "I don't know. Isn't it? Or is it a booty call?"

"Booty call?"

She laughed. "Yes. You know. I'm not doing

anything. You're not doing anything. Why don't we get together and do nothing together."

He shifted on the stool. "I prefer date."

Another laugh. "So do I."

"Do you indulge in a lot of…"

"Booty calls?"

He coughed midway through taking a sip of wine. "Yes."

"This would be my first. You know, if we were classifying it as such."

"But we're not."

"No." Her smile was dazzling. "So I guess that means I've never…indulged in one." She forked a roasted potato and stuck it into her mouth, watching him closely. After finally swallowing, she said, "And in case you're wondering, no, I don't usually sleep with men on first dates, either. They're lucky if they get a kiss."

He hadn't been wondering, but he liked that she'd shared the information. "Then they would be lucky, indeed."

To his delight, she blushed.

He sat back. A woman who had blatantly invited his touch, yet blushed afterward at his mention of it. Intriguing…

"You know, you really should eat something or else I'm going to have to stop."

The chuckle that erupted from him was unexpected and sounded foreign to his own ears. He picked up his fork, speared some lobster meat and then raised it for her consideration. "Happy?"

He put it in his mouth.

She smiled around her potato. "I will be when you swallow."

He did just that. "You couldn't possibly have expected me to spit it out?"

She shrugged. "You never know. You come across some strange people."

He could attest to that. He'd dated a model who would eat nearly everything on the table, including from his and others' plates, and then disappear into the ladies' room, before returning and ordering dessert.

He'd given her the benefit of the doubt…until he'd caught her in the act at his apartment. He'd heard sounds that concerned him, knocked on the door and then opened it to find her crouched before the toilet.

She'd smiled, brushed her teeth and then rejoined him in the living room as if nothing had happened.

But something had. And he'd summarily dismissed her, suggesting she seek out help.

"There was this one guy I went out with who had to trade texts with his mother every five minutes. It would have been okay if he was fifteen, but he was in his thirties." She shook her head. "But that's another taboo topic for me on first dates."

"What is?"

"Having the 'loves that have come before'

discussion. Or, worse, 'those by whom I've been spurned.'"

"And this guy...was he..."

"Oh, God, no. The first date was the last. And if I'm not mistaken, I believe I feigned stomach cramps halfway through the meal."

She picked up another lobster claw and squinted at him. "Seems I'm doing all the talking here. And, again, you're not eating."

That's because Caleb was riveted to the way she fit her lips just so over the red claw.

She caught on to his preoccupation, put the claw down and cleaned up before taking a long sip of wine.

"Shall we move on to dessert?" she asked, snaking a hand around his neck and pulling him in for a kiss unlike any that had come before....

8

CALEB SAT IN HIS OFFICE staring out the windows at downtown Seattle. Though two days had passed since Bryna had stayed the night at his place, he couldn't help revisiting the evening. Remembering the sexy curve of her hip. The sensitivity of the back of her knees. Her soft cries when she'd reached orgasm… again and again.

He'd awakened the following morning with an ache for her the size of Washington State. He'd reached for her across the bed, only to discover she'd gone. No note. No promise of more. No word on whether she'd be back.

He'd finally given in and called her cell phone yesterday morning, but she hadn't picked up. And he hadn't left a message.

"Caleb?"

"Hmm?" He turned from the window and looked

at where Philippidis staff directly accountable to him were wrapping up the morning meeting.

"Anything you'd like to add?"

He straightened in his chair. "No."

"Okay, then," Jason Hasselbeck said. "Then we'll meet again Wednesday morning."

The participants began to disperse, but Caleb asked Hasselbeck to stay behind.

After the last staff member left the room, Caleb took Bryna's proposal from his desk drawer. "I want you to take a look at this for me. Let me know what you think."

Hasselbeck's brows rose as he browsed the first page, but he didn't say anything. Obviously he'd seen the Metaxas name. And if there was one thing Philippidis had accomplished, it was to have anything associated with Ari Metaxas banned from the building... unless it was to help him in his plan for revenge.

Caleb rose to his feet, waiting until Hasselbeck looked at him full in the face. "I don't think I have to tell you that this is to remain between you and me."

Although Caleb had hired Jason, he was ultimately Philippidis's employee, so he knew what he was asking of him was borderline, but he wanted his opinion.

"Are you seriously considering trying to resell him on a company that he's turned on?"

They both knew that the chances of that happening lay somewhere between nil and zero.

"If we can make the numbers work, maybe."

"And if we can't?"

Caleb sat back down in his chair. "We'll cross that bridge when we come to it. This is merely a preliminary look. Nothing official has been offered or agreed to."

Hasselbeck looked suspicious. And he had every right to. Caleb hadn't hired him because he was stupid. He knew that Caleb didn't take anything on, even preliminarily, unless there was a very strong chance he would proceed with it.

He also likely suspected that Caleb had every intention of shopping it around if he couldn't sell Philippidis on the deal.

Hasselbeck left the office and Caleb sat for a long time staring at his empty desktop. He had plenty to do, but he didn't feel particularly interested in pursuing any of the ten other projects waiting for him to okay the next step.

His intercom buzzed. "Sir, Mr. Palmer DeVoe is here to see you."

If anything were capable of nudging him from his current preoccupation, it was his old friend and ally. He told Nancy to send him in and then rose to his feet, buttoning his jacket as he rounded the desk.

The door opened.

"Well, look what the wind just blew in," he said, shaking Palmer's hand and then giving him a rare man hug.

There were few people he respected, either male or female, but Palmer DeVoe was one of them. A renowned business attorney, he worked for some of the most powerful companies out of Boston, starting with nothing but a law degree when he was in his twenties, and building his reputation until he was at the top of the letterhead of a very successful and lucrative law firm.

Caleb had acted on Palmer's behalf many times over the past ten years, usually in the role of aggressor, leveraging competing businesses that didn't want to budge, claiming properties that owners didn't want to sell. Essentially doing the dirty work so Palmer could keep his hands clean. And being well-rewarded for the part.

But it was more than business that bound them. Caleb had never been one for close friends of either sex, but when he and Palmer had found themselves essentially stranded in a small Texas town during the course of their first job together ten years ago—a flash flood had made it impossible for them to get out—they'd gone to the school gym to work out their restlessness on the basketball court...a tradition they continued over the years whenever their paths crossed.

Palmer seemed to know instinctively when to press for more information and when to let a topic lie. Especially when it came to items of a personal nature. And Caleb liked to the think he employed the same tact. And that had allowed a friendship to develop in addition to their professional association.

"I was in the neighborhood and thought I'd stop

by," Palmer said, the same affection that Caleb felt evident in his eyes.

"Bullshit. You're never in the neighborhood, and you never just drop in on anyone."

Was it him, or did Palmer look uncomfortable?

"Correct me if I'm wrong, but wasn't it you who said you weren't interested in losing the two business days it would take to fly halfway across the country to the Pacific NW and back?"

"Yeah, well…"

Another thought occurred to Caleb. One that was easy to forget because he'd only known Palmer in Boston. "Aren't you actually from the area around here somewhere?"

"Yes. A small town south of here."

Caleb raised his brows. "And you've never been back?"

"Not in fifteen years."

Caleb could understand wanting to escape the past. It was why he, himself, rarely returned to his old stomping grounds unless it was absolutely necessary. Even then, it was usually an in-and-out affair.

"Longing for old times?" he asked.

Palmer chuckled. "Not exactly." He looked around the office. "You got time to shoot a few hoops?"

Caleb grinned. "No. But I'll make time. It's been a while since I've enjoyed a little competition on the court.…"

He pushed the intercom for his secretary. "Nancy,

cancel all my appointments for this afternoon. Direct anything urgent to my cell phone."

BRYNA TYPED OUT a report on her laptop at her desk at Metaxas Limited, one eye on the door in case one of her cousins happened by and wanted to know what she was up to. She had an in-box full of menial tasks, but she was busy coming up with counterarguments to what she believed would be Caleb's arguments.

She smiled to herself as she typed up why her numbers should be accepted as was, or perhaps even be adjusted upward rather than down. She hadn't anticipated that having a potential partner would help bolster her confidence.

Potential partner…

Her fingers tripped over the keys. She grimaced and backtracked to delete the line of gibberish. Of course she meant "business" partner. To even consider getting involved with Caleb Payne was only asking for…well, a lot of pain.

She knew guys like him.

Okay, maybe she didn't know them, know them, but she was familiar with them. And was certainly familiar with his mode of operation. Date lady. Be seen dining and out and about with her. And just when others began to memorize her name, drop her cold.

Her research on him had shown he'd never been married. Which was odd, she thought, considering that he came from a very wealthy family back east and he was as traditional as they came in every other aspect. He'd made his own way up the corporate ladder with little or no help from his mother's family, was well-respected, and more than a little feared, which wasn't a bad thing in the business world. Be too nice and too respected and others tended to bulldoze over you.

He kept things on the up-and-up…for the most part.

Bryna chewed her bottom lip. She hadn't liked a couple of bits of info she'd picked up on him. And the fact that he was associated with Philippidis told her that he wasn't beyond selling himself to the highest bidder, no matter his own moral code.

Movement in the hall.

She quickly closed the laptop, only to watch as Elena waved at her as she passed, probably to visit Ari a few doors up.

She gave her a hello-how-do-you-do dismissive wave back.

Why did the woman set her teeth on edge whenever she saw her?

She sighed and opened her laptop again, reviewing what she'd written before saving it.

What she was avoiding very purposely when it came to Caleb was her own chaotic emotions related to what had passed between them the other night.

Quite simply, it was the best damn time she'd ever had.

With a man who was quite possibly even more commit-phobic than her cousin Troy.

She leaned back in her chair and closed her eyes. Since last Friday night, that's all it took for her to remember what it was like to lie in his bed, her back against his soft sheets, his hard body folded into hers.

He'd tried to call her yesterday. She knew that. Knew his number by heart. But she'd been at the brunch table with her cousins, uncle and Elena, nearly choking on her frittata when she'd glanced at her vibrating cell phone. In her hurry to clear the display in case Ari or Troy, who'd been sitting on either side of her, saw it, the expensive piece of equipment had sailed over the opposite side of the table and splintered into three pieces on the deck floor.

She still needed to run to the store to get a replacement.

More movement in the hall.

With a press of a button, she put the laptop to sleep and reached instead for the telephone, picking up the receiver to indicate she was busy.

Elena again.

She raised her hand to wave. But rather than merely returning it and continuing on, Elena stopped on the other side of the door and turned the knob.

Bryna grimaced as she pretended conversation with a supplier.

"That's unacceptable," she said to the dial tone. Afraid the other woman might hear it, she discreetly pushed a button that stopped the infernal sound. But she knew it was only a matter of time before a recording would play informing her to try her number again.

Elena stood smiling in front of her desk. "I'm sorry to interrupt…"

Bryna covered the mouthpiece. "I'm on the line with a supplier. I'm afraid I'm going to be a while."

"That's okay. I'll wait."

The other woman sat down in the single metal green plastic visitor's chair against the wall.

Great.

"What?" Bryna said into the phone. "That's not what I show." She sighed heavily. "Look, let me check my numbers and get back to you."

She hung up the phone just as it began that give-away buzz indicating it was off the hook with no active call.

She smiled. "Hi, Elena. How are you?" She tried for casual.

"Fine. Listen, I don't want to bother you if you're busy, but Ari said something about you needing to run into town to replace the cell phone that broke yesterday, and suggested that since I'm going that way, I might want to offer you a ride. Perhaps we can catch some lunch, as well."

"Lunch?" Bryna said the word as if it were completely foreign to her.

She was about to offer up an excuse about having other plans, or an appointment, or something equally lame and transparent when Ari's handsome head popped into the doorway.

"There you are. I was afraid I missed you."

He came inside and Bryna watched Elena immediately get to her feet to face him. "Did I forget something?"

Ari's grin was so intimate that even Bryna felt compelled to look away. She quietly straightened already straight papers in her in-box.

"Just this," he said, and kissed Elena thoroughly.

Bryna sighed loudly unintentionally, noticing that the other woman was a little unsteady on her feet.

Ari chuckled. "Sorry for the PDA," he said to her. "So, are you girls going into town for lunch, then?"

Bryna opened her mouth to say no, but the look on his face and the hopeful expression that Elena wore stopped the word in its tracks.

"Give me five minutes?" she said to Elena.

"Sure. I'll meet you outside."

The sickeningly sweet couple left her office and Bryna flopped back in her old, squeaky chair, wondering how she got herself into these messes. And how she could go about getting herself out…

9

DRESSED IN SWEATPANTS and a Yale T-shirt, Caleb faked going right and went left, making his way easily around Palmer to earn a jump shot on the half court at his private downtown health club.

"So how's Cissy?" Palmer asked as he went out and caught the ball.

Caleb frowned. He'd forgotten he'd taken Cissy east with him a couple of months ago for some sort of charity event his mother had chaired. The visit had been so brief—overnight—that he'd barely registered it. "You'd probably be better off asking her."

"Ah." Palmer came at him straight on, hooking the ball and scoring before Caleb could get his hands up to block. "Have we reached the cutoff point already?"

Caleb grinned, taking the ball and making Palmer chase him. "How about you? Found yourself a lady to settle down with yet?"

"Settle down? What's that?"

Caleb had figured out fairly quickly a long time ago that one of the reasons the two of them got on so well was they were more similar than different. Ambitious to a fault. Career above all. They were brothers in arms in a world where everything else shifted and changed and often collapsed altogether.

"So it must be something important to bring you out here," Caleb said, claiming another point and then calling a time-out. He led the way to a nearby table and handed Palmer a bottle of iced water and opened one for himself. They toasted each other before taking a sip.

"Philippidis asked me to come out," his friend said.

Caleb's fingers tightened on the plastic bottle. "Since when have you been associated with Philippidis?"

"Since the economy suffered a massive sinkhole and all of us are forced to band together to insure our collective survival."

Caleb narrowed his eyes. Palmer's law firm was one of the most solvent out there. Not given to short-sighted investments or dealings. Surely he wasn't saying he was at risk?

"May I ask what kind of business you two are in together?" His throat tightened, nearly refusing the water he attempted to swallow. Why hadn't Philippidis told him there was a deal in the works with Palmer DeVoe?

Palmer ran his wrist across his forehead and then reached for a towel. "Nothing specific yet. I'm here to feel things out, as it were."

Caleb didn't buy it. Something more specific had to be behind his old friend's visit to bring him back to a place that he'd purposely avoided for fifteen years.

But if Palmer didn't want to tell him, there was nothing he could do to change his mind.

For now.

Caleb tossed him the ball and the two went at it again, with Palmer landing one before he could catch up. He took the ball back and went long, the sounds of their breathing echoing off the high ceiling.

"So are you interviewing for Cissy's position yet?" Palmer asked just as Caleb threw.

The ball hit the backboard and bounced off, no-where near the net.

"Oh! And he loses his composure," Palmer said, getting to the ball first and faking a left before going right around him. "So what's her name? Anyone I know?"

Despite the difference of two time zones, it wasn't an unusual question. In the circles in which they traveled, the pool of well-off singles was small and relatively shallow. Even if they didn't know a person directly, at some point they had likely come in con-tact with direct or extended family. In Cissy's case, her older sister had married a Harvard astrophysicist and now lived in the Boston suburbs with her family, so Palmer had actually met Cissy before he had, although the two had never dated.

In fact, Palmer dated so rarely—except for the requisite woman on his arm at certain events—Caleb had once inquired about his sexual preferences. Palmer had laughed so hard, he'd never had to ask again.

"No."

He left his friend to interpret his response any way he chose to.

No, he wasn't entertaining candidates to take the place Cissy had vacated.

No, he wasn't seeing anyone Palmer would know.

No, he had no interest in discussing the matter.

What had happened between him and the lovely Miss Metaxas was so far outside the norm of his experience that he was reluctant to lump her into some group, dismiss the night as just another one spent with a willing female.

At the same time, he wasn't ready to examine the time they'd spent together too closely. And he certainly wasn't anywhere near to sharing her name with anyone.

Palmer made another shot and then grabbed the ball again, holding it still at his side. "Ready to call it?"

Caleb blinked. He'd lost interest in the game the instant his thoughts had turned to Bryna, which was

funny because he'd taken his friend up on the offer
to play to get his mind off her.

But never let it be said that he'd pass on a challenge
of this nature.

He took the ball. "Not on your life," he said, intent
on making Palmer work for every shot.…

BRYNA PARKED in an angled curb spot in the small,
one-time quaint downtown of Earnest. Unable to
come up with a reason not to go to lunch with Elena
without being inexcusably rude, she'd found herself
insisting that they take her car, because Elena's was
an older model Caprice that looked two hundred
miles away from a total breakdown.

"So many places are boarded up," Elena commented quietly next to her.

"Hmm?"

Bryna glanced at her pale face, then out at the
line of one-time businesses that had thrived in the
town only a few years ago. Now all that remained
of the thirty or so storefronts was an old diner that
had seen better times, two bars at opposing angles,
a cell phone shop that took up only a quarter of the
space of what had once been Hardy's Hardware, and
Chelsea's coffee/book/art shop across the street.

It was a sad sight to see. Sadder still when she
considered the families that had been hurt by the
closings. Sure, they had all taken a hit when strip
malls started popping up some twenty miles outside
of town, with jumbo supermarkets stealing business

from Pop's Market and DeVoe's General Store, and all but dealing a lethal blow to the town's pharmacist. But they'd muddled through the first year and had managed to come out on top, with residents growing weary of the long drive to the other stores, and Earnest businesses reeling them back in with town-wide discounts and savings programs devised by the mayor's office.

Then the mill was forced to close its doors four years ago, imported materials undercutting their ability to turn a profit and federal regulation twisting their arms behind their backs. Her uncle and Troy and Ari had run in the red for two years, trying desperately to find an alternative route, but finally had to admit defeat, giving employees six months' notice and another six months' severance before finally closing the mill's doors for good.

They'd all watched as the town's businesses followed suit, falling like dominos down the block, the closure of one contributing to the bankruptcy of the next.

Then it finally looked as if the deal that she and her cousins had worked so hard to put together with Philippidis was going to happen, like a flower emerging from a crack in the neglected sidewalk.

Until the woman next to her had slept with Ari the night before her wedding to Philippidis.

She took the key from the ignition. "I'm going to run into the communications store. I'll meet you at the diner."

Elena blinked at her. If Bryna had been a bit brusque, she figured she had cause to be. So many lives impacted by out-of-control hormones. It should be illegal.

She got out of the car and walked toward the store, not even glancing in Elena's direction as they parted ways. Too bad she hadn't insisted on driving separately. She could have feigned a forgotten business meeting, or urgent phone call, and gotten out of the lunch altogether. But not even she would consider leaving the pregnant woman to fend for herself.

Within twenty minutes she had a replacement phone, had even managed to have them transfer her phone book, and began walking in the direction of the diner.

It was midday and the rain clouds had briefly parted, allowing the summer sun to shine through, glinting against the wet pavement. She'd spent her teenaged years here in Earnest. Used to enjoy éclairs at the Steinway's Bakery that had closed last year. Attend hayrides and bonfires at Johnson's Feed and Weed located a few blocks north. Her entire adolescence had been shaped by a place that no longer existed.

A dull ache took up residence in her chest even as she felt renewed determination to turn things around.

"Bryna?"

She blinked at a woman standing in front of the

diner wearing a waitress uniform. "Jessica?" she said incredulously.

Jessica Talbot was an old classmate of hers. They were the best of friends one summer, until Jessica had gotten pregnant and married her seventeen-year-old boyfriend. She'd worked at the mill office for a year before it finally closed down.

Now, apparently, she was working at the diner.

And looked at least ten years older than Bryna rather than the same age.

"How are you?" She gave the other woman a quick, awkward hug. "God, it's been ages."

"Yes, it has. I don't think I've seen you since Jason's baptism…what, seven years ago?"

"Surely it can't be that long ago?"

"Wait. You're right. I think I ran into you at the mill once or twice. But we never got a chance to talk."

Bryna felt instantly guilty. She'd been so consumed with her own life at the time, which had been filled with Washington University classes, that she'd barely noticed her old friend.

And had Jessica not said anything, she might have walked right past her now.

A truck pulled up grill first at the curb and an older man in overalls got out, straightening his ball cap. "Jessica," he said, nodding.

She greeted him back and then the instant he was inside, said, "I've really got to get moving. I told Verna I'd be back in fifteen minutes. She'll throw a fit if I leave her in the lurch for too long during the lunch rush."

Bryna smiled. "Actually, I'll probably still be here when you get back. I'm meeting somebody for lunch."

"Oh."

Jessica didn't have to say that catching up had to done now. Upon her return she would go back to work—no time for conversation.

Bryna opened her purse and took out a card. "Here. My cell phone number's on the back. Call me. We'll get together for lunch or something."

She winced at the words, feeling their difference in stations in an acute way she'd never experienced before. She'd always been treated the same as anyone else when they were kids.

Now she was an outsider.

"Sure," Jessica said, already beginning to walk away. "I'll call you."

Bryna stood for a long time on the sidewalk, watching as Jessica hurried up the street and then turned the corner. Was she still living with her mother in the old clapboard house a few blocks up? She hadn't had a chance to ask. She hadn't seen a ring on her finger, but she didn't know if that meant that she'd taken it off for work, or if the marriage that had stood little chance of working had finally reached its end.

Someone waving from the diner window caught her eye. She frowned.

Elena.

God help her get through this lunch without blasting her soon-to-be cousin-in-law for every sin since the beginning of time. For ruining the deal with Philippidis. For making Troy work nonstop to save Metaxas Ltd. For ensuring the town of Earnest had to struggle for another year. But mostly for adding ten years to the young face of her one-time friend....

10

"YOU DIDN'T CALL ME BACK," Caleb's whiskey voice said when Bryna answered her cell.

She relaxed against the dozens of pillows that adorned her childhood bed at the Metaxas estate. For the first time in what felt like days, she smiled an indulgent smile, the sound of Caleb's naughty chuckle tickling more than her ear.

"You didn't leave a message requesting I call you back," she countered.

She debated telling him she'd had to replace her cell phone, then decided against it. Let him think what he wanted. All that mattered was that he had called again. Which meant that last Friday was more than a one-night affair to him.

She looked at her watch. It was a few minutes after ten and she'd just gone up to her room to get out of her work clothes and take a long bath with a good book when her new cell phone rang. It had taken four tries for her to find the right button to answer, bewildered by the latest in technology. Immensely frustrating, since she'd seen his name pop up in the extra-large display.

"Hard day?" he asked.

Bryna bit her bottom lip even as she slid her pumps off. "You have no idea. How about you?"

"No more difficult than any other Monday."

"So it was good, then."

"I never consider a day good. Only challenging or unchallenging. Successful or unsuccessful."

"Shocker."

As for her, her day had taken a nosedive when she'd run into Jessica and hadn't improved a bit from there.

She'd gone in to share a table with Elena only to quickly figure out that lunch had never been the intent all along. Rather, Elena had gone to the diner to confirm rumors that Verna, the owner, was looking to sell or close up shop. And to establish that Elena was interested in buying it.

Bryna couldn't have been more surprised. Yes, she'd known that Elena's family had been in the restaurant business. But Bryna hadn't even imagined that she might return to work. After all, she had seduced one of the state's most eligible bachelors in her cousin Ari. Why would she be interested in working? Especially considering she was preggers?

And Verna's restaurant, The Quality Diner, had been owned by her family for generations. Her grandfather had turned it into the mainstay it was now, making it crisis-proof. It was an Earnest landmark. Surely Elena didn't think it would be that easy to slip in with the locals?

Besides, Verna couldn't be seriously considering selling. The tall redhead might be getting up there in age, but she had two sons and a daughter that were a decade or two older than Bryna. Surely one of them would be interested in running the place? View the restaurant as their rightful legacy.

She began unbuttoning her blouse.

"What are you doing right now?" Caleb asked. "Right this moment?"

Bryna let the light material whisper down her arms. "Why? This couldn't actually be a booty call, now, could it?"

Caleb's burst of laughter told of his surprise. "That depends."

"On what?"

"On how quickly you can get over here."

She shivered from head to foot. "How about you come to me." She popped the catch on her skirt and kicked her legs until it lay on the floor along with her blouse. "I'm at home in Earnest."

"At the Metaxas Estate?"

"That would be home."

A long pause and then, "Oh."

She settled more comfortably against the pillows, one of which was covered with a needlepoint design of daisies that her mother had made just before the crash. "Do I detect a measure of disappointment, Mr. Payne?"

"You definitely detect a measure of disappointment."

She grinned against the mouthpiece. "Good."

"Sadist."

She could get used to this. To Caleb wanting her and not liking not being able to have her. She got the distinct impression that what Caleb Payne wanted he got. Period. No questions asked.

She could certainly attest to that. He was a difficult man to refuse.

Of course, she currently had no reason to turn away his flattering and exciting attentions.

She pursed her lips. "What makes you think I'd respond to your booty call anyway?"

"I never conceded that's what this is."

"Mmm. I'd say it is. What time is it? After ten. You're bored and you picked up the phone to find some company. I'd say that has booty call written all over it."

"All right, then. I concede."

She took a deep breath and released it slowly, wishing she could have responded to his call, gone to his place dressed in nothing but a raincoat and re-enacted the other night with a few new ideas thrown in for good measure. But she was in Earnest until Wednesday night. And unless he had reason to visit the small town—which wasn't a good idea any way you looked at it, because she'd never dare invite him to the house; her cousins would tar and feather him for sure—that meant that she wasn't going to see him until midweek at the earliest.

She told him when she'd be returning to the city and he responded with "Then I'll meet you at my place. Say at around seven?"

Bryna smiled. "Do you really think I'm that easy?"

"No. I'm saying I really want to see you that badly."

"Seven at your place, then. Wednesday."

The word caught in her mind, a niggling voice trying to tell her something. Then it occurred to her why. "Damn. I forgot. I already have a date for that night."

Silence.

She rubbed the arch of one foot against the front of the other, enjoying his speechless reaction.

"I could meet you after," she suggested playfully.

"You could meet me after your date?"

"Mmm-hmm."

He didn't sound pleased. Not pleased at all.

She laughed quietly. "I'm attending a charity ball that night. Something planned way in advance."

"And your date?"

She was surprised he'd asked outright. "My cousins."

She actually heard his sigh of relief.

Which was interesting. She didn't figure Caleb for

the possessive type. Especially considering that they weren't actually dating, much less anywhere near the stage of exclusivity. They'd slept together. Once.

Yet she couldn't help getting a little thrill at the thought that Caleb wanted her for himself.

"What celebrity event might that be?" he asked.

She told him.

"Funny, but I'm also scheduled to be in attendance."

"Is that right?"

"Yes."

"But you were willing to break the date in order to meet me at your place."

"Whereas you are unwilling."

"Only because my cousins view it as an extension of my job. You know, considering the urgency of our plans."

"Mmm."

"So I guess I'll see you there, then," she murmured.

"I guess you will."

"Will you be offering me a ride home afterward, do you think?"

"No."

She lifted her brows.

"I'll be offering you a ride to my place."

"Done."

"Good."

Why did she get the impression that everything

with Caleb was going to amount to a bartering session of sorts?

He cleared his throat. "You never did answer my question earlier…" he said leadingly.

"And which question might that be?"

"What you're wearing…"

"Mmm…you're right," she teased, slipping her free thumb under one bra strap. "How badly do you want to know?"

"Considering I can't see you until Wednesday? Very badly."

"And knowing I'm lying across my canopy bed wearing nothing but a lacy red bra and red panties is going to help?"

She heard his groan and shivered in response to his guttural reaction.

"Immensely."

She enjoyed the sexually charged silence for a few moments, then said, "Well, then, I suppose you might want to know what my right hand is doing right now, wouldn't you?"

"You have no idea…"

11

CALEB SAT ON THE PIANO BENCH before his Steinway grand, running his fingertips over the keys without making a sound as he listened to Bryna's tinkling laughter. He caught a reflection of himself in the glass picture windows, illuminated by the penthouse's soft recessed lighting. The city of Seattle was a constellation of twinkling lights against the dark. He'd taken off his suit coat and tie, rolled up the sleeves and unbuttoned the collar of his crisp broadcloth shirt. His shoulders were hunched slightly over the piano keys and he was…grinning.

The vision was so unusual as to be surprising. About this time of night he might be in his home office going over numbers or catching up on correspondence he'd missed over the course of the day if nothing else was on tap. Or even reading a business journal while watching news and enjoying a finger of whiskey.

Anything but what he was doing. Which was thoroughly enjoying a late-night conversation with Bryna Metaxas while a jazz CD played throughout the penthouse.

"Are you still there?" Her soft voice drifted into his eardrum like the note on the piano.

"I'm still here." He shifted on the bench.

"So do you want to know where my hand is?"

He envisioned her lying back on a big, rough-hewn canopy bed, her red undergarments contrasting against a thick white comforter, her skin smooth, her body curvy.

"Tell me," he said, his voice husky. He told himself it was from the whiskey, but not even he bought it.

"It's lying against my stomach, just above my navel…"

A sexy spot that he'd taken great pleasure in probing with the tip of his tongue last Friday.

"Oh, wait," she whispered. "It just moved…"

As did Caleb. He rose to his feet and neared the windows, trying to concentrate on the skyline.

"My fingertips are inching their way ever so slowly upward…."

"I'd have opted for downward."

A soft laugh. "I wouldn't have thought you an impatient man, Caleb."

Normally, he wasn't. "I don't believe in wasting time."

She hummed. "And is that what you think we're doing? Wasting time?"

"Where is your hand now?"

Silence and then he heard a muffled sound as if she'd moved the phone. Or was, perhaps, stretching out more comfortably on the bed. "My palm just grazed my nipple through the lacy red fabric of my bra...."

His mouthed watered with the desire to claim that same sexy bit between his lips.

"My index finger is working its way under the bottom of the cup...." She hummed. "Naked flesh against naked flesh..."

His temperature rose a couple of degrees. "You read those steamy novels, don't you?"

"I had a date with one tonight, actually. In the bathtub."

She didn't play fair. He had an image of her covered up to her neck in silky bubbles, her skin rosy from the hot water, her nipples poking through, her red-painted toes gripping the opposite edge as her hands did Lord only knew what under the surface.

"Would you like me to continue? Or would you like me to recommend one of those novels?"

His throat was tight. "Continue. Please..."

"Mmm. That's what I thought you'd say...."

He turned from the windows and made his way to the sitting area of the living room, choosing one of the modern brown armchairs to sink down into. He was still facing the windows, as much of the furniture in the apartment was, designed to showcase the penthouse's view to its best advantage. He reached for a remote on the table in front of him and dimmed the overhead lighting until he was little more than a dark silhouette.

"Oops. Seems my hand has, um, a mind of its own. It's no longer satisfied with the juvenile fondling. It's undoing the catch on my bra and…" She sighed. "There. It's gone. Nothing to get in the way of a good, thorough caress…"

Caleb's erection twitched under the fabric of his pants.

"Where are you now?" she asked.

"In my apartment."

He heard her smile. "I know that. Where in your apartment?"

"In the living room."

"Facing the windows?"

"Uh-huh. Sitting in a chair. I was at the piano, but I relocated while you were talking."

"Feeling a bit restless, Mr. Payne?"

A bit didn't come near to covering it.

"And are you…turned on by my verbal exploration?"

"I would be if you shut up and got on with it."

Her laughter touched something deep inside him. "My. We are the impatient one tonight, aren't we?"

If *impatient* meant he was ready to grab his car keys and make his way to Earnest in record time, then, yes, he was very impatient.

"My question to you," she murmured. "Where is *your* free hand?"

"Gripping the arm of the chair. Tightly."

"Mmm...let's see if we can't change that...."

He settled more comfortably into the chair, *comfortable* being a relative term.

"I'm propping the phone against the pillows because one hand just isn't doing it for me..." she said.

Caleb swallowed hard, seeing her run her palms over her full, pert breasts.

"My nipples are so, so hard.... I'm licking my fingers.... Mmm, yes. I can almost imagine that it's your tongue flicking across them...."

Her voice had dropped to a whiskey whisper, encouraging him to follow her into the fantasy she was creating with her words.

He reached down to rearrange his throbbing hard-on in his pants.

"Bad right hand...bad," she said.

Caleb's swallow sounded louder than it should have. "What's bad right hand doing?" he couldn't help asking when she didn't immediately continue.

"Bad right hand is leaving my breasts and sliding slowly, ever so slowly, down my trembling stomach..."

The penthouse around Caleb disappeared, leaving him in an isolated cocoon.

"Oh...oh..." she whispered.

"Tell me," he insisted roughly.

"Bad li'l right hand is cupping me through my panties." He heard her licking her lips and found himself doing the same thing. "My legs are spreading open…yes…"

Before he realized his hand had moved, it had undone the catch on his slacks and tugged down the zipper, not stopping until he clutched his own flesh in his palm.

"The crotch of my panties is dripping with desire…"

Christ, she was going to be the end of him.

He tried to think of the last time he'd even thought about jacking off. Surely not since he was a teenager, before he'd discovered that with a little effort he could have a willing female look after the task for him. But his brain was shutting down, denying him the luxury of rational thought as he slid easily into the sensual web of sensation Bryna created for him.

Her voice sounded raspier still. "My index finger just tunneled under the elastic…mmm…yes. It's stroking the length of my swollen, hungry lips…"

"What's she hungry for?" he asked.

"Why you, Mr. Payne."

Caleb sank down farther into the chair, his arousal standing upright, almost angrily, from the V of his open slacks. He gripped the hard flesh, taken aback by the instant, jerking response.

"I…have…to…take…these…off.…"

She was stripping off her panties. Dear Lord.

"Oh, yessss…"

His mouth went suddenly dry. "Describe the sensations for me, Bry."

"It's... I..."

"Try..."

"The cool air hitting my dampness is so, so sweet...."

He could see her lying spread-eagled, her knees bent, her womanhood bared to him.

"I'm shaking all over..." she whispered.

Amazingly, so was he.

His grip tightened and he drew his hand upward than down again, his mind's eye filled with the image of her parted lips, her pupil-dominated eyes.

"I'm running my hands up the inside of my thighs...no...not yet." He detected the restless chaos in her voice. "I want this to last a little longer..."

Caleb brought his foreskin up over his aching head of his penis and brought it back down, his own gut tightening.

"So wet...so very slick..."

She was stroking herself.

"Oh...oh...oh!"

"Pinch your clit for me, Bry."

"I...can't..."

His own crisis was nearing the boiling point.

"I...it's so sensitive...so hard..."

Caleb's hips bucked involuntarily.

"Oh, yessssss," she hissed.

Her soft cries filled his ear as he came right along with her.

BRYNA LAY SPENT and gasping for breath against the pillows. She'd lost the cell phone at some point but didn't have the energy to search for it just then. She slowly lifted her hand and ran it over her face and hair, unable to believe she'd done what she had. She'd never been so blatantly uninhibited before. But something about Caleb coaxed something out from within her. Something more elemental…more sexual…more animalistic.

She heard a muffled sound and realized it was probably him on the phone.

She rolled over to fish it out from where it had dropped between two pillows.

"Bryna? Are you still there?"

Her smile was so large it nearly hurt her face muscles. "I'm still here. You?"

His sexy chuckle washed over her like a touch.

She lifted herself on her elbows and swayed her feet in the air, pressing her hips tightly against the mattress. Another shiver wend through her.

"So, tell me, Mr. Payne. Did I bring you any pleasure tonight?"

"You brought me a great deal of pleasure."

"But?"

"But it's nowhere near the kind of pleasure I'd like to show you Wednesday night."

She was filled with hot anticipation. "Promises, promises."

"Oh, no, Bry. I don't make promises. I make plans."

"Well, then. I have to say I'm more than a little intrigued."

"How much more?"

"A lot."

A comfortable silence stretched between them as she laid her head down, cradling the phone between her ear and a pillow.

"Would you like to have another go at it?" she whispered. "This time with you in charge of the verbal tour?"

"I'm afraid I wouldn't be nearly as effective as you."

She smiled and found herself yawning. "I find that hard to believe."

He chuckled. "I think this is the part where I bid you a fond good-night, Miss Metaxas."

"Mmm. Good night."

"Sweet dreams."

"Sleep tight."

She reluctantly disconnected the call and tossed the cell to the opposite side of the bed. If he made an appearance in her dreams, they would be very sweet indeed....

12

WEDNESDAY MORNING finally dawned sunny and warm, but Bryna suspected that the day would drag by like an eternity if it was anything like yesterday.

She'd never really gotten into poetry, but a half-remembered fragment from the passage of time rang so true that she'd begun pulling various volumes out of the Metaxas library in search of it. Strangely, rather than help her get through the day, the quest seemed to make the time go even slower.

Of course, the fires that had sparked at work yesterday hadn't helped. The company's head engineer and his five-man team, who were working on retainer until Metaxas Limited secured the funds to continue with their plans, had come in and asked to be released from their contract. It seemed another, rival company was offering him double what they were paying.

It didn't take more than a few phone calls to

confirm their suspicions that Manolis Philippidis was behind the move.

Without the head engineer, they could still squeak by, but not without his team. If all of them left, there would be no moving forward anywhere, with or without funds.

Bryna had stayed late, along with Troy and Ari and a handful of other longtime Metaxas employees, discussing their strategy. If they tried to force the men to honor the contract, they might sue to get out, creating lots of bad blood on both sides. They considered meeting the amount Philippidis offered, no matter how difficult it would be for them to do. And finally placed on the table was the alternative of just letting them go.

Silence had been the response from all.

Now she was snatching a moment of peace with a bowl of Cocoa Puffs and a book of Thoreau's, after spending much of last night working out how she was going to move forward with her own clandestine plans with Caleb, both on a professional and a personal level.

Ari settled himself next to her at the kitchen counter, sighing. Which was never a good thing, because Ari never sighed. Even at the daylong meetings yesterday, he'd never given up hope that they would reach some sort of compromise with the engineers. He'd talk to them, he said, get them to realize that taking Philippidis's offer might appeal in the short term, but in the long, they'd be setting themselves up for disappointment and frustration.

Bryna lifted the spoon to her mouth as Ari sighed for a third time, turning her cereal to little more than chocolate chalk. She finally put her book down and stared sidelong at him as she chewed. After swallowing, she said, "I'm sure I'm going to live to regret this, but what is it?"

His answering grin made her want to swat him with her book. "Elena thinks she's done something to insult you."

"She did. She met you."

Troy entered the kitchen and poured himself a glass of orange juice, and then one for Ari when he asked for it. "She's got you there, Ari."

Bryna smiled triumphantly.

While the three of them getting up together and sharing breakfast had been a regular occurrence a few months ago, lately they seemed to leave the house in stages. Troy was getting up at Lord knew what hour (Bryna suspected that he'd actually slept at the office more than a few nights), while Ari got in late after spending what time he could with Elena every evening. Which left her on her own to eat in a quiet kitchen, as her uncle's summer schedule wrapped around tee-off times that saw him coming and going.

"What are you still doing staying here, anyway?" Bryna asked Ari. "Shouldn't you two lovebirds be shacked up together somewhere? Especially considering that you've already knocked her up?"

Troy broke a couple of eggs into a hot pan. "Can you bring the language up just this side of the gutter?"

She gave him an eye roll. "Don't shoot the messenger. Acknowledge the message."

Troy looked at Ari. "She has a point."

Ari pointed toward the pan. "Smells good. Make a couple for me?"

"If you put on the toast."

"Deal." Ari got up and took a loaf of wheat bread from a drawer, feeding four slices into the eight-piece toaster. "You want one?" he asked her.

"Pass. Thanks."

"Don't mention it. Anyway, the reason why Elena and I aren't living together yet is that she wants to wait until we're married."

"And then?" Troy asked.

Ari stared at him. "Then, what?"

"Oh, God," Bryna said, losing her appetite altogether. Which was tough considering this had always been her favorite cereal. "You're not going to move her in here, are you?"

Ari aimed a glare in her direction. Another rare occurrence that left Bryna feeling guilty. "As luck would have it, Elena doesn't think it's a good idea. But I haven't given up trying. This place is big enough for five full-size families."

Bryna sighed with relief. "I don't think I've given her enough credit."

"Which is exactly the point I'm trying to make," Ari said, pointing at her. "She said you were awfully quiet during lunch the other day."

Bryna got up and dumped the remnants of her bowl down the sink drain and ran the water. "Quiet is better than saying what was on my mind. Trust me."

Troy turned his eggs onto a plate and broke another couple into the pan. "What happened?"

"Happened? Oh, nothing. It was a perfectly nice lunch at The Quality Diner. I caught up with a couple of friends. Was reminded how Verna's open-face roast beef sandwich used to rank as my favorite food group. And then it dawned on me that lunch wasn't the only thing on Elena's agenda."

"How do you mean?"

She sighed. "She wants to buy the place."

The toast popped up, startling Ari. "She doesn't want to buy the place. She was just curious to see if the rumors were true."

"The Quality?" Troy said. "But the Burns have owned that place forever."

Ari took butter out of the refrigerator. "And Verna apparently is feeling as old as the restaurant. Word has it that if the right offer comes along she'll take it."

Troy raised his brows. "What about her kids?"

"Exactly what I want to know," Bryna agreed,

crossing her arms as she stood next to Troy, facing off with Ari from across the island.

He eyed the pan. "You're going to burn those." Troy turned the eggs out onto a fresh plate. "You two are making it sound like this is some kind of conspiracy. Elena isn't doing anything illegal. We're going to be married. She's going to be moving here to Earnest. The only restaurant within a thirty-mile radius is The Quality. And if Verna wants to sell... well, it's as simple as that."

Bryna and Troy stared at him.

"Is she going to buy it?" Bryna asked.

"I'd prefer she didn't," Ari said under his breath, buttering and cutting the toast and then putting the plates in front of two stools on the counter. "Look, I may not like the idea—for entirely different reasons than you—but if it's one thing I've learned, it's that Elena doesn't live by anybody's rules but her own."

"Shocker," Bryna said.

Ari took his seat and accepted the eggs Troy slid his way. "Thanks. And thanks a lot." He sighed heavily. "Elena said this was going to take some time, but, Christ, will you hurry up and get over yourself? We're getting married and there's going to be another Metaxas in seven months."

Troy took his stool next to his brother as Bryna replied, "Maybe if you stopped trying to shove her down our throats, I'd stop reacting as if that's what you were doing."

Ari glowered. "No, Bryna. Shoving her down your

throats would be moving her in here and having her fix breakfast for us all every morning. And dinner every night. And including her in every activity."

Bryna shot Troy a horrified look.

"And if you guys don't start showing some more respect for my wife-to-be, then I swear I'll start doing just that."

Bryna raised her hands in surrender. "I think that's my cue to leave."

Troy took a sip of juice. "Since we're all up, I thought we might drive in together."

Bryna squinted at him. "Sorry. I'll pass."

She rounded the island and kissed each of them on the cheek, her last cousinlike move of the day; from here on out everything would switch to business. "I'm going to have to leave work early in order to get to Seattle in time to make my hair appointment."

Ari blinked at her. "Hair appoint… Damn. I forgot all about that damn charity event tonight."

Bryna tried not to beam. She hadn't forgotten. It was all she'd been able to think about.

"Don't even consider ducking out of it," Troy said. "I need all three of us there. I'll give you a list of the people we need to split up and talk to."

"We already have it," Bryna said.

"I've updated it."

This time she and Ari shared a long-suffering look. "Why am I not surprised?"

"What do you mean—"

"See you at the office, guys. Enjoy your breakfast."

She walked out of the kitchen as quickly as she could without seeming in too much of a hurry, thinking that all would be perfect if she could just fast-forward through the day and have it be night....

IT WAS DIFFICULT TO STAND in the living area of his penthouse without recalling the other night and his risqué phone conversation with Bryna. From the piano bench to the windows to the chair, each made him remember her whispered words and the sizzling impact they'd had on him.

The woman was definitely an intriguing puzzle to be pieced together. She took up more of his thoughts than any of the women he'd dated before combined.

Caleb straightened his tux jacket and checked his cufflinks, turning the idea over in his mind. A warning voice sounded in the back of his head. A voice he ignored. At least for now.

He glanced at his watch, surprised to see he was early. The event didn't start for another half hour. And he made it a point to always arrive late at such gatherings.

He smiled and walked to the bar. He opened a bottle of sparkling water, poured a bit into an etched crystal glass and took a sip. His lack of access to the maddening woman could be partially to blame for his obsession with her. To have had a taste and then be denied seconds was a situation he wasn't used to. He generally opted for uncomplicated women who would rearrange their plans in order to put him first.

But Bryna...

Complicated. Very definitely complicated.

And very definitely irresistible.

The sound of the doorbell filled the room. He looked in the direction of the entry area. Bryna, unable to wait?

The possibility presented all sorts of options on how they might fill the time between now and the charity ball.

He began walking toward the door, but Lionel beat him to it.

"I'll see to it, sir."

Caleb stretched his neck and checked his cufflinks again. "Of course."

He walked back toward the window, glass in hand, attempting nonchalance when all he wanted was to turn and watch her enter the room.

Unfortunately, it wasn't Bryna there to surprise him. It was his mother.

"Is that expression any way to welcome your mother, Caleb?" Phoebe Payne asked with a perfumed smile. "Get over here and give me a hug already, will you? Before I develop a complex..."

13

"IF I DIDN'T KNOW BETTER, I'd think my little surprise visit is unwelcome," Phoebe said as they rode in the limo to the Seattle Center.

Caleb stared out the window at the raindrops that dotted the glass and turned the streets and sidewalks into a dark, shiny mirror that reflected buildings and cars. "Don't be ridiculous, Mother. You are always welcome."

She finished freshening up her lipstick and slid him an amused look. "Now, that was convincing."

Caleb tucked his chin into his chest and chuckled. "I'm sorry. I don't mean to offend you. You know how I feel about surprises."

She tucked her compact back into her clutch and sat back, sliding her hand onto his arm. "I know. That's why I make it a point to keep springing them on you."

Complicated.

Caleb recalled using the same word to describe Bryna even as he looked into the aging but still beautiful face that belonged to his mother. She'd gone completely blonde about eight years ago when, she claimed, she'd surrendered in her battle against gray. It had taken her a few wrong shades to hit the right one, but somehow the golden hue of her almost girlish curls suited her. It helped that she took good care of herself, exercising regularly, watching her weight and getting a discreet nip, tuck, or collagen shot every now and again.

It still boggled the mind that she had never married. Oh, she'd come close a time or two. Even been engaged once when he was thirteen. But when Caleb had voiced his disapproval of the groom-to-be, she'd dropped the man like a hot potato, automatically choosing her son and only child over marriage to a man he didn't like, no matter the reason.

The experience had taught him an important lesson about male-female relationships. Mainly that he could manipulate them, bend them to his will.

And he'd been doing it ever since.

"So will your date be meeting us there?" his mother inquired.

He looked at her. She never referred to the women he dated by name. He'd asked her once why and she'd simply shrugged and said there was no use becoming friendly with someone who would soon be replaced by another.

"And what happens if I ever meet someone who's more than a date?"

She'd raised a perfect eyebrow, considering him for a long moment. "Well, then I guess I'll have to learn her name."

"How will you know?"

She'd laughed quietly. "Oh, I'll know."

"I see. Because you're an expert in matters of the heart."

She'd flinched and he regretted what was meant as a gentle barb. "No. Because I'm an expert on my son."

His formative years hadn't been bad ones. His mother's family had been wealthy, so he'd never lacked for anything and had been brought up in the same house in which she'd been raised, surrounded by extended family. And Phoebe, herself, had been an understanding mother, almost eerily intuitive if not especially doting. She'd always been there when he'd needed her. And did seem to know him better than anyone else, no matter how he often tried to convince himself differently.

"So what brings you out this way?" he asked.

"What? It's not enough that I want to see my one and only child every now and again?"

He smiled. "I'm too much like you to buy that."

"Yes, I guess you are. And I'm still trying to determine if that's a good or bad thing."

"The charity event?"

"Oh, heavens, no. We have plenty of these back east."

"So?" he asked when she didn't continue.

This time she looked out the window. "I've met someone."

Caleb raised his brow at her.

What were the chances that they both would meet someone special within the same time span after having spent so many years happily single?

"And this someone might be?"

She patted his arm and then withdrew her hand. "Now, if I told you, I'd likely jinx the entire thing."

He couldn't help his chuckle. "I've never known you to be the superstitious type, Mother."

The smile on her soft mouth loomed in her eyes. "Lately I find myself wondering if I even know myself as well as I thought."

"As a result of this gentleman?"

She checked her hair. "Who said it was a man?"

Caleb coughed.

His mother laughed. "I always said you were a bit on the stodgy side. Never knew where you picked it up."

Seeing as he'd been raised in one of the most conservative families in the east, despite his mother's rather rebellious behavior when she'd borne him out of wedlock and never married, he guessed he could have learned the behavior from any one of a hundred people that had surrounded him. His maternal grandfather, the late, great industrialist Bedford Payne high up on that list.

"Certainly not from you," he agreed.

"Certainly not."

It wouldn't surprise him if his mother had taken a lady lover. But he got the impression she was pulling his leg, as she had a habit of doing just to get a rise out of him.

Still, he found it curious that she wasn't willing to share her love interest's name.

More curious still that he wasn't willing to share Bryna's name with her…

THE MAN WAS HOTTER than any one man had a right to be.

Bryna stood across the room from the door of the large hall, yet knew the instant Caleb entered. She felt the sensitive skin at the nape of her neck tingle as every nerve ending went on alert. She somehow managed to continue her conversation with one of the matriarchs of Seattle society and the chairwoman of the night's events, but Lord only knew how. Caleb filled her every sense, every thought.

He wore a tux that fit him like a second skin, emphasizing the width of his shoulders, the narrowness of his hips. His smile was wide and generous, his eyes dark and dangerous.

She shivered just knowing that tonight she would again be the recipient of his demanding kiss.

On his arm was a woman who didn't look that much older until they moved a little closer.

"Ms. Payne and Mr. Payne," Ari said at her elbow.

"What?"

"The woman and man that just came in."

"They're married?" she asked, already knowing the answer. Still, it wouldn't hurt to throw her cousin off the scent she was sure she radiated like a perfume.

She wanted Caleb. And she wanted him now.

Ari chuckled. "No. Mother and son. Only son. And some story there, from what I understand."

"Oh?"

A part of Bryna was turned off by inviting gossip related to a man she was seeing, however clandestinely. Another wanted to know every bit of information she could lap up about him.

"Well, Caleb isn't known as The Bastard Payne for no reason," her cousin said.

Troy neared them, deep in conversation with a patron of the arts, and if he had anything to say about it, a patron of Metaxas Limited's future plans.

But not deep enough that he couldn't spare a "Circulate. Circulate," as he walked by.

"Did you hear that?" Ari asked.

"What? The crack of the whip?"

He chuckled. "That would be it." He plucked a champagne flute from the tray of a passing waiter. "Enough fun. Time to do some business."

The problem was, the moment Caleb entered, everything but business was on Bryna's mind. Unless it was monkey business. But there was nothing juvenile about her attraction to Caleb. To the contrary, her thoughts were very, very adult.

"Good evening…Miss Metaxas, isn't it?" Caleb said, standing before her before she'd realized he'd moved across the room.

"Mr. Payne. Nice to see you again." She looked to the woman still on his arm. "Hello. I'm Bryna Metaxas."

The way she lifted her brows was awfully familiar. Bryna realized it was because Caleb did the exact same thing.

"Phoebe Payne. Caleb's mother." She offered her gloved hand and Bryna lightly squeezed her fingers, as was expected at these events. America might not have royalty, much to the chagrin of many in this very room, but they did have a number of wealthy, longstanding families that expected to be treated as such. "A pleasure to meet you."

"Metaxas…that's Greek, isn't it?"

"Yes. I'm third generation Greek-American."

Phoebe sighed. "I adore Greece. I try to get to the islands at least once every couple of years."

Caleb's dark eyes trapped Bryna's. She ordered herself to look everywhere but at him, but found she couldn't escape. Nor did she want to. Reflected in the depths she saw decadent scenes from the last time they were together. Heard her own sighs. Felt his hands on her hips, holding her still as he drove deep into her.

Phoebe Payne cleared her throat. "Caleb, darling, haven't I taught you it's impolite to stare?"

Bryna dropped her gaze, feeling as guilty as if the words had been said to her.

"You're quite right, Mother," he agreed. "But no one ever accused me of being polite."

Phoebe's laugh was low and musical.

"If you'll excuse me," Bryna said, "I've just been ordered to circulate by my overbearing cousin." She nodded her head. "Pleasure to make your acquaintance, Ms. Payne."

Phoebe looked between her and her son, her smile as knowing as any Caleb had ever given her. "I believe the pleasure is all mine, Miss Metaxas."

Rather than homing in on the next target on the list Troy had given her, Bryna headed for the back of the room and the buffet table instead. Why did she suddenly feel as if she'd been put through a head-to-foot MRI? Her pulse was racing, her palms were damp. It seemed she'd completely underestimated her ability to remain detached in public when it came to the sinfully handsome Caleb Payne.

As EXPECTED, Caleb's mother didn't stick with him for long. She had too many friends' cheeks to kiss, too much gossip to share and to hear. They parted ways shortly after he introduced her to Bryna. Which was a good thing, because he was finding it impossible to concentrate on anything other than the snug fit of her scarlet-red dress. It was made of an unforgiving material that would show every flaw unless you had the type of tight body to show off. And Bryna definitely had that body. An hourglass shape that found him taking in the roundness of her breasts, then the fullness of her hips, and back again.

A hand landed on his shoulder. "Looking for a Cissy replacement?" Palmer asked, stepping up next to him and following his gaze.

Caleb frowned and sipped at his champagne even as he looked for a waiter who might bring him something more his style. "Actually, I think I'm going to fly solo for a while." He offered up a grin. "Serial monogamy is taking its toll on me, I think."

"I wouldn't know."

"Of course you wouldn't. You never date the same woman twice."

Palmer looked down at his feet, smiling. "Yes. Something like that."

Caleb began walking and Palmer followed suit.

"You didn't say anything about coming here tonight," Caleb commented.

They'd met at the basketball court over lunch for a sweat-producing one-on-one. "Neither did you."

He chuckled. "No, I guess I didn't. I suppose I've been a little preoccupied lately."

His gaze lingered on Bryna, who was speaking to a matronly woman dripping in pearls. She had her back slightly turned, offering up a tantalizing view of her high, pert bottom, and a smooth length of leg through a side slit.

"And I think I may have just uncovered the cause," Palmer murmured.

Caleb looked at him sharply. "What's that?"

Palmer's eyes opened slightly at the unexpected reaction. "Hey, not my business."

"You're damn right it's not your business."

Palmer shifted him so they were walking in the other direction, his arm across his shoulders so he could speak quietly into his ear.

"I'm just going to say this only once, Caleb. I think it important that you heed it."

His shoulders tightened under Palmer's arm.

"Getting involved with a Metaxas when you have so much riding on Philippidis is not a good idea."

Caleb tried for an amused chuckle. Or at the very least, a smile. Instead, he found himself scowling darkly at his old friend. "My, but you've caught up to speed in a short amount of time."

Palmer stared at him evenly. "Think about how I did that, my friend."

Philippidis.

Caleb recalled Bryna's running into the old man last week.

"That's right. Philippidis suspects something's going on between the two of you. And while I wasn't asked outright to find out what it was, I was discreetly requested to unearth as much information as I could."

Bastard.

They neared the end of the group and stopped, turning to face each other.

"You're not a lover, Caleb. You're a warrior. Remember that. Many men have failed because of a woman. Don't be one of them."

"What the fuck do you know about it?" he asked.

Palmer's gaze dropped. "I know more than you know, buddy. I know more than you...."

14

IT WAS THREE IN THE MORNING, and Caleb had spent the better part of the evening making love to the slumbering woman sprawled naked across his bed in the other room.

Why, then, was he filled with so much restless energy? Why did he still want to go in there and wake her up and start all over again?

Wearing only a pair of drawstring pants, he sat at the piano, the overhead lights turned down to their dimmest setting, his fingers traveling over the keys, one time slowly, then transitioning into a difficult Liszt sonata, and yet again into Chopin. He didn't need sheet music. And didn't play a piece through till the end. He allowed the shadowy, chaotic emotions pulsing within to flow from his fingertips and into the piano.

It had been a good long while since he'd played for more than a few minutes to keep his fingers limber.

Now, eyes closed, his hair fell across his brow and he felt sweat begin to accumulate between his shoulder blades. Like the pieces that he played, snippets of conversations streamed through his mind, nonsensical, little more than gibberish when linked together, but all a part of a whole, a roadmap of sorts leading to a destination foreign to him.

He knew she was there before he saw her.

Caleb opened his eyes. He saw her shadowy reflection in the glass. Like the other night, she was wearing his white dress shirt, the hem hanging to just above her knees, her dark hair a cloud around her sexy face.

He swallowed deeply and continued playing, transitioning into *Moonlight Sonata*.

He felt her hand on his shoulder and tensed, his playing becoming more frenetic.

What was it about this one woman that drove him to distraction? That made him forget about everything but his need to fold himself into her? To claim her mind, body and soul?

He couldn't remember a time when he'd been so moved by another person, much less a woman.

And an alarm of warning sounded deep within him that he didn't want to feel it now.

He abruptly stopped playing and grasped her wrist, pulling her until she lay across his lap, her elbow hitting the keys, filling the room with a discordant din. Surprise rounded her soft mouth, her eyes large in her face.

"I…I thought you never played for anyone?"

Caleb set his jaw, remaining silent as he scanned her face. There was nothing special there. Broken down, her features were fairly normal. But when she smiled, when she spoke, when she called out his name in the heat of climax, she was an object of unbearable beauty.

She lifted a hand to his hair, smoothing it back from his brow. "It's so…haunting."

Haunting.

The word was fitting. For it was as if she was haunting him. Had slid just so under his skin. Always there. Always tempting his senses. Challenging his control.

She leaned forward and kissed him, her lips impossibly sweet.

Caleb kissed her back. Allowing himself a moment without that control he always tried so hard to keep in check.

Before too long, they were both gasping for breath. Bryna repositioned herself so that she straddled him on the bench, the keys she bumped emitting muffled, serene sounds.

She laughed almost silently and then pressed her nose against his, her hands in his hair. "I'm afraid I'm falling in love with you, Mr. Payne," she murmured.

Caleb's heart contracted to the point of pain.

All this was happening too fast. Outside any sort

of timeline he could have envisioned. Beyond any capacity for him to imagine.

He grasped her hips and lifted her to lie on top of the closed piano. Her feet tickled the keys as he held her down with one hand on her stomach. He stood and pushed the hem of his shirt up, spreading her legs, baring her to his hungry gaze.

They'd spent the past four hours in his bed. Surely his appetite for her should have been long since sated.

Yet he wanted her as if for the first time, his balls heavy, his erection so hard it hurt.

Still holding her down, despite her wiggling attempts to free herself, he splayed the fingers of his free hand against the skin just above her womanhood. He swept the pad of his thumb back and forth and then tunneled into her curls, pressing hard against her swollen clit.

She gasped and bucked against his hold, her breathing ragged, her hands reaching for the one that held her still.

"Please," she whispered. "I want to touch you."

He ignored her plea, instead parting her engorged folds with his thumb and finger, taking in the pink portal. His mouth filled with the desire to taste her, to taste them. Instead, he thrust two fingers deep inside her and twisted them around.

She moaned and instantly tried to close her legs, holding him inside her. He released his hold on her stomach and forced her knees back open, thrusting his fingers deep inside her again as she struggled against her own emotions and his touch.

His hard-on throbbed and burned with the need to bury himself inside of her. But he had no condoms on him. They were back in the bedroom where he had left her.

But she had come into the living room, invaded his longing for privacy, for space to put a name to what he was feeling, to find a way to control it.

She tried to sit up and he held her back down. But looking at her in her confused, turned-on state threatened to rip him to shreds.

He could carry her back to the bedroom. But he didn't want to wait that long.

So he pulled her forward, stripped her of his shirt and turned her over so that her bottom was lifted high in the air.

The position allowed him a different perspective. Her tight bottom. Her soft, fleshy womanhood.

He grit his teeth and grabbed her hips, hauling her to the edge of the piano.

This time when his fingers breached her, it wasn't in the place she was expecting. She tightened up on him and cried out. Caleb held himself totally still, leaving his finger where it was until he felt her muscles relax. Slowly he withdrew, moistening the digit with her own juices before returning to forbidden territory.

This time when he entered her, she was ready, her moan low and deep. She remained still, as if not trusting herself to move. Caleb flicked his thumb over the tight nub of her clit and she shivered. He moved his finger slowly in and out, then replaced one finger with two.

Dark desire filled him. A fundamental need to claim her in a way that no man had before. To stamp her in a unique way that would remain with her forever.

He undid the tie on his pants, letting the silky material drop down around his ankles. His member stood in hard relief. He grasped the base of his penis and rubbed the tip of his member along her slick flesh, and then positioned the head against her virginal opening. He gently pushed forward.

Her gasp was part pleasure, part pain as her tight muscles both invited him in and rejected him.

Using every shred of self-control he still possessed, he remained still. So very still. Waiting for her to adjust. For her to open to him. Accept him. Welcome the joining he sought.

Holding her hips still with one hand, he reached round her with the other, slowly stroking her liquid heat. She relaxed almost immediately, opening the way for him to enter her further.

Finally he was in to the hilt.

Jesus…

"Ohhhhh." The sound coming from Bryna's throat was guttural, feral. It reached inside him, grabbing him hard, making his pulse pound, his lungs refuse air. He slowly withdrew and entered her again. She shivered all over, her right hand blindly grasping his hip, holding him in deep.

Her reaction, combined with his heightened sense of arousal, sent him careening over the edge of reason. But rather than hold still, allow the climax free rein, he withdrew again and entered, withdrew again and entered, drawing out his orgasm and causing hers....

LONG AFTER THEY'D RETIRED back to the bedroom, after Caleb had finally drifted off to sleep, Bryna lay curved against him, listening to the sound of his heartbeat. She'd never been made love to so thoroughly. Had never been taken to the heights he'd introduced her to tonight. She felt at one with everything around her...yet oddly apart.

She'd seen a different side of Caleb tonight. A dark, demanding one. She'd glimpsed in his eyes a fierce, deep need that had held her entranced and scared her away all at once.

She understood that he was ruthless in the business arena. But up till now he'd been wonderfully open with her sexually. Tonight she'd realized that the demons that compelled him to succeed at business haunted him on every level.

He'd demanded everything from her. And she'd given it to him.

She was unfamiliar with this Bryna. With the woman who even as she questioned his need to possess her, opened to him nonetheless. He hadn't responded when she'd been compelled to whisper her confession that she believed she might be falling in love with him.

She squeezed her eyes shut. Of course he hadn't. He wasn't a man given to verbal declarations of affection. In fact, she was pretty sure he'd never uttered the words to a woman who wasn't his mother in his life. Or, if he had, he'd been deeply burned as a result.

Too fast…too much…

She bit hard on her bottom lip.

Never had she been swept away so quickly by her emotions. Fallen so hard for a man in such a short time. But she hadn't considered putting on the brakes. It had all been so new. So much fun.

Until now.

Now…

Bryna's heart beat an irregular rhythm in her chest.

Now she was afraid that she wasn't just falling in love with Caleb. But that she already loved him.

And feared that as a result, he wasn't going to welcome her in, draw her closer. He was going to push her away.

The thought was enough to make her feel as if her heart had just cracked into two jagged pieces.

Caleb moved in his sleep. She reluctantly shifted to give him room as he turned away from her.

She lay for long moments, staring at the strong, masculine lines of his back. She longed to snuggle up to him. Hold him for as long as he would allow her.

Instead, she gathered whatever bits of pride she still had left and slipped from the bed.—realizing as she did so that he wasn't asleep at all. Instead, he watched silently as she gathered her clothes and shoes and left the room, deciding to dress in the main bathroom rather than the master. Because she didn't want to have to pass him again. Feel the chest-crushing sensation.

He had withdrawn from her to a place where she'd never be able to reach him again.

15

"OKAY, I'VE BEEN DRONING on for twenty minutes and you haven't heard a single word I've said."

Caleb had been looking at his mother, but now brought her into full focus, his thoughts turned more inside than out.

"I'm enjoying my meal," he said.

He'd reluctantly agreed to meet her for lunch, giving in when she'd played the mother guilt card. "I'm only in town for a couple of days. Lord only knows when we'll see each other again. Speaking of which, when are you going to come back home to the east coast, anyway?"

That question should have told him to do whatever he had to to get out of the lunch date, but she was right. He didn't see her nearly enough. And was it too much to ask to spend an hour of uninterrupted time in her company?

Of course, he'd had no idea when he'd agreed that

his mind would be on other things. More specifically on Bryna.

He rubbed his face with his hands and reached for his water glass.

"So…that Bryna seemed like a nice girl," his mother said.

He nearly choked on the water. He narrowed his gaze, taking in Phoebe's far too smug expression. "Interesting that you should remember her name."

She neatly folded a bit of spinach salad onto her fork and placed it in her mouth, chewing thoughtfully. "I told you that when the time came, I'd remember the girl's name."

Caleb grimaced. "I'm not dating her, Mother."

"No? Oh. Well, I must have it completely wrong, then."

Of course, she didn't believe that. And he wasn't even going to attempt to convince her differently. To do so would only make her dig her heels in deeper.

"And your Mr. or Ms. Right?" he asked. "Was he or she in attendance last night?"

"Oh, heavens, no. Do you think I'd risk someone figuring anything out?"

"You mean like me?"

She smiled sweetly. "Exactly like you."

He pretended an interest in his fish, but the image of Bryna quietly gathering her things in his bedroom last night and leaving the penthouse burned into the back of his eyelids. Every time he blinked, there it was, taunting him, warning him, daring him to do something about the guilt he felt. The remorse that he'd hurt her.

Oh, not physically. Although what he'd done had played a role in establishing the distance he needed to put between the two of them. No. He'd shut himself off from her emotionally. Turning away when she might have snuggled against him. Rolling off as soon as he climaxed instead of lying still for long moments, reveling in the delicious sensations she brought him.

Without saying a word, he'd pounded a wedge between them that she'd at first been surprised by, then hurt.

And, shockingly, her being hurt had hurt him.

"So how do you two know each other?" his mother asked.

Caleb let his fork clatter to his plate and picked up the napkin in his lap. "I'm not seeing Bryna Metaxas, Mother. Leave it be."

"Mmm. That's why your face is so long. You didn't really think I wouldn't see it, did you? The whole room saw it, Caleb. You couldn't keep your eyes off her. And the same applied to her. You could virtually see the electricity that arced between the two of you."

He mutilated a bread roll with quick, irritated jerks.

"If you're not seeing her now, then you should be."

He quirked a sarcastic brow. "Oh? Suddenly you want grandchildren?"

She drew back as if his words had hit her like a blow.

Caleb immediately regretted the remark. There was no need to bring up the statement she'd made ten or so years ago about not wanting to be a grandmother. He hadn't paid much attention to it at the time. Had even put it down to her struggling with the date on the calendar, a showdown with her own mortality. He'd never truly thought she'd meant it.

Funny how he must have filed the throwaway comment away for use in this one moment.

"In fact," she said carefully, "I was thinking how nice it would be to have one or two grandchildren running around that I could spoil."

He stared at her.

She laughed. "I know. I told you that lately it's as if I don't know myself." She shook her head. "Five years ago I would have been horrified by the thought of you having children. Now…"

Caleb buttered one of the bread pieces. "Now…" he repeated.

"I think children would do you good. As well as me."

"And you've come to this conclusion how?"

She twisted her lips. "Sometimes…I don't know, Caleb. It seems as if we're both stuck in some sort of time warp. The image in the mirror changes, but it's a bit like Dorian Gray in that we don't. We go on as if we're going to be young and strong forever."

"So you want grandchildren for legacy reasons."

"No, no." She sighed and tapped her manicured nails against her wineglass before taking a sip. "I guess what I'm trying to say is that a change will do us both good."

Caleb chewed on his roll.

"I've been doing a lot of thinking lately, you know, since the doctor found that cyst on my breast."

He stopped chewing.

"No, no. Nothing like that. Some delayed menopausal reaction that should pass in a month or two. Nothing to worry about. At any rate, I'm being monitored."

He managed to swallow with help from his water.

He remembered his mother saying something about running into some minor health problem a month or so ago, but had no idea it had been a cyst or that it had been on her breast. He'd automatically assumed that it was something aesthetic, an unwanted mole on her arm or something of that nature.

He'd never sat down and considered that there would come a day in the distant or not too distant future that she wouldn't be there for him anymore.

And then he would be completely, utterly alone.

"Anyway, I've been thinking that maybe, all those years ago, I should have listened to my father. That I should have kept the identity of your father to myself. Married that man he tried to match me with and pass you off as his…"

Caleb gave up any pretense of eating altogether.

His mother had always been so strong, so adamant in her stance that the truth was always best. It was a moral code he'd learned early on, so when he was the bastard that he'd been called all his life, the other party couldn't say they weren't warned in advance.

"I don't know," she continued. "I just think that by naming your father publicly, and having him deny it, I placed us both in some sort of social limbo, as if both of us are waiting for something to happen that never will."

Caleb's gaze dropped to the table.

"I know we've talked about the possibility of obtaining a court-ordered DNA test to prove, once and for all, that Theodore Winstead was your biological father, but…" She folded her hands and worried her thumbs together. "What good would it do, really? We both know the truth. Does it really matter what the rest of the world thinks? In the end, does it really make any difference at all?"

Since the prospect of proving paternity had only to do with making his father's family publicly acknowledge his existence, he was surprised by his mother's thoughts.

"And even if we do ultimately decide to proceed… what will change? Will anyone look at either one of us any differently? Would doors that had been closed suddenly open?"

"You and I have never had a problem with closed doors."

She smiled. "No, we haven't, have we? We merely

forced them open." She reached for his hand where it rested next to his water glass. "Which is why I think we should just put this whole thing to bed. Now. Once and for all."

Caleb squinted at her. Whoever this man was she had met, he'd inspired changes in his mother that could never have come about through mere conversation.

He considered telling her about his legal attempts to force a DNA test and proof of paternity, but decided against it. Seeing the fresh light in her eyes, he thought the idea of putting the entire episode to bed, as she'd put it, was increasingly appealing.

"For the first time in my life," she said, "I want to move on. I wanted to forget about that chapter and start writing a new one from scratch."

"You want to forget about me?"

"No!"

Caleb grinned. "It was an attempt at a joke, Mother. I understand."

And, surprisingly, he did.

He'd lived for so long with the shadow of his dead, undeclared father eclipsing his own that he didn't know what it was like to take a breath without it there.

His mother squeezed his hand. "Give it some thought. If you'd like to proceed...of course we will."

A sharp pang sliced through his gut as he looked at her.

How much had she sacrificed for him? She'd borne a child on her own. A child his married father wouldn't publicly attest to. Had turned away suitors when he so much as opened his mouth. Had lived her life trying to heal the pain of his wounds, never considering her own.

She'd hurt when he'd hurt.

And now she didn't want to hurt anymore.

Could he take that away from her?

She began to withdraw her hand, but he held on to it. She blinked, her blue eyes questioning.

"Shall we hold a burial ceremony, I wonder?" he asked.

She held his gaze for a long moment, dampness making her eyes look extra bright.

"I think we just did, baby. I think we just did."

BRYNA SAT IN A CHAIR next to Caleb's secretary's desk clutching her briefcase tightly in both hands. After last night...

She forced air through her tight throat.

After last night she'd feared that Caleb would cancel his business appointment with her. Find some way out of it. Send her proposal back via courier with a terse note that would finish their business as well as personal ties.

He hadn't. But she wasn't altogether convinced that was a good thing....

She swallowed hard, feeling much as she had that first day almost two weeks ago when she'd gathered the courage to make an appointment with him using her real name. She'd been surprised he'd taken it... and then waited a half hour after the time they were to meet only to be told that he wasn't interested in reviewing any ideas from her.

Then she'd changed his mind.

Where just yesterday she might have looked back fondly on the moment, now she knew only fear.

Fear of what she'd see in his eyes when she gazed at him.

Fear of what she might say to erase the look.

Fear of what she might do to coax the one she wanted back.

The secretary picked up the telephone extension and then quietly put it back down.

"He'll see you now, Miss Metaxas."

Bryna got to her feet, feeling as if her knees were suddenly as substantial as the marmalade she'd tried to choke down along with toast for breakfast. She offered up her thanks and a weak smile to the secretary and then crossed to the door, switching her briefcase from her right to her left hand and turning the knob.

He stood at the windows, his back to her.

She knew relief.

"Thank you for not canceling," she said, her voice sounding far more confident than she felt.

She moved to the table and opened her briefcase, pulling out the sheath of papers and the pad she'd brought along.

She heard him turn from the window, but ordered herself not to look up. Not to gaze into his face.

"I'm sorry," he said, his voice so cold that the hair on her arms stood on end. "But I'm going to have to put an end to this now...."

16

BRYNA FELT AS IF the bottom had been cut out of her stomach.

She straightened, fastened a smile to her mouth, then turned to face Caleb.

"I'm sorry?" she said.

He didn't move. Didn't say anything. Merely stood looking at her as if she were an adversary, and not an equal one at that.

She was reminded again of their first meeting. Except then she'd glimpsed attraction in his eyes, sexual challenge. Now…now she saw nothing but distance.

"This proposal isn't viable," he said.

Bryna crossed her arms, searching wildly within for the weapon she needed to pierce his armor. "In which way?"

"In every way."

What did he expect her to do? Turn tail and run?

She felt her spine strengthen. Well, then, he was in for a big disappointment.

"You're going to have to do better than that. I want details."

Was that a quirk of a brow? An upward twitch of the left side of his mouth?

He slowly walked past her. For a moment, she was afraid he was going to go to the door and open it, showing her the way out. She held her breath, battling against the tears that stung the back of her eyes.

Instead, he took something off his desktop and walked to the table, placing the sheath of papers next to hers. He was so near, she could smell the scent of his lime aftershave. It was all she could do not to breath it in, revel in the intimate scent, because she didn't know if she ever would again.

"First, the numbers don't add up," he said, pointing to a column.

Bryna squinted at him. Was he really talking details?

"So…when you said the proposal wasn't viable, you meant as is," she said carefully. "Which means you're willing to hammer out something together."

This close, she could make out the golden specks in his rich brown eyes. "Are you going to focus on what I'm saying?"

"Oh, I'm hearing every word you're saying. Even the silent words in between those words."

He drew up again.

She couldn't help noticing that he appeared to be

steeling himself as much as she was attempting to do against him.

Which was odd. Why would he want to do that?

She forced her gaze away from his, instead pulling a chair out and taking a seat at the table. She pushed her papers aside and pulled his forward, considering the columns he'd pointed to.

"The numbers don't work because you were looking at the wrong numbers," she said simply.

She gave him back his papers and riffled through her own.

"If you take a look here, the end result makes perfect sense."

He didn't move for a long moment. She looked over her shoulder to find his gaze on the back of her neck, left bare by her upswept style. She shivered for an altogether different reason than a few moments ago. His expression was one of those that made her seek out and identify every flat surface in the room. Anything they could use to indulge the incredible attraction that existed between them.

He met her gaze and she saw the same confusion and sizzling chaos that had been there since the beginning.

Finally, he cleared his throat and took a chair a couple up from hers.

Bryna was disappointed by his obvious attempt at physical as well as emotional distance but was determined not to show it. She was here for business. To save Metaxas Limited. To save Earnest.

The rest…well, the rest would have to wait.

He reviewed her papers. "I see what you mean."

They went back and forth, with Bryna presenting him with the counterarguments she had prepared, and Caleb not giving an inch in any point.

The intercom buzzed.

Bryna looked at her watch, surprised that over an hour had passed as Caleb rose to pick up the extension on his desk.

"Yes…I see. Thank you."

They were nowhere near a compromise, the spot that would allow him to take the proposal and approach potential investors on behalf of Metaxas Limited. But Bryna got the distinct impression that the meeting was over.

"My one o'clock is here," he said simply.

Bryna nodded, swallowing past the lump in her throat as she separated her files from his.

"But he can wait."

She jerked to look up at him.

He sighed and walked away from her, then stopped and leaned against a wingback chair. He crossed his arms.

"You have a good proposal here, Bryna…but I'm not sure it's something I can proceed with."

"And the reason for that…"

He ran his hand over his face, surprising her with the exasperated move. "There are many…but the top one is that Metaxas doesn't have enough invested in the proposal."

She got to her feet and faced him, leaning her arm against the back of the table chair. "We have over a year invested in the project. Thirty people contracted and on the payroll working nonstop to make this thing happen."

"I'm talking financially."

"What? Like a monetary investment beyond what I've already proven?"

He nodded. "I don't have to tell you that this is a hard economic environment. You couldn't sell a glass of water to a man crossing the desert." He slid one of his hands into the pocket of his slacks. "Any potential investors will want to know that your company stands to lose as much as they will."

She frowned.

"It's the only thing that will prove that Metaxas Limited is in this for the long haul, not just looking for capital on an iffy venture that may not come to fruition, leaving the investor out and Metaxas Limited untouched financially."

"We have a great deal invested in this project."

"But do you have cash resources?"

"If we had cash resources, we wouldn't need to find a partner."

"But without an even investment, no one's going to sign on, Bryna. Not in this tough environment."

He walked to the table and gathered his own files, stacking them up neatly and moving them to the top of his desk.

"Until you can come up with solid resources

outside that which you've already shown me, I'm afraid there's nowhere for us to go from here."

"Define solid."

"A good seven figures."

"That's outrageous! If we had access to that kind of cash—"

He raised a hand. "You asked."

A sense of doom settled into the pit of her bottomless stomach. She methodically slid her materials into her briefcase.

What scared her even more was the possibility that if she walked out that door without the promise of future discussions, she might never see him again.

"What if I were to come up with those resources?" she asked suddenly.

He narrowed his eyes. "I think it's time you let your cousins in on what you're doing, Bryna."

"I asked you a question."

"Are you talking personally?"

"I'm talking resources. Who cares where they come from?"

He opened his mouth, then closed it again. She suspected he was about to say, "I care." Then changed his mind.

She mentally calculated what she had in her personal accounts. Outside of paying for her small apartment in a quaint section of Seattle, she'd barely touched her inheritance. That combined with the many investments she'd made and savings from her salary, could easily amount to...

"How about mid-six figures," she asked. "Would that be enough to move forward?"

He didn't say anything for a long moment. Merely stood considering her.

She wished she could climb into his head. See the thoughts there. Know what he was thinking. More, learn what he was feeling.

"It would be a start."

"I asked if it's enough to move forward. For you to begin approaching potential investors? To put this deal together? To make it happen?"

The silence of the room seemed to emphasize the hard thud of her heartbeat.

"Yes," he said.

Bryna felt a relief so complete she nearly sat back down in the chair.

Instead, she finished packing her briefcase, snapped it closed and then strode toward the door.

"I'll have the funds together by the end of the working day."

"Bryna?"

She didn't respond. She merely continued out the door and then down the hall, not stopping until she reached the elevators. It was only when the doors whooshed shut that she finally allowed herself to exhale.

And began to hope that this was going to work out...

LATER THAT DAY, Bryna let herself into her apartment, all too aware of its silence. At the Metaxas estate in Earnest, there was always some sort of sound coming from inside the house. Whether it was the housekeeper sweeping one of the rooms, Ari getting something to eat in the kitchen, Troy talking on the phone in his home office, there was always movement, activity.

She found it ironic that while she had purchased the Seattle apartment for peace, now she wanted anything but.

She dropped her briefcase onto the hall table and then took her pumps off one by one, leaving them where they lay against the creamy beige marble tile. She switched on lights as she went, checked the automatic thermostat and then turned on the television, immediately soothed by the sound of a local anchor reporting the news.

After putting on the single-cup coffeemaker to brew in the kitchen, she went into the living room and collapsed onto the overstuffed couch covered with pale green vines and roses, tucking her feet under her even as she shrugged out of her suit jacket.

It was done.

As promised, she'd had her bank put her assets together and managed to squeeze out the amount promised to Caleb. A couple of phone calls later and the resources were deposited into a holding account, and Caleb had guaranteed that he'd have some news—good or bad remained to be seen—for her by next week.

Bryna sighed and leaned her head against her

hand. A tendril of hair had escaped her bun. She reached back and pulled out the pins, her scalp tingling as her hair dropped around her shoulders.

She wasn't sure what was bothering her. She'd accomplished what she'd set out to do—Caleb had agreed to actively solicit an investor in Metaxas Limited's plans. She should be celebrating.

Instead, she felt like doing anything but.

She sighed again and then pushed herself up from the sofa.

"Oh, stop it already. You knew the guy wasn't forever material. So what if he was the best you ever had?" She stomped in her bare feet toward the kitchen and the cup of coffee that waited there, the aroma filling the two-bedroom apartment. "At least you got it. You should be thanking the gods for at least that much."

The problem was how did you go forward knowing that the best you would ever achieve lay in your past?

She added a dollop of cream to the coffee, wrinkled her nose at the sip she took and then added a teaspoon and then another of sugar.

The buzz announcing that someone wanted building access at the front door sounded. She nearly spilled the hot liquid as she was taking another testing sip.

Caleb…

Her heart skipped a beat. She put the cup down and hurried to the hall to press the intercom button.

"Yes?" she said.

"Bryna?"

Ari.

She collapsed against the wall, not realizing how much she'd wanted it to be Caleb until she'd discovered it wasn't him.

17

"Is that any way to welcome your long-lost cousin?" Ari asked, entering her apartment as she held the door open.

"You're neither long nor lost, whatever that means," she said as she closed the door, but not until after a quick peek into the hall. She wasn't sure what she'd hoped to find. Caleb hiding in the shadows, perhaps?

The thought actually made her shudder. Especially in light of the other night and the liberties he'd requested…and that she'd offered up without objection.

"What are you doing in Seattle?" she asked Ari, following him into the kitchen.

He put down the bags he held on the counter and took a sip from her coffee cup. "Damn. How can you drink this stuff?"

"It's easy. I put my lips to the cup and swallow."

He dumped the contents down the drain, much to her despair.

"Hey! I was drinking that."

He opened one of the bags and took out a blue disposable cup with a Greek key design lining the rim. "Try this."

She moved to get the cream from the refrigerator and he blocked her.

"As is first. Then you can alter it…if you still want to."

Bryna popped off the top, sniffed the liquid and then took a slow sip. Okay, so it was good. And it didn't need a single thing added. In fact, cream or sugar would probably mask its deep, rich taste, which would be a shame.

Ari was grinning. "Good, huh?"

Bryna stepped to the counter and peered into the other bags he'd brought. "What else you got?"

He moved them out of range. "Nope. This is not how this works." He grasped her shoulders and steered her toward the butcher-block kitchen table. "You sit. I serve."

Bryna obeyed, if only because she didn't have the energy just then to fight him. Not that it would do her any good, anyway. Ari somehow always got what he wanted.

She sat in a kitchen chair, bending one of her feet under her, and watched as her cousin took two plates from the cupboard. Then he carefully positioned himself so that he blocked her view, keeping her from seeing what he was doing. He took another plate out, and then finally turned and put all three on the table.

"Voilà!" he said.

Bryna looked down at the dishes filled with Greek delicacies, from *dolmades*—stuffed grape leaves—and tzatziki to moussaka and grilled octopus. Just smelling the aromas wafting off the plates was enough to make her mouth water.

She held her hand palm up.

"What?" Ari asked.

"Fork?"

"Oh!" He took two forks from a drawer and then joined her at the table. "Dig in. Every last thing here is as great as it looks."

Bryna did exactly that, humming her approval as she went.

Despite the Metaxas family being Greek-American, it was rare that they actually dined on traditional Greek food. As the octopus melted against her tongue, she wondered why exactly that was. Her mother had always kept a Greek kitchen. And she understood that her aunt, Ari's mother, had, too.

Why, then, was it rare that Greek food was served at home? And when was the last time she'd actually cooked anything remotely Greek?

She frowned. She was having a hard time remembering when she'd actually cooked, period.

Before she knew it, she'd devoured everything on the plates, with a little help from Ari. She hadn't even realized she was hungry. Now she felt stuffed beyond comfort.

"Where'd you get this?" she asked. "Is there a new Greek restaurant here in town I don't know about?"

Ari sat back and grinned that knowing grin of his.

Oh, God.

Bryna made a face. "Elena made this."

"Yep. She's trying out family recipes, testing what she wants to offer on the menu when she opens the restaurant for dinner next week."

Bryna collected the plates, ran them under the faucet and then loaded them into the dishwasher. "She has a Greek place?"

"No. A general restaurant. That's why she needs to pick and choose what Greek dishes she can offer alongside the typical American fare."

"Shame. She should open a Greek place. Everything was delicious."

The compliment wasn't difficult to offer up. The food was great. No matter who had made it.

Ari sat back in his chair. "Don't put any ideas into her head. I'm having a difficult time as it is trying to convince her that she doesn't need to be working so hard. Especially right now."

Bryna poured the cup of coffee he'd brought into two mugs and handed him one. "I thought the restaurant was already open."

"It is. She started with breakfast. And now offers

lunch. But things are going so well, she'd like to open for dinner next week."

She leaned against the counter. "That should put a crimp in your love life."

Ari's long-suffering sigh made her smile. "Tell me about it."

She tapped her fingernails against the cup. "So what happens to this place if she buys the Quality Diner in Earnest?"

He got to his feet and budged her over. She hadn't realized he'd left anything on the counter. "Her mother has been working with her since she reopened and her brother has recently come in. They all worked at the restaurant before when her father ran it, so it's my guess she'll be leaving the restaurant to them, so to speak."

"So the place isn't hers?"

"Technically, no. Her mother inherited it."

Bryna nodded.

"Now for dessert," he said, holding out a plate.

Her groan filled the entire apartment. She didn't think she could possibly swallow another bite of anything...until she got a gander of what the plate held.

"Oh, God! I don't know how long it's been since I've had *sokolatina!*" She eyed the generous piece of chocolate torte. "And baklava!"

She forked a bite of each into her mouth one after another while Ari looked on in amusement.

"Buy...her...that...diner...now!" she told him.

Ari's smile slipped.

"Well, that's the problem."

Bryna didn't respond right away. She was too busy pigging out on the sweets.

Eventually she asked, "But I thought she was interested in buying The Quality."

"She is. With the emphasis on *she*."

Bryna's chewing slowed. "I don't understand."

"I don't either. But there you have it. She wants to be the one to buy the diner. Not me."

Finally Bryna's stomach refused to accept another bite.

How long had it been since she'd eaten that much? God, even her skirt suddenly felt tight.

She sighed, staring longingly at the half-eaten contents of the plate. Then she forced herself to put the plate down, cheering herself up with the fact that it would still be there for her later.

Ari picked up her fork and made to take a bite.

"Touch that, lose a limb." She took the fork out of his hand and put it in the sink and then moved to put the plate in the refrigerator, out of reach.

His chuckle warmed the room at the same time as the buzzer rang for the second time that night.

Ari raised a brow. "Expecting company?"

It took Bryna a moment to force air through the tight passage of her throat. "No," she fairly croaked.

"Well, expected or not, it looks like you've got some."

He began walking toward the door.

"Thanks so much for coming by," she said, wishing there were an easier way to do this. Hand him his coat, his hat, something, anything other than practically snatching the coffee cup from his hands and shoving him through the door.

"Okay. So you might not be expecting company, but I'm getting the impression that you were hoping for it."

Bryna glared at him as the buzzer rang again.

"Thanks for dinner, Ari." She kissed him on the cheek and reached around him to push the buzzer even as she opened the door and shoved him out. "I'll see you at home on Sunday."

"Fine. I can take a hint. But you do realize that I'm going to see who this mystery visitor is, don't you? I think I just might have to introduce myself to him."

Bryna's lungs froze as the man in question appeared in the hall behind her cousin.

"No need," Caleb said. "We've already met...."

_18_

IT WAS OBVIOUS that Caleb hadn't expected to run into Ari at her place. Just as obvious was that he didn't care what his one-time adversary thought. But Bryna did.

She'd always known that there would be problems if her cousins discovered she was seeing Manolis Philippidis's right-hand man. But it was a worry that had vanished earlier that day when she'd stood face-to-face with Caleb in his office and realized that whatever they had shared for so brief a time was over.

Or so she'd thought.

Ari stood staring at the other man, his face frozen in surprise.

"Ari," Caleb said quietly, extending his hand.

Her cousin glanced at him, his outstretched hand, and then at Bryna, obviously trying to piece everything together.

"Come on in, Caleb," Bryna said, her heart beating an erratic rhythm in her chest. A condition caused as much by Caleb's appearance as Ari's accidental discovery.

She quickly kissed her cousin on the cheek. "Talk to you later, Ari. Good night."

And just like that, Caleb was inside the apartment and the door was closed on her cousin, Caleb's hand left untouched.

For long moments they stood silently. She heard Ari's quiet curses as he finally started to descend the stairs.

Caleb cleared his throat as Bryna leaned against the door and closed her eyes.

Please just let him leave in peace, she prayed.

"I hope I didn't cause any problems," Caleb said.

The buzzer sounded and she jumped, her nerves raw.

She bit her bottom lip and then pressed the intercom button. "What do you want, Ari?"

"I want to know what he's doing here."

She took a deep breath. "I don't think this is the time to have this discussion."

Silence. She let go of the button.

The buzzer sounded again.

"Good night, Ari," she said insistently.

"Bryn…if you need anything…"

She turned so that Caleb couldn't see her face, touched by the concern in her cousin's voice, no matter how irritating he was being at that particular moment. "I know where to find you," she whispered. "Drive carefully."

She didn't realize she was still holding the button until Caleb cleared his throat again.

She rubbed her palm against her skirt and turned to face a man she had hoped to see again, but never expected to see in her apartment. Every bite she'd eaten a short time ago sat in her stomach like a pile of pebbles. She searched his face, but was unable to discern what he might be thinking. His demeanor differed very little from what she'd encountered in his office earlier...yet here he was. Standing in her apartment.

She squinted at him. "What are you doing here, Caleb?"

WHAT WAS HE DOING THERE, indeed. Now, that was a good question.

The last place he'd expected to find himself tonight was at Bryna's place. He usually made it a point to keep the ball in his court, in his penthouse, everything going by his rules.

Now...

He looked around the small but smart apartment that undoubtedly had a great view of the city when the curtains were open. Unlike his place, this one spoke of comfort and accessibility. Yes, there was a stereo and a television, but neither was the focus like they were at his home. Instead, two couches and two chairs were positioned around a large, rustic communal coffee table filled with flowers. Floor-to-ceiling bookcases were stuffed with titles ranging from the classics to nonfiction. Magazines and newspapers were stacked on the floor next to one of the couches. Plants were everywhere, as were photographs, both black-and-white prints and color, framed and covering every available surface, faces smiling into the camera lens. There didn't seem to be space for one more thing, yet everything appeared perfectly in place.

Except for him.

He looked back at Bryna, who was still waiting for him to answer.

Her blouse was wrinkled, her feet bare, her hair tousled. And she couldn't have looked more beautiful if she'd tried.

"I don't know," he found himself answering honestly.

With anyone else, he might have offered up an excuse. Perhaps even turned the question on the occupant, inferring from the inquiry that he wasn't welcome in order to elicit a guilt-ridden response. But they'd moved beyond that, hadn't they? Well beyond that.

But since this territory was uncharted for him, he didn't know on what part of the map he stood, much less where he should go from there.

All he knew was that he wanted to kiss her with an intensity that made his groin ache.

He drew closer to her. She moved back, her eyes wide in her face.

"I don't—"

He trapped her objection between his mouth and hers. A silent groan surged upward in his throat. She tasted of honey and coffee and something one hundred percent pure Bryna.

Caleb didn't know what it was about this one woman that brought him to his knees where others had failed. She was smart. She was sexy as hell. But she was as different from him as sunshine was to rain.

Why, then, couldn't he stop thinking about her? Stop wanting her? No matter how many times he kissed her. How many times they had sex. He wanted more. And even more after that.

His hands roamed freely over her hot body even as he pressed himself against her soft belly. The wall supported her from behind as she plunged her fingers into his hair and kissed him back with the same passion that filled him.

Strangely, even now he felt conflicted. He wanted to take her right then, right there. But rather than finding relief in the overpowering emotion, he instead felt…almost rueful somehow.

He thrust his hand between her knees, marveling at the softness of her skin even as he budged her skirt upward. She automatically spread her thighs, gasping as his fingertips met with the damp crotch of her panties.

She was always ready for him. No matter when he reached for her, she was there, waiting. No matter what storm raged, inside or out, she clutched him as tightly as he held her.

Christ, she felt so good. Stroking her like this, hearing her soft sounds, he wanted for nothing else in the world.

Yet he wanted for everything.

With a quick yank, he tore her panties off. When it appeared she might object, he slid two fingers down the dripping channel created by her swollen flesh, quickly entering her, not stopping until her slick muscles trembled around him.

He kissed her deeply again, his breathing hard, his heart beating even harder. Damn it, he wanted to possess her. To bring her to her knees the same way she had so effortlessly done to him. He undid the catch on his slacks and reached in for his throbbing erection. There was no time for condom searching. He wanted her now. And he needed to know that she needed him the same way.

He grasped her hips and lifted her until her calves went around his thighs. Then he entered her in one long stroke, not stopping until he was in to the hilt.

Bryna's nails bit into his shoulders through his jacket and shirt, her eyes hooded, her mouth open in a silent *oh*. He thrust again, reaching for an even deeper meeting. Then again, one hand supporting her peach-shaped ass from behind, the other braced against the wall.

Her tight muscles convulsed around him.

Caleb set his back teeth, determined not to follow. He wanted this to last. Wanted to extend the moment for as long as he could. Because it was only in moments like these, when he was joined with her, that he felt whole. That he felt normal. Like the world made sense in some sort of inexplicable way.

His hips bucked forward and he groaned, his body issuing urgent orders all its own....

BRYNA'S HEART POUNDED so hard she was afraid it might break through the wall of her chest. Chaotic emotions raged through her. When she was in Caleb's arms, felt him inside her, it was easy to forget the rest. But now...now the reality of their situation hit her full force, crowding out everything but confusion and pain.

She slowly slid to stand on her feet and splayed her hands against his chest. She ordered herself to push him away, but instead reveled in the feel of the wall of muscle beneath his shirt, the sound of his ragged breathing filling her ear where his face was still buried in her hair.

Finally she gathered her wits about her and forced him away.

Caleb looked everywhere but into her face as he tucked his still-hard penis back into his slacks and refastened them.

"I...don't understand...." she whispered, feeling ridiculously close to tears.

He still didn't look at her. "I'm sorry. I didn't mean for that to happen."

She bit hard on her bottom lip. "What?" The word came out barely audible. "Are you really apologizing for…"

For what? Having sex with her? Because it hadn't been making love. Caleb had made it very clear that he held no emotion for her whatsoever beyond human need.

He finally met her gaze. She caught her breath. Or did he feel more than he was willing to admit?

She raised her hand as if to ward him off. "Whatever…this…is, Caleb. I don't want it."

He remained silent, watching her.

She swallowed hard against the emotion threatening to choke her. "What we met…it was a mutual thing. Attraction. I wanted you. You wanted me. Simple enough…"

She slid out from between him and the wall and stepped into the living room, putting much needed space between him and her.

"At least that's how it started.…"

His eyes hardened and she stared at him.

"But somewhere down the line…well, it grew into more for me." Her voice cracked on the last word. "I think…no, I know I began falling in love with you.…"

He looked away. She stormed forward.

"Don't you dare pretend like you don't hear me." The floor was cold beneath her feet.

"Don't act like you don't know. I know you know. Because you were feeling the same thing...."

And she did know that. Her knee-jerk reaction to his coldness had blocked out her own sense of the situation, of what had been developing between the two of them, but now...now she understood he felt more, far more, for her than he was letting on.

"Look...I'm guessing there's a good reason why you won't...can't open yourself up to me." A single tear rolled hotly down her cheek. "But this...what just happened...what occurred the other night...it stops here."

She steeled herself. Not against him. But against herself.

"I can't deal with what I'm feeling and your hang-ups at the same time."

They stood staring at each other for what seemed like an eternity. Bryna felt incapable of breathing. Incapable of moving.

Finally he dropped his gaze and nodded.

Bryna knew a pinprick of anticipation.

"I understand," he said simply. When he lifted his head again, the coldness was back in his eyes. "But you're wrong. I don't love you, Bryna."

The pinprick of optimism morphed into a stab in the heart.

"I don't know what love is."

Then he turned and let himself out of the apartment, quietly closing the door and any hope for the future behind him....

19

THE FOLLOWING NIGHT Caleb stood in front of his penthouse window watching rain stream down the smooth glass like liquid beads. The past day had passed in a blur of meetings and phone calls…and he was having a hard time recalling exactly what had been said.

"Sir?"

He turned toward Lionel, his houseman.

"I've put the remainder of your dinner in the refrigerator should you wish to finish it later."

He nodded, thankful for Lionel's unwavering discretion. In truth, he hadn't eaten a bite of the meal. "Thank you. That will be all."

"Very good, sir. Good evening."

"Good evening."

He barely heard the other man make preparations to leave the penthouse for the night and return to his own apartment on a lower floor. He'd already turned back toward the windows, his mind virtually paralyzed, his body strangely numb.

He thought about calling one of the many names of friendly females in what amounted to his little black book. Preferably someone who would take his mind off Bryna, but wouldn't want anything beyond tonight.

A booty call.

He smiled slightly at the reference, a moment that was gone as quickly as it appeared.

He slid his hands into his pockets. No music played. No drink waited. He had no plans. And he couldn't seem to bring himself to change one thing. It was as if a switch had been toggled, holding him in place. Forcing him to look at something he was missing.

But he saw nothing.

Finally he turned away from the window and went to the foyer closet, taking his coat out. He considered calling his driver James to take him somewhere. But he didn't know where he'd go. Instead, he shrugged into his overcoat, bypassed an umbrella and took the elevator down to the lobby, barely acknowledging the front doorman as he hurried to open the door for him.

He stopped in the middle of the sidewalk, closed his eyes and tilted his face up toward the sky. Raindrops, cool and steady, fell down his skin. For a moment, one sweet moment, he was offered relief from his thoughts and he grabbed at it, only to lose it the instant he did.

"Mr. Payne?"

He didn't acknowledge the doorman.

"Is everything all right, sir?"

Caleb took a deep breath, opened his eyes and glanced in his general direction. "Fine. Everything's fine."

He began walking. He wasn't sure where. He just didn't want to be interrupted again.

Seattle's streets were dark and oily, lights reflecting off the wet surfaces. Within five minutes, he was soaked to the bone, but he couldn't bring himself to care.

Imprinted on his mind was the image of Bryna's face the last time he'd seen her. The tortured expression she'd worn.

Anger he could deal with. And was usually what he encountered when a relationship reached its natural conclusion. But he'd never gotten such sadness.

He smoothed his wet hair back from his forehead several times. What had he been thinking when he'd taken her into his bed? When he'd wrongly assumed that Bryna Metaxas could be an intriguing diversion between more suitable dates?

He'd never meant to hurt her.

He winced.

What was he saying? He'd never cared one iota if he'd hurt anyone before. Why the guilty conscience now?

She was so young. More than chronologically. While she was as smart as anyone he'd come across, he had at least a decade's life experience on her.

And that was it, wasn't it? She'd mistaken great sex for love.

An honest mistake, to be sure. Because the sex had been phenomenal. In fact, he couldn't remember a time when he'd enjoyed a woman's body more. But sex was just sex. It wasn't a relationship.

His jaw tensed. If that's what he believed, then why in the hell was he out walking in the goddamn rain on a Friday night by himself with no destination in mind?

BY LATE SATURDAY AFTERNOON, Bryna was concerned her family was on the verge of staging an intervention. In a part of her brain that still worked, she figured she wouldn't blame them if they did. After Caleb had left her Thursday, she'd paced her apartment for a couple of hours and then finally locked the place up and headed to Earnest and home, where she'd promptly shut herself into her bedroom and hadn't ventured out since.

Ari, Troy and her uncle had all made appearances at the door, with Ari even making it as far as the bed.

She lay under those same covers now, blocking out the early-evening sunlight that burst through the clouds, slanting in her windows. She sniffed. Then sniffed again. Then quickly folded the covers back.

She needed a shower something terrible. But she couldn't bring herself to leave the bed for more than the necessary runs to her connected bathroom.

She wasn't physically ill. At least not with anything that a doctor could help her with. No, no antibiotic or medication could help her with what she was suffering through. Not unless they'd discovered a magical elixir that would help heal her broken heart.

She eyed the untouched food tray on her bedside table. She couldn't remember anyone bringing it, but like clockwork, one was delivered three times a day. Ari? Likely. She couldn't imagine Troy doing it. Then again, the men in her life seemed to be surprising her a lot lately.

Especially Caleb.

The problem was that Caleb wasn't really in her life, was he? Had never been. To him, she'd been nothing more interesting than an amusement park ride he could leave behind when he became bored in search of the next one.

She grimaced. Now, there was analogy for you. She was a roller coaster. Or at the very least, she felt like she was riding one. And had just come to the end without hope of ever mounting it again.

Mounting it. Ugh.

From out of the blue, a sob rose in her throat and again she was crying.

Okay, even she was getting tired of this. So he'd hurt her. She'd known the dangers going in. A man like Caleb Payne wasn't one to be thrown by simple emotion. And, after all, he had that "love 'em and leave 'em" reputation to live up to. Plus his name.

Payne. Pain.

It couldn't have been clearer had it been tattooed across his handsome forehead.

But that didn't make it any easier to take.

She reached for the box of tissues next to her bed only to find it empty. She looked around for a semi-used one, only to find them littering the floor on either side of her bed. She stared at the linen napkin on the food tray and pulled it out from under the silverware, loudly blowing her nose into the starchy fabric.

She needed to go on a tissue run.

Stripping back the covers, she padded barefoot to the bathroom. Even the toilet paper roll was empty. And there wasn't an extra under the sink.

Great.

She went back into her bedroom and pulled her robe on. She couldn't find her slippers so she left them as she went in search of more tissue.

"…that son of a bitch doesn't know who he's messing with." She heard Troy's voice as she neared the kitchen. "If this is some kind of game Philippidis has arranged, I swear—"

"It didn't look like a game to me," Ari said. "I mean, I couldn't tell you exactly what was going on between the two of them, but I can assure you that Bryna is a smart girl. She would never allow someone like Caleb Payne to hurt her."

Troy snorted. "Oh, yeah? Then why has she been locked inside her room for two days straight crying her heart out? I'm going to kill him."

Bryna stood in the doorway looking at her cousins, who sat on stools at the kitchen island. Her uncle was drinking a cup of coffee on the other side, while Elena was loading the dishwasher.

Bryna squinted at them, her heart beating an impossible rhythm in her chest.

It was one thing to deal with all this on her own. Adding her cousin's concerns to the mix was almost more than she could bear.

Her throat refused her voice. She turned on her heel to go back upstairs, remembered she'd come for a reason, and then stalked to the supply closet and grabbed a box of tissues and a roll of toilet paper. Then she stalked back through the room, the path in front of her blurry.

"Bryna, wait," Elena called.

She kept going, not stopping until after she'd slammed her bedroom door and run for her bed, once again burying herself under the covers....

BRYNA COULDN'T BE SURE how long she'd slept. All she knew was that when she opened her eyes sometime later, the sun had set…and Elena was walking into her bedroom with a fresh food tray.

She moved to cover her face with the blankets, then decided differently and left them where they were.

She did, however, close her eyes, deciding to act like she was still asleep.

She listened as Elena replaced the tray with the fresh one. She waited to hear the door close after her.

"I know you're awake," Elena said instead.

Bryna made a face. "You must be psychic."

Elena laughed quietly and then Bryna felt her weight on the large bed. She opened one eye, peering at the other woman.

"Did the guys put you up to this?" she asked.

Elena's eyes widened. "The guys…? Oh. No."

She didn't say anything more.

Bryna stared at her openly now. Couldn't she tell that she didn't want company? A closed bedroom door should certainly be a clear sign that she wanted some privacy, if not the covers over her face?

Elena smiled awkwardly then plucked at the hem of her shirt. "Look, Bryna, I know you don't care for me much."

Definitely psychic.

"I'm not entirely certain why, but that doesn't matter. Not this minute. We can work all that out later."

Why not now?

Bryna grimaced at her silent side of the conversation.

"But seeing you like this…in bed, shutting out the world…well, reminds me of what I went through such a short time ago."

What she was experiencing was nothing like what had happened between Elena and Ari, Bryna silently maintained.

Her hope was that if she remained quiet, the other woman would finally get up and leave.

"I know you probably don't think it does, but..." She tucked a strand of hair that had escaped her ponytail behind her ear. Was her hand shaking, or was Bryna imagining things? Elena laughed thinly. "It isn't easy to one moment think you have the world all figured out, then the next be thrown into another reality by what amounts to little more than a sucker punch to the chest."

Bryna sucked her lips into her mouth; the description nailed her own feelings dead on.

"Add on top of that the fact that your family is completely against your relationship and...well, you have a clear recipe for disaster."

"Your family was against you being with Ari?" Bryna found herself asking.

Elena gaped at her. "Are you kidding me? My...affair with him ruined everything they'd ever wanted." Her gaze fell to where she rubbed her palms against the legs of her jeans. "I didn't figure out until sometime later that it wasn't what they wanted for me, but rather what they needed for themselves."

"I don't understand...."

Elena raised a hand and waved it. "That doesn't matter now. None of it does. Although my mother still occasionally insists that Manolis Philippidis will take me back."

"Even though you're pregnant with Ari's child?"

"That's usually my response. But mostly I just ignore her because her comments typically come after a long shift spent at the restaurant when she's been on her feet all day."

Bryna folded the blankets down even farther. "I don't understand. I mean you could marry Ari now, move in here, and have enough money to take care of your family, too. Why don't you do it? I know Ari wants that."

Elena smiled sadly and her hand went to her still-flat belly, a seemingly unconscious move that touched Bryna. "Because I don't want to make the same mistake twice. This time I want to go into my marriage with my own independent means. I want to pursue my own interests. And I don't ever want Ari or anyone else to think that I'm marrying him only for the money."

"And Philippidis? Weren't you going to marry him just for the money?"

Elena's expression was rueful. "See. That's exactly the reason why I don't run off to the county judge's today, this instant, and marry the man I love with all my heart. Because everyone questions and probably will always question what my motivations were in agreeing to be Philippidis's wife."

"An honest reaction."

"Perhaps. But I would never consider marrying

anyone for money." She smiled. "Which brings me around to the point I came in here to make."

"I thought you'd come in here to bug me."

She laughed. "If it chases you out of your bed, then it would be just as effective."

By now Bryna was actually sitting up, the covers bunched around her crossed legs as she considered the other woman.

"You see, Manolis had been a friend of our family for as long as I can remember. He and my father came over here from Greece at around the same time. He was more like an uncle to me than anything. And then my father died and…"

She trailed off and Bryna sat waiting patiently.

"And, well, Manolis was like an angel to me and my family. Before I knew what was happening, we'd begun dating. And when he asked me to marry him, I saw no reason why I shouldn't…"

Bryna wanted to ask questions, but Elena was in her own world now.

"Until I met Ari. Until I understood…love."

"You didn't love Manolis?"

Elena half smiled. "I thought I did. I was convinced I did. But what Ari inspired in me…" She sighed wistfully. "Well, I knew immediately that while I might love Manolis—then, anyway—I wasn't in love with him. Not with the soul-stirring passion that I love Ari."

"And you knew that immediately?"

"Yes."

Bryna nodded.

"So I guess what I'm trying to say, Bryna, is that you shouldn't let anyone else influence how you feel about someone." She reached out and took Bryna's hand where it rested against her knee, already resembling the mother she would soon be. "You can't choose who you love no sooner than you can change the color of the sky."

Bryna stared at her, speechless.

"What you can choose, however, is how that love will manifest itself."

"I don't understand."

"I didn't either. At least not until Ari refused to let me go…" She sighed. "What I mean is, this… whatever you're feeling for Caleb Payne? It's up to you to decide what to do with it. You can either go the rest of your life knowing that you had that once-in-a-lifetime love within your grasp and let it get away… or you can grab it tightly with both hands and refuse to let it go. Because to do so would be a sin against the gods of the highest order."

Bryna held her breath, wanting to tell her that the choice wasn't hers. That Caleb had made the decision for both of them. But she couldn't seem to force the words from her throat.

Instead, she suddenly threw her arms around Elena and held her close. "Thank you," she whispered into the shocked woman's ear.

"Don't mention it. We Metaxas women are few. We should stick together, don't you think?"

Bryna leaned back and looked into her smiling eyes. "I do now...."

20

"OKAY, NOW I'm really starting to worry about you," Phoebe Payne said across the table from Caleb over Sunday brunch.

He looked at her. So he'd barely said a word. That wasn't so unusual. Especially lately. Really, he shouldn't have come to the upscale restaurant. But the thought of staying in that empty apartment for one more minute alone had been even less appealing.

"Are you going to tell me what's going on?" his mother asked. "Or am I going to have to get up and leave you to eat alone?"

Caleb tensed, his chaotic emotions coalescing briefly in anger. "Do what you have to."

Phoebe leaned forward, not about to back down on this one. "Don't think that I won't," she threatened.

This was her last day in town. Later in the evening she was catching a red-eye back to New York. If he allowed her to stay upset with him now, he knew he was in for months of strained relations.

He grasped the napkin in his lap with his right hand, wringing it tightly. "Actually, I do have a question for you…" he began, unsure what he was going to say or exactly how to say it.

Phoebe gave him a full minute while she sprinkled a sugar substitute on her grapefruit. Then she glanced at him pointedly. "I've never known you to be so reticent about anything, Caleb. Just spit it out already so we can get on with our meal."

He met her gaze head-on. "Did you love my father?" he finally asked.

She sat back as if pushed, blinking at him for several long moments. Then, slowly, a smile spread across her face. "Is this about your father? Or about love?"

He quickly looked down at the napkin he held in his lap.

"I'll be damned. Finally."

"What?"

She waved her hand for the waiter. "I've been waiting for this talk for the past twenty years."

"What talk?"

The waiter bowed next to the table. His mother told him that they had an urgent matter to attend to and could he please arrange for the check to be billed to her room, along with a generous tip.

"But we haven't eaten," Caleb said, looking at the full table.

She ignored him as she put her own napkin on her plate and rose to her feet. "Come on. We need to find a nice, quiet spot to have this conversation...."

THE FOLLOWING MORNING at the office, Caleb was still mulling over that long-awaited conversation.

"Why did you wait so long to tell me all this?" he'd asked his mother after they'd spent several hours at his penthouse. Lionel had arranged for brunch to be served to just the two of them at a table set up in front of the floor-to-ceiling windows.

"I was waiting for you to ask, son," she'd said, warmth radiating from her blue eyes. "What I've told you today, I couldn't have shared until you were ready to hear it. And, thank God, you're finally ready...."

Caleb leaned forward and attempted to concentrate on the contract on the desk in front of him. But he'd read two words and his mind would wander again to the day before.

"I loved your father more than any other man—outside of you—in my life," she'd admitted quietly.

He'd never really asked about his father. The only conversations they'd ever had about him were always related to legitimacy issues, not matters of the heart.

"A part of me wants to say, 'Of course I loved him!' I mean, why else would I have gotten involved with a married man?" she'd asked. "I was young and naive and believed every word he said, every promise he made." Her smile had been wistful and made her look decades younger, probably much like that woman who had fallen for a married man. "And I still believe he meant both."

She'd fallen silent then, as she apparently recalled moments from that time that she would never share with anyone, not even him.

"He loved me. I know he did. But life is not always that simple. He was married and had three teenage children. When I told him I was pregnant…"

Caleb had been sitting back, coffee cup in hand, trying not to rush her.

She'd finally smiled. "When I told him I was pregnant with you, he was the happiest man in the world. He wanted both of us to take off to the west coast, leave our lives in the east behind. He would get a divorce, we would get married and we'd live happily ever after.…"

She'd never told him any of this. For some reason, he'd always gotten the impression that he was the result of a one-night stand, not a full-blown love affair where promises were made, and broken.

"One week. He asked for one week to get his affairs in order. Then we would leave. We even had the tickets.…"

He could have guessed the rest. One week passed and his father never made that flight, had left her sitting at the airport, alone and pregnant, with nothing but a short note saying that he was staying with his family…along with a considerable check for her to do with as she wished.

"And the checks kept coming. Every month like clockwork. Even after he passed," she'd said. "I put them all in an account for you. The account you received as a gift on the occasion of your college graduation...."

Caleb's entire reality, what he'd thought was the truth, all changed during that one conversation.

Love...

He'd had no idea that it had been connected in any way to his conception. If Theodore Winstead hadn't died would things have turned out differently? At some point, would Winstead and him have become at least friends, if not the traditional father and son?

All that was water under the bridge now.

Slowly, the contract in front of Caleb came back into focus and he looked around, having forgotten where he was. Then he reached to pick up the phone, asking Nancy to put him through to the bank where the company did all their business.

He told the account manager what he was looking for and was put on hold. Moments later, he came back on the line.

"I'm sorry, Mr. Payne, but it appears that account has been closed."

"Closed? But that's impossible."

The clicking of a keyboard and then, "No. It was closed first thing last Friday."

Bryna? Had she retrieved her funds from the escrow account after that night at her apartment?

"Could you please tell me who authorized the transaction?" he asked.

The manager shared a name with him that was not Bryna's....

"Up, up, sleepyhead...time to go to work."

Ari's voice reached Bryna in the bathroom connected to her bedroom. She tiptoed to the open doorway as he approached the bed. She hadn't made it yet, so the covers were bunched up, and apparently he thought she was still under them.

"Bryna?" he said more tentatively.

She crossed her arms over her chest.

He poked a finger at the blankets, likely expecting another groan that would send him running for the hall. Or maybe this time he was prepared for it.

"Time to get up," he said, grasping the end of the comforter in his hand.

At the same time he yanked it down, Bryna tapped him on the shoulder from behind, nearly causing him to jump out of his skin.

"Damn, Bryna! Let a guy know you're creeping up on him, will ya?"

She laughed and walked around him to make the bed. "Since you're here, make yourself useful and get the other side, will you?"

"You're dressed," he said, looking over her slacks and blouse. Not her usual work attire of skirt suit. "Good, we can ride in together."

She tugged the comforter out of his hands. "I'm not going into the office. I'm taking a sick day."

"Haven't you already taken a couple?"

She eyed him as they made quick work of the bed. "I took one. Last Friday."

"Oh. That's right. It only felt like more." They finished and he stood straight. "Would the weekend count as family sick days?"

She tossed a throw pillow at him even as she piled up the dozen or so others on top of the bed.

There. Done.

Bryna stood looking at the bed she'd spent so much of her time in over the past three days. She was glad to be out of it. While she still wasn't one hundred percent, and the ache in her chest had grown rather than diminished, at least she felt she had the energy to do something other than roll over and pull the covers above her head.

It wasn't much. But it was something.

"So," Ari said. "What do you have planned for today? Are you going to stay around the house?"

Bryna gave him a half smile. "I'm going into Seattle."

He shifted his weight from foot to foot. "To do what, exactly?"

"Wouldn't you like to know?"

"Yes, I would. Because Troy left to drive into the city, oh, about…" He glanced at his watch. "About twenty minutes ago."

Bryna grabbed the things she needed and passed Ari on her way out the door.

"Good luck," he called after her.

"Luck has nothing to do with it," she replied as she took the stairs two at a time, estimating just how fast she would have to speed in order to beat Troy to Caleb's office.…

21

"YOU CAN'T LEAVE Philippidis," Palmer told Caleb as he threw the basketball at him on the private club court, hitting him hard in the chest.

Caleb dribbled the ball back and forth. The scene between him and Hasselbeck had not been a pretty one. He'd confronted him with the seizure of the account, expecting remorse. Instead, he'd received a cold smile and an explanation that he'd been directed to take it.

Directed by whom? Philippidis himself, whom Hasselbeck had admitted to reporting to since the moment Manolis had run into Bryna outside Caleb's office. He'd used information gleaned from rifling through Caleb's desk to fraudulently access the account.

The man he'd personally hired had betrayed him. Not that he was surprised. Was it so very long ago when he might have done the same thing in order to get a leg up? Hasselbeck was only looking after himself.

But he had done it at the expense of any ties with Caleb. And the first thing he had done was fire the smug bastard, since that power had yet to be taken away from him. He didn't want to see him anywhere within a mile radius of his work environment. Ever.

Now he shot the ball and missed, letting rip a string of profanities that made Palmer laugh and club members passing by stare.

"Good thing I caught you outside Hasselbeck's office or else that pent-up aggression you're showing might have ended up being directed in the wrong place," Palmer said.

Caleb guarded him, forcefully reaching around his old friend and knocking the ball from his grip.

"Whoa! Foul."

"The only rule in our games is that there are no rules." Caleb dribbled the basketball out and shot again, hitting it off the rim. "And if you think this game will stop me from confronting Philippidis, you've got another think coming."

Palmer stood still, dribbling the ball but not making any attempt at shooting. "All this over a woman?"

Anger flashed through Caleb as he stood staring at his friend. "All this over his meddling in matters that are none of his business."

"Matters concerning a woman."

"Matters concerning an independent business deal."

"With a woman. A woman with whom you were sleeping."

Caleb had never struck another person in his life and was surprised by his desire to clock Palmer.

"Whoa! Foul," his friend said for the second time, holding up his hands and backing away.

Caleb trapped the dropped ball against his side. "Tell me, Palmer. How did you happen to be at the offices to stop me from charging Philippidis, anyway?"

He hadn't considered the reason why his friend had shown up out of the blue at the time. He'd assumed he'd stopped by to invite him for a lunch b-ball session. Now he wasn't so sure.

Palmer wiped sweat from his brow with the back of his hand and then put the same hand on his hip. "I have an office there. Up the hallway from yours. Today was my first day in it." He grinned. "Looks like perfect timing."

"A little too perfect." Caleb gripped the ball in both his hands. "Since when have you had a permanent office?"

"I don't. It's not permanent," he said. "It's just until I can arrange for a place in Earnest."

Earnest. Where the Metaxases were from. Where the business deal he hoped to put together for Bryna would focus, more specifically on the Metaxas mill.

"Why Earnest?" he asked.

Palmer shrugged. "Why not Earnest?" But Caleb was having none of it. He shot the ball at him.

"Okay, okay. Earnest happens to be where I'm from." Palmer threw the ball back.

He raised a brow. "So your return has nothing to do with Philippidis."

"I didn't say that...."

Caleb rubbed his free hand over his face and then pushed his hair back. Was there nothing the Greek would stop at in order to wreak his revenge against that family?

As it was, he had dipped into his own resources to return Bryna's money to her account, his intention that she not ever know what had happened...and for him to get that same money back from Philippidis himself.

"Caleb Payne!"

His name echoed through the basketball court and commanded his complete attention. He turned to face none other than Bryna where she stood in the doorway, hands on her shapely hips.

"Your ass is mine, bud...."

BRYNA'S BLOOD PUMPED HARD through her veins, allowing her a measure of confidence that she didn't feel. At least not to the extent that she pretended.

But after having raced to Seattle at the risk of a major speeding ticket, and cutting Troy off at Caleb's offices, she was just relieved that she'd reached him before her cousin had.

The scene had been nerve-racking. Troy standing before Caleb's secretary demanding to know where he was, the possibility high that he might run into Philippidis as she had a week before. Her unsure what he wanted and unconvinced of her own ability to chase him away.

"What are you doing here?" her cousin had demanded of her.

"I could ask the same of you."

"I'm here because that son of a bitch in there did something to you that made you dive for cover in your bedroom for the past three days."

Caleb's secretary said, "Sir, I've already told you, he's not in there."

"I don't believe you."

Bryna stared at him. "What, you can't seriously think that Caleb Payne is actually afraid to see you?" she asked.

She strode toward the closed door.

"Miss Metaxas," the secretary began, getting to her feet.

But there was no need for intervention. Bryna had swung open the door, revealing an empty office.

Troy's stare could have frozen a tropical wind.

She closed the door again and went to stand in front of him. "While I'm touched by your display of…affection for me, I don't need you to fight my fights." She squared her shoulders. "I'm quite capable of fighting them myself."

"If that were true, you would never have gotten

involved with the likes of that man in the first place."

He had her there. But she wasn't going to let him know that. "What would you know about anything related to relationships, Troy? Of the man-woman variety? Last I checked, you haven't been on a date in over two years."

He cocked a brow. "I didn't realize anyone was counting."

"That's because you're incapable of seeing anything outside your hell-bent obsession with saving Earnest." She took a deep breath, knowing she was treading dangerous waters and might go under at any moment. "Did it ever occur to you that Earnest might have to take care of itself? Who died and left you savior?"

He winced at that and she immediately felt guilty. But didn't back down one iota.

"Go back home, Troy. I can handle this myself," she said more quietly. "Please."

He stared at her for a long moment and then finally his expression softened and he nodded. "You're right. I'm butting in where I don't belong."

She smiled at him.

"But if you need anything—"

"You'll be the first person I call," she'd assured him.

Who else would she turn to? The first place she'd gone when she was in desperate need of licking her wounds was the house in Earnest. The one she shared with her uncle and cousins. Home.

Thankfully, he'd left the office…and then Bryna had beseeched Caleb's secretary for his whereabouts. Surprisingly, she'd told her straight out.

And now she stood at the entrance to the private club's basketball court staring at the man in question.

How was it remotely possible that she'd forgotten how dynamic he was? The only time she'd seen him without every hair in place was in bed. But now he wore a college T-shirt and sweat pants, the soft cotton hugging his every muscle. Sweat dampened the front and the back of the shirt, and his skin color was high. His eyes glistened like black onyx, taking her in from head to foot much the same way she was him.

He looked like a dangerous predator who had just returned from a long hunt to find an unwanted animal waiting in his den. A small, defenseless animal that he could render history with one clean snap of his powerful jaws.

Why did she suddenly feel as if she'd much rather dive back under her bedcovers…?

22

THE LAST PERSON Caleb had expected to see appear in that doorway was Bryna. Yet there she stood, her glossy black hair loose around her shoulders, contrasting against her cream-colored blouse and matching slacks, the hue highlighting her naturally tanned skin.

"Speak of the she-devil," Palmer murmured.

Caleb wanted to shoot him a look of warning, but he couldn't seem to tear his gaze away from the spectacular creature striding across the court in her high heels as if she owned it. And she did. At least in that one moment. There wasn't a man alive who could be untouched by the image she cut.

A sexy female on a mission.

Then he remembered what could have made her angry enough to seek him out instead of waiting for him to return to the office or contact him via some other means: she must have discovered her money had gone missing before he'd replaced it.

She advanced on him…and kept on coming, backing him up against the wall behind the net.

"I'm sorry about the money," he said quietly, taking in her beautiful green eyes and her soft, provocative mouth, feeling an overpowering urge to kiss her.

She blinked. "What money?"

Christ, she wasn't there because of the missing resources. He grimaced. So much for keeping her from learning about the mishap.

"Are you pulling out of our professional agreement?" she asked. "For personal reasons?"

This one had a fire inside her that not even a bastard like him could extinguish. A strength that matched and might even better his.

He could barely stop himself from grinning.

"No," he said.

She propped her fists on her hips. "Then what money are you sorry about?"

"It's nothing with which to be concerned. Not anymore. Everything is as it should be."

She looked unconvinced. "Everything?"

"Mmm." God help him, if she moved any closer to him, he *was* going to kiss her.

Out of the corner of his eye he saw Palmer near them.

"You must be Miss Metaxas," his friend said, extending his hand. "I'm Palmer DeVoe."

Bryna tugged the basketball out of Caleb's hand and shoved it at him. "Nice to meet you, Palmer.

Now, if you'll excuse us, Mr. Payne and I have a few things we must discuss. Privately."

Palmer held up a hand. "Sure. Never mind me." He looked at Caleb, an amused expression on his face. "I'll just hit the showers...."

Bryna never took her gaze from Caleb.

He cleared his throat. "Would you like to go somewhere...private to have this conversation?"

She squinted at him. "Why? So you can distract me with sex and then play games with me afterward?" She shook her head. "Oh, no, buster. We're going to have this talk here and now."

One of the symptoms of love that his mother had shared with him was a painful expansion just behind the solar plexus, as if you couldn't take another breath if your life depended on it. Caleb recognized the sensation as exactly what he was feeling.

Quite simply, Bryna took his breath away.

And he'd been stupid not to admit the truth before now. Before he'd hurt her.

"I know you said you didn't love me," she began.

Her voice hitched slightly, revealing an undercurrent of emotion she was obviously trying to keep under control.

"But I know differently."

She swallowed hard.

"I felt in my bones. Felt it in your every touch. Saw the love I was feeling reflected in your eyes. You were feeling every last emotion I was—"

"Feel," he corrected, his own throat growing unbearably tight.

Her mouth snapped shut and she searched his face. "Pardon me?"

He'd hurt this woman more than any person deserved to be hurt. All because he'd been unable to open his eyes to his own true feelings for her. He'd been a bastard for so long, he didn't know how to be anything different. A scarred child incapable of moving beyond his own imaginary constraints.

And in a strange way, it had taken hurting Bryna to finally come to terms with that. To see what love really looked like. Not just in his own heart, but in hers.

No matter what he said, what he did to her, she never blinked. She stood up against him just as she was now, determined to make him see what he'd refused to.

She was apparently waiting for him to explain himself. And he did.

"You referred to what you believed I'm feeling in the past tense. I merely corrected you."

Her eyes shone brightly as she considered his words.

Caleb couldn't help himself. He knew that she had a lot to get off her chest. But he needed to touch her.

He reached out a hand and cupped the side of her face. At her small sound of delighted surprise, emotion surged sure and strong within him. A desire he suspected would never be satisfied, no matter how many times he marked his brand on the fascinating woman before him.

"I'm sorry for what I said the other night," he whispered, wanting desperately to convince her. "I…"

She leaned her head into his palm and he suppressed a groan.

"Damn it all to hell, Bryna, I don't deserve you.…"

He watched her absently lick her bottom lip, threatening to sidetrack him.

"The truth is, I don't know much about love."

She tried to look away, but he denied her the escape.

"Even though I don't rate another chance…would you be willing to show me?"

He'd lived for so long in an emotional vacuum, consumed with his career at the expense of all else, proving himself to a father who had died long ago, he didn't know how she or anyone else was going to change that.

But it wasn't up to them to bring about a change. It was up to him. And after suffering for the better part of the past week without the touch of Bryna's skin against his, distracted to hell and back by the thought that he might never see her again, he knew he needed to make that change. Or risk becoming the type of man he despised, not respected.

To his relief and surprise, the corners of Bryna's

mouth turned up slightly into a smile and her gemlike eyes shone even more brightly. "Oh, I don't know. I think you're doing a pretty good job of it right now."

Caleb hauled her into his arms, tunneling the fingers of one hand into her hair even as he crowded her against his body with his other against her lower back. She smelled so damn good. Felt even better.

"God, I don't deserve you," he murmured, kissing her hair, then her forehead, then her nose.

She tilted her face up, her expression full of fire and need. "Don't you think I should be the one who decides that?"

Caleb's gaze moved from her eyes to her mouth and then back again. Then he finally did what he'd been hungering to since the moment he'd first spotted her standing in the doorway—he kissed her.

Any words he was unable to say he conveyed through his kiss. And he realized that it was what he'd been doing all along. While his conscious mind and lifelong hang-ups had kept him from seeing what was right in front of him, his heart and body had known all along.

A desire so strong that it blocked out everything and everyone around them took hold until a club patron cleared his throat nearby.

"Get a room," he said in disapproval.

Caleb drew his head back from Bryna, his hand pressed against her rounded bottom.

She laughed. "Where's the closest hotel…?"

Epilogue

PALMER DEVOE WAITED for Caleb outside the office building housing Philippidis's current international headquarters. The morning sunlight speared the dark rain clouds, creating a rainbow to the south. His mother might have said it was a harbinger of good things to come; of course, she'd have to be alive in order to say it. And she hadn't been around for a good long time. Too long.

That Earnest lay to the south didn't escape Palmer's attention.

Earnest…his hometown…

The place where Penelope Weaver still resided…

Caleb burst through the front doors as if they'd been blown open by a strong wind gust, his face as dark as the sky.

A scathing line of obscenities erupted from his mouth. "I could have killed the son of a bitch."

Palmer crossed his arms and considered his

longtime friend and sometime business associate from under lowered brows. "I'm guessing that went well."

Caleb paced back and forth several times, as restless as he'd ever seen him. "I never in a million years imagined I'd fall victim to a power play."

Palmer grinned, amused. "Yes, well, that's because you're usually the one making the plays."

His friend stared at him. "My point exactly."

He paced again.

Palmer weighed whether it was wise to let this play out right there or if it was better to suggest they take it to the club. He cast a long look at the building behind him and considered his own business with the man Caleb held in such low regard.

He'd never seen his friend so worked up. "You didn't do anything stupid, did you?" he asked.

Caleb stopped, aiming that glare at him.

Palmer raised his hands. "Whoa. I'm not him."

"Define *stupid*."

"Wrong choice of words. Perhaps I should have said *unprofessional*."

"Oh, what I did in there was professional, all right. I professionally told him where he could get off."

Palmer winced. Not good.

He looked back at the front doors. It probably wasn't a good idea to stick around where they could be seen in plain sight. While he sympathized with his friend's plight, he had plans of his own to implement…and that included keeping the wily Greek on his side.

"Why don't we work this out on the basketball court?" he suggested.

"I'd rather go in and clock him…."

Palmer slapped a hand on his back and propelled him toward the street instead.

"I should have given in to the urge while I was in there."

"Probably best that you didn't. You don't want to burn any bridges."

"Burn them?" Caleb asked, a glint of humor sparking for the first time since he'd come outside. "I loaded the damn things with explosives and blew them the hell up."

Christ…

"That's right. I wouldn't work with that lowdown, scum-sucking son of a bitch again for all the money in the world. If my life depended on it. If the end of the world was nigh and he was the only one who could save me…"

Wow. Palmer put his arm loosely around Caleb's shoulders as his driver pulled up. "Don't be drastic, now."

He opened the door and Caleb climbed in the back; Palmer followed.

"I'm sure whatever happened in there isn't anything a little distance, time and clearer thinking can't fix."

Caleb squinted. "Surely you jest. Aren't you hearing a word I'm saying?"

"I'm hearing every word," he assured him. "I just don't have to like them."

Caleb paused, then asked, "You're not seriously considering continuing to work with that asshole?"

Palmer carefully weighed his words. "I'm certainly not about to dump everything I've worked so hard for over a girl."

Caleb looked ready to sock him.

He lifted his hands again. "Hey, just stating facts as I see them."

Caleb must have read something in his reaction. He drew in a deep breath and then let it out slowly, running his fingers through his hair several times before sitting back. This external manifestation of his friend's internal turmoil wasn't something he was used to seeing off the court. Caleb usually had iron-willed self-control. Most had no idea what was going on in his head.

Now you could read his every emotion like a brightly lit billboard.

"You know what?" Caleb asked. "You're right—this is about a girl."

He turned to face him; Palmer wondered if he should put up his hands to block a surprise assault.

But Caleb wasn't scowling…he was grinning.

"And it's the best damn thing I've ever done in my life."

Palmer blinked.

"Think about it," Caleb said. "When was the last time you did something that wasn't dictated by your head, but rather your heart?"

"Never," he said without hesitation.

Caleb laughed. "Me either."

This time Palmer was the one who ran his fingers through his hair, finding the unfamiliar action contagious. "You picked a helluva time to start."

"Yes, well, I think in this matter, you don't pick the time, it picks you."

He considered his friend for a long moment. "And if things don't work out?"

Caleb looked at him. "With Bryna and I?"

Palmer nodded.

He appeared to give it consideration as the car navigated the distance to the club. Finally Caleb smiled. "Then it doesn't work out."

Okay, he'd lost it.

"All I know is that I cannot not do this, Palmer. Everything in me is telling me she is the one."

Great.

A loud chuckle. "If you'd told me a week ago I'd be saying this, I'd have said you were crazy."

"Now you're the one sounding crazy."

"Maybe. But, oh, does it feel good...."

Palmer looked out the window at Seattle, trying to get a handle on the situation. The rainbow still arced in the south. He wanted to say he had no idea how his friend felt, but the fact was, he did know…and in a few short days, he'd find out if the combination of time and distance had been enough to destroy it.…

* * * * *

A sneaky peek at next month...

Blaze®

SCORCHING HOT, SEXY READS

My wish list for next month's titles...

In stores from 21st October 2011:

❏ Private Affairs – Tori Carrington

& Simon Says... – Donna Kauffman

❏ Northern Encounter – Jennifer LaBrecque

❏ Santa, Baby – Lisa Renee Jones

Available at WHSmith, Tesco, Asda, Eason, Amazon and Apple

Just can't wait?

Visit us Online

You can buy our books online a month before they hit the shops! **www.millsandboon.co.uk**

1011/

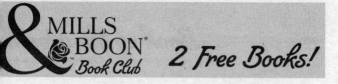

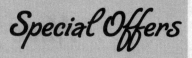

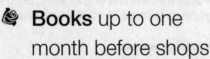